More praise for *All Things, All at O*

"Abbott is the rare writer who doesn't fee[...] into accepting his narrative idiosyncrasies. [...] in. . . . From the very start, we're engaged by the entertainment and vitality of Abbott's prose, by its local color. Then, right in the middle of a typically eccentric and loose-limbed story, he often grabs us with a moment that becomes sharply moving—and then almost unbearably so. . . . Despite all the loquacious banter in this impressive collection, the most important moments turn out to be the ones in which, even briefly, words aren't enough."
—Meg Wolitzer, *New York Times Book Review*

"Picking up one of Mr. Abbott's stories is like stepping into a rushing stream. Before you know it, you've been thrown up on the bank in a place you never anticipated, because you, like his characters, felt you knew what was happening, and that you had control. In his stories, no one ever does, not really." —Anne Morris, *Dallas Morning News*

"A writer's writer, Abbott has honed his craft to a glinty, dangerous sharpness. . . . *All Things, All at Once* is a powerful mix of 25 tales full of bittersweet emotion and the low-level suffering that comes from not having or not knowing what you most need. Abbott's stories are the stuff of everyday life wrought crisply and with clarity as visual as it is visceral. . . . [Abbott writes] in a style both off-handed and go-for-the-jugular bloody. . . . There are no so-so stories in *All Things, All at Once*; each piece resonates its own complex chords of loss, suffering, betrayal, redemption. . . . These stories capture the language, color and incestuousness of small-town desert life with brutal, flinty clarity."
—Victoria A. Brownworth, *Baltimore Sun*

"Abbott is a fine writer, who, like Cheever, seeks out the sublime on the back nine, where the mundane real estate of the suburbs turns into something magical and cosmic. But something wilder lurks in his pages, even less mainstream than Cheever. . . . Few writers show us the interior life of the man stumbling away—poised between that 'enchanted province of paradise and dread' that is the future—quite so honestly as Abbott does here."

  —John Freeman, *Sunday Denver Post and Rocky Mountain News*

"Complex character is the core of Abbott's stories, but it is the voice that carries you irresistibly along; it is a rhythm, a riff, a rap that makes you smile at least every two pages with recognition or reconciliation, or both. . . . Like Raymond Carver, Andre Dubus and Alice Munro, who remained faithful to the powerful but neglected form, he is a master of its particular poetic demands."

          —Charles E. May, *Milwaukee Journal Sentinel*

"The interesting aspect of these 25 Southwestern-based stories by Abbott (*The Heart Never Fits Its Wanting*) is the range of themes he fits into each story. . . . Abbott brilliantly manipulates the narrative. . . . Highly recommended."   —Joshua Cohen, *Library Journal*

"*All Things, All at Once* is rightly titled. It's a florid and rich cornucopia of stories, full of exuberance, passion, gravity, consolation, and utter zaniness. It is a rare collection and puts Abbott's great versatility and masterful narrative skills on vivid display."   —Richard Ford

"Lee Abbott's stories are *fiction* of the age—of a time and place so palpably real you feel you can step into it—funny, grave, written with wit and high lyricism, and dialogue so rich and real that lives move at high speed, swiftly defined, always heading toward the far edge of reality, or just beyond. This is *fiction* in the mode of John Cheever, written for the long run, marking out those days when all you love hovers right there—maybe forever, or maybe it's about to disappear. Lee Abbott is one terrific writer."   —William Kennedy

"Lee K. Abbott is a true American original, the owner of an unmistakable voice—at once funny, wise, loopy, and utterly unique. Abbott is one of our finest short story writers, and the arrival of this long-awaited volume of his collected stories is cause for celebration."

          —Tom Perrotta

"Lee Abbot's is a unique voice. You think he's writing, say, about a boozy golf player who mismanages his love life. But you soon enough realize that you are enthralled in a dark descent into the very essence of what it means to be an American and in despair. There is often a glimmer of light in his stories, and Abbott's absolutely individual voice broadens that glimmer to a gleam as his characters work at finding a way to live. His sense of shape, and the voice that drives his narrative, are the achievements of a master of the form."   —Frederick Busch

"What a magnificent and necessary collection. I think, if God in his heaven decides to do it all again, he ought to read this one. What he got right. What he got wrong. The glorious imperfections of his little perfections. We strange beings of the human variety. He might just change his mind and move to earth, buy him a truck and get a real nice girl because there is truly life down here and joy and sadness attend and no one can do better or worse or bear the burden more than we do for ourselves. Lee K. Abbott's *All Things, All at Once* is a splendid triumph—salutary, edifying, radiant."   —Robert Olmstead

OTHER BOOKS BY LEE K. ABBOTT

The Heart Never Fits Its Wanting

Love Is the Crooked Thing

Strangers in Paradise

Dreams of Distant Lives

Living After Midnight

Wet Places at Noon

LEE K. ABBOTT

ALL THINGS, ALL AT ONCE

New and Selected Stories

W. W. NORTON & COMPANY

New York / London

For Max and Mia

Copyright © 2006 by Lee K. Abbott

For information about permission to reproduce selections from this book,
write to Permissions, W. W. Norton & Company, Inc., 500 Fifth Avenue,
New York, NY 10110

Manufacturing by RR Donnelley, Bloomsburg
Book design by Brooke Koven
Production manager: Andrew Marasia

Library of Congress Cataloging-in-Publication Data

Abbott, Lee K.
All things, all at once : new and selected stories / Lee K. Abbott.—1st edition
p. cm
ISBN-13: 978-0-393-06137-6
ISBN-10: 0-393-06137-X
I. Title
PS3551.B262A79 2006
813'.54—dc22
2005027348

ISBN 978-0-393-33012-0 pbk.

W. W. Norton & Company, Inc.
500 Fifth Avenue, New York, N.Y. 10110
www.wwnorton.com

W. W. Norton & Company Ltd.
Castle House, 75/76 Wells Street, London W1T 3QT

1 2 3 4 5 6 7 8 9 0

CONTENTS

. . . hardly anything happens except the world.
—A. R. Ammons, *"Right Call"*

ACKNOWLEDGMENTS

These stories, some in different form, appeared in the following periodicals to whose editors I am as indebted now as I was the day they said "yes": *The Atlantic* ("Ninety Nights on Mercury" as "All Things, All at Once," "Category Z," "Revolutionaries," "The End of Grief"); *Agni Review* ("Love Is the Crooked Thing"); *Boulevard* ("As Fate Would Have It," "The Who, the What, and the Why"); *Carolina Quarterly* ("The Valley of Sin"); *Crazyhorse* ("The Eldest of Things"); *Daedelus* ("Men of Rough Persuasion"); *Georgia Review* ("One of *Star Wars*, One of *Doom*," "The Final Proof of Fate and Circumstance," "The Talk Talked Between Worms," "*X*," "Gravity"); *Harper's* ("Dreams of Distant Lives," "Sweet Cheeks," "The View of Me from Mars"); *Kenyon Review* ("How Love Is Lived in Paradise"); *North American Review* ("Martians"); *Southwest Review* ("The Human Use of Inhuman Beings"); *Story* ("The Way Sin Is Said in Wonderland"); *The Idaho Review* ("What *Y* Was"); *The New Orleans Review* ("When Our Dream World Finds Us, and These Hard Times Are Gone").

I am also indebted, as all readers should be, to Susan Kenney, whose story "Mirrors," first published in *Epoch* and later collected in *In Another Country*, is in part the story badly paraphrased by the narrator of "The View of Me from Mars."

ALL THINGS,
ALL AT ONCE

NINETY NIGHTS ON MERCURY

for JSP

SHE WAS BETTY PORTER, a being as much of magic as of muscle, and I who I ever am—Heath "Pokey" Howell (Junior), banker, Luna County commissioner and, as events will prove, the dimmest of sinners, male type. We'd known each other, yes, as acquaintances in this commodious desert, she a widow and me a recently estranged husband, and then, at the Valentine's Dance at the Mimbrs Valley Country Club not so very long ago, we shed the selves ordinary folks had said howdy to, and, fumbling fiercely at each other, we took up the private half of lived life.

It was quick as heat lightning, wicked and unpredicted—odd, I say, as ninety nights on Mercury. I'd taken a break from the boogaloo, or whatever it was that Uncle Roy and his Red Creek Wranglers were hollering at us, and made for the door to the men's locker. I was hunting quiet, plus at least one damp towel for my face. Betty Porter was, it appeared, keen for much of the same, and so we came upon each other, she in hesitation at the door to the ladies', me using the wall for a handrail. I was not drunk, I hold. Just smitten. By her dress, which was blue as heaven's bottom and at least four times more sparkly than a poet's idea of nighttime; and by her legs, which were long as hope itself; and by her skin, which seemed to glow like moonlight; and by her shoulder, which was bare and which something crooked in me wanted to lick.

I said nothing, and I would tell a jury now that I had nothing to say—not, at least, in this feeble language. Rather, I was listening: to Uncle Roy in mid-yowl and to cocktail chatter annoying as power tools, not to mention to my own loose heart and to my bones as they ground against the considerable meat I am, and to my breathing which was certifiably gasp-like, and to her own swish-swish as she marched deliberately toward me. Even when it had started, when we had pushed our way down the hall to the trophy room and had locked its door and, by several weak but happy lights, I had touched her face and felt certain fibers in my chest snapping free, I didn't talk. Did not wonder. To that jury that sits ever more in my brain—and to the one in your very own—I would say that Heath Howell was but a bystander, no smarter about this than is a dog about democracy.

Deep down, of course, your narrator knew exactly what he was doing. He knew the fever that swamped him and the midnight hour and the green of her eyes and the hoopla outside. He knew, even between her legs and afterward, the sourness of his breath and where he'd come from in the world and how, a dozen years before, he'd gotten his wife to say "yes," never mind the three children they had once vowed to rear together. Yes, Pokey Howell knew it all. And he expected it would come back to him, like a tide pent up in the oils and other liquids he was, when Betty Maxine Porter, in the hall, cocked her head as if sizing him up for an old suit she had, before she took his hand, her own cool as tap water, and placed it hard against her own hard crotch. But nothing came back to that man—unless you count, as I must, the cruelest hunger and the vulgarest thirst.

So yonder we went, Betty Porter in the lead, me an animal eager to catch up. Ours had been a sudden recognition, I say, and not knowledge you can have twice about the simplest thing you are. Behind us the door clicked and we, like butchers or other workaday folks with common business to conduct, stripped ourselves, eye to eye like sophomores about to fistfight. Time was not moving by in ticks and tocks but in whooshes and chunks, fast as a nightmare you partly enjoy the terror of. A moment later, I was in a chair sufficiently comfortable for a man five times fatter than I, and she was more or less astride me, still not saying her say nor asking me mine. I was erect as a fence pole, hard as I've ever been and thoroughly amazed by it, and for a moment, before I let myself go and waited to see her slip over her own crumbly cliff, nothing was happening between my head and my hoof but wind and fire and thudding organs.

A week later, she would tell me why, but in those minutes then, when I had started to sweat and when I could see her face go slack but before various notions became plain, she said nothing. Inside her, I was still stiff, spectacularly so, and she was wet in a way spooky to me as travel in space. The world was coming back now, piece by piece— a screechy voice perilously close, another Uncle Roy tune I could sing two-thirds of, the light in the farthermost trophy case flickering, my cigarettes smashed in my shirt pocket, her weight on my thighs adding up pound by pound by pound until, nearly out of breath, I had to shift. Then I could see it, a thought sift through her face and almost get to her lips. She seemed to have settled something, a concern or an insight she'd just found the sentence for, and I could feel her let me loose down below.

She would be off me in a second, I knew. She would be off and gathering up her pantyhose and slipping on her high heels and messing at her hair very professionally, but first she leaned close to me, almost nose to nose, the light behind her as harsh as the word *no,* and she spoke, hers a sly smile to wonder about, hers a voice with as much rue in it as there is in mine when I tell a debtor the goddamn end is nigh.

"So you're a naughty so-and-so, too," she said. "Goody."

This is why. The next time we met—at her place on Fir Street, a ranchette-like spread that seemed to have been decorated by spirits too angry to have names in English—she said it was fate, a word she even bothered to spell for the houseguest in the three-piece suit.

"We were destined for each other, Pokey. You and me, a cosmic conspiracy."

I didn't know about such business, I told her. I was average, as undistinguished as white bread, plus burdened with a laugh like Daffy Duck's.

"Don't be modest, Pokey," she said, all but wagging her finger. "You're just enthusiastic, that's all."

I had been to college, I told her, where I had memorized enough about real estate and arithmetic to be my father's partner at the Farmers and Merchants Savings Bank, plus I was pretty fair at snooker, but about fate—a word I now believe too puny to describe what happens boy to girl—I knew only what you know when you tear up Sunday morning that lottery ticket you bought Saturday night.

Here it was then that she asked about Lizzie, the wife I was apart from but who, unbeknownst to me in the days I was to paw over Betty Porter, was pregnant with our fourth child.

"There's nothing to know," I said. Lizzie was average, too, just better than I with the please and thank-you necessary among our kind.

This was a weird afternoon, I tell you. Like events out of *The Twilight Zone* or the second page of the *National Enquirer.* Betty Porter had met me at the door in an outfit from the peignoir pages of the catalogue, and the instant I stepped inside she had roiled over me like a dust devil, pulling and tugging, her skin hot as a fry pan, both in and out of reach, on my neck when I thought she was about to tackle my knees, or at my ear with a whisper or two when I paused to get my balance. Then, as quickly as she'd begun, she stopped. Became downright business-like—more a tea-time hostess than somebody who means to slap your naked butt like a farmyard beast to be shooed out of the way.

I was directed to sit on her couch, a leather monstrosity red as the Devil's hindmost. She put a drink in my hand, lemonade with too little sugar to get down easily; and, sitting across from me, prim as Sunday school itself, she ordered me to shut my trap—her phrase, exactly.

"I got something to say," she said. "You got something to hear."

I was recently separated from a sweetheart I didn't understand any more than I do hijinks in Hungary; I was a father who sought to cross the *t*'s and dot the *i*'s children are said to have need of, plus a taxpayer with a checking account big enough to pay for the minor disasters of bad weather and poor planning; but mainly I was a man wobbly in the departments our public moralists like to yatter about, and so, not suspecting that in exactly fifty-one days I would say no, I said "yes" and waited to hear what Betty Porter, mistress and friend of fate, had to say about the to and fro that was she and me and Planet Earth.

"Heath Howell," she began, "I intend to have you one hundred percent."

I was looking at the dozen or so candles on the coffee table between us, thinking myself suave as Yancy Derringer himself, when most of that round, usually nice, number caught up with me.

"Don't be scared," she said.

I wasn't, I said. Big old thing like me.

"Then swallow," she said, "before you dribble on yourself."

She told me then, the whole kit and caboodle. How, after Marv died, she was adrift, jumpy, et cetera. Not especially aggrieved. Just couldn't focus. Couldn't sleep. Like a person waving to America from the moon. More words per minute than I could keep up with.

"That was tough," I said. "About Marvin, I mean."

She was getting something out of her eye—stage business, I think now, if a stage can be a living room echoey as a hotel lobby.

"Marvin Porter was a high school principal," she said, another tone completely. "About as exciting as Velveeta cheese."

I looked into my lemonade, found nothing there to study.

"He was company," she was saying. "And good enough, I guess. Now I want something more. I deserve it."

I should've got up. Honest. When she began talking about Marv— how he was a penny-pincher, for example, or not much of a poon hound, how he ironed his hankies, or what in the rest of our desert was a flat-out disappointment to a woman with appetites big as the outdoors itself—I should've risen, fled for the front door; but Betty Porter was heat and light and water—all things, all at once—and I something dumb in nature did not want one without the others.

"I have a proposal to make," she said at last.

She had candles. Furniture heavy enough to hurt you. A coat rack that all but picked your pocket when you came in the door. And now she had a proposal.

"I'm giving you six months," she said.

I took a drink here, counted my way toward August, using both hands. "For what?"

She laughed, sharp as gunfire. "For you and me, silly. I'll be your girlfriend for six months. Then you've got to make up your mind. Elizabeth Howell or me."

In retrospect, here's another place for your narrator to rise. To button his cuffs. To reknot his tie. But in those days, there was no 'spect' —retro or otherwise—just Betty Porter, strange and forbidden and fetched up only eight feet away, and yours truly, over six feet of flesh that had somehow learned its ABCs and how to drive a pickup truck on the right side of the road.

"I've been watching you," she said. "Hell, I know which pump you use at Ray Bill's Texaco. Your shirt size. How much you paid for that house."

I chuckled. Your classic BMOC. "You've been busy," I said.

She sniffed—an allergy, I thought.

"I've been lonely, Howell."

I heard my blood then, buzzy as a box of bees, and waited for my arm or hand or leg to act in some significant way. I could've thought of Lizzie, I suppose. Of my boys, Brad and Lonnie. Of their toddling sister, Mary Beth. But I didn't. The Widow Porter had her own drink at her lips now, her slender throat yet another fine creature feature that Heath Howell could see himself crawling toward. I could smell her, too. Roses and mint and what the skin gives off on its own. Then I wasn't thinking at all, my head hollow as a gourd you could shoot a BB clean through, and I was standing—impossibly lonely my own self— and stepping toward her, behind me a million doors slamming shut.

Lizzie has since said it was the sex. Well, sure. It was going into a room and knowing you had a surprise to find—a bomb, a flying saucer, Old King Cole with his fiddlers three. It was being blindfolded and turned a hundred times about, our desert a new vista to behold when it stopped spinning. It was a pulse, loud as an ooomm-pah from a Sousa march, and the shriek time makes when you are yanked from it. Hell, yes, it was the sex—what Lizzie's preacher, the Reverend Oram Tins-ley, M.Div., once called the den and lair and roost of us. And for nearly two months it was more of everything than you're supposed to have in this vale. More of more.

And then one day—our fiftieth, I'm guessing—it was something else, too.

"Pokey," she said. "Answer me this."

We'd been at it for an hour, us the litter on her queen-size bed, her reclined on her elbows and me on all fours ready for round two. I felt I hadn't taken a breath since the previous Monday.

"What's the capital of Peru?" she said, yet another new person to tussle with.

I looked around, me like a hungry pound dog ordered away from the dinner table. "What?"

"Peru," she said. "It's in South America."

I knew where it was, I said. Just—ha, ha, ha—didn't know where the mayhem was made.

"What about this?" she said, sitting up, me so close to her breasts I could see their network of veins, plus a hickey I was awfully proud of being responsible for. "Where are King Solomon's mines?"

"Betty, what is this, a test?"

She was looking at me hard then, yours truly a goopy mess on the rug you'll have to spend the whole afternoon scrubbing up.

"Just answer the question, Mr. Howell."

I made a show of checking my watch. I had to be at Lizzie's in two more hours to take the kids to the movies, an agreement we'd thought civilized way back when.

"This is a game, right?" I said.

"What about yogurt?" she said. "What's it made of?"

Didn't know, I told her. Yogurt—like hummus and couscous—wasn't food I cared to fret much about.

She was out of bed now, tying the belt to her robe, and suddenly Heath Howell, the guy with the watch and the devil-may-care atti-tude, felt stupid to be naked and alone. Just another peckerwood caught picking his shorts off the floor.

"What about the Seven Dwarfs?" she said. "Can you name them?"

I could, I declared, though a moment later I found myself two short. "Who's after Dopey?"

She was in her dressing room, she that lovely thing in the mirror dabbing on lipstick. Evidently, we were done today.

"I suppose," she was saying, "you don't know the dates of Chester A. Arthur, right?"

I aimed to say something clever then, but didn't. Couldn't. Instead, I suffered a vision of Marvin Porter, dead husband, cross-legged in the chair at the other end of the bedroom, an ironed hankie in the pocket of his sport coat and the answers to all questions on the tip of his silent tongue.

"Did you hear me?" Betty was saying. "I asked you to name the longest river."

I had my pants on now. Socks, too. I had a shirt somewhere and was hoping to locate it soon.

Then it came, more questions about X and Y and Z than I had heard since Deming Senior High School. What's the formula for determining the circumference of a circle? Who wrote *The King and I*? Who was the fifth Beatle? Where is Madagascar? How high is Mt. Everest? When did Neil Armstrong land on the moon?

"1969," I told her.

"What month?" she said.

I was dressed now, completely presentable, and Marvin Porter, former assistant principal in charge of attendance and discipline, had disappeared.

June was my guess. Maybe July.

She'd come out of the dressing room, no evidence in her eyes or expression to indicate what had happened elsewhere in her house that afternoon. She looked as she would were she to appear before the Luna County Commission to ask young Chairman Howell, and his white-collar cronies, for an emergency zoning variance.

"Pokey," she began, "how do you make it in the world?"

I thought about what I'd be doing an hour from now—me in the dark with three young people, before us in images thirty feet tall the world as it looked to somebody with a movie camera and an imagination peculiar as the imagination itself.

"I manage, Betty. I do very well."

She had her arms crossed, her head tilted, and I had the temptation to wipe my face, get the lints—or the spiders—off. It was a full minute, I say, time enough anyway to suck in the belly and square the shoulders for whatever came next.

"Heath, honey," she began, "you have to know stuff to get around. You got to have some facts. Some ideas."

I was looking at the picture above her bed, a chunky sweetie pie on a horse leaning over to kiss a guy got up in the armor Lancelot wore. "Stuff?" I said.

"That's right, darling." Hers was the high-wattage smile you see on folks who believe they'll live to be one hundred. "Knowledge of the world."

And then, convinced I knew what the dickens she was talking about, I was smiling, too, me one day to be a very old man with this equally old woman, and she was ushering me to the door, hand at my elbow. "Girls' night out," she was saying. "Uncle Roy's playing at the Hitching Post." Next, she had given me a good, if too brief, kiss on the cheek and I was out in the sunlight, it only hot as the fifth floor of Hades, and making my way down the walk to my Ford. She'd call me tomorrow, she was saying, tell me when to come over, tell me what—stuff, I hoped, glorious and wanton stuff—we'd do then.

Lizzie found me in the front yard, sitting on Mary Beth's tricycle, every now and then ringing the bell on the handlebars.

"How long you been here?" she said.

I hadn't seen her in nearly a week, having picked up the children the time before this at her mother's house on Zinc, so for an instant she looked like somebody I only recognized from a magazine. An instant later, naturally, she wasn't. There was her hair, which was brown and snatched up in a clip behind her ears. There was her chin, which was strong, a cute dimple in the center of it. There were her eyes, which behind those sunglasses were blue as lake water on picture postcards from Colorado. Then, finally, every other inch of her, heel to hair—another of us critters I presumed to know the actual in and out of.

"You all right?" she said. "You look a little goofy, Pokey."

Screwy, isn't it? Like living at the whim of crackpots named Zeus and Thor and Athena. Like having your back and forth managed by, oh, ghosts or gremlins or twinkly items who show up on your doorstep with wings flapping from their backsides. What I'm saying is that at the moment she found her wayward husband spread-legged on her daughter's trike, Lizzie already had her news. For three whole days, she'd had it—that she was pregnant with what has turned out to be John Robert, now a child with two permanent teeth and a modest ability to run; for three whole days, news from grumpy Dr. Forest, a young fart who—so Lizzie once said—liked to practice his college Español over those women with seven or eight or nine pounds of squalling, red-faced life to deliver; for three whole days, while I was shagging with Betty Porter, Lizzie Elaine Howell, honors graduate of the University of New Mexico and onetime assistant director of services for the city of Deming, had had her news—her own secret—and she'd already made up her mind about both it and the other human it might grow to resemble. Fate? Whatever. Watch it come.

"Where are the kids?" was what I said next.

"Brushing their teeth." She was standing between me and sunset, hers a shadow that went from me to the street and halfway up the door panel of my four-by-four. "I fed them earlier, so don't buy too much junk. No more than one Coke each, okay?"

That was dandy, I said, and then—on account of the unaccountable parts of me, I assume—I was talking this talk: "Lizzie, you know the capital of Peru?"

She looked at me the way I imagined I had looked at Betty only an hour before: perplexed, as if the joker in front of her were wearing an arrow through his ears.

"Lima," she said. "I'm not sure."

I nodded then, thankful, and found myself ringing the bell one last time. "That's what I thought," I said, rising to my feet. Time to see what Walt Disney knew about things. "I'll have them back by nine, okay?"

It's coming, her news. Quick and dire and three days old. Or, rather, it's already come. Heath Howell just hasn't heard it. He's been thinking about his socks, the intricate pattern the machines at Gold Toe had sewn together. Socks and the tassels on his loafers, plus a black bug thick as his thumb making its way through the Bermuda grass between his feet.

"It's a boy," she said.

Socks and shoes, a bug and something that was a boy.

"What?" I said.

"I'm pregnant, Pokey. About three months, Sherman says."

Sherman Forest. Dr. Buenos Dias himself. "When?" I said.

She wasn't sure, she said, her shadow not moving even one iota. In January, probably. Maybe at the Commissioners Congress in Gallup. Maybe after that champagne reception. Maybe in that Holiday Inn. Maybe on that bed in that Holiday Inn. Maybe.

"You're crying," I said, it something harmless to say.

"It's a cold, Heath. Pay attention."

I was. I was paying attention to the heat. And to the wind. And to our daughter, Mary Beth, now behind the screen door, ready to go. Yes, I was paying attention—to the gravel and grain of us, the string and the spit, the mud and melt we are.

"I'm keeping it, Pokey. Him, I mean."

I was hearing everything clearly now. Her words. My breath. The ugly thump of one heart.

"What about me?" I said, not the only selfish sentiment Heath Howell had that evening.

"What about you?" she said.

The children came out of the house then, as wooden as play soldiers, and went straight for my truck. "Hi, Dad," Lonnie said on his way by, he the oldest one in charge. "Hi, son," I said—my words, given the fist in my gullet, way too loud. They climbed in, boys in the back, Mary Beth buckled in the front, three small citizens for Pokey Howell to keep track of.

"You're going to be late," Lizzie said.

I'd put the shot in high school. Me, a Wildcat in warm-up pants and a green and white shirt. Me, with eight pounds of lead cradled in my right hand. Me, in the circle, the shot between my chin and shoulder, crouching, coiled. Me, strong enough for second place. I was thinking about that. And about Lizzie one day in the stands, in her lap an algebra book she would later conk me on the head with for getting fresh.

"Why'd we go bust, Lizzie?"

She was beside me now, the two of us hip to hip, watching our well-behaved heirs.

"I don't know," she said. "You got bored, honey."

You could see the arm of one shadow then, mine, rise to the shoulder of the other, a sight worth a picture or two.

"I'll see you later, Lizzie."

Then those shadows parted—one to the house, the other to the rest of the story.

It was *The Lion King* that evening. Simba and Scar and Timon, and four Howells howling from the front row. It was rope licorice and Paydays and jumbo buttered popcorn, the junkiest of junk. Yes, it was the Howell clan, and a hundred others probably, all going "ooohhh" and "aaahhh" and rooting hard for the good guys.

Then it was the house on Palace Circle and three little ones saying, "Night, Dad," followed by the apartment on Olive Street and the dad there in the night. Then it was hours—more than a few, so the clock claimed—and me moving among them, chair to stool to bed to chair again, the world without a root or a hook to hang on to.

Newsweek had come, in it typing about Clinton and Saddam and that sappy Russian drunk, Yeltsin—more woe you're relieved to see happening to the other fellow—but I kept losing my place, something about Syria becoming something about a homegrown villain becoming something about a wolf in Wisconsin. On the dining room table, my briefcase was open, in there spreadsheets that I was known to be the master of. Tomorrow, my father and Bert Cummins, our treasurer, would want to know what the numbers said, but in these minutes those figures seemed about as familiar to me as the Persian our enemies speak.

To my credit, I did stay away from the whiskey. At midnight I was away from it, as I was when the clock next gonged and gonged again.

At three, however, I was with it, a juice glass with a lone cube of ice to keep myself respectable. After that, I was respectable at least a dozen more times. I considered the small things nearabouts—the table holding me up, the floor holding it. I considered, too, the big—love, and the inward idiots we are because of it. I even thought about that sizable black bug, wondering if it had gotten where it was going. Then it was morning and, remarkably, Heath Howell was ready for it—buttoned and zipped, buckled and buffed—him that go-getter at the well-waxed conference table across from two cigar-puffing coots with bankbooks as thick as the Yellow Pages and hair white as storybook Christmas snow.

"I can't say," I was saying into the phone.

To which she, Betty Porter, was saying, "Go on, Pokey. Guess."

Across from me, my father and Bert Cummins were grinning and whacking each other on the back—textbook wheeler-dealers. The numbers, a piece of me understood, were exceptional. For all they cared, the youngster in the room could've been exchanging confidences with the Count of Monte Cristo.

"I really can't talk now, ma'am," I said, aiming to be a customer so cool he'd just arrived from frozen Alaska.

"I'm looking in the mirror," she whispered. "Know what I see?"

I could imagine, a bolt thick as my wrist twisting in my stomach.

"I'm wearing a corset, Pokey. I look good enough to eat."

Bert Cummins was hacking now, a wiry man with a length of wire to spit out. Really excited. Umpteen umpteens ago, he'd given me my nickname—for the sensible way I go from hither to yon—and suddenly I hated him for it.

"That's a joke, Pokey."

"Yes, ma'am," I said, still pretending I wasn't talking to a woman with so many ideas.

"You come by at seven," she said. "I got something for you, too. A silk something."

Again, I said my say, still hoping the right side was still right side up.

"Seven sharp, Pokey. You don't keep a lady waiting."

And then I was through. The phone was down, Bert Cummins had got his breath back from wherever it went, the elder Howell was fir-ing up another stogie, and the younger was waiting for the pulleys and wheels of himself to stop squeaking.

You don't keep a lady waiting. Yes, that was true. You don't a lot of things for a lady. You don't carp and bitch and do the runaround. You don't, no matter the matter, lie and cheat and scold. You don't over-look or undersay or give offense. You don't wheedle. You don't whine. You don't fuss and fume. You don't. You really, really don't.

But, regular as sunset, you do.

Your morning goes by, and you do. Your lunch, and you do. Your afternoon. Your close of business. Your drive home. Your open door. And then you are collapsed in your easy chair, a big boy still dressed for the working world, and beside you the phone is ringing—you, luckily, with an answering machine modern enough to do all the talk-ing for you.

"Pokey," she said. "Are you there? It's quarter after, darling. Mys-teries await."

She went on, giggly as a schoolgirl, for another minute—she'd driven to El Paso, shopped at the Luv Connection, got us some good-ies to play with—but I didn't pick up. Instead, I watched the tape go around and took note of the shapes that were my loyal companions in the dark. My TV, my coffee table, my unlit lamps. I was thinking about Lizzie, about the bit of me dividing inside her. Maybe, à la his old man, he'd be able to roll his tongue. Maybe he'd have my cowlick, my teeny ears. Maybe, him a chip from a chip from a chip, he'd be inclined to sloth. Lordy, I thought. Heath Howell knew some stuff, now, didn't he?

By eight o'clock, I still hadn't moved. And the phone was ringing again.

"Are you sick?" she was saying. "I'm worried about you, Pokey. You want me to come over?"

No, I was not sick. I was, in fact, not anything. Not blood. Not bone. I was empty, one me for ten me's to rattle around in.

"Pokey, you don't move, okay? I'll be right there."

Smoke, I told myself. And did, me and the Marlboro Man estab-lishing a relationship in the dark. Outside, I supposed the stars were twinkling, up where up ought to be. I supposed that on Palace Circle TV was being watched and noise being made by three extraordinary noisemakers. I supposed my father, behind the wheel of his brand-new Lincoln Town Car, was taking his supper at Del Cruz's Triangle Drive-in. I supposed my wife, Elizabeth Howell, was folding laundry or balancing her checkbook. But about here—the Olive Street Apartments, number 6—I had nothing to suppose: It was just a man, now four cigarettes older, and somebody rapping on his front door.

"It's Betty," she was saying. "Pokey?"

That would be me, I supposed.

"Open the door, baby," she said. "I'll perk you right up."

That Valentine's Day Dance. I was hearing Uncle Roy again, him a string-bean cowpoke with a guitar he'd named Dynamite. I was seeing again that squishy chair occupied by Mrs. Porter and Mr. Howell. And those trophies, silver and gold and bronze, on several shelves behind them. I was thinking about Mr. Howell's brain, the lobes and knuckles of it, the fancy thoughts it cooked up. About the man's self, the narrow and wide of it. About the man, his good fortune on earth.

"I know you're in there," she said. "I can see you smoking."

Mr. Howell. Born in February 1957. Mother deceased. An only child. Christened Heath after an uncle on the father's side. Married in 1982. A double-ring ceremony. Hundreds in attendance. Hundreds, I say.

"Betty," I began, each word to follow twice the weight of the last, "I think I'll stay put tonight."

For an instant, and for another, I imagined the hole to heaven, which was small and tight and already closing fast on my tail.

"You're dumping me, aren't you?" Betty said. "I absolutely do not believe this, Heath Howell."

I lit another cigarette. This time of night, I could be home in fifteen minutes. Twelve, if I made the light at Iron.

"When I leave," she was saying, "I'm not coming back. It will be over, you understand?"

Mrs. Porter. The edge after the edge. The other side. The way beyond the way.

"You won't be welcome at my place, either, mister. You know that, don't you?"

I could see her silhouette, and I tried to imagine why she hadn't moved, left. She was a woman with a big house. A woman with big furniture. She had ideas. She knew about the Tigris, the why of a zillion what's. She knew atomic numbers. She could say words from the least-visited pages of the dictionary.

And then, bless her, she had moved. And—a little sadly, I thought—she had spoken.

"Pokey Howell, you're a coward."

One final fact.

You think you know how this turns out, but you're wrong. Yes, yours truly does go home, but it's too late—"Too too," the wife tells him— so by December of that year, Lizzie and Heath are no longer Mr. and Mrs., Bert Cummins having done the legal paperwork on both sides of the fence. Then, inexplicably, it is January, raw with cold; then March, windy but good for sleeping; then June, and Pokey Howell sports a beard he looks sixty percent sharp with.

Of an evening, you can find him sharing a meal with his kids or his father, or enjoying a snack from the grill at the country club. During the day, you can find him behind his desk, still a big man on the outside. Some nights you can find him playing draw poker with four fellows from the bank or watching what CNN thinks is useful for him to know. Sometimes, you even find him with his nose in a book, him for a chapter or two shaking his head over some made-up hero's hardbound ups and downs.

Then, one day in late July, you can find him parked outside Betty Porter's house on Fir Street, waiting for his body to catch up with his mind. A minute later, he's on her doorstep, ringing her bell, his dialogue about three-quarters memorized. He's there for old times, he thinks. Maybe—har-de-har-har—new times, too.

And then the door has been opened and there she stands, "Pokey," a greeting about as heartfelt as heatstroke.

"Betty," he says, the next thing to say not the next thing he says. "Can I come in?"

She looks over her shoulder, back in the house, before turning to him again, a little mischief in her eye.

"This is not a good time, Pokey."

Behind her, down the hall toward the bedroom, someone is singing a tune peppy enough to tap your toes to. A man—too yodely for this time of day.

"Got company," he says.

She does, she says, and it hits him. With a whomp.

"Uncle Roy," he says, to which she nods.

"The one and only."

Heath Howell studies the street then. He knows this road. He knows the house next door, too. And the scraggly trees. And the dusty cars parked in the driveway.

"Is there something on your mind, Pokey?"

Oh, there is, and, the gears of him grinding and banging, he says as much.

"Bashful," he begins. "People forget about him. Doc, most folks remember. Grumpy, too. Sleepy, all the rest. But Bashful, well—"

For a moment, she seems puzzled, and Heath Howell has the urge, a shiver from his toes to his teeth, to touch her hair, to hold her breast, to taste her neck. Just once more, he wants to be inside her— hot and wild and falling free.

"Bashful," she says.

"The one and only."

Christ, he's doing a lot of nodding now. This street. This house. This door. Fate has put a lot here for him to nod at.

"Is that all, Pokey? I've got a guest."

The ground is moving now. Only a little time left.

"You didn't say anything about the beard," he says.

She's giving him one of her looks again, hard and dry and pointed as a bullet.

That's right, she says. She didn't.

AS FATE WOULD HAVE IT

WHEN YOU MEET, she should be mightily charmed by the gestures you practiced in the mirror an hour before—your bon vivant's smile, for starters, or the Eastwood-like tilt of your head. She has to adore your hair, your cologne, the Italian loafers you paid too much for on the PCH in Long Beach. All day long, from the instant you rolled out of the rack, you should have felt yourself moving toward a possibly providential discovery, something as momentous to you as was the apple to Adam. It should be a party in the hills, Halloween on Devonshire Court, the crowd a throng of geeks and witches and gremlins, but it should not be too noisy at first—a celebration subdued, in this case, by the news, revealed only minutes before you tossed your keys to the kid from valet parking, that your host has a mistress.

His wife, lipstick smeared red on her teeth, ought to be moderately drunk—frantic and edgy, a woman who kisses hello too hard, then jams a breast in your arm. Dressed like Marie Antoinette, she should be sloppy, outrageous as a voodoo queen, her hug almost fierce enough to crack your back. "Ooooh-la-la," she should squeal to the air beyond your ear, evidently tickled to see you—tickled to see, in fact,

Kong and Nero and Sweet Betsy from Pike, all of whom followed you up the walk.

Immediately, a beverage must be spilled, Marie a sudden whirlwind of parasol and petticoats to clean it up, so this then will be the instant you see her—your new sweetheart. She might be standing next to a gray-haired guy who seems overwhelmed by his cape, the Count of Monte Cristo. In any event, you should feel your ribs cracking open, an astounding amount of light pouring in on your quivering, oily organs. You are about to gasp, you should think. In her eyes, she will have a glint that suggests that, like your own eager self, she has come to this party with no more to lose than time and terror.

"A tart," Marie should be saying to the room at large. "At forty-six, Mr. Big Shot's got himself a floozy."

She—your dream girl, your angel, nothing whatsoever like your ex-wife—should be close-pored and deep-socketed, her skin like mayonnaise. With a handshake implying, even in costume, that she could bench-press you to the ceiling, she should have beautiful hands—you've always liked women with nails too long to be practical in the real world. Without the tee-hee-hee and the annoying trail of dream dust, she should be Tinkerbelle, her outfit the choice of her girlfriend Roxanne, who will turn out to be the tall redhead in the gold lamé swimsuit with the banner reading MISS CONGENIALITY across the bosom. They're starlets, Roxanne and your true love, Sandi. They've been in commercials, industrial videos, even a feature at Paramount—which is good to hear because, as fate would have it, you're in the business, too.

"A musician," you should say. "A drummer."

A half hour, spent in splendid conversation, should go by. Eventually, you must be introduced to Roxanne. They have a duplex down Eagle Rock Boulevard from Occidental College, you will learn. Roxanne has a Siamese, Mr. Mister. It came with her from Oklahoma.

Loud as a tuba, she will be the kind of woman that's always scared you a little—too chatty, too brash, too many parts to keep track of, a woman with too much past—so you should concentrate instead on Sandi: slow, quiet, steady, perfect Sandi.

You've worked with Kenny Loggins, you will say. Toured with

Glenn Frey. Jackson—Browne, not Michael—is an acquaintance of yours.

"I want a drink," Roxanne should be saying. "Miss Congeniality wants a whole lake of drinks."

At some point well before you catch yourself crashing through the landscaping, before your fancy shirt is torn at the elbow, before you fumble with your keys so you can start the car and get the hell out of here, you will stand on the balcony with Freddy Krueger, your host. He should've known you nearly five years—"a friendship of long-standing in these parts," he will remark.

You're buddies, he is to remind you. You Tonto, him the Lone fucking Ranger.

You should wonder about Sandi. She had gone to the powder room and then you thought you saw her talking to one of the Munsters.

Impatiently, Freddy should ask you if you're listening.

You have to be gazing at the lights in the valley, a sea of flickers and winks you still remain awed by, and it should not surprise you that you're thinking about your future—about being out there, in a car, going somewhere special, the horizon lit up like highest heaven.

"Roxanne," Freddy will be telling you, "she's the girlfriend."

You like Freddy, you should tell yourself. He's a facilitator, you will have heard many times. He puts deals together—"like nitro and glycerin," he should've said once. "Watch for the flash and see what's left when the dust clears."

They met at the Red and the Black, Freddy should be saying. Roxanne was having a cocktail with her agent, an ogre from ICM. The wife doesn't know the particulars, at least not that he's been laying pipe two afternoons a week above the Main Bar at the old Beverly Wilshire.

"Right," you will say, trying to keep up your share of the discussion.

Torrid should be a word used a lot. *Passionate.* You will be asked, more than once, how you feel about passion.

You favor it, you should think. Really, you do.

"The whomp of it," Freddy must keep saying. "It's like hitting a goddamn wall in a bus."

Freddy will have a joint—one whose name you've never heard before: Crunch or Crud—eighteen percent THC, it should be said.

"The marihoonie," he will call it. "Rhymes with moony." Stoned, Freddy should hold forth on a number of subjects—the points he almost had in *Aladdin*, plus a crisis with ASCAP and getting old—but he should keep returning to passion. With a capital *P.*

"Roxanne," he will confide to you, "is an animal. A lynx. A tiger."

"Terrific," you are to remark. "Honest."

Here Freddy should be working his lips as if his teeth hurt.

They're breaking up, he should say at last. Complications. Tumult. It's tough shit, but there it is. Roxanne doesn't know yet.

Now Freddy should seem soured, divided into fifteen, or fifty, parts—no flash anywhere. In a brotherly fashion, you might clap him on the shoulder, concerned. Besides having found you the most ruthless divorce lawyer in California, he's thrown significant studio work your way over the years. He's an independent, he will have reminded you often, indebted to no man. With connections to everybody but the Ace of fucking Spades.

Did he mention how invigorated he feels with Roxanne, he should be saying to you. "A new man," he should insist over and over. "The corpuscles fairly hum. Honest to goodness, it's like the Vienna Boys' Choir set up shop in the belly."

You must like the idea of that, but days and days and days from now, even a month after you've sent candy and flowers to apologize for the ruckus, passion will seem as wanton to you as weather, as much a matter of fear as of beauty, a frenzy as much to flee from as to wallow in.

When the silence sets in, a few seconds after Freddy has explained his views concerning God and the blessings that are steadfastness and tough genes, you will make to excuse yourself. You've spotted Sandi, you should think, in animated conversation with Jesus of Nazareth.

"What's she doing now?" Freddy should ask you.

"Roxanne?" you will guess.

Freddy's reaction—part shrug, part wince—has to be semi-painful to behold.

"No, man," he should sigh. "Marie Antoinette."

You mustn't know how to answer. Before you came out here, Marie will have been in the den, scissors in hand, snipping methodically at the seams in one of Freddy's jackets, her audience—two of the

Stooges and nearly half of the Ten Little Indians—as enthralled as cavemen at a science fair. "It's a *vestimenta*," she should have been saying. "Four figures from Sami Dinar."

"She gets crazed," Freddy should inform you. "Always takes it out on the clothes."

You ought not to know many other people at the party—they're suits mostly, management hustlers or A&R types on the prowl—though the fellow dressed like a pumpkin seems familiar. At the bar, shoulder to shoulder with Cabeza de Vaca and one of the Four Horsemen of the Apocalypse—Pestilence, you think—you must keep an eye out for Sandi, and try to stay out of the path of the more serious hoopla. Freddy's wife, her massive powdered wig slipping over her eyes, will be yelling into the telephone in the kitchen. In spite of her fury—or perhaps because of it—she should appear unspeakably gorgeous, much of her chest exposed, her breastbone so milky white you can't help the low-life ideas that assault you five and six at a time.

"She weeps," Freddy will have said to you. "She yowls. Swear on a stack, she gnashes. It's like being married to Minnie Mouse."

The CD will have come on again, a whole house system it probably took a month to install, and when Popeye has begun demonstrating something frug-like to a creature that could be Pocahontas, you should think of your ex-wife, Darla—to dancing, you have to note, what bullets are to gunplay.

She should be in Texas, a suburb of Dallas, with your son and namesake, the boy—what?—fifteen or sixteen. That you are uncertain will embarrass you. Drink in hand, you should remember his hair, surfer blond like his mother's, and his eyes, which are yours, blue as a kind of ice. Although you send the child support yourself, you should try to recall when you yourself actually talked to him, or Darla. It could have been Easter. Or Memorial Day. Very probably, you should guess, you were on the road. St. Louis, maybe. Or Kansas City.

At this moment, Little Bo Peep will be advancing on you, behind her a man in gauzy robes and a scary quantity of white, windswept hair. She should ask what you are, your costume. Her companion, his fake beard frosted white and crooked underneath his nose, has to be wild-eyed, a snow-covered cannibal fresh from a rampage.

Old Man Winter, he should tell you. That's what he is.

You will try to clear your head, but your thoughts, usually ordered as infantry, have to be competing for space with the wails the Breeders, at 110 dbs, are blasting into your brain. Not for the last time will you wonder where Sandi is, your long-lost true love. Like a weapon, Bo Peep should be carrying a staff, large and hooked at one end.

You've forgotten, you should tell them. You've been out of town. You aren't dressed as anything.

Puzzled, they must consult with each other, Bo Peep and Old Man Winter. They're surprised. They thought you were a cowboy. A young Bat Masterson, for example. Or a younger Lee Van Cleef.

A week from now, when you are nearly asleep and when you feel like a sickly child who's seen a bad shape skulking in the trees, you should remember that time, at this point in your adventure, passed in a disturbing way, as broken and ill-fitting as space was in the aggressively silly art Darla once dragged you around Brentwood to gawk at. Freddy's place will have become more crowded. Attended by a Nubian slave, Nefertiti should arrive. The crew of the starship *Enterprise,* Mr. Spock on crutches, must materialize.

You're a cowboy, you will tell George and Martha Washington. You've just mislaid your pistols.

You'll have another drink—and another—and when you hear the name Harrison Ford, you should wonder if he's here as well, or just his Han Solo look-alike. Sandi will have said she'd had a part—itsy-bitsy, albeit—in *The Fugitive,* but while you dread for the ten thousandth time that she's run off with Colonel Sanders or the Michelin Tire Man, you should glimpse Roxanne trapped on the couch at the far end of Freddy's lobby-like living room, her expression completely stricken, absolutely helpless while a woman heaves and sobs in her lap. It will be Marie Antoinette, her hoop skirt fanned up over her shoulders like a turkey's tail, while behind them Frankenstein is doing a handstand for Heckle and Jeckle.

Here it must occur to you, in the frighteningly corny way all insight has occurred in your middle years, that you are ravaged. Thoroughly trashed.

·   ·   ·

Near the door to the bathroom, you should lean against the wall, an effort to take stock of yourself. Something is missing, you have to feel. Your wallet. Or that interior tissue, the result of many centuries of natural selection, that's meant to keep humankind from slobbering all over itself. Your hands, normally light and strong, should feel clumsy as crates and too heavy to carry around for the next hour, but in them you should find not one, but two drinks. Yours and—whose? You should endeavor to reconstruct the last five minutes of your life, an exercise that proves as futile as trying to swim to Siam. The marihoonie, you decide. The Crud.

You will imagine yourself elsewhere—at the beach, or the gym on Pasadena Boulevard. Christ Almighty, you should be in bed. You have a session in the morning, Julio Iglesias or the like. The producer—an inconceivably hairy guy, a virtual Wolfman, another of Freddy's connections—will expect you to be sharp. Really, you ought to leave now, but between you and your car stand several munchkins and famous murderers, all of them amused by your ability to keep the wall from crashing down over your head.

And then the bathroom door has to open. It will be Sandi, the only person in the world able to renew you with a single wave of her wand.

"There's a problem," she has to tell you.

You should repeat the word, startled to find what could only be snakes at the bottom of it.

"The ex-boyfriend," she will say.

A bone creaking inside, you should remember what you learned about Sandi before the Aga Khan, on the claw of a Maine lobster, interrupted you earlier. The ex-boyfriend should be named Jake—or Slate: a name as contrived as are hats on hyenas—and he should be an actor notorious for off-screen escapades involving sports cars and semiautomatic pistols. Like a billboard for tanning butter, he should be handsome, and mean as a hammer. Sandi is afraid of him. Really. Before rehab, he ran with the Brat Pack—Judd Nelson, Emilio, that bunch. A certifiable brute.

This was totally unpredictable, she should be saying now. Typical Slate. The story of her life.

You should groan, more truth bearing down on you.

"What about a rain check?" she should ask. There's a place in Burbank. The Palace of Mystery. Maybe you could meet her there?

Like someone shown the modern world with the lid yanked loose and the gears inside spitting off grease and flame, you should understand that, among the arachnids and yammering vegetables, among the living dead and the various extraterrestrials, Slate has just appeared, the latest of Freddy's guests.

"Burbank," you have to say. "The Palace."

Events will unfold very swiftly now. You may find yourself dancing, your partner a vigorous blonde you believe you rooted for on *Baywatch*. Wobbly on her high heels, Roxanne may break in with news about Freddy and Marie. In one of the bedrooms, so it should be reported, they are sitting calmly on a settee, sharing a joint Freddy has speared on one of the gleaming knife blades that are his fingers; apparently reconciled, they are said to be singing a verse of "Some Enchanted Evening." Without question, this image should move you. You are not insensitive, no matter Darla's opinion on the issue. You do have a sentimental side, and for a moment, while Roxanne struggles to tear her banner off, you should imagine having slept with Sandi, the different things you could have learned—about her body, sure, or her habits in bed, but also about your own self at its best. She will have told you that, as a triple Virgo, she is trustworthy, but, apart from behavior to read about in the Calendar section of the *Times*, you have to wonder, as a Scorpio, if that ever boded well for you.

Meanwhile, Roxanne, at war with her outfit, will have attracted a crowd. Dracula, Porky Pig, Jimmy Carter, Thelma and Louise. Nearby should stand the fellow in the pumpkin outfit, his expression composed and abstract, as if he's chanced upon a problem he could solve with his calculator and graph paper. At last, you should recognize him—the Virgin exec you worked overdubs for at Groove Masters in Santa Monica—Fenton, or Felton. He wanted to be called Finn, you should remember. He desired more boom-boom, or comparable effects. More hi-hat. More chuffa-chuffa. More of what you didn't have that day.

The bottom is out of you now, you ought to realize. Lordy, you're litter inside, a wretched wind howling through the center of you.

"Help," Roxanne should be yelping, slapping and swatting at the glittery script of her banner. She wants this thing off. Right fucking now.

"Calm down," you should tell her. But at the instant you prepare to wade in to assist her, which is also the instant Sandi appears with Slate, you should realize you are about to do something both stupid and violent. Your heart suddenly frozen, you pause, dumbstruck by your own goofiness. You won't believe it. You're the peaceable kind, you should think. Once upon a time, ages ago, you marched.

Nevertheless, as dazzled by your own lunacy as you might be were a Martian to land on the stage of the Dorothy Chandler Pavilion on Oscar night, you should turn away from Roxanne: You are now, against all odds, a man with one last good office to perform. You are the nitro, you should think. And the glycerin.

"Mr. Drummer," Roxanne will be saying, tears in her voice. "Where the hell are you going?"

Near the foyer, Slate and Sandi will have appeared. Notwithstanding what you've heard from Sandi's own luscious lips, they should present themselves as sufficiently arm-in-arm to convince you that the world has rules as twisted and bassackward as are its ruled. It's the Crud, you should believe, that's making you think this way. It is not, you feel certain, a permanent but heretofore unacknowledged feature of your character. Nor is it a condition, like a pimple on your ass, you can ignore or forget about. As if seeing this episode from the rafters, or on Freddy's big-screen TV in his media room, you should be amazed. Utterly bamboozled. You are, clearly, a man in need of some help yourself. If Roxanne—or anybody—is hollering at you, they ought to be doing so now. In a kind of stupor, you should look about. If there's someone to save you—Attila the Hun, maybe, or the June Taylor Dancers—they should be doing so now, before the ground opens beneath you, before the lights start flashing and the banshees break into song.

"Hey, pal," someone should be saying. "Long time, no see."

Distracted, Slate has to be looking elsewhere, but Sandi—beautiful, tasty, faithless Tinkerbelle—should be trying to warn you off with her eyes. Bravely, you are to attempt to ignore her. A principle is involved here, you will be telling yourself. Something big—bigger than the two of you, more monstrous than happiness itself—is at stake, and if you could summon them up, you should like to say a few words about it.

Still, halfway to Slate—which, to you, is halfway between one life and another, halfway between fate and circumstance—you have to discover that you are, remarkably, only halfhearted about what's befallen you. You are, God help you, resigned. You are motion, not movement; activity, not action. Your blood running cold in your throat, your fist should be cocked, but you should feel powerless, dutiful, obliged. Once again, you should wait for your brain to catch up to your feet. The world, you have to decide, is almost rotten, and there's only one thing you, alas, can do about it: You—Noley James Gilmore, formerly of Star Route 2, Luna County, New Mexico, Western Hemisphere, Planet Earth—are about to throw a punch.

You should be face to face now with Slate. Sandi should have been only partly right: He is a Nazi, yes, but with a smile from a toothpaste ad.

"Is this the guy?" he should be asking Sandi. "This can't be the guy. Say this ain't the guy."

With a shudder, you should understand now that the punch, the first you've thrown in anger since the Alameda Junior High School lunchroom, has no chance of connecting—for a thick-legged mesomorph, Slate will be fast as a flyweight—and that, slack-minded and off balance, you will tumble past St. Francis of Assisi and crack your head against the tile-covered stairs.

Your punch still unthrown, you should see yourself moaning like an infant on the floor, your universe muffled and swirly and murky, colors running gooey at the margins of your vision. You should see yourself crawling, slowly at first, then with greater determination. Briefly, you should imagine something sharp attacking your ankles and knees, a mob going after your kidneys and thighs. Then, your flung fist flying feebly in the air to nowhere and the focus coming back to your eyes, you should envision being later assailed from on high.

It will be the pumpkin man, bent over you like an orange Florence Nightingale. Whispering over and over, "Hey, pal," he will be trying to help you up, and, like a bullet into your forehead, knowledge will be reaching you that, a knot throbbing over your eye and your shoulder bruised, you are leaving here with a tiger.

Roxanne.

In the car, she will have something to tell you. A secret.

Behind the wheel, you should be taking an inventory of yourself. The stinging in your wrist. The faint ringing you should hope, however stupidly, is coming from an ice-cream truck lost way after dark. Amazingly, you should be in good spirits. Pumped and jittery—wasted, sure, but somehow shriven—as athletes are said to feel on the other side of victory. But then you should recall your shameful exit from Freddy's house, in particular that pathetic attempt from the floor to explain yourself, the sneers of contempt from Little Red Riding Hood and the Big Bad Wolf beside her, and here your heart will give an ugly lurch sideways, the steering wheel about the only thing in free America to hang on to.

Her real name is Alma, she should tell you. After the city in Oklahoma, her parents' idea of cute. "Near Muskogee," she should say. "Where Merle Haggard comes from."

Now you should yearn for other things to happen tonight. A drive-by, say. Or a flash fire roaring in the canyons leading out of here. A catastrophe equal to the hour and atmosphere. An earthquake.

Roxanne is so much more evocative, she will be telling you. She could just strangle her mother.

You are in this together, you must realize, two fools in fantasyland. So you should ask her what she'd like to do now. You will know a dozen clubs you could get to in twenty minutes—Sparky's Melon Patch, for example, the Frog and the Peach, the Crest Café on Sunset—but you should assume she'd be embarrassed to show up in a swimsuit and see-through raincoat. You could shoot pool, you will think. Maybe sneak down to the beach. It will be past midnight, the sky cloudless all the way to China, the ocean somewhere dark and forever in front of you, the desert over the scrub-covered mountains behind, and you will say okay, a part of you cold and brittle, when she says, in a tone both mischievous and business-like, that you should surprise her.

"Freddy Krueger," she should say. "What a dipshit."

At your place—the bungalow on Valencia Street in La Canada, the house Darla will have left in a huff one spring so long ago you can't remember your reaction—Roxanne will be thrilled that you're so tidy.

"A neatnik," she should call you. "Not like you-know-who."

Here events should become roiled, disordered as war itself. One minute, Roxanne might be inspecting your drum set, maybe timidly trying her hand at banging the floor tom; the next, she is drinking Quervo, sniffling over how crooked life has turned out. One minute you might be kissing her—she will almost be too tall for you, the kiss curiously without current and heat—and the next, she is chattering about calligraphy, hers a language about nibs and strokes you struggle to make sense of. It will be morning late and morning early. A streaky dawn and deepest darkness. Tumbledown and upright, the air smelling clean as Clorox. You will find yourself ahead of her and behind, both smarter and dumber—maybe, you have to concede, as you've been with all women—and then a moment will arrive, unexpected as lightning, when you find yourself in your hot tub beneath the gazebo in the backyard, only hundreds and hundreds of gallons of bubbling, frothy water separating you from a sodden woman who, as Miss Oklahoma Rodeo of 1986, once barrel-raced astride a quarterhorse named Hardhat.

"Poor Julio," you will say. It should be obvious to you now that you're in no condition to go anywhere.

"Yes," she will hasten to agree. "Poor Señor Iglesias."

The Crud should have seemed to wear off, but there will be a vast space between your ears you fear was once filled with memories and plans.

Roxanne will ask about your eye.

"It's sore," you will have to admit.

"Here's to that," she will say, and from somewhere previously out of sight a bottle of Dos Equis will rise in salute.

On the outside speakers, your only album, *Wet Places at Noon,* has to be playing. John Hiatt, himself a wild man in those days, should've helped you with chord changes and horn arrangements. This should've been your drug years—Percodan, Xanax, the exports of Mexico and Peru. Back then, it might seem to you, you had no trouble with words.

"Who's Finn?" Roxanne will want to know.

"The pumpkin," you should answer. "Another music mogul."

She has to look at once bedraggled and revivified, her red hair slicked back like a seal's, and then you should realize that you, your brow still thumping, probably don't look so swell, either.

Finn gave her his card, she will announce. Tucked it in the top of her suit when he was leading you out the door. She's to call his service next week. Tuesday.

You should study the evidence, soggy in her fingers.

"Poor Señor Finn," you will say, and, taking the card from her, you have to drop it over the edge of the steamy tub, where it should lie for nearly a week until the maid, Mrs. Dominguez, picks it up and asks Señorita Roxanne, the last lady in your life, if it is *importante*.

Deliberately, you are approaching the end of something, you should conclude. Not an era, certainly. Merely a phase. A confusing but not unimpressive period of warp and woof, of riot and silence, of ruin and rain.

"Noley," she will say. "What kind of name is that?"

"It's a ranch name," you should answer, and several images will spring to mind of you and your father discussing T-posts and salt rubs and spavin in the cattle you have grown up tending.

With the awful clarity of a clairvoyant, you should foresee what's to happen next. An hour from now, Roxanne will have asked you if you want to make love, a prospect that will have struck you as inevitable and necessary and sad. You should say yes, but at the moment the two of you rise from the tub—Roxanne still hasn't gotten her banner off and it should droop from her shoulder, water dripping as you walk toward the house—she will say she has a story to tell.

You like stories, you should remind her. Hell, you've told a few in your own life.

She was in an auto accident, she should begin. On the Ventura freeway, near the Laurel Canyon turnoff. Last August. A pretty nasty affair. A three-car pileup. Somebody died, the idiot who caused it.

You should be in your bedroom now, both of you looking at your bed, a car alarm woo-wooing nearabouts.

It's afterward she will need to tell you about. When the ambulance arrived.

You should have your soggy pants off at last, your shirt somewhere you will laugh to discover when you awake ten hours hence.

It's the paramedic, she should continue. He was so gentle, so careful. He talked to her like a lover. Held her head, went through her hair slowly, searching for glass. For the cut that would account for the blood beside her ear.

The alarm should be gone now, but another noise will have become clear to you—a clanking, rattling sound that could be an engine, something infernal and wrong.

His name was Ric, Roxanne should tell you. With a *c*, not a *k*. She'll remember that forever. His tenderness.

It is your heart, you will decide. At the moment the two of you climb into your bed from opposite sides, still wet, still slow and cautious, that noise, thunderous and leaden, is your heart.

His touch, she should say. She wanted Ric Martin Pettibone to take her home. She almost asked.

The whomp of it, you should think. It's like hitting a brick wall.

But this scene shouldn't have happened yet. Time a fluid as likely to travel one way as another, you will still be back in the tub, the future an hour away from history, and you should be telling Roxanne about Darla. On the stereo your most famous song should be playing, "All Things, All at Once," a ballad, complicated as any poem you studied in college, that peaked at 84 on *Billboard*. The advent of a Santa Ana, a breeze should have arisen, hot and dry as air from a grave, and you must be telling a story about your mother, how you once saw her slug a horse. Another story should occur to you, this about backing up Jeff Beck years ago at the Coliseum outside Cleveland, and you should describe how it felt, spooky and exhilarating, like being able to fly, when the crowd applauded and you couldn't get the shouting out of your ears.

Water burbling under your armpits and between your legs, you should speculate aloud about Sandi, even about Slate. You're planning a vacation, you should say. Aruba, the Azores. Australia, maybe. You should fetch Roxanne another drink—Ron Rico now, you're out of tequila—and, on the way back, you should notice how doughy you look, how you didn't have a gut even a month ago.

You don't smoke, you should tell her. Generally, you're law-abiding, considerate. You owned a dog once, a collie, and would again were you home regular hours. You vote, mainly Democrat. You've given money to United Way, to the AIDS people. For a couple of days, you were a Boy Scout. You tried college, Arizona State, but you were—are—a musician. A drummer. You've played with Jackson Browne. With Ray Davies, from the Kinks. Bonnie Raitt, God bless her, is a pal of yours.

"You're shaking," Roxanne should say to you.

With effort, you ought to be able to bring yourself under control. You should have experienced the first of many flashbacks, this one the moment that you lay crumpled more or less at Slate's feet while Little Bo Peep, urged on by the squeaky cheers of Old Man Winter himself, whacked at your knees with her terrible staff.

"What happened?" Roxanne will be saying to you. "To the horse your momma socked."

"Nothing," you have to say. "She busted two knuckles."

It will happen now. Or not at all. Head back, looking at the stars, Roxanne will say the magic words, those few unique to all matters of love and loss.

She's lonely, she should admit. Flat-out pissed off.

Awkwardly, you should reach across the tub to her. Something, you should feel, hangs in the balance between you. A compact having more to do with the soul than with the flesh. Her skin should be water-wrinkled, like your own. She will be Miss Congeniality, you a young cowboy after all. Your mind, which you have always thought of as a cluttered storage attic, should be clear, nothing between the first and the next thing to do but water and air and time. You have to feel for-tified, stalwart even.

"Please," she will say to you. "Put it on again. That song."

And you should.

You will.

You have to.

CATEGORY Z

for Dorcey Wingo

AT SIX A.M., the sergeant ordered us to board the bus. He spit a lot, called us pansies, ladies, queerbait. He wore his garrison cap like a hoodlum, was built like a hammer, and had the whitewall haircut Uncle Sam preferred. He took away our lunches and radios, told us to shut up; this was the Army's day.

"For the next twenty hours," he shouted at us, "you're mine." I looked out the window. We would be going from Lordsburg through Deming and Las Cruces to Fort Bliss, in El Paso, almost two hundred miles of desert, lonely and stark as the moon. "Do nothing, girls, abso-goddamn-lutely nothing to make me mad. Am I clear?"

This guy is a joke, I was thinking. He is John Wayne, Sergeant Rock, a doofus.

We were twelve, all Chicanos except for my pal Ray Reed, me, and Cooter Brown, a kid we knew from high school. For some, me among them, this was only "preinduction," but for others, including Ray Reed and Brown, this was induction itself; we were all IA, which in 1969, the year some of this takes place, meant what Cooter called "Veetnam."

"I ain't going," he said. "No way."

35

He sat in front of us, and Ray asked what made him so special. The sergeant—Krebs was his name—sat by the driver, drinking coffee from a thermos.

"I got a note," Cooter said. He unfolded a square of paper—from a Big Chief tablet, I think—and I took a peek. "Dear United States Army," it read. "Please excuse Master Wm. A. Brown from his draft physical. He has ringworm, tetanus, and a little polio. Yours sincerely, Dr. August T. Weems, M.D., Esq." It read like a tardy note at school.

"You wrote this," I said.

His was the smile of a first-time father.

"Damn straight," he said. "Pretty good, huh?"

Ray Reed and I were a lot alike, often excellent in the subjects we liked, and handsome enough to be in love every year, but this boy Cooter was what we called a *dweeze,* a word for which we knew no synonym in the English that teachers ask for. One month he was fat (put you in mind of the Pillsbury Doughboy); another, he was skinny. He'd graduated a year before us and worked sometimes as a night irrigator for my father, Avis Buell, who's the pro at our country club. I had also seen Cooter a few times at the Elks Lodge, playing drums for Uncle Roy and the Red Creek Wranglers. Cooter had the singing voice of a chicken.

"Between you and me," he was saying, "I gotta know."

"What's that?" I said.

"You scared?"

I'd been reclassified for two months, but this was my first physical and I had a back problem. Besides, I was going to college.

"What about him?"

Ray Reed was asleep, his mouth open. He had the expression of a man dreaming about money. Or women. Ray weighed about two hundred, All District (AA) outside linebacker, and had fist-fought Coach Mirmanian during two-a-days last September. He rode cycles—motocross, mostly—and I could think of nothing that frightened him.

"What about you, Cooter? You scared?"

"Hell, no," he said. "This is political, man. I'm a peacenik, honest. What about you, dove or hawk?"

In those days, I'll admit now, I was nothing but a semi-grown teenager, a B-minus student, fair in algebra and such world history as we had, a reader of books that made the brain race, and, best of all, a recipient of a full golf scholarship to the University of Houston. I was a lot like the fourteen-year-old son I have now: nice-minded as, say, your first barber and unable to see farther than the hundred miles I knew here in my desert. I had a love of the game, a girlfriend named Sally Whittles, a brand-new set of Arnold Palmer irons, and no larger desire than to be one of those tanned sportsmen you see on our country's most famous links.

"I'm conscientious," Cooter was telling me. "I'm tapped in the SDS, the Venceremos Brigade, Yippie Defense Front, the whole works. This is protest, Buell. Jimi Hendrix, Country Joe, Abbie Hoffman, the Chicago thing—it's a collective, man. We have a common soul."

Sergeant Krebs had turned around.

"Brown," he yelled.

Cooter waved his hand. "Back here."

"Shut your face."

In Las Cruces, the bus pulled into the 70-80 truck stop near the Palms Motel.

"You may use the latrine," Krebs told us. "You may smoke, you may shoot the breeze. You have fifteen minutes."

In the men's room, Cooter described us as meat, fodder, dog leavings. He mentioned Che Guevara, Emerson, and Thoreau, a California professor named Marcuse. We heard language like "proletariat" and "serving class," and listened to what Cooter knew about crime and about the dread DuPont was doing to us.

"Where'd you get all this?" Ray Reed asked.

"Books," Cooter said. "*The New York Times*. I'm radical, man, an objector."

"Cooter Brown," Ray said, "you're a dipstick."

In the toilet, I could hear Cooter telling a couple of the Chicanos about "the heritage of the oppressed." Like them, he said, he was disenfranchised, fit for consuming only, a 3-D thing that ate, slept, and lived in debt. "I'm displaced," he said. "Dispossessed, too." His older sister, Francine, was a waitress at the Ramada Inn—"a victim of sexual politics!" His father, Tully, was a working stiff, a mechanic at Ellis Lincoln-Ford. "No profit-sharing," he said. "We're the underkind, boys. We want peace, am I right?"

In the next few minutes, I learned his mother had died of cancer two years before. He'd had a dog once, a pound breed named Fuzzy, part collie, maybe part sheep—"a big sucker."

After I washed my hands, he dropped his jeans.

"Holy Christ," I said, "what's that?"

The two Chicanos were backing out the door, flabbergasted. Outside, Sergeant Krebs was telling Ray Reed a war story that seemed to take place in a Baltimore slum.

"These, my friend," Cooter was saying, "are one hundred percent pure India silk, hand-sewn, reinforced-crotch ladies' bikini underpants."

Here it was that two thoughts came to me and I took one step backward. Indeed, Cooter Brown was scared; he was frightened for his life—and, Jesus H., I liked him. There, in one of America's nasty men's rooms, a kid with the high forehead of a comic-book egghead and the pinched lips of a milk snake, he had seen something—himself, I guess—in a vision, in a nightmare. He had seen himself, I believe, as a smear of blasted flesh, a crawling, drooling, weeping thing; and I had this question: If he's scared, why aren't I?

"Those Army medics," Cooter told me, "are going to take one look at me and throw me out as 4F, count on it. I'm twenty million F, Buell. They're gonna put me in the Z category, as positively undesirable as a human can be."

Back on the bus, Ray Reed sat by himself on the seat behind Krebs. They were having a conversation that involved rope and what man is.

"What's his problem?" Cooter asked me.

"He's a patriot." I remember trying to make the word sound sensible. "He wants to get out of town, see other places. His recruiter told him he could go to Germany, Greece."

Just south of Las Cruces, where I-10 lay out flat and straight on the mesa above the Mesilla Valley, Cooter asked if I smoked reefer.

"Sure," I said. "A little Mexican weed."

"I had some this morning," he said. "Pure Colombian. Really screws up the coordination."

Up front, Ray Reed was laughing with Krebs, so I told Cooter about my back, how I'd had five vertebrae fused when I was in the ninth grade. I'd been in a car wreck on the way to the Phoenix Open with my father.

"I did some speed, too," Cooter whispered. "That's why I'm blabbing so much. My blood pressure's gonna ring bells."

I was thinking about my girlfriend, Sally Whittles, and where we might be in ten years, when Cooter told me what was in his overnight bag. Candy, he said. M&M's, Mars bars, Three Musketeers.

"Gets the blood sugar up," he said. "They'll think I'm diabetic. A certified vampire."

I'd heard they kept you overnight, I said.

"I'll be blind," he told me, rolling his head and slapping the seat. "I won't talk. I'll French-kiss somebody, a general."

For the next hour, Cooter went on about the things he'd do—spit in his urine sample, masturbate, grab ass—but I was watching the landscape, the scrub-covered Franklin Mountains on the left and that part of my world on the right that went on parched and white and lit up forever. I couldn't imagine Vietnam. The TV I watched made it seem unbelievably lush—too green and wet and noisy. It was Oz, I thought. It was old, and full of murder. Mr. Cronkite said its people believed in tree spirits. It rained, plants had souls, and in it were 500,000 young people like me that I was glad I would not join.

About nine-thirty, we reached the outskirts of Fort Bliss, and Cooter rose up in his seat. Outside stood ranks and ranks of barracks, wooden and identical, no place at all to live. We could see signs with official lettering that made no sense as language folks ought to use. We rolled by an obstacle course—hurdles, tires, barbed wire—and Cooter tapped me on the shoulder.

"I don't think I can do it, Archie."

He might have been ready to cry, and I knew what he was talking about.

"I know what's going to happen," he said. "They're going to tell me to jump and I'm going to say, 'How high?' I ain't political, Archie. I'm a wuss."

Sweat was running down his temples, a lot of it.

"What about the panties?"

He shook his head. "Took 'em off," he said. "They're Francine's, my sister's."

We turned a corner, and a group of recruits—a platoon, maybe—came into view, marching and chanting about gore and how happy they were to be sons of bitches.

"Jerks," Cooter sighed.

He uttered it the way you and I say "Amen" in church, half swallowed and not at all encouraged; but I didn't hear any more until the bus stopped and Krebs, calling us females, told us to grab our gear and get the hell out of his limousine.

You could say my day turned out fine. A doctor with freckles named Finkel took one look at me, told me go away. I was putting on my sneakers when Ray Reed found me.

"I'm in," he said.

"What about Brown?"

Ray didn't know. I'd heard Cooter's voice a couple times. He had been saying "Yes, sir" with real enthusiasm.

"Here," Ray Reed said, a key in his hand. "You take my bike. I'm staying, they can have me now."

And that was it. I went home that evening, me and a few Chicanos who were missing fingers or had the misfortune to be deeply ignorant, and in time I put aside most of the foregoing. That fall, I left for Houston, playing three years on the golf team, then went to Florida for PGA school. I took a month qualifying; but got my A card, played on what was then the satellite tour in Honduras and Guatemala, twice in Mexico City. Only once did I hear from Ray Reed. In his letter, he spoke of Army Mickey Mouse and where he wanted to be in the next life. "Every day," he wrote, "is as lousy as the last."

As everyone expected, Sally Whittles and I married, and after my dad put together a syndicate of club men—Dr. Weems, Buzz King, Freddy Newell—I spent two years trying to make a living as a professional. At the Tallahassee Open, I won enough for a new Buick and real meal money; in 1973, I qualified for the U.S. Open at Winged Foot but didn't make the cut. Then, following my father's heart attack, I came back here, to Lordsburg, to be the assistant pro. I sold cardigans, NuTonic spikes, gave lessons, bought a house near the course, and thought little about Ray Reed and Cooter Brown.

Ray must have been back about a month when I saw him at the Labor Day party at the club. He was working for his dad on their ranch north of town.

"Still got the Yamaha?" he asked me.

He was thinner, losing hair at the temples, no lines at all in his face to say what he'd seen, what he'd done.

"Yes," I told him. I hadn't ridden much but kept the cycle in good repair. "It's in my garage. When you gonna come by?"

"Soon," he said, "real soon."

He didn't turn up, of course. A year went by. And another. And sometimes I'd go out in the garage, start up his cycle, lose myself in the racket it made. In high school, we'd been best friends. We'd partied together, cruised Main Street, even lost our cherries to the same Juarez whore. One summer we'd gone to Pacific Beach in San Diego, took Ray's old Nash. We had known each other since first grade, and now that was all gone. So one Saturday I bought a helmet, gloves, and steel-toed boots for my son, Eric, and took him into the desert to show him how to ride fast and not get hurt.

Then Cooter Brown appeared.

I was on the practice tee, trying to keep Mrs. Baird's right elbow from flying out on her backswing, when I saw a guy by the door to the men's locker. It was late afternoon, the sunlight sharp and white enough for the hell a terrible God might have made, and for a time, while Mrs. Baird flung herself at a bucket of balls, I kept my mouth shut and wondered who it was.

I thought about my wife, Sally, and how she looks waking up, sleep-soaked and radiant. I listened to the wind, studied the contrail of a plane miles overhead, and wondered if I was cold and only alone.

Who are you? I asked myself. Who are you now?

I told Mrs. Baird she could finish by herself—"head down," I said, "tuck that elbow"—and walked toward that man in the sunlight.

"Cooter Brown," I said. "Long time."

He had the well-cut hair and square shoulders of someone who is very proud now.

"William," he said. "I'm called William now, or Will."

I had my hand out for a shake and he took it.

"Ray Reed said you'd be out here. You're doing all right, he says."

There were fifteen cars in the lot and I could hear Casper Lutz in the pro shop singing a ballad he liked. I felt awkward, stupid as a cow, and wanted to apologize for the too-colorful clothes I wore.

"I'm in Hollywood now," he said, "flying choppers."

The Army had made him a warrant officer, given him a million jobs to do in the air. He had the touch, he said. The aptitude, the facility. A superior sense of equilibrium, good eyes, poise. Now he was flying stunts for the movies. TV and commercials, too.

"You ever see *Reruns*? Or *Going Away*?"

I said no, then he told me Ray Reed was going to meet us at the Grange, a bar on Ormond.

"You knew Ray over there?"

"Some," he said. "Ray was at Tay Ninh for a time. We were tight."

At the bar, I called Sally, said I'd be home late.

"What's wrong, Archie? You sound weird."

Except for Cooter, me and the bartender, Jimmy Sample, the place was empty, and I had nothing to look at but the scribbling on the wall by the pay phone. I saw the names of some I knew, and I felt as I had when I stood over a five-foot birdie putt I knew I would not sink.

"You remember Cooter Brown?" I asked.

"The guy in the panties?"

He was standing by the jukebox. He would play something twangy, I thought. A tune a Nashville cowboy had invented about bad love.

"I'm having a drink with him now."

"Oh," she said, and that was all until I said goodbye.

Ray Reed walked in about eight, and he and Cooter made a little war noise saying hello. We had a table in the corner, from which we could see the Grange fill up and grow smoky.

"How's your dad?" Ray wondered.

"Good," Cooter told him. "Retiring in three years. Francine's in Albuquerque married to a guy named Wilson. Got two kids."

We drank to that and to several other things in the next hour—good health, money, having women—then they told Vietnam stories. I heard about a black corporal named Philly Dog and a place called LZ Thelma. Some names I recognized: DMZ, Westmoreland, Saigon. But most were unfamiliar, private: First Corinthians, the Battle of Bob Hope, Firebase Maggie. Ray Reed told about life in II Corps, how the land lay, what you sweated when you heard the wrong sound in the wrong place at the wrong time. Cooter Brown told about his remarkable life in the skies—descent, rotor wash, skids, China Beach. Once they toasted a woman named Madam Q.

"Right on," Ray Reed said.

"You bet your ass," Cooter said.

Many beers later I told them I'd been a rabbit.

"What's that?" Cooter asked.

It was a golfer, I said, who showed up on Monday to qualify for the few open spots in the tournament that began on Thursday. "I played with Jack Nicklaus once," I said, "at the Kemper."

"I'll drink to that," Cooter said, and I went on.

I liked being married, I said, being a father. And for a time, as I talked and in a way I can't explain, I felt the years had fallen away between them and me. It was practically spiritual, I think now, as if, as kids do, I could say anything and wishing would make it so. I felt dumb, too—dumb as are lucky men when the jackpot comes their way for the second time.

Then Ray Reed said he was going home.

"Take care," Cooter told him.

"You, too," Ray said. "Good to see you."

Cooter's Chrysler was large and had every gadget he could afford—power windows, automatic door locks, and a computer that figured how far you could go on the gas you had. On the way to my house, he played the tape deck, rock 'n' roll, particularly a song that rhymed, in a manner I thought wonderful, *docket* and *rocket*. Cooter told me he knew lots of actors—Lee Majors, Fess Parker, the guy who played Batman.

"California," he said. "Party state, Arch. You ought to come out."

He was nervous, embarrassed, and I didn't want to say much until I said adios.

"Turn here," I told him, and in a few minutes we stopped outside my house. A light was on in the garage.

"I did the right thing," Cooter said. A few doors down the block, the Risners were having a party, and for an instant I wanted to be there with the two men on the porch. They held drinks and were looking eastward with smiles.

"You want to come in?" I asked. "Say hello?"

He held a cigarette he didn't seem to enjoy.

"Your wife's Sally, right?"

The two men on the porch were joined by another who looked just as content.

"I remember her," Cooter said. "You're lucky, Arch."

He had more he wanted me to know, and for the longest time, while the men went inside, I waited to hear it. I aimed to count stars and attend to what my heart was doing, but for some reason—perhaps because of the moon we had and the blackness everywhere—I thought about Sergeant Krebs and the war he'd be fighting next.

"I'm a prole, Archie," Cooter told me at last. "I do what I'm told."

Then he left, and I had my familiar indoors to look forward to.

There is a moment in golf, as there must be in other sports, or what in life sports stand for, when you strike the ball with such authority and accuracy that you know it will be where you planned it to be. I have described it to Sally as a moment of purest intelligence—poetry, if you will—when nothing at all stands between you and what you imagine. It is more mystic than what gurus practice, and often more religious than the state of mind Baptists have. More than luck, it is a peacefulness—whole as we think love to be—and, for a time, it is able to spread its shine to all you do thereafter. It is the way I felt, in the year this occurs, when I walked down the hall in my house to find my son, Eric, in the garage.

"What's the matter?" I said.

Spread out, in a pattern that would make you say a Buell had done it, were dozens of parts from Ray Reed's motorcycle.

"It was misfiring pretty bad today," Eric said. "Besides, it needed cleaning."

"Kind of late, don't you think?"

He was scrubbing part of the clutch assembly with an old toothbrush and turpentine, and doing a good job.

"Yeah," he said. "I'll put this away."

"Never mind," I told him. "I'll do it."

I waited until he went inside before I sat in the midst of the parts of Ray Reed's motorcycle. The party at the Risners' was breaking up, nothing would be on TV, and it seemed suddenly that I had a lot of time. Working the rest of the night, I believed I could get the Yamaha back together. Then tomorrow—or the next day, or the day after that—I could take it south in the desert, toward Hatchita, maybe twenty miles. I'd have a helmet, work boots, a jacket, and I'd see how fast I could go getting back.

DREAMS OF DISTANT LIVES

THE OTHER VICTIM the summer my wife left me was my dreamlife, which, like a mirage, dried up completely the closer we came to the absolute end of us. In the fourteen years we were married, I had been a ferocious dreamer, drawing all I knew or feared or loved about the waking world into my sleep life. If I had seen a neighbor's animal— Les Fletcher's horse, say, or Newt Grider's collie dog—in my dreams that night I would see dozens of them, beasts whose language I understood and respected, animals whose own stories I heard and wept over just as one day I would weep over my private misfortune.

One night—actually the early morning hours after our first son was born—I watched a flock of pigeons from my wife's hospital room. There were hundreds, mindless as those swivel-eyed birds can be, flapping and swirling in a hurly-burly over the massive air conditioners, their bird-chatter an unhappy, loud whirring, constant as party talk. It was a noise I heard distinctly hours later when I fell asleep at home. They were yammering, those dreambirds, and what they said to each other, and would say to others yet to arrive, seemed so sensible to me in my sleep that I awoke smiling, as if I had heard secrets vital enough to live by. I had been where they had been—north and south, in good weather and bad—all the places they visit, into trees and onto ledges, on rooftops and in parks. I was, in the few hours I dozed, a pigeon.

Another time, on a vacation to Disneyland, I became the folks we met on the road—those who pumped our gas, or cooked burgers for us, or stood behind the desks at the Holiday Inns we stayed in. I was the boy who bused our table in Phoenix, the blond woman outside the entrance of the San Diego Zoo whose own child was colicky or too well fed; I was the motorists we passed by at seventy miles an hour, and I was those citizens whose communities we circled on the atlas: Santa Barbara, Laguna Beach, San Mateo. I paid their utility bills (PG&E, water, and garbage), shopped and ate and hollered for them. At the end of our four weeks, as we drove south from San Francisco to our home in Las Cruces, I was even the pilots overhead, whose lingo was as remarkable and private as that, yes, spoken by birds.

But when Karen left, my dreams stopped—not abruptly, as if the tape that was my inner life had finally ended, but gradually, as if the world inside were subject to erosion by the common elements of wind and water, and by the uncommon elements of lovelessness and despair. My first night alone, I was a general—a George Armstrong Custer. I had blond heroic hair, plus heavy gold braid on a tight broad-cloth tunic that flattened the lazy-man's belly I have. My dream voice was stern, gifted as what stage actors aim for; and for that voice I used a vocabulary as fancy and important as one in any schoolbook. In that dream, I issued orders which were ungrudgingly obeyed and had my name called so often that, when my alarm clanged, I woke saying, "Yes, how may I help?" I remember standing—at attention, I suppose—at my bedside, alert as a sentinel, listening for what was needed of me, what emergency had fetched me into daylight again. "Karen?" I said. "What is it?" I was awake, but part of me—the part, clearly, that she had left when she went to her sister's in El Paso—part of me believed that she was still here, if not in the bathroom next door then in the kitchen.

Searching for her, I opened Danny's door, and then that of Mark, his younger brother. Their bedrooms seemed empty, not abandoned. Beds were made, closets organized, their toys put away. Still, hearing her name over and over in my memory, I looked for her. Her plants were here—the Boston fern, the overwatered rhododendron—as were her books and most of her clothes, but she was not; and it was only when I opened the patio door and stood in the backyard, studying the rank of rosebushes she'd planted the year before, that I snapped to. I had been slugged, I felt. I actually staggered, thrown backward by a force like horror. "Karen?" I said again, but by then I did not mean it: Her name was only a word given to an object that wasn't here anymore. It was a word that stood for an absence, like darkness itself, that had made way for the waking life.

In the weeks that followed, my dreams came quickly, but with parts missing or poorly joined. They had no beginnings and their endings seemed less like conclusions than, well, interruptions. Not nightmares exactly, they were like slide exhibits, flashing picture shows thrown together by the weary, unthinking heart of me. The family came and went: my boys were born, grew, and went into adulthood in minutes. My father, dead many years, appeared dressed for golf, in the too-colorful plus fours he favored, and in his happy Panama hat. He did not speak, nor did I see him, as I often had, in front of the TV, his expression fixed and baleful. Instead, he was swinging his Walter Hagen driver, in slide after slide, his stroke an enviable display of coordination and strength. I saw my mother, too. In every frame that rose out of the night, she sat at the shallow end of the country club pool, her bathing suit an unflattering one-piece affair whose wide shoulder straps hung down her arms and whose skirt seemed more appropriate to a child. She was fluttering her feet in the water, again and again and again, and pointing, in obvious joy, to a soaked figure in the baby pool—me, I think—a skinny, clumsily diapered toddler. One night I saw the few friends I had as a youngster—Mark Runyan, John Risner, Jay Bullard—and I saw the first house we lived in, 111 West Gallagher, behind which was a cotton field where we raced our Schwinn bicycles and, later, a rusted two-door Ford we bought. I saw the girl I loved first, a high school sophomore named Michelle Parker, and I saw the way she was now, which was sad and too perplexing to sleep through. I saw the Texas college I could not graduate from, the cramped dorm room I lived in, and the Lake Dallas oilman's house I was violently drunk in once. And often, too often to be unimportant, I saw faces and events placed side by side, as if between them I were to make comparisons; as if between, on the left, my wife at home in her nightwear, and on the right, me in the caddy room at the country club, I were to see a connection.

I saw nothing. No meaning, no significance. I was uninvolved, as distant from what was being shown to me in sleep as from what I had once seen in time. In these days, I climbed into bed after the ten o'clock news, and before setting the alarm and switching off the bed-stand light, I asked myself what silliness, what oddball's concoction of delight and misery, I would dream. Nothing of my job as a ninth-grade math teacher came to me, nor did I recognize anyone from the present—not Herb Swetman, my principal and best pal; not Emily Probert, his secretary; not any of the youngsters I coach on the freshman soccer team. Puzzled and partly stunned, I conceived of my unconscious, the thing we are told our dreams spill from, as a fishing net whose weave was too wide for the current world.

By September, my dreams involved me in tasks. Night after night, I picked up leaves from trees I don't have, one by one, and stacked them in piles as high as my ears. I wrote my name, with one hand then the other, in ink and in pencil, on ruled and on unlined paper. One time, after a phone call from Karen (a conversation whose last lines were so impersonal they could have been uttered by Martians), I sleepwalked. My dream concerned thirst, and when the alarm went off, on my nightstand I found not one but five glasses of water; and I report to you now that I drank each of them, slowly and seriously, as if I dared not, as if the penalty for neglecting what our dreams bid us do is not less than death itself. Yes, I drank them; and after each, in the silent moment between the putting down of one and the taking up of another, I had a vision of myself as I was when Karen and I married—an eager beaver ignorant of what time can do to love.

The last of these dreams—when they ran out and never came back—was almost a year later, after our divorce was final and I knew I ought to go forward again. This was several years ago, when I regularly played stud poker in the men's locker at the country club. There were five of us, all married but me, and the most you could lose in our quarter-limit game was twenty dollars; we would drink and order roast beef sandwiches from the second-floor snack bar and, if we planned to be late, we could shower or, as we once did, we could dive into the pool or go out to the driving range to be crazy. On the night of this dream, I was the last to leave. I'd won, but the sight of my winnings, folding money and change, didn't impress me. There was no place to go. Ed had driven home to Bonnie, Max to Jean, the rest to their wives, and I was there, in a chair, a drink at my elbow, listening to the showers drip and the satisfying musical whoosh-whoosh the outdoor sprinklers made.

Almost directly, I went to the pool and tumbled in, clothes and lace-up shoes and all, and as I had as a kid, I pulled straight for the deep end, down fifteen feet to the drain where, for the child I recalled, the pressure and heavy silence of the water overhead seemed as reassuring as gravity. Several times I plunged down, suspending myself as long as I could before crawling up for air. I felt good, I say. I had a former wife who lived elsewhere, sons who would not be too much damaged by what had happened, and a job I was fine enough at; more important, I had this night to myself—a spread of stars whole nations could wish upon, and clouds that say rain is on the way, and breezes that bring with them the smells of what we plant hereabouts in the Mesilla Valley. I think I sang; or I wish I had sung, and now— in the wistful half of me that's putting this on paper—I hear that singing again, as if I were out on the course at night, and say to myself, as a stranger, that there is a man singing over yonder, in a scratchy voice that certainly has some liquor and cigarettes in it, and that man is happy.

I folded my soggy clothes over the chain-link fence and, alone like one of the first smart creatures on our planet, I considered this place. I studied the buildings—the pro shop, the ballroom, the women's locker a floor above our own—and beyond them, the third of my town that wasn't asleep or had no work to do. I could see Hiebert's Drive-in, the Rocket Theater, and the curve of North Main Street that swept by the Loretto Shopping Center. I could hear cars, faint and steady, and I wondered who was out there. I imagined moving the one hill in front of me and being able to point out the house I owned as well as those I pass every day on my way to Alameda Junior High School. I was putting together my world as my dreams had once put me together, and everywhere I looked I spotted something—a willow tree, someone's Lincoln Continental, a garage—that might look better over there. Or there. Or there. Naked, common sense stripped away by the Jack Daniel's booze I like, I saw the world I could construct for the sixty thousand souls I share it with. A house became a castle; a streetlight, a tower. I put X with Y, A with B, and by the time, an hour later, I sat down in a ratty chaise by the pool, this largest town in Dona Ana County had become as quaint and patchwork as those we yearn for from olden times that never were. Joy—and mirth and bliss and virtue—had many faces that night, I say; for I put in pockets or hearts or minds whatever over time had been stolen or broken or made sad.

And then I dreamed.

We are told, I believe, too many truisms about our inner lives. In books, magazines, and on TV, in all the yakety-yak that comes our way, we hear too much about the selves we are. We are good, we hear; or we are bad; like dogs, or not; like angels, or not; flawed, or perfected. Our swamis tell us—our preachers and teachers, politicians and doctors, all the tattling experts loose among us. But it is in dreams—of pigeons, of the past, of people long gone—that we attend to the inner life itself, hear it in its own words, at its own pitch.

My last dream featured the desert we have, the thousands of square miles of sand and rock and scrawny brush that doomsayers tell us will one day be your home, too. It was a flat world, infertile as a skillet, with lightning flashing at the horizon. It was a world of red and yellow and green skies, all the colors poets love, a place whose light was liquid and melting all around. I was in it, I dreamed, at an unmarked crossroads, the age I am now, thirty-nine, and in good health. I could go left, or right, or straight, but to the man I was then, the choice made no real difference. I was to see something, I knew, and soon enough it appeared in the shimmering, indistinct distance. Out there was myself, black against white, too tall in an otherwise diminished land.

"Fine," I said. "All right."

And I waited—waited on me. My inner life, the world constructed from what I'd been or done, was speaking to me, patiently and calmly. I would hear what it had to say, and I would understand. And so I came to myself—observed the man I am now walk forward to the man I was then and take him, as you take your children, into his arms. The one held the other—the future cradling the present— and the one who had been left, the one whose interior hooks and hasps and snaps had come undone, gave himself up utterly. They were both there, in dreamland, under heaven and over hell, two versions of the same man, clasped in an embrace that would only end when the world came up again.

GRAVITY

THEY GRAB HER—Tanya, my fourteen year-old daughter—early in the afternoon from the sidewalk outside the north entrance to J. C. Penney's at the Mimbres Valley Mall.

At that moment, I, her father, Lonnie Nees, am in my office in the county administration building, putting together the agenda items for the road department, in particular the details for abandoning a bladed road in southeast Luna County adjacent to Panky Scott's O Bar O Ranch, so, of course, I don't know that Tanya isn't, as she told me before she left for school in the morning, at her friend's house. "You can pick me up at Segen's," she said. Her mother, my ex-wife Ginny, thinks Tanya is at basketball practice, the JV team. In any event, neither of us knows that while I'm putting the polish on the wherefore's and whereunto's and Ginny is taking a nap to the sounds of *One Life to Live,* Tanya is being dragged into a late-model pickup in front of what Sheriff Milton will say are nearly fifty witnesses.

The call comes at four-thirty. From Milty himself. Here in Deming, New Mexico, no one is a stranger. You want to talk to the editor of the *Headlight,* you call up Dwight Eddy and say your say. Ditto with the fire chief, B. J. "Butch" Punch. Our state representative, Monte Zamora, a Democrat, lives down the block from my office on Fir Street. Sylvia Chavez owns the El Corral Bar, Earl Spencer the Ford-Mercury dealership on Iron. Dr. Friedman will come to your house, night or day. Eight Thousand Smiling Faces, so says the billboard on I-10.

"You know anybody drives a dually—maybe a Chevy—red over white?" Milty asks. "Texas plates?"

Hereabouts, pickups are common as horseflies. I even have one, an F-150 I use to haul trash and the like out at my mother's spread toward Hatchita.

"What's up?" I ask.

Milty takes a second, too long for this call to be about an auction or the benefit rodeo. He's polite, our sheriff, especially if your collar is white and you make a living, as I do, talking about writs of mumbo-jumbo and using your large legal genius to keep on the sunny side of Uncle Sam.

"We think it's Tanya," he says. "That's what a couple of girls are telling us."

Okay, I think. An accident.

"Is she all right?"

Milty clears his throat, another habit he has when hard words are to come next.

"She was kidnapped," he says.

I have my pen out—a birthday present from Carly Barnes, my girl-friend—and, Christ, I have the *k* written down before my brain gets too big for my head.

"Lonnie, you there?"

I am here: rooted, it seems, stuck between standing and sitting, the air in my office suddenly too thick, me like a dog listening for thunder.

"How long ago?" I ask.

An hour, he says. Maybe longer. His people and the Deming PD are out the mall right now, interviewing witnesses.

"Give me five minutes," I tell him.

Outside my office, my secretary, Margie, is telling her son-in-law over her phone that her plumber, Delton Shirley, still hasn't covered the trench for her new septic system, a complaint she's refined for a week.

"Meet me at your place in an hour," Milty says. "You can't do any good out here."

That makes sense. I'm a practical man, few of my ideas ever half-baked. I brush my teeth three times a day, gargle with mouthwash, change my drawers in the morning—as ordinary a citizen as you can find in the funny pages. I, as my mother insisted, mind my p's and q's. "If X knows Y, and Z doesn't," my father used to say before his heart went "blooey" two years ago, "let X do his damn job." Milton's the sheriff: X. Lonnie Nees is a county manager, as at home with statue and regulation and such as is a tailor with needle and thread: Z.

"You tell Ginny yet?" I ask him.

Here's that necessary second again, Milty—like too many of us men, I suspect—far more comfortable with what cusses and spits than with what only shakes its head and clucks its tongue.

"I thought I'd leave that to you," he tells me.

He's right, but for the next few minutes—time enough, anyway, to find my seat again and put my breathing in order—I don't call. Instead, trying to put English to the thoughts I have, I listen to Margie chattering on about what a miserable, low-down skunk Delton Shirley is for not putting the cap on the clean-out and tearing up the chain-link fence so she has to keep Sugar, her spaniel, in the house all the durn time. And then, nothing new to learn about leach lines and the ethic of today's workingman, I punch in Ginny's number and tell myself that here isn't Albuquerque or El Paso, or even Las Cruces. Here we just beat the stuffings out of each other and drive into a utility pole or take the ugly times out on a stop sign with a .22. This is Nowhere, New Mexico, folks, home of the duck races and five-acre "ranchettes" and a handful of families, mine among them, that pretty much own everything you can see from Devil Bill's Texaco station all the way to Lordsburg in the west. But Ginny has come on the line, her new baby in the background fussing, and I find myself, as per usual with her, hoping for the roundabout way to get at what needs getting to.

"I knew you'd call," she says.

She's said something, but I can't make heads or tails of it.

"I told you," she's saying, "Tanya can't stay this weekend. Billy's taking us to the dog races in Juarez."

Billy—William Teaford—is her husband, the cowboy she left me for three years ago, and as good a guy as you could wish for your ex-wife. Good stepfather, too, to hear Tanya tell it. Generous. Always ready with a laugh.

"This is not about the weekend," I tell her.

"What is it, then?" she says. "Little Billy has the colic or something, so I'm kind of pressed for time."

We have an arrangement, Ginny and I. Though she has custody, Tanya stays with me Monday night through Friday morning because the Teafords—Billy's a son in one of the five families—live forty miles south of town, too far for Tanya to participate in any extracurricular activities; Friday afternoon, Ginny picks her up after shopping and getting groceries, and that's that until Monday when Tanya climbs in the front seat of my Suburban outside the ninth-grade wing of Deming High School. We're civilized, we tell ourselves. Making the best out of times that once upon a time seemed only bad.

"It's Tanya," I say, a little louder than I'd planned.

"She sick?" Ginny asks. "She get hurt?"

I'm getting ready to tell her, but before I do, I have a moment with myself—just me and the sharp parts inside that have gone loose.

"She's missing," I say.

Ginny named her Tanya, said it was exotic, suggestive of times better and elsewhere—Shangri-la and the like, a picture-book paradise with soft breezes and homes with five bathrooms; not this hardscrabble desert and everything sad as dirt—said it gave her a place in the world that was already full of Ashleys and Mallorys and Kaylas. Me, I'd wanted a name with some history to it—Sally, say, or Virginia, aunts of mine I'm partial to.

"Outside the mall," I tell her. "Milton called."

The forty miles between our ears are hissing and crackling, time grinding like a flywheel, and I imagine Ginny putting my words in a pile, one atop another, until she's got her breath back, her tongue ready to come out with it.

"You son of a bitch," she says.

Tanya's not really missing. I won't learn this for a month. I won't learn
that she's only run away, vanished herself, headed elsewhere in a cloud
of dust. No, this news is coming, thirty days hence, me in the mean-
time jumpy and scared, the America outside my windows as remote
and cruel as Mars. Instead, see me that afternoon, pulling into my
driveway, Sheriff Milton already there, his car the biggest eyesore in
the zip code.

"This hers?" he says, holding a Baggie with a flip-flop inside.

Who knows? I want to say. *It's a flip-flop, for crying out loud.*

"What's going on?" I ask, the simplest question on the planet.

He's not sure, he says. Could've been wetbacks, cholos, anybody.
Could've been the dually. Could've been a four-door Dodge, maybe a
Ram. Hell, everybody's got a different story. Some joker set off fireworks about the same time. Helen Harrison, from the Mode O'Day,
thinks it was a flatbed with winch and a light bar. Two guys. Maybe a
third driving. Older. Grown-ups. Went east on Country Club.

Milty's put the Baggie back in his car, and we're standing outside
the gate to my yard, the sun beating down hard and nothing between
us and the next thing to do but time and footsteps.

"I got to ask," he says.

"What?"

Milty looks a lot like a Ben Franklin without all the bad habits, eye-
glasses on the tip of his nose, his the rosy cheeks of the fat man he's
sure to become.

"Can I look at her room?"

Another bit of good sense, so a minute later we're standing at the
door to Tanya's bedroom, little so far to say that life has now completely wobbled out of groove.

"Well kept," he says, nodding.

He's right: Bed's made, drawers are closed, no clothes on the floor,
her dresser organized. Daddy's good girl.

"Mind if I look around?"

Hanging from one corner of the ceiling is a hammock filled with
stuffed animals—a buffalo, a jackalope, a moose, a lizard, a bear the

size of a steamer trunk that I got her on a trip to Yellowstone. "Consult the bear," she used to say when a choice had to be made—green beans, say, or peas—her voice swami-like, her eyes rolling dreamily. Beneath her boombox are her CDs—Eight States Away, Savage Garden, Shudder to Think, Thrasher, groups that look angry and starved. Her TV has a tape in it—*Moulin Rouge*, I think, a longtime favorite—and hanging like bunting from one mirror are her ribbons for swimming, even a mini-marathon at Elephant Butte. Sure, I tell Milton. Look around.

"I'll help," I tell him.

Milton holds up a hand, a new being entirely.

"It's official, Lonnie," he says. "I've got to do this by the book."

A book, I think. The book. The one with the whyfore's and such. The book that says the loved one—the father, in this case—should wait in the living room, or the den, while the peace officer conducts his search. That book.

"You want something to drink?" I say. "Coke. Iced tea."

"Just give me a few minutes, Lonnie," he says.

In the kitchen, I help myself to a glass of water, attend to the scrapes and creaks that say Milton is opening drawers. Held on the fridge by a magnet is the roster for Tanya's basketball squad, so I think, what the hell, and pick up the phone. A mistake's been made, I'm telling myself. Not Tanya. Someone else.

I get Ruth Peterson, Sissy's mother, on the second ring.

"I'm wondering if Tanya's there," I say. "Could you put her on, please?"

"Lonnie?"

Only this morning, the refrigerator was semi-interesting to read. Pictures of Carly and me in the swine barn at the county fair last autumn. A wallet-size of Tanya in her away uniform. Number 25. Her hair in a ponytail. A to-do list. Fix the water softener. Treat the brick in the sunroom. The toll-free number of the Pegasus satellite people.

"She's not here, Lonnie."

"Do you know—"

"Lonnie," Ruth says, some steel in her voice. "She's not welcome anymore. She was supposed to tell you."

"Ruth, I—"

"You need to watch her, Lonnie. That's all I'm going to say."

Sissy, I'm thinking. A homely creature. A dinosaur's wicked teeth. Hair like a tumbleweed. Tall, elbows like doorknobs—just the specimen of girlhood you need in the paint to clear a little landing area.

Nobody answers at the Sanders' house, so, while Milty is banging around in Tanya's room, I try Cassie Moore's number, people I don't know. Moved from California a year or so earlier. The father's in real estate.

"Mrs. Moore?" I say to the woman who answers.

Her "hello" was cautious, wary, sixty percent *We don't want any.*

"This is Lonnie Nees," I say, "Tanya's father."

An ocean of silence, and for instant I wonder if there's anyone at all her end of the line.

"I'm looking for Tanya," I say. "We've got kind of an emergency."

The Moore family's big, I hear. Five kids, Cassie the oldest. A looker, so the gossip goes. Too full in the bosom for fourteen. Hell, too full in the bosom for forty.

"I haven't seen her," Mrs. Moore says, her tone ice and darkness.

"Maybe I could talk to Cassie," I say. "Is she there?"

More silence, this downright toothy. And I find myself staring at the phone, half convinced I haven't been speaking English, but a foreign tongue much burdened by x's and m's, the language of fits or permanent panic, what you see in the cartoons when life in 2-D gets runny at the edges, when faith gives way to gravity.

"Tanya's off-limits," Mrs. Moore is saying. "We don't condone that kind of behavior, Mr. Nees. We're Baptist people."

Behavior—yet more vocabulary from the animal kingdom.

"Mrs. Moore," I begin, "I—"

"Please don't call again, Mr. Nees. Our Cassie has nothing to do with your Tanya."

I'll remember this exchange forever, as I will remember all that arises out of these events, me still unable to sort sense from silliness. I've got the phone in hand when I catch a glimpse of myself in the den mirror, a massive thing with an honest-to-goodness lariat as its frame next to my gun case. There's Lonnie, I think. Square-shouldered, nose

a little bent courtesy of Wildcat football (junior year). He's going to
seed in the gut, not the worst fate that can befall a man in middle age.
He has an impressive loaf of hair, none of it gone gray, and eyes that
say he's stepped through a seam into a world cockeyed and tumbledown, this day the wrong day for folks with money in the bank and
diplomas on the wall at work.

Which is when Milton appears in the doorway, a metal box in
hand.

"Does Tanya do drugs?" he asks. "Marijuana, pills—that sort of
thing?"

Tylenol, I'm thinking. She wouldn't swallow Tylenol until the
fourth grade.

"Found this in the closet, hidden behind some shoe boxes."

He's holding the thing as if it were a bomb, which I suppose it
more or less is, big as a cash box you'd buy at Staples.

"She hates smoking," I tell him. "Made me quit before we went to
Yellowstone that summer."

"Look inside," he says, the top now back on its hinge.

Here's something else to remember: the father approaching, the
news clearly bad, time seizing up, the outside turning black as coal,
the links and straps of him letting go, his heartbeat the only sound for
miles.

"I believe that's crank, Lonnie. Crystal meth."

She's in a street gang. Vatos Locos. She's a Pee Wee, well down the
ladder from the O.G. There's an affiliation with the Insane Pope
Nation. She hangs with Queen Lefty, Mopi, Molla, Cuzz 211—Shorty
Folks with a desire to go Lil AK. They squawb and tag and pretend to
front for the Anglo Queens. She speaks punk and Aramaic and voodoo
and all else foreign to the round world of God-fearing Christians.
There's no JV basketball. No "gee" and "golly" and "tee-hee-hee."
Instead, it's piercing and doo-rags and low-riders, children with nothing between their ears but fear and woe.

I learn these facts over the next few days, Sheriff Milton appearing in my office doorway or on my porch. The third morning, he puts

his Stetson on the corner of my desk and says, "I've got something to show you."

I drop the paperwork I really haven't been reading and give Milty the once-over.

"How long have I known you?" I ask.

He gets which-away in the eyes and looks briefly over his shoulder—maybe for the bogeyman.

"Hell, Lonnie, we go back to grade school. I don't remember ever not knowing you."

True. We go back to the Alameda Falcons, back to freeze-tag with Kay Stevenson and Michelle Parker and the Newell brothers, back to swimming the flooms and racing ATVs over Jimmy Bullard's lettuce field, back to the time when days were only and always twenty-four hours long and the sun—always yellow, always hot—rose routinely in the east.

"You like this, don't you?"

"Lonnie, what're you talking about?"

"The action," I say, meaning to include in my tone all of America that can hear me. "Getting on the radio, talking the cop talk, turning on the siren, ten-four and Roger that."

He's got his hat in hand again, giving it a thorough look-see.

"Hear me out," I tell him. "This is my daughter we're talking about. This is not a case, a fucking investigation. We're people you know. You've eaten barbecue in my backyard. We fucking play golf together. Jesus H. Christ."

He doesn't know what I'm hollering about and, truth to tell, neither do I. I sit in the office and try to appear busy, my inside absolutely unrelated to my out. I read the paper but have no idea what those marks on the pages mean. I drive my car, uncertain about I how I get from hither to yon. I eat what's set before me. I doze in front of the TV and wake to find myself still stupid, still fond of us at our best.

"Sorry," I tell him. "I'm not thinking straight."

You can see him get his corners tight, the hat back on my desk.

"I have some pictures," he says. "We opened her locker at school."

For the first time, I notice an envelope next to the hat.

"They're pretty rough," he says. "Just wanted to warn you."

While he closes the door—no more complaints today from Margie about Delton Shirley or his common kind—I consider the envelope, standard issue interoffice.

"Put these on," he says, handing me a pair of latex gloves.

He's shaking a bit when he takes out the pictures, Polaroids, more than a handful in an evidence bag. Sheriff Barry Milton, I think. Milty. Just the sort of stick-'em-in-the-eye, clean-shaven meat-eater you want around when there's a warning to heed.

"Take your time," he says.

The first is of five girls—early teens, I'm guessing—all in ordinary school clothes, shirts too tight, pants their mothers couldn't wear. In the middle stands Tanya, scowling like the others, all throwing the finger. One has the bored expression of a viper. They look sore-minded, defiant, girls bidding adios to high heaven.

"You recognize any of them?"

Not a one, I tell him. They're aliens, witches.

"Keep looking," he says.

In the next, they've taken off their shirts. They're wearing brassieres, fancy colors for modern times, their bodies still ten percent baby fat, five girls in thrall to the same simple idea.

"I didn't realize she was so big," I say. "Tanya. Her breasts."

Milty shrugs, clearly embarrassed as much for himself as for me.

In the third, they've dropped their pants, the five of them in their underclothes, panties from the hard-breathing pages of the catalogue.

"Who's this?" I say, pointing to an arm—the photographer's, I assume—in the lower left corner of the photo. On the back of the hand is a tattoo, what looks like a stylized unicorn with bat wings, a Technicolor nightmare from a comic book evil genius.

"We think it's a guy calls himself Trey Dog. Real name Douglas Posey. He's a punk, runs with a gang called the 8th Street Bombers. Dropped out after the ninth grade. In and out of the juvenile system pretty regularly. Mainly first- and second-degree misdemeanors, but we think he boosts cars for the Rolling 60s out of Tucson."

"You interview him?"

He nods. "Claims he was at his mother's, babysitting some nephews."

Oddly, I think of Ginny, the way she can whistle loud enough to get the attention of most of West Texas.

"Why am I looking at these, Milty?"

Maybe something will ring a bell, he says. You never know.

And maybe it's all a mistake, a practical joke gone haywire, every roof beam of the planet now snapping free. Or maybe it's the right time to see the creatures we are, to reckon with the sorrowful and crooked kind you've raised, to throw back the lid and consider, moiling before you, the motes and mites my old man said we are.

"You're strong," Carly told me last night.

She's a sizable piece of work, a former Miss New Mexico Rodeo in the late seventies, but at that moment—her at the stove, me at the breakfast table—she seemed tiny, less of what more had once been.

"Say it," she told me. "Say, 'I'm strong.'"

I beheld her, Carly Louise Barnes, orthodontist: hair from a fairy tale, teeth out of Hollywood, a laugh that can move furniture.

"I'm strong," I said, yet more chatter from Mars.

Now I'm holding the fifth photograph. The girls, Tanya in the center, have turned their backs to the camera, their rear ends thrust out. Cheesecake, is all. A harmless two-page spread from my old man's *Swank* or *Playboy* magazines—another instance of what the tribe is thought to pant for.

"Nothing," I tell Milty.

In the next, they've unclasped their bras, their backs still to the camera. Muscles, I notice, skin the many hues we white ones come in. They're coquettes, vamps, so grown-up they're strangers. One looks like she's sucking on a jawbreaker.

"It gets worse," Milty says, taking no pleasure at all in the fact.

The panties vanish next, five asses from dreamland. They'll turn, I am thinking, and in the next one they have, their bellies flat, Tanya clearly proud of how much she's left behind, none of them with pubic hair, all bald as their first birthday.

"It's an initiation," Milty tells me. "A ritual, we're guessing."

Like church, I think. Like varsity football. Like pledging Greek. Take off your clothes, show the outsiders your goodies. Amen.

At last, then, we've come to the picture Lonnie Nees has not lived enough life to see: Tanya alone, evidently on her knees, her head back, her frizzy hair pulled away from her face, eyes wide open, mouth set straight as a ruler.

"What's that on her face?" I ask.

Later, I will tell Carly, her own face turning stony, her eyes glassy and flat, the air between us dry as ash.

"Ejaculate," Milty says, a catch in his throat. "It's semen."

"She's lazy," I tell Carly that evening.

We're on the porch, cocktails in hand, most of New Mexico to the east a cheap shade of purple. In Carly's lap are the Yellow Pages, another night of takeout.

"Ginny cuts her goddamn food for her," I say. "Peels her banana. Jesus."

"Don't," says Carly.

"Watches TV all the damn time. Takes a half-hour shower. Christ, I've never seen her read anything that wasn't a school assignment."

Carly closes the phone book, stage business meant to dramatize her impatience with me.

"What's your point, Lonnie?"

I don't have a point. I have facts. The height and weight of us. Our odd and low needs. Tanya Virginia Nees. Libra. Southpaw. Brown eyes. Braces once upon a time. Can't sing worth a hoot.

"Chinese or pizza?" Carly asks.

I swallow a drink, high-dollar bourbon that's not nearly potent enough.

"You wouldn't think she'd have the imagination to be a punk," I tell Carly. "How can you be a bad ass if your mother still cuts your meat for you?"

A minute passes, arctic and miserable. To the south a coyote barks—not with enthusiasm, I think—and more night descends upon us, another terrible morning only hours away.

"I'm going home," Carly says. "You're not fit company." An hour later, I'm in the kitchen when the phone rings, a huge sound in an oth-erwise diminished world.

"Carly?" I say, me ready with an apology, but in return only come the hiss and ticks of an open line, your county manager connected to outer space.

On the counter sits the bids for the elevator retrofit at the court-house, numbers and words I haven't the sobriety to comprehend.

"Hello?" I say again.

The silence has heft and hue and heat.

"Tanya?" I say, now on the tottery side of fear.

I hear it then: breathing, deep and steady, what the perky heroine puzzles over before the front door busts open and the psychopath charges in with the miner's pick.

"Lonnie Nees?" a man says.

"Who is this?"

Shortly, when I am shooting my .22 at the hay bales stacked between T-posts next to the pump house, I will congratulate myself for my calm, my cool—for not losing my temper with the owner of a voice that is as much sand as sound.

"She's gone," the man is saying.

"Who are you?"

Laughter now—faint and fading—the chuckle of the hombre who holds the deed to dreamland.

"Posey?"

But the call has ended, me with a million more questions to ask. I hit *69, the callback function, but all I get is a handful of rings, and a handful more. I punch it again, and again, until, the inside of me filled with ice and echoes, I find myself at the gun cabinet, replica six-shooter in hand. And then I've scrambled outside, bourbon for company, and I'm plugging away at hay bales I have no other use for—just me, Jim Beam, and the Man in the Moon.

Not a minute later, Ginny Teaford, ex-wife, appears on the ditch road you take to my house, her Explorer raising considerable dust in the starlight, and I spend some quality time with my hands and feet until she brakes to a stop a couple of giant steps away.

"Billy the Kid," she says through the open window.

I doff an imaginary ten-gallon. "At your service, little lady."

She eyes me hard, as if I'm a stain that won't wash out.

"You're drunk," she declares.

I look around, take in the far and near. "I'm trying," I say.

Here she gets out of the car, shakes her head—a real production.

"What're you doing in town?" I ask.

Her face tightens, and for a second I think she might smack me.

"How about a drink?" she asks.

I hold out the bottle, neighborly and generous.

"On ice," she says. "In a glass. Civilized, Lonnie. Let's go in the house."

Is it here where I tell you that, not three civilized drinks from now, we'll be having sex? Yes: Wrong as God on horseback, we, Billy the Kid and the little lady, will be mostly naked on a bed big enough for a stage show and that not a word will be spoken, nothing but rutting sounds forthcoming, us but friction and flesh, the two of us having gone mean and wicked against each other.

"You haven't decorated much," she says when we sit in the living room.

"Not much to decorate with," I say.

We're going to fight, I think. A storybook shouting match, the sort we had so surprisingly little of when the end was finally upon us.

"How's Carly?" she says.

I make a wave that indicates Dr. Barnes is fine.

"Where's the baby?" I ask.

Her mother's, she says. "I'm in town for a few days, maybe a week."

"And Billy?"

We've arrived at a fork in the road. One way leads to a cave where the monsters roar, the other to a version of this room, in easy chairs an old couple with one last complaint to register. In any event, this is the end of what the weepy call high tide and green grass.

"Billy thinks I'm fat," she announces.

Even with all the hooch, I'm smart enough to keep my trap shut.

"I nag, he says. Fuss at him."

In the half-light she looks tired, as if she's run all the way here, and a part of me remembers why I fell in love with her back in the Dark Ages.

"You should go home, Ginny."

She gives me that high-handed look again: I'm an interesting smudge she's found on the tip of her boot.

"And you should pour me another drink, Lonnie Nees."

The wind is up now, acres of Arizona blowing our way, time getting gooey at the edges.

"One more," I tell her. "Then you go home."

But, of course, she won't, a certainty I don't grasp until, standing at the bar, my thoughts going whichaway in a whirl, she tells me to close my eyes, turn around.

"Ginny," I begin, helpless to know what to say next.

"Just do it," she says. "Just do this one thing."

So I, eyes closed, turn, me the most obedient being in the desert.

"We had it good, didn't we, Lonnie? We had the best, you and me. You made me laugh. You made me feel smart."

Hers is the voice from yesteryear, all the age out of it, all the bite gone.

"Open your eyes," she says.

She's got her shirt off, an honest-to-goodness western affair with yoke and mother-of-pearl snaps. Her jeans are on the back of the easy chair by the fireplace. Except for her underclothes, she is white as light itself.

"Say 'yes,' Lonnie."

It's not a word I know, and then, because this is Oz and Wonderland and Atlantis and that parallel universe the eggheads yack about, it is the only word I know, and I am following her toward the bedroom where, as driven by grief and fear and helplessness as I, she will, grabbing me by the belt, ask, "Why didn't we know, Lonnie? About Tanya."

To which question I will have no answer. Except rage.

Midmorning the next day, Milty calls, tells me to come out to the county dump.

"You found something," I say.

Just come, he tells me. He doesn't want to talk about it over the phone.

At her desk, Margie my secretary is on the phone herself. "Delton Shirley," she mouths. "The bum."

I take the phone from her, wind myself up.

"Mr. Shirley," I begin, mine the voice you hear from the Republican Party when there's a war to fight.

I ask him if he likes working for the county on occasion, to which question he says, sure, why not, the checks don't bounce, so I tell him about the "exceptions and exclusions" clause in the county charter, which information gives him pause, and I can picture him scratching his noggin, eyes crinkled with suspicion, trying to figure out which field I'm coming from.

"It's a great day," I tell him. "No clouds, no wind. Couldn't be any better."

"Where's this going, Mr. Nees?"

To Margie's house, I tell him. A fence needs mending, the clean-out needs a cap.

"This ain't right," he grumbles, which sentiment I agree with, but, hey, what can a body do, county has good work for good workers, not fellows who can't seem to get themselves motivated, certainly not for folks who say one thing and do another.

"You understand me, Mr. Shirley?"

This is prejudice, he informs me. Outright discrimination.

"Have a nice day, Delton."

I hand Margie the phone, me the newest version of the Big Bad Wolf.

"Call the courthouse," I tell her. "I want the property records for people named Posey—addresses, taxes, the whole thing."

On the way out to the dump, I catch a glimpse of myself in the rearview mirror: Mine is the smile of a man who's not smiling, me your dandy hero with the heart of coal. Still, I'm right about the day: The wind coming out of the south is cool, something in Mexico gone to ice. Scattered clouds: September as imagined by a Mr. Rogers on a toot.

At the gate, Milty has posted a deputy, who flags me down, gets in the car.

"Take a right beyond the appliances." He's pointing to rank after rank of dryers and stoves and refrigerators, durable goods that will take centuries to rust. Maybe a quarter mile on, Milty's leaning against his car, the light bar flashing, more than a dozen of his deputies walking in line away from him toward the bypass. Not too far away a front-end loader idles, the driver one of my guys from the road department, while yonder a couple of bulldozers are burying what Deming threw away yesterday.

"We got a backpack and some clothing," he says, leading me toward a pit the size of the municipal swimming pool on Birch Street.

"You hurt me," Ginny said last night, only a minute or two before she left.

She was standing by the end of the bed, mostly dressed, showing me the bruises on her forearms.

"Sorry," I said. "I don't know what happened."

She was still for a second, little in her face to suggest she knew me at all.

"Get him, Lonnie," she said. "Get the bastard who took our Tanya."

Yes, I was thinking. That terrible word again.

Then she was at the dresser, my six-shooter in hand.

"Whoever he is, you find him," she said, "and you shoot him a hundred times."

Now I'm side by side with Milty, police tape between us and what might be the place Tanya turns up.

"The state patrol is bringing a cadaver dog," Milty is explaining. "Meanwhile, my people are poking around. We have no idea when the dozers were in this area."

I have nothing to say, nor anything to say it with. I'm just the parts God left behind, more mud than mind, a mummy but for the coat and tie and cell phone.

"You recognize this?"

He has a paper bag—Safeway, of all things—and he's spilled its contents on the hood of his cruiser, spreads the stuff out as if it's closing time at the flea market and he's got some slightly worn items he can make me a really good deal on. A backpack. A T-shirt that says TUFF GRRRL. A pair of denim shorts frayed at the legs. A hair scrunchy. A textbook, *Patterns for a Purpose*, that looks like it's been abused by every freshman in the Western Hemisphere. A pair of Adidas sneakers sizable enough for the Hulk.

"Doesn't look familiar," I tell Milty.

Milty seems to chew this over, his the expression of an accountant finally coming to the end of a foolishly long number.

"We talked to some kids at school," Milty says. "They remember the T-shirt, but hell, nobody knows for sure."

"We're at a dead end, right?"

He nods, obviously offended by how this corner of the republic has turned out.

"I thought we might catch a break from the security cameras at the mall," he says. "But the one outside Penney's was on the fritz."

"The feds?"

He shrugs, tilts his Stetson back a mite. "I called Fred Beeker, the special agent in Cruces, but he says his hands are tied. No actual evidence of a snatch. No evidence that she's crossed state lines. Just a lot of what-if's and maybe's."

I'm thinking of Ginny, her bucking beneath me last night, the pair of us dropped from the sky, and how later, composed as a nun, she walked from the dresser to the bed, gave me a granny's kiss on the forehead, and put the six-shooter on the sheet across my lap, the thing heavy as a clothes iron. "Shoot him dead," she whispered. "Shoot him, shoot him, shoot him."

"Tanya's a runaway," I tell Milty, now certain of it myself.

Our sheriff gives me the look he probably reserves for UFOs.

"I got a call," I tell him, the particulars of which need only a single deep breath.

"Caller ID?"

Nothing, I say. Just yours truly and Mr. Sandman.

"Could be a prank," he suggests, the hopeful half of me eager to agree with him.

"Could be," I say.

And that's the way we leave it—two yahoos from the Elks Club leaning against the fender of a Ford Crown Victoria, a line of lawmen meandering its way across a moonscape of disposable diapers and bed frames and buckets and tin cans, at our feet a crater at the bottom of which might lie anything you had fear enough to imagine.

"Stopping power," the kid says, the phrase clearly as suspicious as poetry.

"It's from law enforcement," I tell him, and thereafter we exchange the looks you see on people who've come a long way and realize they have a long way yet to go.

I've been thinking about this moment—the pace and texture of it, its shape and shine—since I left the dump and while I was briefly home. I've been wondering what's going to happen. And if whatever's going to happen will happen enough. I am two, it seems: a man watching a father about to deliver a boy to Kingdom Come.

"It's having the power," I tell him, "to kill or maim a man—*stop* him—before he kills or maims you or hurts someone you love."

He nods, this a concept he's evidently familiar with.

"You bring a slingshot," I tell him, "I bring a crossbow. You bring a hammer, I bring a howitzer."

"This going somewhere?" he asks, not a squeak in his voice—a kid named Trey Dog being tough for the chump in the Suburban.

"This is what I'm bringing," I say, and hold up my replica single-action revolver, a Ruger .45 Vaquero with a hog-wallow sight and rosewood grips, a weapon as wicked as it is heavy, what muscle can make given an understanding of our kind's lower needs.

He nods again, still another fact of life he knows the up and down of.

"My ex-wife gave this to me years ago," I tell him, me keeping the squeak out of my voice now. "You know the Wild West Shootout and Barbecue at the Fairgrounds every July?"

He does.

"I'm in the posse that chases down the outlaws."

As I talk, I am not seeing anything but him—not the no-account house with the chain-link fencing that, according to Margie and the tax assessor of Luna County, belongs to one Elena Gomez Posey, probably his mother; not the kid, a toddler in diapers wrestling a Big

Wheels across the lawn behind him, maybe one of the nephews Milty told me about; not the car on blocks, an ancient Dodge, in the driveway; not the windows covered in tinfoil, not the beat-up lawn furniture, not flower pots on the front steps—just him: Douglas, skin and bones in baggy shorts and a wife-beater T-shirt, a slump-shouldered ectomorph even Gandhi might want to kick around for an hour. And I'm seeing Tanya on her knees in front of him, the world a place thereafter in which you are obligated to find the time to make time stop.

"We're just a bunch of college kids and businessmen and cowboys having fun," I tell him. "Three times an evening for four days, we're riding horses and dying like you see in the movies—lots of grunting and moaning and staggering and whooping and falling down. You ever go?"

He takes a second to say no, him looking hard at me, too.

"We use blanks for the playacting," I say, "but today I'm using CCI Blazer Brass 230-grain TMJ. It's good for snakes. Coyotes. Assholes who want to break in your house and hurt you."

I've come to end of my speech, and he seems ready to begin his.

"Bito," he says, "go inside."

The toddler, dark-eyed and already tending toward fatso, gives Posey the "huh" look, me another, shrugs dramatically enough to suggest he, too, might have had a speech to make, and starts toward the front door, Big Wheels dragging behind. Everything is happening in slow motion—the weather, the words, the turn of the planet.

"It's short for Alberto," Posey says to me, one guy chatting with another on a street corner. "On my mother's side, we're Mex."

It almost happens here, that part of the drama Ginny wanted. In fact, for a moment I think it has—the boom, impossibly big, and the bad guy flying backward onto a plastic patio table, the good guy with nothing else to do but chew gum and put his heart away. But nothing's happened, and we are who we used to be before there were devils and dragons loose in the land.

"Where is she?" I ask.

He considers his hands, the marvels they appear to be. "Who?"

"Tanya," I say.

He's smiling. Evidently, I've said something that's amused him.

"T-girl," he says. "Nice piece, that one."

Here's the second time it almost happens—the noise God makes when He smites, the big become small and the wrong made everlastingly right—but I am not the person I was only a moment ago. I am not this flesh. Not this tongue. Not this finger on the trigger.

"I ain't seen her in a couple of months," Posey is saying. "She a friend to you, too?"

I can't wait to tell Carly about this instant. It's like discovering you have a tail or that you can bend flatware with your mind.

"I'm her father," I tell him.

He shrugs, body language he's obviously learned from Bito. "Sorry, mister, I don't see no resemblance."

An hour ago, I was sitting on Tanya's bed, her huge teddy bear in my hands. I was telling myself the hopeful things you tell yourself when hope is the last thing you have. And then I had opened the back of the bear, the modern world soon to be another fact hard to argue with. Inside were bank receipts, dozens of them, for an account in the name of Tanya Nees. Deposits. Then a withdrawal—over six thousand dollars—six weeks earlier. T-girl before she vanished.

"You know where she went?" I ask Posey.

"Last I heard, L.A.," he says. "Maybe San Diego. Can't say, really."

And here, at last, is the last time it can happen. I consider my revolver, its weight and the magic it can be made to make. I can do this, I tell myself. I have the skill, the steady hand. I take the breath I need. I have made peace with the clouds that bear witness. The trees are telling me to do this. The grass is telling me. And then Sheriff Milton, having made his way from the cruiser parked behind me, is telling me not to.

"Margie," I say, two and two making four.

"She was worried," Milty says, as much friend as lawman. "Said you sounded weird."

The trees aren't talking to me anymore.

"It's over, Lonnie."

And it is: Nothing is new or different between my ears except the whole world.

"Posey," Milton says to the kid, "go inside."

The kid gives me the bored, flat look of a snake—the trees aren't talking to him, either—before he turns toward his door.

"Give me the gun, Lonnie."

At his door, Posey gives me a wave and a grin, another monster to share the twenty-first century with.

"I could've done it, Milty."

"And then what?" he says.

It's a good question, one I ask myself after I've given him the revolver, one I ask when I pull away from the curb, one I'll ask Ginny someday, one I might ask Tanya if she ever comes back from whatever L.A. is, a question I hope Carly has the answer to.

HOW LOVE IS LIVED
IN PARADISE

THOUGH I AM still called Bubba by some I do and do not like, my real name is Cecil Fitzgerald Toomer, and this adventure that's happened to me starts with the idea, no doubt loony to ordinary citizens in the big world, that what I know about love comes not from falling in it once, but from watching, years and years ago now, nearly one thousand yards of Super-8 movie in the cinder-block film room at the University of New Mexico and seeing something in football that, by the end of it, had me quietly, well, weeping over the 265 pounds I was.

This was 1970, a year that seems like "yore" to the conspicuous sentimentalist I am, and I was in my second year as the linebacker coach for the Lobos. I'd graduated three years before, played a season and a half with the St. Louis football Cardinals as a late-round draft choice, blew up one knee, then its partner, and spent a summer wondering what would become of me, until my old head coach, Mr. Emery Ewing, called up and asked how'd I like to work for him—which meant finding and thereafter teaching huge American youngsters to be semi-bloodthirsty and entirely reckless.

I could have the linebackers, he said, and be as fierce with them as Baytagh was with his Tartars. He was always fond of me, he said, considered me prime this-and-that, claimed I possessed a first-rate mind—the flattery of which I was happy to agree with.

"You think about it, Bubba," he said, his voice perhaps the tenth human thing I'd heard since the previous May. "You're a born teacher, boy. I can see you now—kicking tail, rousing passions, the works."

Coach Ewing had a colonel's shaved head and an unlucky man's violent temper, and he was enough like my own father, who was dead then and probably mayor of the harps-and-honey afterlife he believed in, that I said yes too loud and drove eighteen miles to tell a girl I'd haphazardly courted that we ought to get married.

That August I stood around in the sunlight and yelled at muscular teenagers. "Hit that sumbitch," I'd holler. "That pissant is insulting you, son."

They were named Ickey and Tongue and Herkie—nearly a hundred who thought nothing of mud and hurly-burly as the medium to be distinguished in. They'd squat, heave, make mostly chest-derived noise, and afterward hie themselves to me for more high-decibel instruction. When they were good, I'd snatch up a bullhorn and say so to all of downwind Albuquerque; when they were not, as they often were, I'd invent belittling names for their male parts, plus urge them, then and forever, to contemplate their miserable inadequacies.

Once the season started, though, I hit the road, recruiting high schoolers in those portions of Texas that Coach Ewing had given me. I tossed my bags in my Fairlane, said adios to my wife, Stacy, and spent the next four of every seven days driving Interstate-this and FM-that, knocking on the depressingly flimsy doors of folks who lived in Marble Falls—or De Leon or Jacksboro or Devine—any town, one horse or more, that had a kid playing football and dreaming he was a Cleveland Brown or a Ram from L.A.

I preferred these boys to be big and quick, with eyes that didn't roll much, and I'd sit in their living rooms, or at their coach's house, and tell them what I and the University of New Mexico might offer— which was meals, books, and tuition waivers. Lordy, these were exceptional moments: Mudflap or Ricky T. or the Prince of Frigging

Darkness sitting across from me, Ma and Pa Darkness gussied up as if for a job interview, and me saying how goddamned grand it was to be bushy-tailed and strong and unafraid of headlong contact.

Yet it wasn't football I was talking about, really; it was having a way in the world: somewhere to go and the means to go there. I was talking, as Coach Ewing and my father had once talked to me, about a point of view, sensible and righteous, to have; and how, as interested folks, we admired the self-reliance that Thoreau wrote of, plus what is underlined in such volumes as *The Pathfinder* and *Huckleberry Finn*. In living rooms in Crockett and Woodville and Baytown, anywhere plastic pads and Riddell headgear were common, I'd tell about weight rooms and adequate housing and the eggheaded tutors who could make Goonch or Elvis or Tattley know, and care about, Geoffrey Chaucer and, say, thermal transfer and what the kings and queens of England meant to freedom.

Letters of commitment in hand, I'd talk—my voice scratchy and cracking from the effort—about how physical prowess, the business of jumping high or running far, was just a chance to know the world by throwing your body at it; that what Jimmy Jeff or Poot or Del Ray might sweat on the gridiron was given in fair exchange for the delight it is to know the achievements of Hannibal and Hammurabi and Mr. Thomas Stearns Eliot, plus conflicting views of us as hollow men or reeds that cerebrate. That old flimflam, I'd say, of a football player being dumb was just plain wrong. A noseguard, I'd insist, was a psychology major with stump-size thighs, a Lambda Chi minus the body fat. "A linebacker," I declared once, "is a scholar who learns his Trotsky on the scrimmage field." Football, yes, was meaning, too, just swifter and largely ignorant of please-and-thank-you.

Then there was the film, the miles and miles of it I studied when I was not driving one flatland or another. Shut up in the film room, deaf to the chatter of the antique Bell & Howell projector, I looked for those who were fleet or passably nimble-witted, studying—in slow motion or backward sometimes—a Tiger or a Rocket or a Red Raider who had girth and but one violent notion on his mind. I'd receive a half-dozen film cans a week, usually with a note attached from the high school coach: "Look at Morris," it might read. "He's pure-D remarkable. He wants nothing more than to whack the wigglies out of everybody on your schedule."

They had personalities, these boys from the hinterlands. Despite grainy film stock and no sound, they revealed themselves as bewitched, eccentric, often inspired sportsmen. Rained or hailed on, slogging in mud or red dust, they said, as one's actions can, that they, in this heap or that, were vain or Republican or downright evil. R. C. "Gumball" Weed might be a lunatic with only six yellow teeth and the engaging disposition of a catfish, but he recognized a misdirection when one was tried and you could see the umbrage he suffered from it. Tall and short, black and white, thick through the middle or bottom-heavy like bowling pins, they were what you and I are—a percentage wicked and childishly joyful when triumph calls.

Such was the boy, indeed, I was watching the night, years and years gone, when I ended up alone blubbering. A left outside linebacker for the Flowers, Texas, ISD Rebels, Boyce Fowler had speed that seemed inconceivable to the porky sort he was. He possessed "great feet," which is coaching argot for the tiptoe that is necessary among twisting and toppling bodies, not to mention sufficient strength through the chest to pitch aside those dim-witted enough to take him on straight ahead and manlike. You needed to be sly with him, I thought once. You needed to trap-block, leg-whip when the back judge was blowing his nose. You needed to call him "Queerbait" or puke in his ear hole—anything to make him leave you alone and go back to the wet waste he'd oozed from.

I don't remember when I stopped watching him, only that at some point a sound burst from me—what the word *agog* suggests—and I put down a ham sandwich perhaps I'd taken one bite from. This wasn't a large moment, I tell you, no bells or "aha" of surprise—just a moment when I heard from, as we now and then do, that vigilant creature inside of us whose job it is, when we can't, to look behind and above and afar.

While the film rewound, I approached the window, eyed the way the Sandia Mountains were raised and how, north of us, the light at dusk had turned almost wintry and thoroughly depressing. For the last

half hour, I had been watching not the virtually Marine-like Boyce
Fowler and the savage services he performed; rather, I'd been watching—or that creature in the heart of me was watching—a youngster
from the other team, a runty black wingback about the age then of my
own son now. Eventually, I discovered his name, Purvis Watkins, and
came to know how he wanted his steak cooked and what Motown
records he sang along to best, but in 1970 he was mere arms and legs,
a whirl my Boyce Fowler collided with fifteen, twenty, twenty-five
times one dry Friday in November umpteen umpteens ago. I was
drawn to this Watkins kid not because he was so good, though good he
was, but because, in ways romantics understand, he had chosen this
night to be a hero, to lead his much-overmatched, poorly outfitted
team against the big and the pretty and the rich. It was the melodrama
I was captivated by, a modern equivalent of the big-little set-to that
was David and Goliath.

More than once, after I started the film anew, I found myself abandoning the high perch my disinterest was supposed to be—the one
from which I was supposed to say, as scientists and the really wise do,
this is this, that that; more than once I put aside analysis and dispas-
sion to slip instead straight into the silent, black-and-white world that
Purvis L. Watkins, Cougar senior and piece of work, was being excellent in. Folks, I flat-out identified with that sport-mad juvenile, dashed
where he dashed, hopped when he did. I scooted hither with him,
and thither, felt hostile flesh flatten me; and when he saw stars, as he
did a couple of times, I saw them, too—twinkling and liquid, not at all
where they ought to be in God's heaven.

Through the first and second quarters, when his Cougars were
being crunched and made laughable to the five hundred farmland
Texans who'd gathered to watch, I trudged with him to the huddle
and regarded most sympathetically the beleaguered faces of his,
and my, teammates. I wasn't film-watching any longer; I was there,
on a chewed-up playing field in Borger, Texas, eyeballing my
skinned knuckles, picking clots of turf out of my face mask, and
muttering to myself, as Purvis Louis Watkins was muttering to himself, "What's going to become of us here?" A measure was being
taken that had to do with the misconceived notions of distinction

and honor and personal worth. A standard was at work here, a goofy code he'd absorbed from Marvel comic books or what grown men habitually yammer in locker rooms. A line was being drawn, as in epics lines are drawn and drawn again, and Purvis Watkins, not to mention the parts of him that were me, was saying that it—all the things in him and me and us that lines stand for and that are the butt of mean-spirited Hollywood humor—would not be crossed or violated. Purvis L. Watkins, I say to you, hauled himself back to the huddle after one disastrous play, and I knew, from his bobbing head and what finger-pointing signifies, that he was saying, "Boys, this shit's got to stop."

And, come the second half, it did. Stopped cold. Those Cougar boys, what eleven kinds of motley are, returned from halftime with only victory on their minds. They hit, they ran, they blocked, they tackled, and presently it became clear even to the talented felon Boyce Fowler that this wasn't sport alone: It was evidence of what we aspire to without vanity or pettiness. Clearly, this was beauty, which is composed of all you love and cannot survive without, and time after time I found myself rocking back in my chair to holler the wildest words I knew about the bliss that warmed me. I pounded the table I leaned against and the wall that also kept me upright. I cried "Shit-fire!" and "Hot damn!" and other things that are mostly the ooh and aah of our best nature, and then all that remained was my fist in the air, pumping like a piston, and the throaty, strangled sound my joy was.

There would come a moment, soon enough and terrible, when I would be absolutely goddamned hobbled by the void left behind when this joy vanished, but for twenty minutes yet, I got to climb up, as Purvis was doing, those mountains Coach Ewing said challenges were; and up there, jubilant and not at all mindful of what tragedy teaches us, I said, "Well, ain't this something?"

I hooted, I hollered, and twice, swept up as in verse the radiant are, I laughed—from the deepest nooks of me, without regard for where my spit was going. Purvis scored. Dived over a feeble free safety and scored. Purvis threw a block, using everything but his toe-nails, and let another score. And there occurred that dancing now popular on every gridiron in America: what shameless grind the

hips do when you are alone and mirthful—half humping and half
hootchie-koo, the effect of it purely gratifying to the portions of you
that don't think.

I ran the film in slow motion; I wanted to see—and scribble down,
maybe—how his parts worked, what could be made language about
the bones and muscle and wind he was. It was the creature in him, and
me, I was attending to—the thing that in flight looks smooth and
intent and imperturbable. The meat of us that turns toward light
and sound and shrinks from an unfriendly touch. "Yes, indeed," I
remarked several times. "All right and amen."

Later that night, over the big man's meal of pot roast and carrots
my wife had cooked, I tried to explain what had happened. I described
how I sat there, more in the action than out, while Purvis led his people. I mentioned the scores, which grew closer and closer. I mentioned how those home fans—every Sadie and Edna Mae and
Bucky-boy of them!—had suddenly gone church-quiet and wholly
respectful, and how the light lay in that ticky-tacky stadium. I used the
word *grace* to say the noises we eek when we see meaning moving this
way and that.

Stacy was herself gracious during these minutes, encouraging and
tolerant of my mumblings. She fetched me more Coors beer and sat
across from me and did not go ha-ha-ha when I described how Purvis,
for what would have been the tying touchdown, went flying for eight
yards. I thought he had scored and was halfway out of my chair, a war
whoop coming to me, before I realized that he'd fumbled; and in that
moment—and the many moments afterward, I told Stacy—I broke, as
Purvis L. Watkins never did, into a dozen widespread pieces. I could
see it all: the ball there, Purvis yonder, that Fowler boy leaping in
ecstasy. I could see what had befallen him, and me. We had done
everything—been smart, been courageous, been hopeful—and then
there we were, on our knees, not slumped yet, staring in the direction
we had come from so heroically. We—he in his time, me in mine—
were dumbfounded: The object we loved and prized, a fifteen-dollar
oblong of leather and string and heavy thread that said who we were
in the world and what could be done, was way gone and we were only
stupid again, a thousand miles from the lights of wonderland.

He was cold, I think; I know I suddenly was. He was not sad yet, nor to my knowledge did he ever become sad. He was simply astonished that life had turned out this way. But if he was not sad, I, his distant confederate, was. I was thinking again, is what: I was being the history major I once was. I was recollecting the A's I had and the dates I was graduated for repeating. Compare, I may have told myself. Contrast. But the brain in me—those folded pink tissues that could say this was only football after all—had just stopped sending what it conveys to the thing in us that is monkey or lizard or slop we eons ago crawled from. I couldn't move. I had hands that weighed twenty pounds and would not close when I begged them to. I had a heart that went thump-thump and breathing that sounded far away and labored.

And then I heard it, which is the pronoun for the me I was. It was crying, folks. It—with its flat tummy and its sportsman's crew cut and its twice-broken nose and its weight-lifter's chest—was sobbing, silently but steadily. For itself and not. For Purvis and not. It wanted help, I tried to tell Stacy. It wanted knowledge. It wanted to know, for example, why time couldn't be turned back and suspended at the moment Purvis L. Watkins and his faraway fan were shining and smart and true.

That year Purvis L. Watkins went off to East Carolina State University, and I went forward, too—a man with a job, two babies, a wife who looked tasty in expensive South Seas swimwear, and a worldview thought to be generous and informed. Yes: Forward. And, I hold, generally upward, which is one metaphor I learned for those improvements we endeavor to make in ourselves and the world we crisscross. I am in a looking-back humor now, a state of mind that wonders how we come to this intersection of the here-and-now and not another. First, it is 1972 and your narrator resides in Ames, Iowa, the recruiting coordinator for the Iowa State Cyclones. He is happy, he believes, and learning to cook meals like Roti au Vol, Legumes Garnis; he is losing a little hair, watching his weight go, and learning how it is to live with snow and four months of falling temperatures. Then it is 1976, and he is in Fayetteville, Arkansas, one defensive coach for the Razor-backs, and he is watching his wife, blond as straw, walk toward him in a bias-cut Patou tea gown he has ordered from I. Magnin of Califor-nia. It is another year, and he is doubled up with worry about govern-ment and the secret, dangerous deeds done to preserve it. His oldest boy, Bobby, has braces, and then he does not. His youngest, Samuel, breaks his arm, then it is healed. Next it is 1981 and Bubba Toomer lives in Dallas, recruiting for Southern Methodist University. He is drinking too much and not drinking at all. He is smart, then not. A TV watcher and not. A book reader and not. A Democrat and not. Look-ing back, I wonder who this Bubba Fitzgerald Toomer was. Is that his crooked smile? Is that his opinion about party etiquette and how anger is definitively expressed? And then it is 1986, and he is in Albu-querque again, the defensive coordinator, and, Lordy, Coach Toomer is in love.

As we are told in that old song that birds must sing, so was I meant, I think, to fall in love. It was in my nature, I believe. Maybe it was my nature itself, the huffing and puffing and going to and fro I am, the blue eyes I have and the way (not becoming) that my arms hang and swing too far like a march. Corny it might be, but I may have fallen in love with Mary Louise Tipton the instant she entered my office to announce that though she was a tutor, a Ph.D. in literature, she had only the most meager respect for the teaching that coaches did. It was a corrupt and demeaning undertaking, this football thing. One class, an underkind, which served another. It was stupid as recreation and retrograde as ideology—words which, as they came from what is a beautiful mouth, seemed alien as chatter from space.

My hand, I remember, shot up, and again, as if to say *Wait* or *Hold on a minute, missy,* but she was eight places at once in my office—picking at the knickknacks I'd lugged through the years, trophies and goodies and inspirational speeches, plus a pile of news clippings that confirmed, more rather than less, what purpose and direction I could give youngsters—and then, settled at last in an easy chair, she said, "I hear you're smart. Let's have lunch."

She had a smile that involved the whole of her face, plus a bent-forward posture that implied she could be lively on a million other subjects—foreign policy, say, or price indexing—and before another second went past, I said, "Hell, yes."

Maybe I fell in love with her on another day in a different restaurant when she said, almost clinically, that she liked the way I attacked my food, which was like the way her dogs—a boxer named Lucy and foundling Dane-like monster named Luther—went at theirs.

I was de-light-ed, a word it takes mouth and heart to say correctly. I was de-light-ed to learn that she was from Shreveport and that her daddy, by whom she was still enthralled (though he'd been dead for five years), was the sort of man who climbed into his pajamas at six-thirty in the evening, a man who liked *Ivanhoe*, a quarterhorse named Nellie First and the happy company of fellow millionaires. I was de-light-ed by her age, thirty-six, and the years she'd worked as a waitress, or as a bartender, or as a pubic relations gofer in Hermann Hospital at the Texas Medical Center in Houston.

I was as well de-light-ed by the tragedies that had struck her, age-old troubles like alcoholism and a passel of brothers and sisters as swamp-infected and priss-minded as any creation from William Faulkner. I was charmed by her drawl and the singsong my whole name became when she thrust open my door to declare that one player I had was, regrettably, dense as igneous rock. I took de-light, which is mental pleasure that does not lessen over time, in how damned intelligent she was, in the way she could just stand up and say, "This is shit; this Shinola." She knew, and I let her teach me, what texts are and how we are better for losing ourselves in them. In lunch after lunch, Bubba, who was "Cecil" to her, learned what slips of the tongue meant and how, through manner and word, we act out the horrors and miseries of our youth. In one hour, I learned the two words we have from Old High German; in another, what politics have to do with the art we consume; in another, how pride is related to sloth, gluttony to greed, and the several things that goeth before the fall.

One day, in addition to the palaver and eye-looks that are part of love, came the actual making of love. We had gone to her house, a ranch-style stucco on Bennet off Menaul, a house she cherished as if it, too, knew about fear and failure and human wishes, and in the middle of looking for something—a book, I think, whose thesis concerned the personality sloppy handwriting reveals—she said, "Cecil, it's time we had sex."

Miss Mary Louise Tipton was serious and laughing at the same time. She had done all the thinking, I realize now, as she always did the thinking for the two of us: In her mind, where there was already so much about males and females and what they've done to each other, she had seized the subject of us, debated its pros and cons. She had the facts, among them old prohibitions against sin, and she had shaped the pain, or happiness, they might foretell: She had decided, of a Thursday afternoon, that Cecil Fitzgerald Toomer, sometime nitwit, was the man she could best mean love with by making it to.

I, on the other hand, was not thinking at all. Like a schoolboy asked to cha-cha at cotillion, my hands were stuffed in my pockets, and I was doing well not to shuffle my feet or hem-haw too loud.

"When?" I asked, a question so pathetic I am still embarrassed to have uttered it.

"Now," she said.

I thought of her room, which she had said was back yonder, and the black lacquer bed she claimed was the biggest in Bernalillo County. I wondered, too, about the amused looks her dogs were giving me.

"Where?" I asked, the last of my clever responses. I considered her kitchen, which was small, and its cold tile floor, and her dining room, whose every flat surface seemed covered with papers related to the inheritance she was pointedly indifferent to. I saw the corner of a rug that appeared now tattered and certainly too scratchy. And then I came back to her eyes and the irresistible invitation they were.

"Here," she said.

Neither was I thinking when Miss Mary Louise unzipped my Levi's and urged me down on top of her, a cane chair shoved sidelong to make space for us. It is only now—in this summer two years later when I am divorced, when Coach Ewing is dead, when my former family has moved back to Deming in Luna County to live with its faithful relations, and when Mary Louise and I are planning the honeymoon Paris, France, is supposed to be—it is only now, thousands of hours removed from the events herein, that I am thinking, really thinking; and what I see, in the film I close my eyes to watch, is a man unaware but wholehearted—a man a bit like Purvis L. Watkins before he fumbled.

Silly as it sounds, this man I was, whose body always seemed too big for the indoors, was giving her, like a model sportsman, all the things and conditions and states of mind he was: He was muscle and grit, the greasy foods he hated but gobbled down anyway, the dreams he half remembered, the shitkicker music his boots tapped to, the marvels (good and bad) he was always shocked by, the real and made-up histories he was, the Catholic growing-up he'd had. He, the me I used to be, was giving her, in the square yards of floor they lay on, all he knew: his first kiss and the winter he'd run his fastest, the drunk he'd too often been, the only fist he'd thrown in a fight that had blood in it.

Then we were finished, sweaty and sore and altogether light-headed. Time had started again. The walls went straight again, then clamped down like the lid to a box.

"Oooohhh-weee," Miss Mary Louise Tipton said, like a cowgirl.

Lordy, those next months were weird—those before Bubba woke to Cecil the way, years and years earlier, Purvis L. Watkins had awakened to his own peculiar world of woe. Your hero, I say, had two lives. In one I could be seen in Allworth's Drugstore, in tow the versions of myself that are Bobby and Samuel, buying Crest toothpaste and Mennen deodorant, paying from the sixth-grade shop project in leather that is my wallet; in the other life, by twilight or noon itself, I could be seen in Vincent's Blue Moon Lounge or Butera's Café, the hairier part of a snuggle or the louder half of a ho-ho-ho. In one life, itself not craven or deprived or ruined, I paid a mortgage and bills from Southwestern Bell and Dillard's; in the other, I held a tumbler of Jack Daniel's and lounged most agreeably in a green deck chair constructed by the best hammer-and-nail socialists in Sweden. In one life, itself fine enough and honest, I got to grab an undergraduate by the face mask and announce what it is rover backs are obliged to do on Saturdays—which is to sunder and to rend and generally to stuff an opponent into the foul middle of the next month; in the other life, I was myself snatched by the cheeks or ears and told where the self sits and how meaning is refracted—that was Mary Louise Tipton's word, indeed—through the lens of our limited perception. Peculiar to say—yes: strange, strange, strange—I passed nimbly life to life. I want to add, if I can be only sixty percent sappy about it, that in one life I was a fish; in the other, a bird. A rock in one; a tree in the other. Finally, because of the way insight works, particularly that which (as my father used to say) smites us hard and quick, I was nothing.

"Do you have something to tell me?" Stacy asked that week in October my marriage was to stop and I was to find myself blubbering again like an infant. We sat in our family room, Stacy reading a good-versus-evil spy novel she liked and me making the X's and O's and arrows and lines that illustrate what piling on and crackback blocks can do. I had lines scrawled here and lines wriggled there and, until Stacy directed me to tell her what was going on and why I was as distant from her as the moon is from Miami, I was completely beguiled by a vision of football as precious and tidy as college philosophy.

"Something's bothering you," she said.

My head snapped up as if I'd been clobbered, and I found myself, as if awakened by a siren, in the real world again. I would like to report that she asked me if there was another woman or if I loved her still, but she didn't. I looked ill, she said. Maybe I needed a checkup? I was tossing and turning in bed, I was stumbling into furniture, I was babbling—facts I was totally ignorant of.

"I'm fine," your hero told her, mostly not an untruth.

Here it was that I took her in, this longtime wife of mine. I thought of the sixteen years we'd been together, the presents I'd given her and how rough I could sometimes be. I thought of the fancy underwear she looked appealing in and the eight cuss words she used as effectively as teachers use chalk. I thought of her folks, Winona and Bill, and how, as ranchers, they were wholesome as milk. She was good, I thought. She liked to garden. She had patience with the lamebrained and foolhardy.

That was Monday. On Tuesday, as she is now someone you are reading about, so she seemed to me to be a person I had only read of, a character out of Hardy or Charles Dickens or Tom Clancy. She ate spaghetti with a fork, forsook dancing when the Watusi came in, could make a fist the littleness of which could make you gasp. She was a heroine about whom I knew many things—her birth weight at the Mimbres Valley Hospital in 1948, her green-and-white Wildcat cheerleader outfit, the Yamaha motorcycle she once liked to ride, the enduring contempt she had for Richard Nixon, the ups and downs she suffered; but except for the final chapter, those pages having to do with her dumbstruck, wayward husband and his bye-bye to her, I had, Lordy, finished my reading of Stacy Richards Toomer.

On Wednesday, so it has been reported to me, I assembled my players on the practice field to harangue them about love. Our opponent that Saturday was Colorado State, so there were many, I gather, who were befuddled by a speech that never once mentioned valor or the digging down that victory comes from. I don't recall any of this, I confess. Not the slightest word. But even now, from boys who are juniors and seniors, I hear how I climbed the tower to holler down at them, how I used a bullhorn and appeared deeply angry. There was fall sunlight and a bell ringing and New Mexico noises elsewhere, and there was, I am told, this crazy man shouting about affection and what a withered landscape we wander in. There were linebackers and nose tackles and defensive ends, and there was this fellow dressed in shorts and a UNM Department of Athletics T-shirt bellowing about the swell and warp love could be in those the bushwhacked victims of it.

This exhausted an hour, I hear. Coach Toomer, I hear, talked about sapsuckers and dipsticks and those who are mollycoddled overmuch. I hear that Coach Toomer, wearing dark glasses and a baseball cap that looked slept on, made fists and pointed in the high and low directions wisdom comes from. He called for reason and its antithesis. He called for a breaking apart and a putting together again. Geez, he called for sowing and reaping.

These were boys from Alpine and DeWitt and Forest City, boys who majored in poly sci and bio and comp lit, and they were urged to consider all that stood apart from elections and paramecia and foreign gobbledygook. They were introduced, instead, to creatures named Stacy and Mary Louise. They got to hear about Little Leaguers named Robert William and Samuel Beck. These players, students big as refrigerators and violent as hailstorms, heard about dreams, which are the waste of you; and actions, which are not. They heard how much greater they were than the sum of their no-account parts. The word *spirit* was used, as were the gestures said to be occasioned by it.

A cloud whisked by. And a second. You could hear raspy, shallow breathing and watch athlete eyeballs shift around and around nervously. The bullhorn clicked off, clicked on. Then it went tumbling in the direction of Section H, Rows 9 through 15. Coach Toomer called for a glass of Gatorade, I understand, and one was brought him.

"Coach was loco," was what I heard later; is what, in fact, I still hear from time to time. Coach was off his rocker, his marbles spilled, the inside of him fractured and collapsed. Coach, in his tower and wobbling, was most out of touch, as cut loose and moil-minded a human as is possible in sunlight. He mentioned rain and related elements from the sky, and screamed down at one huh-faced boy, "See?" And that boy, who was from Espanola in the north and was no smarter at football than was Daffy Duck at dancing, went "yes" with his head in a fashion that made you fear what muscles "no" used.

In the next minute, Coach talked about the body, which was vehicle and medium and incarnation of the goo your mind invented. "Do you dingleberries see?" Coach asked, clearly displeased they did not. "You understand, Bigmouth?"

And Bigmouth, a spoon-faced safety with feet the size of pontoons and a three-speed brain shaped, it was believed, like a loaf of bread, said, "Hell, yes, Coach!"

And so commenced another paragraph, the sharpest points of which were Coach's opinions about dress-wearing and the miracle hips are, plus what we are inclined to feel when spring rolls around.

"I am trying to account for things here," Coach said, now using a second bullhorn so those still asleep in North Dakota could hear.

Another hour had gone by, in the tick-tock way time can, and nobody had moved a lick. Even in the silent seconds, when Coach seemed especially cockeyed and heaven-sent, his players, all ninety-six of them, were paralyzed, a contraption he had built, dismantled, and flung the makings of all around.

"Love," Coach Toomer said, giving the word eight syllables and half the color wheel. Why not call it hair? he wondered. Or teeth? Or the food you had for breakfast? What was wanted was a new word, one shook free of the la-la-la Romeos swoon over. For that purpose, he said, football was a fine word, too, and a fairer approximation of what havoc happens between boys and girls.

Foot-goddamn-ball. Love needed some rules, he declared, along with impartial folks in stripes whose job it was to say when, and how badly, you messed up. Hell, some structure was called for, some cheek-popping whistle-blowing that signaled you had a half minute to conjure up new plans for going headlong at it.

"Ha," Coach said, in what may or may not have been a laugh. "Ha-goddamn-ha."

Later that evening, much as I had on another evening in the "yore" I spoke of earlier, I tried to explain to Stacy what had happened to me. I described how I had climbed down from my tower, the going up an exercise I did not remember at all. I mentioned how I'd suddenly whipped into wakefulness, finding myself walking through a clot of my players, theirs the faces you see on those who've witnessed a car wreck or similar calamity. I used the word *goggle-eyed* to describe my own expression and mentioned the roundabout path I'd taken to my Toyota in the parking lot. I used the word *tired* to say how I'd felt; *nothing* to say what I knew. I had regarded the sun, which had been orange as a flagman's vest, and wondered how love is lived in paradise.

Stacy was solicitous, asking if I wanted a drink and what would I say to a visit from Dr. Weymann, our GP. I had her one hand in mine, and in my mind three-quarters of a sentence in regard to the bags I'd pack in a few minutes, and then—about the moment, I think, when she plainly understood what I had not yet said—I heard it: that blubbering me.

As I had been years ago, I was again cold. And cogitating, too. I was wondering about the rattling insides of me, the clatter my hooks and hasps made breaking loose. Wait, I told myself. Consider. I had a "why" question, and a "how" and a "when."

"Bubba?" Stacy said, a name I could not for the life of me make sensible.

As before, the it in me was crying: a tear on one cheek, a second on the other. Its mouth dropped open and its face, I suppose, was like Purvis L. Watkins's own, wonder-filled and baffled, the victim of ten or ten thousand ideas at once. As before, it, the me I was, desired answers. To questions about the forward movement of living life. About what to do with weakness. About why it is we have the hearts we do, and how it is they work.

LOVE IS THE CROOKED THING

ALL OF THIS happened years ago when I was the son of a bitch I am not now.

I was Number 56 then, your gruesome outside linebacker, and; dressed up in my workingman's clothes of plastic thigh pad and Riddell headgear, I had this purpose on earth: to sunder (as in render) flesh and make it lie down quietly.

Which is how you become when you share your plot of turf with mud named Jitter and Dokie and the Prince of Fucking Darkness.

This is how I sounded then:

"Son," I would snarl at the tackle across from me, "do you know who I am?" And he, after swallowing hard the way the observant do when they recognize doom itching to mash them, would say, "Uh, of course," pent up with the fear I meant to put in him. Whereupon I'd turn to my compatriots and speak: "Did you boys hear what this pissant called me?" They did, adding that such was neither pretty nor fair-minded, especially coming from, as the case might be, a TCU Horned Frog or Bear from Baylor. "Well," I would say, "don't come my way on account of this." Which was my massive arm and its inflexible cast, which might take the daylights and sense of him and put them in outer goddamn Mongolia.

More about me before we come to what I'm here about:

At my graduation, I moseyed across the platform in Razorback Stadium and greeted the president in the customary manner, then surprised him by saying thus: "Archie, I'd like to speak a few words to these folks."

You could see he did not wish to quarrel with even one of the three hundred pounds I was. Plus, I was cum laude from this place, an expert among their groves of multiple choice and true-false.

"Burl Perteet," he said, "I would be honored," and he went wisely to his appointed chair.

I let the thousands gathered to watch bask in the shine of my smile.

"Citizens," I said, "you're looking at meat worth four hundred thousand dollars to the Lions of Detroit, ain't that grand?"

Picture the ooohh's and aaahhh's that followed.

"Here, look at this."

Whereupon Jitter and Dokie and several sophomores I'd browbeat conveyed my bedroom of trophies up here with me, the mass of which glimmered, as is said, unto such gold as is worshipped by minions everywhere. In addition, there was sunshine that May afternoon worthy of Brothers Homer and Wordsworth.

"These are what I got," I announced, "for being mean and excellent at it. Citizens, I can't imagine living another way, thank you."

Which brings us to the present moment, a dozen years from the above event, and how I come to be the charitable gent I am now.

In 1968, at the same instant your rookie Burl Perteet was called upon to sing his alma mater for all those veterans at training camp, a woman from the west side of Cleveland, Inna Lee DuFoys, was learning that her husband, an E-4 named Coy in the service of Uncle Sam, was dead many thousands of miles from her, slain by illiterate fourteen-year-olds in pajama-like outfits who did not, as we are wont to believe in these olden days, appreciate life in the precious sense those in America did.

At first there was no conflict: Coy came home in a box and was buried with a ceremony which included a flag and a chaplain's handshake, as well as words aimed at healing over such scorched areas as those surrounding the heart and in the brain where memory lurks.

Then, about the time our hero Perteet was making his first start against the '49ers, Eddie Ivory, Coy's best pal, came back and said how it was over there—who was who, for instance, and what was what, and how to distinguish between them—telling enough so that Inna Lee could summon up a picture of her man among whirling rotors and the whomp-de-whomp of incoming and the dozen colored smokes used to mark the LZs.

"Tell me more," she said, famished for details of this event which seemed so underhanded.

"Well," Eddie said, "we went in-country R&R one time, at China Beach. I suppose you know about that."

She did, to be true, but had to know more—about the war food they ate, and what a piaster was, and how they slept standing up or in a squat; so, evening after evening, she learned about hardware which could melt a building, and the heart-stopping clank the wrong sound in the wrong place might make in those hearing it, and the spectacle of teenagers calling for intervention of the divine kind.

"What were those sounds again?" she said.

They were these: Splat and Aarrrggghhh and Boom-boom-boom.

And every night, after Eddie Ivory left, when she was particularly sore-hearted, she went deeper into the spot she was coming to know so well—a convergence of jungle and bug and random, hurly-burly violence. Some nights she could see Coy sprawled, all the limbs of him flung outward, his resting ground of leaves and soil as white and large as a Niagara Falls wedding bed. What's more, she even shared his thoughts—those unique to storm and flying metal and the calamity of phosphorus, thoughts that were four, then forty, then four million horrors at once.

She could see him walking, not at all the figure who'd married her in Cobb County, Georgia, and brought her to Cleveland so he could split steel at Republic and maybe make a little money. Skinny, looking made of bristle and spit, Coy was first in line, wearing a much-too-large helmet, his apparel scribbled over with words she didn't know he knew: *futile* and *fenestrate*. He had a calendar drawn in Magic Marker on his fatigue shirt, all the June and July days X'd out. He seemed awfully burdened, Coy did, what with flak jacket and well-oiled weapon and his face a mask of Avon horror-show, his features rubbed out in favor of the deep shadows common to this action he lived in. Inna Lee could plainly see his amigos and hear their brave chitchat and smell that Cambodian weed Coy said they smoked to keep their wits up. Always, she was in his blood, it seemed, when the turmoil commenced; and she felt, as he must've, his private alarms go off when the flora they hiked among burst into flame or became a hail that made an ooommmpphh noise piercing them. She heard him ask his leg for a thing it could not do; nor could his arm, it having been given a too-vicious wrench by something that sped past it buzzing like a wasp. She had his thoughts, too—those that were made into such speech as "Shit" and "My Lord!" and "Holy Mother!"

And then—at the moment Burl Perteet was easing a Dallas Cowboy into never-fucking-never land—she was down and crawling, scurrying from shriek to howl and then stopping, knowing (with bleak amusement, even) that everything light and uplifting was being swamped by an onrushing dark tide which carried above it such trash as wife and home and living to an old age.

In 1974, Burl Perteet, twice an All-Pro, found himself in a court of law, his crime a prank the city couldn't accept the humor of. His was behavior, the *Free Press* wrote, such as required correction, on account of athletes being heroes to the young among us.

Yes, he and his roomie, Harold Walls (Southern Mississippi, '71), had raided mostly white suburbs, stealing porch plants—in particular several poinsettias which belonged to the mayor of Grosse Pointe Woods.

"Aren't you ashamed of yourself?" the prosecutor wondered.

Burl turned his lavish smile upon those shopkeepers who were convicting him.

"You did see Mr. Walls take those decorations, didn't you?"

Our linebacker said he'd seen Mr. Walls do a hundred laugh-worthy deeds, but little with plant life.

"Like what?" that man said.

"Like dally with your wife, I believe."

That man rose up as if punched: "Your Honor!"

"You want to hear the noise she uttered?"

That man got ahold of himself in a hurry: "Perteet, what kind of person are you?"

They were waiting, so he told them: "Mr. Prosecutor, I like to romp and care profoundly little about you and your ilk."

Which was how, in a week, he found himself the property of the Cleveland Browns. It was a trade designed to make everyone look smart, plus get a troublemaking mesomorph out of town; and Burl Perteet went hither as a man partial to jest and hurling his unwelcome bulk at the other guy's breastbones.

Six years later, one summer might, late, Inna Lee DuFoys woke up beside a man who was wearing a diamond earring shaped like the numbers 5 and 6 and who had such weight to him that, for an instant, the world seemed to tilt in his direction. It took her a minute to remember his name and that they'd left together after she got off work at the Crazyhorse, where she served drinks and sauntered about in a costume best described as skimpy. He'd said she had a body that those at *Time* magazine write about: all sinew, with the girth of Snow White. Lord, he had been a presence in that place, like clatter in a grave, those fellows with him given to whooping and slapping of the thick parts. He was a football player, he'd said, on that gridiron downtown, where he did mayhem and got paid for it. Mostly, she remembered that being under him had been like being buried in an avalanche which shook and spoke of itself as violence made living meat: "I like you plenty," he'd said. "Here, put up your fingers like this."

Now, up and about in this room, she wondered where she was. There was evidence of a wife, perhaps, somebody whose pictures made her look punched and bruised, with hair upswept like a Roman helmet. Inna Lee's clothes were everywhere, as if stripped from her by a hurricane. This was a palace, she figured, big as a roller rink with everything in it—fuzzy carpet, furniture, even decorative doodad—courtesy of Kmart. "What is that stuff?" she said once. "Tufts on suede, is what."

She was half dressed before she thought of the men she'd known since her time with Coy. There'd been that attorney who'd handled the GI insurance and other work she couldn't get the hang of. His name, she believed, was Tom and he liked to beat his chest afterward and brag about the explosions in his head. That had lasted a year. Then there was a period without companionship during which she worked as a teller at National City until Mr. Hensley made her feel like a hillbilly, which led to work at the Big O store on Chester Street. Afterward came these fellows: Lamar Fike, and that Pepper Pike person named Schilling who drove the Mercedes, and two best friends named Gee Gee Gambill and "Hamburger James" (who said they worked for Elvis Presley once), and Hodge who used to take her to the Shoreway Holiday Inn, and that affair she got into with what's-his name, the astronomy professor at Reserve.

Then Eddie Ivory came back into her life. He'd been working at the Twinsburg plant for Chrysler and said he hadn't done squat with his life except buy such vehicles as motorcycles and four-wheel drive Broncos and drink to the point of forgetfulness.

"I know what you want," she said; to her, life was as simple as grade school arithmetic. "Okay," she said, "here."

Whereupon her shirt came open and his face became like daylight again.

Lord, this Ivory boy did weep a lot, even naked when such would seem impossible. He'd come to the door, at her Ohio City apartment, always with a bottle of George Dickel, his expression full of bad news and pity he hadn't earned.

"Come in," she'd say, and in minutes they'd be at it, that embrace they were doing part wrestling, part hanging on.

"What're your thoughts?" he said once.

"I wasn't having any," she said, right away having plenty.

Eddie was staring at the ceiling, specifically the water stain which resembled another man's angry face. Eddie was thinking about Coy, that time in March they were on loan to Hotel Company and visiting a pal of theirs, a mortar man with 1/26.

"This guy was a killer," Eddie said. "He could be eating cheddar cheese and cling peaches and talking about greasing Charlie the whole while. You know what Coy said?"

Inna Lee did not.

"He said dying was shit to him. He said this was the United States Marine Corps we were talking about and death wasn't no more to it than TOC latrine."

Which was when Inna Lee slugged Eddie Ivory, her fist catching him on the eye socket, releasing blood enough for the two of them to wipe up.

"Eddie Ivory," she said, "I don't want to hear no more about it."

Thereafter, she had a hard time imagining her husband Coy—which was, she assumed, how true heartache worked in those suffering a serious case of it. Once she pulled her wedding album out and flipped through its snapshots like a detective wondering where a clue would appear. This album, she thought, was like her high school yearbook, Coy no more to her than that pimply know-it-all in geometry class who used to warn of war with Fidel Castro. She read some names: J. D. Summers, Missy Hess; R. W. and Cecil Blackwood, Billie Jean LaTook—wedding guests who seemed as unfamiliar now as those places on the moon which have names. She looked at the presents she'd received way back then as an eighteen-year-old: J. C. Penney gift certificate, three-speed blender, steak knives with real wood handles, seventy-five dollars from Ellen Tharpe. "Well," she said many times, "well, how about this."

The only clear memory she had of Coy was the night they had sex, after homecoming, at Dick and Joe Anderson's house, Coy in the shirt he believed made him look like Johnny Carson. He was already talking about joining Uncle Sam and tried to take it to her as he believed a Marine ought—with much growling and a flurry of handwork.

"Hold on," she said, "here, help me out of this."

There were a hundred things to take off, it seemed, girdle and beaver-cheaters and real silk hose and those lilac panties she felt so special in.

"I couldn't ask for any more than this," Coy said.

"That sure is true," she said.

Then, seeing her spread out on Mr. and Mrs. Anderson's bed, his face a mostly animal display of thankfulness, he'd said, "Oh, Jesus. Oh, God."

"When he got on," she told Eddie Ivory, "I was thinking of other things."

This was the night Eddie said he wouldn't be coming around anymore, there being an attraction on the West Coast he would see about.

"I was thinking how much my dress cost and what time it was, and Coy was just sweating and making faces at me below him."

She said she stopped thinking entirely when Coy went inside her and there was nothing to do but push back and make the same noises he did. Which were all about love and this tempest they were and being unable to hold back.

"I think he went 'oh-oh-oh-oh' and I did the same."

Eddie Ivory already had his underpants on and was hunting for his shoes.

"Coy said touch him here and here and kiss him, which I did. I could hear Dick and Joe Anderson in the living room with their dates. They were dancing, Dick singing along with the Rolling Stones."

Inna Lee hummed a little for Eddie, that section which talked about having to have it and what the effect is.

"Then I had an orgasm, too," she said.

She didn't care where Eddie was now, for she was pretty much speaking for herself, saying that in the liquid rush of lights and tingles, because of the fear it wrought, she knew this boy atop her was already dead; it would just take another year or so and maybe fifteen thousand miles between them for Coy to flop down and realize it.

Which is how—at the same instant Burl Perteet was addressing a Dolphin tight end on which point of the spectrum to dream on—love and death became linked in her mind, not to mention fixed to that spot she'd imagined so often: that spot presided over by the friendly shining moon and now soaked with body liquors most of us only read about.

.   .   .

When I woke up, she was studying the picture on my nightstand.

"That's Eva," I said. "She gets twenty-six percent of everything. Alimony."

Whereupon I heard the foregoing tale of boys named Coy and Eddie, and, surviving it, that creature who was here with me. It was a story, I did believe, such as told by drunks about their first pet or lost riches.

"After Coy got off me," she was saying, "I was as wet as you have made me now."

She had eyes which seemed composed of oil and coal.

"Say, why don't I call you sometime?" I said. I was going fishing up in Canada with the defensive backfield but would call when I got back. To be true, and I am now ashamed to say so, it was a lie to ease her out of here and my life forever. I should've known.

"Here," I said, "write down your number."

Time moved on as it will in my world, and in August I went into another Baldwin-Wallace training camp, that beef of me much older, my knees held fast by gizmos of stainless steel and miracle fabric; and I thought little about Ms. DuFoys until that afternoon, during two-a-days, when three from the Blue squad, including a lunatic rookie who desired to be the new edition of yours truly, sought to batter old Burl's kidneys and shiver his thinking parts so that Number 56 would go down in a pile the size of an economy sedan.

They—Knots Weaver, Mossy Cade, Moe Bias—lined up across from me, each grimy with professional NFL sweats. You could tell they had hearts of fire, plus smug daytime visions of fame.

"Old man," they said, "your time has arrived." They spoke as one, their minds evidently from the same gutter.

Your hero was idle upstairs. He was pooped, what he was, with no hope save that which would later come with rest and one million calories of food.

"Here we come," they snarled.

You're right in thinking they were as savage as Burl Perteet himself had been in the faraway world of his youth.

There was a whistle and in an instant of tremor, crunch, and riot, they were atop that man who was me—one nattering, "Whoop,

whoop, whoop!" in the ear, another chewing the hand, the third babbling of the mists and dim lights of the Great Elsewhere. I had the
feeling there were one thousand folks on the sidelines—and in homes
across ruined America—going, "Hoot, hoot, hoot!"

"I can't breathe," I gasped. "Honest, it's growing dark down here."

Someone was spitting. There was heard consternation and discouraging language, and your hero felt himself being squashed, sod
squeezing into his ear hole. I was on the brink, I know now, of a vision
of Old Testament proportions—swift, unbidden and full of awe.

"I can't feel my arm," I hollered.

Somebody was pummeling my tender parts.

"I can't feel my leg, either!"

And here it was, while flopped down and spread out, that I thought
of that woman, Inna Lee DuFoys, and the story she told—a story
about a heedless man such as Burl Perteet who might have stood over
a naked woman, saying *Oh, God* and *Jesus,* never guessing what
awaited in the darksome world of the future.

"Wait," I yelled from the bottom of the mound I was. "Don't be
bending my nose, I've got something to say."

One of them, Mossy Cade, was eyeballing me, his face suspicious
like what happens at a Mexican rodeo: "What you want to say?"

There were nerve noises in my head: I could imagine Inna Lee as
she had been her homecoming night, that now-dead boy of hers fling-
ing himself at her like she was a wall he had to get over. I saw her
naked and smiling and pointing to herself, saying, "You don't want to
do nothing else, boy. You just want to come on over here and have this
and these and all they do stand for." I was stunned as no Bear or Colt
or Ram had ever whacked me.

"Hey," Mossy Cade was saying, "what's wrong with your face, it's
crawling!"

I imagined her the night Eddie Ivory visited and her shirt fell open
and her eyes said something like, *Look what I have to give, give, and
give.* I imagined her skin, which was fine as new money, and her eyes,
which were bright and proper places to hide in. And then, an instant
before those boys stomped my wits into a blackout, I saw myself just
as Inna Lee had seen Coy: bedraggled and flung into a vaster world of

woe, flesh forever exiled from a love so fierce it could survive distance, time, and even mortal misfortune.

That night the Turk knocked at my door. (The Turk's the beast who bears the bad news—which is usually that you ain't wanted no more or have gone in trade for that which is younger, faster, stronger, and cheaper.)

"How you feel about playing in Dallas?" Coach Sam said.

"I could use my option," I said.

"Yes, you could, Burl."

My contract said I could choose: Did I want to stay here, a brooding presence pacing the sidelines, or did I want to play sports with blondes from *People* magazine named Lance and Dougie, or did I want to quit?

Which was when I conceived of this woman who is now my wife and what we are here for in this world.

"Coach, I retire."

It took forty minutes for me to pack and be out of there toward her doorstep. I felt as remarkable as I had that afternoon the GM for the Lions phoned and said how'd I like being a number one draft pick, of which there were only eighteen on this planet. This was my thought, exactly: Burl, that thing you see is the future with its arms open and waiting to smother you in luxury. I felt as Coy must've when he shed his Johnny Carson outfit: chosen, powerful, and clean as an angel.

I banged on her apartment door at one-thirty P.M. A minute later I'd pitched the other fellow out.

"Miss DuFoys," I said. Yes, I was on bended knee. "Would you marry me?"

She eyed me like I was something dark which she recognized from her past.

I would be generous, I said, would never go off, would carry her around on my shoulders day and night if such pleased.

"Where would we live?"

I was right: She did have a practical mind.

"We can go anywhere," I said.

"I'd like to go home, to Georgia."

That was fine, I said. Budweiser had promised me a beer distributorship, and didn't they drink that stuff down there?

"Please, say yes."

She held her arms apart, and I stumbled into them like one of those halfbacks I'd dispatched in my other life.

"Now, why would I want to do that?" she said. "You tell me."

As I say, this was ages gone. We were married four years ago in the Presbyterian manner, dozens of my erstwhile coworkers in attendance with their tarts, and then we came down here where I stand around in a drafty warehouse ten hours a day, six days a week, and holler at whiskered delinquents named Tippy and Joe Bob, or sometimes eat roast chicken and cold peas at a high school honors athletic dinner. At these events, I get to talk about that which I have little affection for: prowess and how it feels to imperil the other fellow.

We have a toddling girl, Marvine, and one on the way which, if male, will be the Junior of me. We have a swimming pool Esther Williams might like and a rec room such as is favored by Italian movie gangsters. I drive a Ford pickup and can be often seen lost in its wraparound stereo music; and nothing lifts my heart to a higher point than pulling into my driveway and seeing this woman I love waving to me from the kitchen like I'd been gone years and had to live through wild happenstance to get here.

But you want to know, don't you, what I said to her that night my life took a turn for the splendid item it is now.

What I said was this—the gist of it, at least: I wasn't nothing but overlarge and rewarded for it, a modern monster which lumbered left and right mostly, and did no good except for others' pocketbooks.

I said, "I want to be with you, Inna Lee DuFoys."

I said, "I need that thing you gave your boy Coy."

Yes, I was holding her just as you would hold your own hope if it had heart and leg and tongue.

At last, I said I intended to expire in that spot she imagined so completely—that spot, as I comprehend it now, where I am young and beautiful and eternally loved even though I am dead.

MARTIANS

Several years ago, about the time my wife Vicki began talking about suing me for divorce, my best friend, Newt Grider—who had to him all the virtues you expect from men in middle age—told me he believed in UFOs. We were on the sixth green of the Mimbres Valley Country Club, only half serious about our two-dollar Nassau but thirsty as Arabs for the beers we would get at the turn, and for an instant, because he had the tendency to mumble or clown, I thought he was speaking French or trying out on me that Howdy-Doody double-talk he used to invent for the entertainment of his daughters.

"Boy, you don't believe in nothing," I said; this was banter, like that between Butch and Sundance. He had just smacked a driver and was watching his ball soar off into one of those sunsets our New Mexico has a reputation for, extreme and scary to the animal in us.

"Lamar Hoyt," he was saying, "I have known you a long time, right?"

We had been pals of the lifelong sort, since teenagers when we had been in the same Wildcat front court. We had done everything together, lost our virginity to the same Pine Street hairdresser, took in the same experiences I hear described as necessary but usual. We even lived, in the time I am writing about, on the same block and had the same thoughts about what Vicki used to call the great themes of our age—how to vote, where love comes from, and what to do with the weaknesses in you.

For a second—as long, I suspect, as it took for his ball to land in the way-off fairway—he just looked at me, eyes bright as new pennies, then he said that last night, while all of Deming town was asleep or rolled up next to its TVs, he was in his backyard, wearing only pajama bottoms and being addressed by beings from outer goddamn space.

"Shit," I said, "what're you talking about?" I was looking around for the joke, the way you do on April first when your children tell you the car's on fire.

"I'm serious," he said.

He had the full-speed-ahead forward posture he'd get when we played cards and a full house would suddenly appear in his hands— earnest as a Baptist, humor a thing for lesser souls who believed in luck.

"What do they look like?" I wondered. I was, of course, imagining the common alien: green, perhaps slime-dipped, plus the large, lop-sided brain of a genius.

"They're luminous," he said, "like angels." They were about the size of my oldest boy Taylor, he said, which meant they resembled fifth-graders, and they traveled from what we now know is the Vega galaxy, a swirl of planets and dust older than time itself, and they were coming here just as they had been coming all along over the centuries, in magnificent vehicles which made our efforts at combustion and top-secret propulsion look feeble as campfires. "You believe me, don't you?" he said.

His voice was dreamy as sleep and, yes, because he was my best friend, I was believing him, just as I have learned to believe, for exam-ple, those born-again folks who say that in their swimming pool one afternoon or sitting behind a desk at the Farmers and Merchants Bank there was first a thunderous crack, then something like firmament opening, and finally Christ Himself beckoning forth, all the choirs of the afterworld singing about love and wooden arks.

"You ever lose anything, Lamar?"

You should know that we weren't playing golf any longer; in fact, we were just standing to one side of the fairway, letting Mrs. Hal Thibodeaux and three of her lady friends play through.

Well, I told him, I'd lost a wallet one time and my high school graduation ring and the keys to the Monte Carlo disappeared at least once a week.

"That's not what I'm thinking about," he said.

He was thinking about, specifically, people and objects, all those things which were said to vanish in spooky places—boats and planes, and all the people aboard them, plus citizens who were supposed to go to the movies or shopping at the Piggly Wiggly, or big animals, like cows and horses, which are one day there but gone the next.

"They got 'em," he said. We were being probed, he told me, and mentioned many names from history of those who knew: a whiskered lunatic named Trismegistus, not to mention a tribe of fifth-century Hebrews, as well as most deep-thinking Orientals of modern times.

"How do you know all this?" I wondered

They had told him, his small visitors. He had stood in his backyard, watched in breathless suspense as this vehicle had landed silent as snow, and they had popped out of something you would call a port and went up to him without the inconvenience of walking and put in his mind, instantly as magic, everything which could be read or spoken or thought. "You know what's up there now?" He was pointing at his own temples and eyeing me as if from a hundred miles away.

Near us, in an outfit most folks only wear on Sundays, Mrs. Thibodeaux was flailing with her five iron; and for a time, I confess, I wished I was part of her foursome talking about bridge or what to do with Green Stamps.

"Up here," Newt was saying, "is stuff about Lemnos and animus and quote the blood-dimmed tide unquote."

He was scaring me, he was, as he had frightened me months before when, soaked with Smirnoff's and overtired, he'd shouted that what this republic needed was a good shitstorm, one which would bury the lot of us—him and me, too!—and thus teach us a thing or three about the small, damp beginnings of everything.

"What's Alice Mary say?" I asked. She was his wife and, from my view, sweet as any man deserved.

"She thinks like you do, that I'm loco."

He was fingering his head bones again and making up such language, he said, as is exchanged between galaxies and the stark reaches of far-off orbs, utterances you can hear anytime from pigs or barnyard fowl. "They want me," he said, "and I do want them."

His plan, I learned, was to be swept up this very evening.

"I'm going out in my backyard," he said, "look for them in twilight and go up when they say to." In his face was that divine look which, I suppose, has come over mystics in every age: bright flesh and eyes watery with bliss.

"What about the girls?" I said. I was trying to turn his mind to the practical. This was merely upset, I told myself. He was only angry, as we all get, or fretful about money matters.

"Lamar," he said, "come over here." He was like me in every respect, so I did as told. He threw his arms around me in that male way, part grapple and part clasp.

"These people are my destiny, Lamar. They've known me before I was born, goddammit."

All the way back to the clubhouse, one arm still hung over my shoulder, he told me what a delightful world awaited him—air and rare mists and peace—all those words that sound great when you're drunk but in the full light of day, especially in the shitkicker paradise of our desert, sound sentimental as baby talk.

"I'm going to be moving in another dimension," he said when we reached his pickup. He was still wearing his spikes, plus those shiny green slacks which always brought to mind Pinky Lee. "Say bye-bye to me, Lamar."

He was shaking my hand, vigorously, and if I was thinking, I was doing so more as jelly than as vertebrate, looking at him as if he were a fresh work of creation, something as shocking as another sun. And then, after he opened his door, he did a brave thing, which was to kiss me on the cheek.

"I'll miss you, Lamar," he said, "but I'll be keeping an eye on you from where I am."

.   .   .

This next part is the hard stuff, for I ask you to join me in forgetting for a moment that this is 1994 and that we have been to space itself and do have the Air Force and thousands of Ph.D.'s to tell us otherwise. I want you to think as I have read that Indians and other ancient people do—which, as I understand it, is with their hearts and in the company of wise if grumpy sorts from the icy underworld. What you already suspect is true: Nearly a decade ago, as it has been reconstructed by our police, Newt Grider, smiling like a ninny and dressed up (Alice Mary says) in a costume which was mostly bedsheet, did wander through his TV room, said *No, thanks* to a macaroni-and-cheese casserole, and drifted like an ardent juvenile into his backyard from which—in a second or an hour—after some mumbling about twinkles and the cosmic items we are, he utterly and instantly vanished.

For several days, Alice Mary was in the panic this deserved. No, she told Sergeant Krebs, there had been no fight, at least not a big one; and no, there was no other woman or any some such, as who would desire something doomed to be a fatso like Jackie Gleason. If they wanted to know, she said, why didn't they talk to old Lamar Hoyt?

"I bet he knows where Newt is," she said, "he's a son of a bitch, too."

For a week, exactly as I'd heard it, I told what I knew. I repeated it for Krebs and to a detective (who sported the Fu Man Chu mustache State Farm men wear) and once to an FBI fellow who wondered how long I'd had my Chevrolet dealership and was it true I'd once attended SMU?

One afternoon, I even gave the story to a reporter from the *Headlight*, a lady with a lively haircut which would have looked sharp on the corpse of Elvis Presley. It was a "profile" article, she said, but when it appeared, the Newt I loved was nowhere in it. I read stuff we all knew but had forgotten about: his setting fire, as a teenager, to a cotton field behind the Triangle Drive-in; his opening an irrigation canal and flooding Mr. Bullard's lettuce field; his having a certain drinking prob-

lem after the infant death of his only son. There was talk, too, of out-
of-body travel and the belief in astrology, plus how you could divine
the future in special leg bones. All of which, wrote that lady writer I
was liking less and less, sounded like a voodoo smokescreen for a man
who, like thousands and thousands of others in America, was just a
plain, matter-of-fact runaway, vamoosed to Peru or another romantic
kingdom in search of his lost youth.

It was in here, you must know, that Vicki moved out, taking our
sons with her, and time (of which I am somewhat concerned) became
mixed and fluid and dreadful. One day, I am saying, she was here and
merely wrought up with the usual strife and dissatisfactions; the next
day, she was off in Las Cruces, sixty miles east, living with a club pro
named Ivy Cooper and telling my children, Buddy and Taylor, that I
was a beast and a dimwit and absolutely without ambition. On another
day, I was divorced and lighter the fifteen thousand dollars it cost; and
on still another, I say, a year had gone by and I was skinnier by many
pounds and lonely as a castaway; and I'd look up from my reading and
see the walls move (as they do when, for forty-eight hours, you haven't
talked to anything except your own stubbed toe). I'd phone my boys
every Sunday and hear about their soccer and that soon Ivy was taking them to Fort Worth to rub elbows with Ben Crenshaw and Justin
Leonard and that Mother, my Vicki, was working at Mode O'Day and
maybe looked a little like one of Charlie's Angels, all blouse and flyaway hair.

Then one day I grew the beard my shop foreman Poot Tipton said
I ought to and started to go out. The first time, I remember, I stood in
front of the mirror for an hour perhaps, studying myself as I have seen
others look at my automobiles they can't afford. I said to myself such
hopeful phrases as "You look good, Lamar, you really do," and
splashed myself with a modern fragrance Buddy had sent for Xmas. I
smelled like a jungle, I thought, which was maybe right for this world.
Poot said I got lucky as that evening I met a woman at the Thunder-
bird (which is bowling alley and lounge, both); but she was herself
divorced ("His name was Veloy and I hope he rots!") and miserable
from it.

At my house, she walked around and made faces at the knickknacks I hadn't thrown out. Her name was Merri Lu, I learned, but she was contemplating changing it in favor of one which complemented the exotic sense she now had of herself.

"How 'bout Reva?" she said.

She was out by the pool, already unbuttoning her shirt.

"C'mere, you bastard," she said, "call me Mia and you can have all of this."

At that moment, I took a look at myself and saw this: almost forty years old, a little bit Episcopalian, Libra to those who cared, modest about my money, and once upon a time a fair linkster.

"Miss Reva," I said, "why don't I take you on home?"

A month later I went out with Poot's sister, Randi.

"You're looking studly, boss," he'd said, "you'd be doing her a favor."

She had cheekbones I hadn't seen before, severe and red, and the posture of a hat rack. She smoked red-dirt marijuana and claimed she wanted me to join her in the hinterlands of spirit.

"What're you thinking about?" she said. "I'm thinking about the Father of all Hindrance."

We were in the El Corral Bar, a place of cowboy motif and welcome darkness, and I felt as apart from her as I had from Newt the day he disappeared.

"You want to hear about me," she said, "before we get back to your place?"

From the bar across the way, two guys, both dressed like buckaroos, were making liquor noises. I heard the word *woo,* I believe, and then a string of words, every other one of which was either Mex or obscene.

"I look older than twenty-two, don't I?" Randi was speaking to me. "It's carriage and knowing your own mind."

She had my chin in her fingers, my lips mashed together; and she had the eyes you see on starved Hindus in *National Geographic*— forty thousand years old and not tired.

"I like you," she whispered, "you're going to be good for my mind; I can tell."

Exactly here it was, in this story I am telling you, that I excused myself, said I had to go to the toilet, and then left by the front door. I was heading, I think, to that place I had been tending toward all along.

"Well, I'll be damned," Alice Mary said. "Look what's here on my doorstep."

In jeans and an old T-shirt that could have been Newt's, she appeared young, and I was hoping she was still sweet, too.

"I like that beard," she said, "gives you an air."

In the light, she was touch-worthy and I had the urge, which I felt like a fist in the chest, to have her neck and bosom next to mine.

"Where are the girls?" I said.

They were at the Shelbys'. A sleepover.

I must've said a hundred things then, all forgettable and overused elsewhere, about what a tragedy our world was and what a pecker-wood I'd become and how, when something broke, I didn't fix it; and then—bless her—she said, "You're letting the bugs in, close the door," and I followed her inside to a living room that had no trace at all of her absent husband Newt Grider. Something was swimming in me, stomach or neighbor organ.

"You'd like to have me, wouldn't you?"

What I said came out choked, but affirmative.

"You believe I'd like to have you, too, don't you?"

That was true, also.

"It won't be any good, you know."

She was being tough, which this deserved, and I was grateful.

"I had a guy in here last week," she said. "Told me I was the sad-dest piece of ass he'd ever known."

I'd seen the truck. A Blazer, gray over white, one of its headlamps cockeyed. Plus a muffler my people could repair for fewer than thirty dollars.

"Okay," she said, "let's try this thing."

Folks, there is something in a man, independent of his lustful under-half, which loosens and grows light when a woman shows him that she's a creature, too; time stops and even before clothes are shed, or noises made, there is something—composed of gland and the way you are taught, I suspect—that makes you think you are wise when you are dumb, able when you are not. Alice Mary was right: We were witless and fumble-fingered as virgins, shy and fearful. We tried for an hour, I think, even kissing a labor. As lovers are supposed to do, we went after each other in a fury, but, I am telling you now, all the heart was out of it. She was brave, and I was brave, and then, after it became certain that courage wasn't the substance called for, she said, "Lamar, I think you ought to go home now."

She had my underpants in her fist, being helpful.

"I could come over tomorrow," I said.

"No, you couldn't," she said.

She was right about this, too: There wasn't anything between us but her husband and my wife, and they were in the distant world.

"You're a cute guy," she said, "don't be a fool." She gripped me by the ears and kissed my nose, which is the feature most people see first.

And then, in what I know to be the end of this narrative, I was outside, my house down the street lit up like a ballpark. Its neighbors were all dark and middle-class, here and there a lightbulb glowing. My heart felt as if it belonged to another man, leaky and floppy at the valves, and thoughts were reaching me as if by telegraph, clipped but steady. "Okay, Newt Grider," I said, "where are you now?" Everywhere the sky was random twinkle and black as the Devil's carpet. I was ready, I knew, as Newt had been ready for our advanced visitors to hover near and draw your hero up into their world. I wanted to be where everything which is ever lost or put aside or misplaced is gathered together, waiting.

MEN OF ROUGH PERSUASION

ALMOST LOST AMONG the gabbies and goombahs, fakeloos and fun-
nel-heads, Catamites and hypes, rajahs and ringers, and can openers
and Visigoths in the twenty-plus chapters that are *The Gates of Hell,* a
semi-sci-fi mystery with no little tally-ho at the end of it, is the skel
Harbee Hakim Hazar—Triple H himself—an Ur-Dravidian whose
opening line of dialogue, addressed to his image in a mirror, is this:
"Behold, dips and dewheads, the baddest, blackest bindle-bopper to
bo your peep."

He's a dropper, contract-style, working this evening for the Solatzo
sect. Blades are his specialty—the shiv, the ice pick, the Flora Dora.
His mark is Terry "Little T" Blount, a thief built like a flagpole, and an
hour before Triple H guts him in the alley, the half-loaf is camped at
a burp-n-urp on Euclid Avenue in New Cleveland, Khalid and Ling's
O-Town of Music, nearly twenty large in the breast pocket of his Omar
Sharif. The stotinki, of course, is ill-gotten gelt, two K of which are the
tala-taka for a patty-cake Open Sesame at a poobah's palace off the
Forbidden Square. Little T is jumpy—"sweating bullets," you're
tempted to say—and is medicating himself with corn from the well.

When he's not making too loud chitchat with the bar rag, Lonesome Abe, he's trying to figure out, given the givens of the wide and craven world, who to hose first. Seventeen thousand samolians, after all, buys a lot of loose. A lot of uptown leg. A lot of downtown boogaloo. A Shoofly as financially fit as he could trip some beaucoup light fantastic. Still, what complicates his thinking is that of late he, too, has been in the employ, albeit sporadic, of the Solatzos, in particular the High Pillows himself, Don Marco, an elder too wrathful even for the Old Testament. A "hard man," the Brunos say. Specifically, the Don has put the fear of God into Little T, fear with a head and tail and impressively large teeth. It's fear with lots of x's and y's in it, a parlez-vous more spit than speech. So here the hooch-head is, Little T, breath ragged, heart rattling, gorge in the gullet—only time, he suspects, between him and an ugly end. And here he comes, out of the dive, looking both ways—at once, if possible—him a disease with mucus and red eyes and clammy feet.

The atmospherics are minimal—mizzling rain, light sufficient enough to see how alone you are, the scrape and hiss and clatter the effects you expect in the genre—and Little T is making his way to his bucket, a bona fide land yacht (a Volgograd with custom largo and rust on the kootenai), which is parked around the corner. Several steps behind, hewing to the shadows, follows Triple H, whose brain, we're to infer, is part fish, part ferret. You can't imagine him as a boy, at least not an unarmed boy or otherwise coffee-and-doughnut. When Little T reaches his iron—you can all but hear his quote big sigh of relief unquote—Triple H makes his move: the Damascus high in the back, free arm around the neck, trap close to the trapper.

"Into the alley, sweat sock," he growls.

Little T goes wet in the whistle. What else can he do? A force of nature, irrational and heartless as a hurricane, has him throttled, something perilously sharp digging hard into the tender flesh between his wings.

"The Don?" he says.

"None other," says Triple H, spinning Little T around. Harbee prefers the face-to-face, respects the various truths, ripe or raw, you can read in the eyes of an Opie about to land mug up well outside the locked gates to paradise. Little T, Harbee is pleased to think, looks like a Jasper eager to take direction, to curry favor.

"You Harbee Hazar?" Little T asks. "Triple H?"

"Chains and chips," he says.

"I heard about you."

It's repartee you find under *D*, Triple H thinks. *D* for Despair—yip to yap when the ipso gets facto.

"Figured you were Fiji. Maybe somebody's outback."

"African-American," Harbee tells him.

It's a movie, you got a sound track here—strings, Mother Nature rinsing her delicate underthings.

"I suppose I got no choice," Little T says. "I suppose we couldn't negotiate, say."

Little T is doing a lot of supposing, Harbee says.

"It's curtains," Little T says. "Supposing's called for."

Harbee can appreciate that. Truly. A humanoid, even gink as pubic and inconsequential as Little T, is entitled. You got your bottom-feeders. But, not unhappily, you got your bottom-feeders with backbone. The low-down getting upright.

"You a family man?" Little T asks.

Past tense, Triple H tells him. The cupcake and carnage didn't work out. There were tensions, obvious points of contention—hairs split, nits picked. Now it's just chippies, bims, tea bags and the like, Janes no longer worrying about their choice in chuck.

"Me, too," Little T says. "Got a daughter somewhere, though. Margaret. Her mother named her after the saint."

There's another page and a half of biography, the bulk of it touchingly ordinary (Little T owns a cat, it turns out, a monster with one ear named Mister Pitiful; Triple H prefers Knott's Berry Farm over Disneyland, cartoons make him nervous—"It's a syndrome," he says, "you can look it up"), before Triple H orders Little T to fork over the moola, whereupon Little T, The End rushing at him in bold type and exclamation points, grows emotional—a catch in the throat, several tears, some pathetic trembling of the flippers.

"Get a grip," Triple H says with exasperation. "This isn't becoming at all."

"Sorry," Little T says, sniffling. But, Uncle Jesus, this is a dire moment—gloom and doom, expiration and such, the Kibosh itself. "Yardarms and lampposts," he says. "The Big Sleep."

"Too true," Harbee says.

Here Little T pulls out the Knox, a wad the size of a welterweight's fist, enough geetus to put some satisfying distance between you and the vulgar life.

"You don't have to do this," Little T says.

A contract is a contract, Triple H says. Plus, there's a reputation, pride in the job and related issues. Passion and action, Heidegger puts it.

"A mope, this Hi-guy?"

"Light reading," Triple H tells him. A paragraph or two before bedtime. Religiously. Data to crunch before the Sandman visits and it's thereafter cataracts and Coney dogs.

The mazuma has changed hands now, disappeared into the Adam & Eve Triple H is wearing.

"Why me?" Little T says.

Our hero shrugs, the question more schoolroom than clubhouse. "You're a loose end," he says. "The Don prefers the tidy. Duck soup and getaway sticks."

Little T seems to take this information in, pick it over for dry spots, maybe glom a way to leave the air.

"How you going to do it?" Little T asks.

Harbee says, "With dispatch."

Little T looks around. No Angels of Mercy. No Tartars. No Air Cav. Just night as the arty-farties at MGM imagine it, the last of his allotted thousands.

And then, quick as the weasel pops, Little T is zotzed, efficiently if brutally, the blade thrust under the breastbone, beneath the right nipple and through the pump, Little T to bleed out in less than a half hour while Harbee Hakim Hazar, nothing between his ears but three bars from what he thinks is an old-timey Isle of Dogs bootleg, walks with purpose right out of Chapter Two.

.   .   .

You don't read about Harbee again until the middle of *To Hell and Gone*. Years have passed. The Don is dust, a stroke in the middle of a sit-down across from a precinct Viceroy dressed in Vulcanized go-go boots and a leather breastplate, so the High Pillow now is the Don's nephew, Jake Fox, for whom, dingus or no, Harbee is effecting a necessary diplomatic service on the eighth floor of the Downtown Hyatt, the particulars of which the dish had been quizzing him on only seconds before she said she could stand some skee. "Parched."

"Help yourself," Harbee says, indicating the minibar.

Her sashay from the sofa in the suite is a story with four endings, three of them unique to doomsday. Lots of if-only and holy-cow in those hips. Lots of swear-to-God upon that full-sprung hindmost.

"So the deal is—" she starts, which exposition Harbee once again tries to detail by saying that they, the Ozzie and Harriet they are, stay put, watch the paint peel, pass the time, until the phone call, maybe a couple hours from now, whereupon she returns to her four score as Mrs. Ernest Hoom, mobster's housefrau, and he, fully recompensed, goes back to his as the proud owner of a Gold's Gym franchise on Euclid near the Clinic and the Plaza of Previous Humiliations.

"You ever met my brother?" she says.

"Seen pictures," Harbee tells her.

The croak's got hands the size of shovelheads. Deals in hop and ice and snow, has a back-scratching arrangement with the Greene gang from the Kingdome of Lyndhurst and parts. Represented by a lip named Leach with a nest in the Terminal Tower. Shags a looker—Doreen or Noreen, some such—lives in Bay Village, Miss Pneumatic Tool and Die once upon a time.

"He's an animal," the sister is saying. "My high school prom, the kid who takes me out doesn't get me back by midnight or whatever. Jake takes a bat to his knees. The Rocky Colavito model, if I remember. Thirty-six ounces."

A family man, Harbee thinks.

"The Neck—my husband?—he's no better." The sultana is pointing at the minibar, door open, hers a profile that is all mutton and handful of ideas as wonderful as they are woeful. "You want?"

Harbee shakes his head. "Business before pleasure."

"Your loss," she says.

Triple H pulls the book out of his pocket, *Harlem Sunset,* flips to the page where the Ralphie, dark meat named Feet, is crawling free from still another instance of dire straits. The chapter before featured a two-ply, C. J. Pucker—"the hostess with the mostest"—and Brother Hazar is hoping she'll show up again, heater in hand and hitting on all eight.

"So, technically," the kitten is saying, "I'm a hostage, right?"

Harbee lays it out—the sukiyaki *and* the succotash. "Insurance," he tells her. "My guy and your guy are in pow-wow, setting parameters. Your brother's plugs got one of ours, we got you—a way of guaranteeing that nobody gets jobbed."

She's back to the sofa now, legs crossed, and Harbee's having a hard time thinking about anything that isn't blond, shimmy, and sassafras. She's pure rumble, she is, a biped with slant and hoorah and wire, a torcher you wouldn't object to finding in your wikiup.

"So what do you want to do?" she says.

He points to his book. C. J. has just put in an appearance, thoroughly darb and dolly.

"We could—you know," she says, like a clerk or a teller, funny business evidently still business after all, and Harbee is trusting his puss doesn't say too much about the racket his thumper is making. "I mean, I never had a black man before."

"African-American," Harbee says, his pants suddenly too tight.

"No offense," she says.

"None taken," he tells her, having lost interest in the to and fro of C. J. Pucker and her Look-Ma-no-hands attitude.

"I'm a Democrat," Mrs. Hoom is saying, turning off the floor lamp next to the sofa, whereupon the ambience morphs from Broadway to boudoir almost immediately. Heat's not rising anymore; it's settled, close and wet, nothing to do but sweat and try not to breathe overmuch.

"Look, Mrs. Hoom—"

"Doris," she says, a given name finally for the 3-D havoc he is guessing will follow.

"You ever been to the House of Slaves?" he asks. "It's in Goree, an island off western Africa."

She's never been anywhere, she tells him. New York City, sure. Florida. The Neck's got a condo near the Shula compound in Miami. But anyplace without nocturnes and Neptunites—who's kidding who?

"They speak Wolof there," he's saying, hoping to pile up sufficient je-ne-sais-quoi to hide behind, scoot in low and score some hey from the diddle-diddle before the cock-a-doodle does. "I've been to Banjul, too. The mouth of Gambia River. They got hibiscus you would not believe."

"If you say so," she says, all the angles here now Chinese and outer space, and Harbee feels too large for himself, the mob inside him ready to riot, especially now that she, mostly belly and kneecap and ooh-la-la, has abandoned the sofa for parts spectacularly unknown.

"So I'm saying," our hero begins, "that I'm a serious man. Maybe you shouldn't be trifling with me."

She's not trifling, she insists. She's the bulge and the breeze, a clean sneak with no nasties to fret about, keen to pitch woo.

"And Ernest?" he asks.

"The Neck?" She's not a giant step away, a red-hot in high heels. "The Neck—Ernest—is a gourd, Mr. Skipout in the flesh, a loogan with nix in his noodle. He's my concern, not yours."

Tripe H has a moment with his higher self here, weighing the right against the not-so. He suffers no special affection for the Neck, sure. He also suffers no special desire to be a sharper himself. You got the tomato, he tells himself. Or you got trip for biscuits. Your call. Maybe somebody throws lead one day. Maybe you toot the wrong ringer. Or, chicken and cheese, you get ribbed up and it's thereafter glad rags and eggs in the coffee. Harbee consults the book again. What would Feet do?

"Time's a-wasting," Doris is saying. "Let's hootchy-koo, Mr. Hazar. My pump is primed."

Another light has gone off—she's part electrical storm, he decides, part work of art—and, what with the curtains closed, it's dark as a French movie.

"My tribe was the Dinka," he says. "A very proud people."

Doris has made a noise, sound with muscle in it. And gland.

"My tribe was the O'Boyles," she says. "A very drunk people."

Without any more "but" and "might," they've made contact, and soon the physics have begun, tabs and slots everywhere, everything coming to hand either hot or easily pushed out of the way, seconds falling away from the future in handfuls, the landscape in Harbee's mind seventy-five percent storybook oasis, Doris Hoom a secret a country or two might fight over, and the only word going back and forth too vowelly for English—one and one not making two anymore, just a last act full of blocking peculiar to desperation and glee both, their clothes the product of forces of inconvenience, a stone to pray to behind that big swirling mass overhead, the telephone—noisy as the sixteenth century itself—ringing berries and buttons and bings, Harbee grabbing the thing, his a "hello" in spirit only, not another "ugh" to utter before he is to vanish into space white as the walls of Wonderland.

"It's the Neck," the voice grumbles, full of nails and sandpaper. "Put Doris on."

Which Harbee does, the phone disappearing into the bedding as if into quicksand.

The last time you see Triple H is in *Hell's Hounds,* where he's just left a can house, the scent of a redhead catfish named Charisse in every crease and pore of him. His ashes have been hauled, his clock cleaned, his buck wheated, and now, less than a half block from his boiler, last year's Anglo-Saxon, his head is stuffed with images of a bop most horizontal, the heels round and the sugar sweet. Threw down enough spondilux to make her squeak "Eefff," and then tipped his mitts to say, "Who's your daddy, cheeks?" At which point, Charisse, to the possible what the tongue is to taste, went all but jingle-brained with delight, a lid to be lost if she were wearing one. So here he walks, the memory of her get-along getting nicely along, a fit to be pitched and a hoity gone toity, until he's reached his crate, opened the door, and settled himself behind the wheel, when from the inexplicable darkness of the back seat comes a voice as unexpected as it is feminine: "Grab a little air, Brother Hazar."

Triple H needs a moment to get his breathing in order, rake the sand back on his beach.

"You gave me a fright, miss," he says.

"Ms.," she says. "I'm a modern girlie."

Nothing in the rearview mirror, just the suggestion of a shape, darkness measurably darker than usual. A ghost, he thinks. Probably what you see when you've gone over the edge with the rams or hit the pipe, when the gas is Nevada and the cap snapped. Still, he's hearing things, too, specifically the direction to put his hands on the steering wheel.

"That the crop?" he says. "This a bump?"

Harbee doesn't know, and won't for several minutes, that this is his final hour. He's about to exit—an "adios" attended by gunpowder and badinage—so we won't know, for example, much more about his fondness for seafood, grouper foremost, or his many but anonymous donations to PAL and the Fund for the Terribly Wistful. He's a Leo, too, and taking an extension class in Personal Expression at Tri-C—the "wanton word," says the teacher, a Dagwood with flesh the shade of week-old pork. His mother's dead, a lunger, and all that's left of the Hazar clan is a cousin with a fondness for bangtails and an uncle—Fergus maybe, or Ferdie—more ding than dong. Why, but for a blip or a broderick, Triple H is virtually retired.

"How's Charisse?" the skirt asks. "She still all high hat and happenstance?"

Here Harbee takes an inventory—head, heart, the Alderman, all the parts he could count on only a second ago.

"So you know the lady," Harbee says, keeping the mustard off his cornbread.

"We used to drink out of the same bottle," the modern girlie says. "Worked the Argentine squeeze one time. Did doobs in Chi-town. Habeas, Mr. Hazar, and corpus."

Still nothing specific in the back seat. Not a kisser. Not a mush. Not a map. Just the voice, doubtlessly a rod attached. Jumping Jesse James, a Vincent Price scenario and who-knows-what in the offing.

"You remember a wrong number named Terry Blount?" the woman asks. "Little T?"

"This in the Dark Ages?" Harbee wonders.

"The darkest," she says.

"Could be."

"Take your time, slip knot."

He does, his time getting bunched and tumbledown, too many yesterdays to paw through. There's a derrick named Goodnight and a clout called Shirttail Shelly, never mind various conks and flatties and frails, Mustang Sally among them, but, so far, nothing T-related.

"A sap, mostly B&E," the woman is saying, "a little goosey, I'm told. Liked the eel juice too much, the pins when he could afford the luxury. Had a pan with blue eyes."

"You're *told*, you say?"

"My father," she says. "Terrence Xavier Blount."

Harbee tries again. Less who's who, though, than what's what. Lots of Big's, however. Biggie Smalls, for instance. Big Bob Harris from Harrisburg, as much gaycat as gonif. And a horn-head called His Bigness, raised bees, hustled a lot of jack for the Philly folks. But no Little's, not for the longest time, until, a rock having tumbled free in his brain, Harbee Hakim Hazar remembers, and the root of him goes grainy and rank. The Don. The many large. The burble of blood. Uncle Jesus.

"You're Margaret," he says. "After the saint."

"The one and only," she tells him.

"That's, what—mid-Nineties?"

"'Ninety-one," she says. "I'm twelve at the time. Go to St. Mary's of the Weeping Wood. The plaid jumper, the white blouse—the whole bit. Vocabulary champ three years running."

Harbee's ready to blow. Out the door, up the street—climb the beanstalk if necessary.

"Legerdemain," Margaret says. "That was one of my words."

The threads are popping now, the seams of him giving way. After all, he knows up from up, the kite from the string, what one whizzer whispers to another.

"Staphylococcus," she is saying. "Any of various spherical parasitic bacteria occurring in grapelike clusters—"

"I could apologize," Harbee offers, considering his what-if's.

The silence back there has hair and heartbeat.

"Make restitution," she says eventually.

"Exactly. Put you next to respectable cush. We dip the bill, an hour passes with some chin, I work the blower, and—bingo—you're lousy with lint. No peach. No Shoshone."

"Everything silk and swift."

"Indeed," he says. "The world wise and white."

This time the silence is frigid, the bad air at the bottom of a grave.

"You're forgetting the Shakespeare," she says.

"The tit for tat, you mean?"

That's precisely what she means. The bossa and the nova. The eye for an eye. Not to mention the teeth and hair and hands.

Now it's Harbee's turn to turn yapless. He's in a corner, Dutch any way he cuts it, his whip lashed and his shot put. Modern Margaret has the hooey on him, the powder very nearly dry in his vitals. He finds himself wishing for a lucky star, a ding-a-ling—any hombre with supernatural powers and more than common compassion for a smoke being fitted for a wooden kimono.

"So I'm wondering," he says.

"How you and me come to be in your heap on the last night of your life, right?"

She's on the nut there, he tells her. Right as a hook.

"You remember Doris Hoom?" she says. "Downtown Hyatt. You and her and a rumpled king-size."

How could he forget? he says. She was jip and juju both, mesca and marbles, the hubba-hubba and the alaban left.

"Then you remember the Neck, too?"

Instantly, Triple H has no need for any additional up-and-down. The picture's clear to him—savvy and sin and singular. You got your Numero Uno, Jake Fox, and your Butter and Beans Buster, the Neck. You got the rap and the details that bring it to life, your poke and your preaching. You mix it together, let sit for three decades or so, and, quicker than you can cop a smell from the barrel, you got a tin-talking tamale in the dark and a dinge about to be filled with daylight.

"You ready?" Margaret says.

Harbee nods. "But not willing."

She's got a butt lit, and in the rearview Harbee sees she's more speed trap than parking lot, something in the eyes that says, *Happy*

Birthday, Mr. President. He's pinched now, unwanted tonnage collapsed atop his innermosts, time grinding forward with a screech, his pipes starting to clog.

"Zucchetto," he says, a light way at the end of the tunnel.

She gives him a pointedly amused look—one part margarita, one part mother-of-pearl. Buck, yeah, but no Rogers.

"From the Italian," she begins. "A skullcap worn by Roman Catholic clergymen." She sighs—too much air, too little space. "You finished, Harbee?"

Triple H consults that tunnel anew. Yeah, he guesses he is.

ONE OF *STAR WARS*, ONE OF *DOOM*

THE SLAUGHTER HASN'T started yet.

Tango and Whiskey, in fact, have just left bowling class at the Mimbres Valley Lanes off Iron Street. No one knows about the Intratec DC 9 or the Savage sawed-off double-barreled twelve-gauge. No one knows about Little Boy and FAT MAN, the propane tank bombs set up with egg timers and gallon gasoline cans. Even Mr. DeWine, who's famous for believing he knows everything about anything any kid does, doesn't know that right now, nearly nine in the morning, Tango and Whiskey are parking their cars, a black VW Golf and a blue Camry, in their assigned places in the student lot across from the gym. Sadly, Mr. DeWine can't even guess that in several minutes—maybe ten—Tango, Marlboro in hand, will stop Mike Richardson outside the cafeteria.

"Richardson, I like you," he will say. "Now get out of here. Go home."

No, Mr. DeWine knows only that it's too early for lunch and that he has a mountain of civics exams to grade before seventh period. His gut is churning—too much coffee too early, he guesses—and, come four-thirty this afternoon, he'll be in his Jockey shorts in a room at the Red Roof Inn off I-10, listening to Ms. Petty—Ms. Leanne Elizabeth Petty, late of Tularosa—crying in the bathroom. Before or after—hell, often both—she cries in the bathroom: No one is listening to her, she sobs, no one values her opinion, she's a fireplug for all anyone cares. Just a truck or a root or a box of rocks. She'll be wearing a garter belt and seamed hose, the fetish wear Mr. DeWine drools over, and she'll be sitting on the closed toilet lid, sniffling and boo-hooing that even Mr. DeWine, the guy she's been screwing for the last ten months—Christ, probably the only heterosexual in this goddamn Land of Enchantment who can get from one to ten without using his goddamn fingers, a guy who regularly made her laugh right out loud—even he doesn't listen to her. No, that crumb just climbs on and hollers "Whoopee!," not a "yes" or "no" or civilized phrase to go back and forth between them until, at six-thirty, he says adios so he can hustle back before Sue Ellen, the wife, gets home from Pioneer Realty, Associates.

So there is Mr. DeWine—Frank to his pals, Francis to the Social Security Administration and the DMV, Shitbird to the likes of Tango and Whiskey—in the hall, for eight minutes merely another cop slash cowboy obliged to herd Brianna (all forty of her) and Jason (the fifty or so he is) and Niki (the dozen she's turned out to be) into the right holding pens slash classrooms, to prevent them from stampeding over one another. He's got the "Declaration" to teach, for crying out loud. And attendance to take. A zillion announcements to make, plus homework to hand back—No, Tiffany, not on the curve—a whole briefcase of ideas he'd like to tell the world about if only the natives weren't so damn pimply and tall and loud, if only they didn't dress like lumberjacks and toddlers and thugs, if only they had more on their minds than Friday night and Duke Nukem and where to barf up that turkey sandwich.

The world? Fuck the world, he wants to say. Wants to stand in the center of the hall—right there, in fact, right where Colin is messing with Trisha who's messing with Erika who's messing with Misty who's probably wishing that Joshua were messing with her and not that skanky April May Lester—yeah, stand right there in between Mr. Geller (History II) at his door hither and Mrs. Fletcher (History I) at her door yon, and shout that it's the millennium, for God's sake, that

there's got to be something else to do for forty-eight thousand two
hundred and sixty-one dollars a year; that he was once young, too, a
skinny Virgo with an acceptable jumper from the top of the key, not to
mention an expert way with power tools and a singing voice that did-
n't pain you too much to hear in St. Paul's version of youth choir. "Hey,
look," he wants to holler, "Mr. Masters-degree himself can burp the
entire first verse of 'Silent Night'!" Yeah, Frank Round-Yon-Virgin
DeWine, you moles. Frank you-just-would-not-get-it, don't-you-wish-
you-did DeWine.

So, okay, it's crowded and noisy, the air thick and institutional, the
air smelly and damp and bad for learning, rotten for anything except
virulence and nightmares, and right now, while Rammstein and Nine-
Inch Nails and Creed and Tupac and Little Fascist Panties and the
Holy Modal Rounders are on that Walkman and that CD player and
between those ears, and someone—Fishboy, maybe, he's the type,
subtle as a circus clown—is bellowing "ho-ho-ho," and while all of the
Mountain Time Zone is getting stupid and cranky and old, Whiskey
and Tango are unloading their duffels.

Jesus Lord, they are in possession of some seriously impressive
ordnance—hand grenades and pipe bombs, all homemade with glass
and nails and jacks and BBs—and these guys, breathless and teary-
eyed, are practically punch-drunk with glee. The plan, amigo. Everything's proceeding according to plan, approximately a year in the
making. Months and months downloading the data from the Net, the
only other shit keeping you sane being Buckhorn specialty knives and
natural selection and seeing white trash wreck their brand-new cars.
Nearly a year, man, of putting up with jerks who mispronounce words,
plus O. J. Simpson and weathermen and slow people in line in front
of you and paying for car insurance. So it's now time for five—and five
more, bro—and five on the dark side, too. The time, motherfuckers,
is nigh. Oh, sweet Jesus, is it ever.

Which is ten on the dot, and the bell is ringing, the tardy bell, and
the doors are closing—boom, boom, boom echoing in the hall—and
soon Mr. DeWine, the image of Ms. Petty on all fours fixed like a photograph behind his eyes, takes roll. Surprisingly often of late, he's
imagined the room with a Ms. Petty in each of the twenty-six seats. A

Ms. Petty in a tiger print corset, growling. A Ms. Petty bound hand and foot, duct tape over the mouth, hands down the naughtiest wench in the area code. A Ms. Petty on her knees, tears dripping from her cheeks, her lower lip trembling, hers the grunts farm animals make. *Ugh. Baw. Eef.* A Ms. Petty laughing, then choking because, hell, if you didn't laugh, really bust a gut, you'd just end up banging your head against the nearest brick wall—the government, for starters, and the freeways, *Friends* and the hopeless porkers at the free weights in Gold's. Oh, man, a Ms. Petty in the back of the room, pulling down the map of the Gadsden Purchase, her fanny shiny and smooth and broad, the ass of a former rodeo queen of Otero County now with unspeakable credit card debt.

But today, no. No frills to fondle. No silk or satin or whatever the dickens it is that brings his blood so quickly to boil and makes his thigh muscles twitch. Today, seat 6A, we find Amanda, too sparkly in the eye, busy as a hamster. And Chelsea, 4F, with earrings and bracelets in industrial quantities—probably couldn't get through an airport with all that hardware. And Todd, his best citizen, A's on everything, including his high-dollar hair. They're all here, it seems. Tarika? Yes, as usual, about as far from Mister Teacher as she can possibly be without leaving the room altogether. Tyson? A simple "here" would do, but, Christ on a crutch, this drama club president and his "present," a response that under his care and feeding seems to have eight—possibly ten—syllables. Bethany? Ah, practically under his feet again, eye shadow like poster paint, but a rack you wouldn't mind warming yourself against during the next ice age.

"Anybody know where Kathi is?" It's the "i" that kills him, hanging off the end like a tail, a smiley face above it on all her written work. A letter like a lollipop. "Kathi? Anybody?"

"I saw her in physics." It's Harrison, Todd's foot slave, a junior with the fertile imagination of a dumpster. "That was second period."

"Thanks, Harrison," Mr. DeWine says. "Anybody else?"

They're studying the floor, every blessed one of them. Or the ceiling. Maybe that fascinating crack in the drywall. They don't look at you anymore, these kids. They mumble, they shrug, and they cough. Eye contact? A new social disease.

"She's on the Spirit Committee." That's Suzanne—not Suzy or Sue, if that's all right with you, Mr. DeWine—and she possesses a smile that all but blinds him: more teeth than *Jaws,* pearly as the path to paradise itself.

The committee, he mutters. A second later, shazam, it has hit him. It's Free Cookie Day, The cafeteria. All the chocolate chip and peanut butter and ginger snaps you can eat. Fight, you Wildcats, fight.

"All right, then," he says. "Turn to page 194."

And so that's the way it goes—"When in the course of human events" blah-blah-blah—time a drip to torture yourself with, time a stick to poke into your eyes, time you wouldn't want to meet alone in an alley. Until it's time—no matter the ifs, ands, and buts—to serve up generous portions of Life, Liberty and the pursuit of ever-loving Happiness, precisely as Master Tom described it. Time, in fact, to turn the page, please.

". . . Appealing to the Supreme Judge of the world for the rectitude of our intentions," Todd is saying—in*ton*ing is more the hell like it. Good Lord, the kid is a senator already. A justice of the Supreme Court. King Todd is straight out of the Charlton Heston edition of the Old Testament, the words raining down on Room 144B like murrain and flies and frogs, and, while Ben Franklin and John Hancock and the rest of the colonies' ruling class are mutually pledging their lives and fortunes and sacred honor, Mr. Frank DeWine is doing his damnedest to concentrate, to keep his eyes open, to hold himself upright and not, weakened by boredom and surprisingly epic fatigue, to lay his impossibly heavy head in Marcy Hightower's fetchingly ample lap.

"Mr. DeWine?"

Our hero finds himself looking straight at Harrison, eyeball to eyeball. The boy has spoken. He has brought Mr. Frank DeWine, our onetime recording secretary for Lambda Chi Alpha and full-time yellow dog Democrat, back to the here and now. Evidently—and this, Mr. DeWine thinks, is truly alarming—he was somewhere else, a there and a then well distant from the rhetoric of revolution, a place and time you most assuredly did not want to visit in the company of humanoids as aggressively disinterested as these.

"Page 208," he says. "Manners, Query XVIII—for man is an imitative animal."

They're good, these children. They appreciate knowing what to do next. They appreciate knowing what's to be done in, say, November— even in a November a decade from now. They're big fans of clean laundry and recreation rooms and pool parties. They like pizza and keggers and Old Navy. Not like Whiskey and Tango—code names, in case of capture behind enemy lines. Whiskey and Tango don't like people who bump into them or country music or freedom of the press. Especially Whiskey, who wants to haul all those who are against the death penalty and who dig commercials and who cut in line and— well, he doesn't know exactly where he'd haul their sorry asses, except that it would be forever, the outer darkness and way beyond here, beyond even time and God and any idea that can't be made plain in four words.

It's the Luvox, Whiskey sometimes thinks. The shit gets in him deep, soaks his bones. It blasts him out there, really out there, where the stars creak and the slop drips off the sun and the angels dress like Baron Frank-N-Furter. But that's no reason, never has been. Instead, the reasons are Fishboy calling you "pussy" and "pansy" and Clinton— the fucking president—blowing his wad on that intern, that Monica. Yeah: Kellogg's and lard-butts and the crap they're spraying on your food. And against that, in opposition to all that stupefies and enrages and disappoints, stand himself—the Whiskey man—and his loyal sidekick, the Tangster. Hi-ho, Silver, you dipshits. Hi the hell ho.

Which is more or less what Mr. DeWine has come to think in the last ten minutes. He thinks to tell them he was in a rock band once, Dr. Filth and the Leather Cup—neat, huh? They specialized in Vanilla Fudge covers, Iron Butterfly. He played drums—the perididdle, the flam, the rim shot—no Ginger Baker, sure, but Ringo enough. Nineteen, freshman year at State, and he's on the stage at El Patio Bar in Old Mesilla, pounding out the beat for "Hey, Joe," and urging the unwashed to shake their tail-feathers, joints the size of cigars going back and forth, the singer—man, what was his name?—humping the air, humping the organ, humping the Peavey amp, humping the bass player one time. That's what he wants to say, here, out loud, from atop the desk, having dropped an atlas or two to focus everybody on the present: "Once upon a time," the speech would go, "in a world far, far away, Mr. DeWine, no kidding, had a topless ZTA from Roswell ride him pony-style while he, the selfsame son of a gun huffing and puffing before you, kicked over a cymbal and generally wreaked havoc on the stage décor." Here he would look around, taking stock, with that celebrated pregnant pause. "Ended up on the floor, ladies and germs, a pair of Bermuda shorts between the teeth."

But he won't. Can't. A line, you see, lies between them—a Maginot Line, practically. You are the teacher, the incarnation of decrepit, laughingly out of touch with cool, yours the clothes that even Larry, Curly, and Moe said "yuck" to. You all but wear your hair in a combover, you've gone spongy in the belly, and you gobble goddamn Lipitor and Prinivil because your body—some temple it is, Bunky—has turned on you in outright revolt. And they are the students, the rulers of the wasteland, the tribe yattering in Martian.

And then, thank God, the bell has rung and, only a moment short of a moment that doubtless would have shamed you eternally, you have not told them anything actionable, haven't told them anything at all except that they should know, with the same certainty they know their names, Jefferson's September 25, 1785, letter to Abigail Adams—"Yes, Tiffany, this will be on the test"—and, instantaneously of a single mind, they rise, legs and arms everywhere, backpacks strapped on, their chatter a noise that becomes a roar, then insensible as static, then nothing for the next few minutes but elbows and ball caps and ponytails, nothing except time diving at you like a missile, you just something else goopy, slow, and warm-blooded that can talk.

The carnage? Still an hour away.

Erika's in orchestra, third flute, trying to catch up, her foot having found a rhythm for some fa-la-la that, duh, there isn't ick to like. Misty's pretending she's not in English, at least not in any English that demands you read such brainless typing as *The Bluest Eye,* not to mention all the footnotes and commas and infinitives they make you use. Todd? He's in the library, study hall, doing math homework and another scholarship essay. The Kiwanis, the Optimists, the Lions—all the do-gooders. They're all looking for heartfelt words and a winning way of saying squat. Harrison, sitting across from Todd, seconds that opinion. Suzanne would as well, but right now she's trying to figure out why Mr. Hart, Latin (fourth period), hates her so much. After all, forty kinds of ablative, ninety noun cases, never mind Horace and Virgil and Cicero—who are these mushmouths anyway? *Mehercle, qui dies!* Which sentiment Alicia would understand were she present, but she's gone to the cafeteria to help Kathi, who's managed to get rid of all the sprinkles and the butterscotch and who's made—"Sorry, Ally"—a sizeable dent of her own in the gingerbread men. Which leaves April May Lester, who's not really a skank but just wants one of the cool kids— Bethany, for example, or that prep Tyson—to like her, to ask her a question she can say "sure" to.

So back we are to Mr. DeWine. "Francis Michael," his mother used to bark, a genuine drill sergeant. "Francis Michael, you have been a profound frustration today." He can imagine her here, at attention beside his desk, a switch or a fly swatter in her hand. Her plastic hairbrush, more likely. "Francis Michael, I trust we'll have no more of such tomfoolery." Yes, ma'am, no more. No foolery of any kind, Mother. At which promise, she disappears, and Francis Michael finds himself with little to imagine but what, in the first place, his father, not a saint himself, ever saw in her—the former Mary Cobb, of Silver City. Her hair, maybe? She had great hair, a thundercloud of it, hair to spare, all of it fine as cotton candy. Plus, she could take shorthand, did so right in front of the TV, one January the pages that were reportedly a faithful transcription of *Gunsmoke* piling up beside her armchair. *Bonanza,* too. She liked the rough-and-tumble, sodbusters blazing at each other with pistols, dust swirling, horses going to panic in the eyes. But other than that—the bang-bang and the frenzy, and, okay, modest expertise in the kitchen arts—what? Oddly, Mr. DeWine can't conjure her now, not a single feature. Just the hair, floating in midair, atop the head of a ghost maybe.

A vision which would scare him if, without warning, he hadn't been distracted by a hard and sharp thing that's settled in him—a bone, he fears. Something small and heavy has tumbled to the flat bottom of him, the thunk like a bolt in a bucket, and right now, before Jason appears to discuss his overdue research paper, Mr. DeWine would like to smoke a cigarette, the first in, oh, ten years. A cigarette. Menthol. Nothing at this instant (and for the several to follow) strikes him as a finer idea. At the very least, business to occupy the hands. An activity to keep them from banging here and here on the desk before him. Another flaw in character, albeit tiny and common, to lie about. And, magically, just when Francis Michael needs him, there he stands, Jason, the most earnest Caucasian youngster since Johnny Appleseed.

"Come in, son," Mr. DeWine says, startled he sounds at all like himself, relieved as well that he speaks any language other than Urdu.

"Something wrong, sir?"

Mr. DeWine, most recently of Planet Earth, sneaks a peek at his watch. Eleven on the nose. T minus Tuesday and counting.

"I'm fine, Jason. Why do you ask?"

The boy knows everything, Mr. DeWine has heard. The periodic table, the succession of England's kings and queens. Who kicked hindmost in the Tang Dynasty, how law is made in Kafiristan. So what now?

"It's your face, sir," Jason begins. "It was like you weren't here."

All right, Mr. Frank DeWine thinks. They know he hollers and the comely Ms. Petty from mathematics weeps, and that old Ben Franklin has helped himself to all the tarts in Paris. They gab among themselves, these creatures. They know his dog, the pound-bred Rex, and his weakness for bourbon. They know the sorry state of his socks, his wayward heart. They know the rusting piston in his chest, the sump above his shoulders. They have, indeed, found him out.

"Let's begin, shall we?" Mr. DeWine gestures to a chair and, a minute later, time with shape and weight and sound, they have begun.

As have Tango and Whiskey. It's a pop quiz, right there on the hill overlooking the cafeteria. One Stevens pump-action, sawed-off shotgun? "Check, Tangster." One Hi-Point 9mm semiautomatic carbine with the sixteen-inch barrel? "Double-check." One of this, one of that, one of everything they'd started whispering about the summer before. One childhood of *Star Wars*, one of *Doom*. They're wearing their outfits—the flannel shirt, the camo pants, the lace-up boots, the ghoulish smirk. They're about to engage hostile forces, the fitness fuckheads and those geezers who don't use their turn signals. Whiskey has done what he needed to do. He's washed his hands, he touched his ear six times when he got out of the car, prayed to the four corners, touched his other ear six times—the hocus-pocus you do on Tuesday so that on Wednesday you won't find yourself naked in your closet begging the pardon of an audience of Klingons and druids and the Four Horsemen of the Apocalypse. In his room, he identified everything that began with the letter c—his carpet, his cat, his cap, his Cap'n Crunch, his cudgel.

And now, goddamn, there's more to inventory. The ammo, the Molotov cocktails in the Piggly Wiggly bag at your feet, the notes that tell the civilians you've morphed, you're about to jump through the only open seam in the universe to join the master race, and so here you are, Attila himself, a BFG 9000 in hand, decay dust in one pocket and in the other a potion from the Wicked Witch of the West, warp speed the means by which you hurtle from A to B, you and your buddy now Knights Jedi and Errant and Black, you and your buddy now the most special of special effects, founding members of the ninth circle, the inner sanctum, the grave, you and your buddy now specters brought into the full light of day by rage and by the heartening prospect of a prodigious volume of gore. Oh, Tango, it is April, the cruelest month. Oh, Tango, it is seventy fucking degrees. Oh, Tango, it is the end of the world as you know it and you feel fine.

"You ready?" Whiskey says. "I am go for liftoff."

To which, for the longest time—a century, it feels like—Tango says nothing, his mouth chewing crazily at the air. His eyes have become narrow and dark, his ski cap down over his ears like a bank robber. He could be thinking about heaven, about saints to goose-step with, nectar to sip. He could be thinking about crows that tap-dance or storybook Apaches to send on the warpath or a feat impossible to do like carry the ocean across the desert in his hands.

"I'm scared," he says. "Really scared."

Yes, it's springtime, the bell about to ring, a few kids on the lawn, smoking, a few walking in from the lot. Schoolmates, they are called. Peers. Whiskey loves them. No kidding. He must take their lives because he loves them, which fact they will comprehend when he walks among them. This is his lesson. They have been shallow, these Wildcats. They have been arrogant. They have given offense. And now, lo and verily, he will smite them.

"Afterward," Whiskey says, "we'll get nachos."

Tango knows this is not true, can never be true. Afterward is not in the plan. The before has already ended, and nothing will follow but smoke and blood and debris and dreams never to wake from.

"Tango," Whiskey says, a question.

Foot. It is the only word Tango can utter, the only word he remembers from a lifetime of words. Wait, there's another. *Tree.* Which he says and says again until enough minutes have passed for him to say, with nearly incredible relief, *Insect.* Then: *Wolf.* Then: *Night.* Whereupon Whiskey touches his shoulder, and, miraculously, Tango has other words to say, all of them big and new and remarkable as the day itself.

"Pizza, too," he says. "Pepperoni."

The world has already turned red and swirly at the edges, an arctic cold settling at their feet. The world is about to tilt, to wobble out of its groove, about to shrink. The world is cracking, a splintering you can hear in heaven.

"Ready?" Whiskey asks.

This time Tango can answer. His shit is squared away. The epic wind has left his mind. He's copacetic. He salutes, stiff-armed and urgent.

"Heil Hitler," he says.

And now the doors are near, a handle for each to grasp. They have only to pull, which they have done, and they have only to march past several classrooms, Ms. Petty's among them, and toward the library like soldiers, which they are doing, and they have only to arrive at the circulation desk, which they have, and they have only to squeeze off a round, which each does into the ceiling tiles, and at last, the clock ticking toward 11:45, to the dozens of now thoroughly why-faced Wildcats in front of them, those trembling like Todd and those not, those like Harrison wide-eyed with awe and those thinking they ought to be able to claw through their notes for the answer to this unreasonably complicated question, the warriors Tango and Whiskey have only to speak.

"Here we are now," they say. "Entertain us."

He's got a half hour, Mr. DeWine does.

He could eat. Mystery meat in the cafeteria or the tuna sandwich in the refrigerator in the teachers' lounge. He could pay a bill or two, maybe. He's got his checkbook, a week's worth to pay up in his briefcase. Instead, he puts his feet on his desk, rocks back in his chair. Why not visit Leanne, a surprise? She's got this period free, too. He could sneak up behind her, grab her at the waist. He's done it before, though only once. The whole time, not more than five minutes, he was overwhelmed by the fear that somebody—a student having forgotten a book, or a teacher searching for the new calculators—would walk in on them. His skin had felt too small, his head too big. He thought he might fall over, his heart like a ferret in his chest, all claws and climbing. Besides, she was herself spooked, slapping at his head like a spaz, hissing—Honest Injun—hissing like a goose or some such. Fucking fowl, for Pete's sake. No, he'll stay put. He takes his deepest breath of the day. He'll do a push-up or two. Work on that spare tire. Tend to the mind and body both, he thinks. Your familiar heart-and-head imbalance. Man, is it quiet. Eerily quiet, only the a.c. cycling and the clock and the creak of a middle-aged middleweight hauling himself to his feet. It's the quiet from the moon, the quiet where time ends.

Outside, there's nothing, just the school flag, all that theme-park blue. He walks among the desks. "Abandon all hope," someone has scribbled. Dante—what a bozo. Blamed the whole fiasco on Beatrice. At another desk—here is where the lovely Sherry parks her lovely butt—he finds a hair. Blond. Not Sherry's, though. No, this is the blond of a practicing protestant. This blonde drives an Explorer. Doubtless, this blonde aced the ACT. Red would be something else, he guesses. Honest work to be done on a ranch. A career on the stage. He turns on his heel, Mr. DeWine does. And brown, Sue Ellen's color? He doesn't want to think. That's a smart mouth, a wiseacre.

Brown's a story with an unhappy ending. Brown is boredom. Brown is a mannequin that drinks Vodka gimlets.

Now he's really curious. What have they left behind, these kids? Last fall, he found a spiral notebook with writing in it so peculiar, so detailed and figurative, it could have only come from the hand of an egghead's egghead. Squiggles gave way to squares and those to bouquets of dashes and those to a series of capital *L*'s, the whole of it bizarrely architectural—the castle of a dark-minded wizard, he thought, or a Byzantine metropolis of gnomes and haunts, or a low country in ruin. Yeah, it was a civilization to dig up, you and ten thousand other zombies looking for the reason you can't sleep. He wonders now what happened to the notebook. It might have led to treasure. Jesus H., if only you were fluent in runes and glyphs and smudges and symbols, it might have led you out of Deming, New Mexico, and right to the golden threshold of Shangri-la itself.

Gracious, there's so much to know about Mr. DeWine, especially now that elsewhere the shooting has started. That topless Zeta Tau Alpha, for example, at El Patio those many years ago? That was Sue Ellen, his wife. Sue Ellen Bates then. Older by a year. A sophomore business major. But she wasn't really topless. She wore a Moby Grape T-shirt. He likes to embellish—makes the real realer, he thinks. The Bermuda shorts? Those he didn't invent. He didn't invent Roswell, either, or the cymbal, or the wreckage in his wake. Nor, later than night, at his apartment off Solano Street, did he invent the clumsy sex he and Sue Ellen had, or that hour, toward dawn, when he felt that he'd been dropped on the planet for all the wrong reasons. He didn't invent Catherine, either, the baby who died six years later. A miscarriage, actually, the first of two. Eons ago, it feels like, when beasts ruled and we were but fish or flesh that crawled.

What else should we consider before he makes up his mind to drop in on Ms. Petty? He was runner-up in the fourth-grade spelling bee, *terpsichorean* the word that got between him and the silver trophy Kay Stevenson bragged about. His first girlfriend? Michelle "Mickey" Barker. Went steady the whole summer the Beatles came to America. Behind Timmy Bullard's house, in the onion field, she let him touch her breasts—"For a count of five, Frankie, no more"—the surprising weight of them something he swears he can still feel. Oh, this as well: He wrote a whole book in high school, in Las Cruces. Well, eighty-some pages. But hand-illustrated, lots of forest scenes and a mountain range that looked like eyeteeth. His version of Sir Gawain and the Green Knight. Lots of derring-do in that. Nick-of-time stuff, too. An alluring maiden in distress, of course. He was the Sir, naturally. *Vanquished*—man, he loved that word, that and *dispatched* and *woe betide he who,* all the fancy talk you nowadays don't hear much at Del Cruz's Triangle Drive-in—yes, he vanquished a dragon. Slew the sucker silly. Afterward the Sir found himself bedecked—right, another word stuck-up Kay Stevenson wouldn't know the up from down of—with a sash and more medals than Bayer has aspirin, the king (the maiden's father) the most grateful potentate in all of Pip-pip, Cheerio, and vicinity. Got some serfs out of the deal as well. Mrs. Chew let him read a chapter to his English class, Mickey Barker right under his nose. Made it all the way to the part where Sir Gawain and his friends—the vaunted Sir Fitzroy and the steadfast Sir Palmetto, mainly—lay siege to the manor house of the dastardly Archduke Fussface before the bell rang. Yeah, dastardly. "I think," Mrs. Chew said to everybody, "there's a lesson in this for all of us." It was this event, he still thinks, that made him want to become a teacher—to find lessons everywhere, even in his own needy heart.

Not terrible lessons, though, like those being delivered right now a hundred yards away in the library, where Whiskey, clomping through a tangle of overturned chairs and scattered papers, has announced that he is the Lord Humongous, the Ayatollah of Rock 'n' rolla, and Tango has discovered underneath a reading table a girl, Tiffany, to play peek-a-boo with.

"You like me, don't you?" he says, his the grotesque grin you carve on a pumpkin.

What a silly question. Of course she likes him. He has the gun. Dark and greasy-looking with May Day streamers hanging from it and maybe actual human ribs, gobbledygook like Arabic or graffiti scribbled with Marks-a-Lot on the stock, the gun is pointed at her.

"So," Tango begins, "if I asked you for a kiss, you'd give it to me, right?"

Another asinine question. He can have her purse, her hair, her hands.

But now it appears that all he wants is for that noise—an animal howling in pain, Tiffany thinks—to stop.

"It's a cat," she says, trying to help.

The gun goes off again, another boom wrong for books and study hall and Free Cookie Day, and Tiffany understands that it is she, the only daughter from the house of Hudspeth, who is crying. She is the cat, howling.

"Do her," Whiskey is shouting. "Do the bitch."

But she can't be done, she thinks. After all, she is home, under the covers. She has her pj's on, in her headphones Jack Diesel's greatest hits. A novel lies in her lap, a tearjerker Oprah wanted her to read. She can't be done. No, she certainly can't.

And, mysteriously, she isn't. Instead, the boy—she's seen him before, James or something, from the soccer team—crouching behind a desk chair is done. He has a cute haircut, close at the sides, then he doesn't. Unmoving only a moment before, he is flying—snatched by the collar, it seems, and hurled against a bookshelf, the reference section crashing down to bury him.

"Targets of opportunity," Whiskey is calling them.

He's firing into the floor—*pow, pow, pow*—his shotgun like a pogo stick bouncing him through the room, real astonishment in his eyes. The firepower. The fucking firepower. He's hanging on to the smart end of a contraption that spews out blood and justice, cordite and delicious disorder.

"Dance, tenderfoot," he orders, now Billy the fucking Kid and Triple H and Prince Jericho and Mr. Blue, and immediately one unlucky gomez—gee, Harrison, fancy meeting you here—is dancing, snot smeared across his lips, clearly the loneliest fellow in the hemisphere.

"It's the hucklebuck," Tango says, delighted to be the new host of *MTV World*. "Shake a leg, dude. Trip the light fantastic."

Arms spread as if in ecstasy, Harrison dances, knees higher than a desk, nothing beneath him now that the floor has disappeared, now that Whiskey, giggling, is keeping promises. Now that the present, simple as Simon, is giving way so easily to the even simpler past.

"The hokeypokey," Tango has said. "Turn yourself around."

Events are moving swiftly, many at the same instant. Todd intends to rise, to dash for the door. He's thinking it, yes, but a moment later he's not thinking anything at all, the organ to think with having unexpectedly gone mealy and cold. The world smells sour and sulfuric. A blizzard has roared through here, dust roiling, shreds of paper falling like snowflakes. The floor is pocked and pitted, as if gouged by jackhammers and the picks of giants. Shattered glass lies everywhere—in your hair, down your shirt, in your Nikes. Wood splinters have stabbed you in the arm, the neck, the backs of your thighs. Remarkably, you've heard not a single sound. The muzzle flashes are unmistakable, a spray of wadding and sparks, a window pouring over a desk like a shimmering waterfall, but, huddled behind the body of a girl whose misfortune—thank you, Mr. Hart—was to need the Latin for *Never cut class again, Miss Suzanne Winters*, you can't hear anything. Except your own heart, its fitful thud-thud the rhythm vampires are aroused by. Yes, Tango is speaking—his mouth is working, his awful tongue—but the audio is on MUTE. You want the remote control. But the instant the sound thunders over you like a tidal wave and you have glimpsed Miss Petty at the door, you don't want anything except for time to snap backward so that you'd have a century to warn her, nasty old DeWine's girlfriend, not to come in here, that she can read this week's edition of *Time* tomorrow or the next day. Please, Miss Petty, don't come in here for anything.

But she has. And Tango—his shirt off, his bird-like chest glistening with a war paint of blood and paste and ink—has already, with the formal bow of a Beau Brummel, welcomed her to his intimate get-together.

"You're just in time," he says.

For Whiskey, there's too much to account for. The wall, the floor, the wall again. At this point, he had hoped to be well into Beta phase. The main event. Little Boy and FAT MAN themselves. But his ear has to be checked, and his wrist, followed by his boot and his ankle, before he can move on to his knee and his eye socket. "Say the words," he tells himself. And, soon enough, from his prepared list, he does: "Reason, virtue, plenitude." He glances around. Evidently, he has been shouting. "Being," he hollers, "is not different from nothingness."

"Put that down, James Crawford." Ms. Petty is addressing Tango, stern as a movie actress. "What do you think you're doing?"

What lunacy. Which can't be helped, unfortunately. Ms. Petty is, figuratively speaking, beside herself. She's watching herself stamp her foot—yes, actually stamp her right foot—and put her hands on her hips, a schoolmarm from ancient America. She should shake herself, slap some sense into her pretty head, but she can't because Leanne Petty is not really there. Instead, dumb and foolish and proud, standing not a giant step from the barbarian with the rifle, is a lunatic female using her name and wearing her clothes and saying what would be said if the universe had not so completely melted.

"I said to put that down, Mr. Crawford."

He can't, he says. He's committed. Totally.

Committed. It's an expression she's heard before, our fussbudget with the wagging finger and the profound respect for propriety.

"I mean," Tango is saying, "fifteen minutes ago, maybe. But now? Jesus God, Miss Petty, we're, like, in the second act here."

Against the far wall, still wringing his hands as if scrubbing them in air, Whiskey has almost reached the end of his speech. "Give us this day our daily bread," he is reciting. "The horror, the horror. One if by land, two if by sea. Merry Christmas to all, and to all a good night."

Ms. Petty slowly surveys the room. If only Frank could see this. These kids worship new gods now. They speak a new tongue. They will eat a new food in a new world and grow old in the new way.

"Miss Petty?" It's Tango, his the shrug of youthful impatience. He has work to do now, okay? And little time to do it in.

"What's that on your forehead?"

It's sandpaper, he says. To strike matches on. For the fuses, you know?

"James, you were such a nice boy. I can't believe this."

Another shrug, this one of eighteen-karat sadness. "I still am nice, Miss Petty. You just don't know me, is all."

She's desperate to return to herself, to step into the person still staring at James Crawford, nice boy. The situation demands organization. She should be telling that girl—Misty or Jewel, something perky anyway—that she can leave now, poor thing. She should be calling the authorities, the principal at the very least. A thousand tasks need attention, if she could only climb back into her own skin. But she can't. Never will. For James Crawford has finished his work, Whiskey having hustled over to observe, and the old self of Ms. Leanne Petty is collapsed on the floor, one leg twisted under her hips, the last of her dribbling out of the shockingly ragged hole in her head.

Whiskey squats down, lifts her limp hand. "Goodnight, air."

The plan. It's Tango's turn to talk. "Goodnight, noises everywhere."

For weeks and weeks afterward, Sue Ellen DeWine will wonder what Frank was doing near the library. She's visited his classroom and it's—what?—a good hundred yards, could be more, from where the murders happened. The papers—the *Headlight,* even the *Journal* from Albuquerque; TV, too, Channel 4 from El Paso, and CBS—have called him a hero, running in to rescue those students that way, but all Sue Ellen will puzzle about, when she goes back to work a week after the funeral, is what Frank was doing there. He should have been on lunch break, the other direction exactly, but he was headed toward the library. In June, admittedly embarrassed to be obsessed with such an inconsequential detail, she will nonetheless phone Dick Spivey, the assistant principal, to ask him, but all he will be able to tell her is that he hasn't the slightest idea. "Maybe he had to return a book," he'll tell her, and, okay, that will be her answer—a book to return, another mystery solved—until the following August when, steering her Camry into the lot of Zia Title for a closing, the merciless logic of curiosity and intuition and suspicion still hard at work in her, she will say "Leanne Petty" aloud, and Sue Ellen DeWine, the widow of a hero, will know. Francis DeWine, the son of a bitch, was on his way to see Leanne Petty.

Which is no more than Frank himself knows as he yanks open the door to the math wing. He's got his tie loose now and he's making good time, bum knee and all, more or less skipping, in his mind a dumber-than-dumb image of gimpy Chester shouting "Mr. Dillon! Mr. Dillon!" in the middle of a Dodge City street. Sir Francis has a personal matter to attend to, a furtive and private concern, so more than several seconds pass before he notices that he's the only person heading toward the weird banging noises. Everybody else, students and grown-ups alike, is scrambling to get by him. It's an honest-to-goodness fire this time, he thinks. It's not a drill, not a bomb scare like last Halloween. Adjacent to the men's toilet, he spots a kid he recognizes, one of the Goliaths from the lacrosse team, April Lester tugging on his arm.

"What's wrong?" he asks. "Richardson, what's going on?"

The kid's head goes back and forth. It seems to be the only part of him that works. The rest of him is frozen, seized.

"Well?"

Richardson needs a second, clearly. He has the expression of a landlubber crawling out of shark-infested waters. (*A moment will arrive, soon, when Mr. DeWine will remember this Q-and-A with greatest sorrow. How boneheaded he has been, he will scold himself. What a stone. How could he not have known?*)

"April?"

Mr. DeWine grabs her arm, gets her attention. Good Lord, she's thin, like a ballerina. What, he wonders, is she doing with a behemoth like Richardson? It's like finding Tinkerbell keeping company with the Incredible Hulk.

"The library." She's whispering, as if she has to tell the whole school the dirty word some creep in homeroom yelled at her. "They're in the library."

Somebody is smacking a wall somewhere, Frank thinks. With a bat, sounds like. Really giving it the business.

"Who's in the library?"

She shakes her head, her tiny head. She doesn't know. All she can do is point, another of the species with seemingly only two or three moving parts. (*And this, too, is another instant he will regret when his moment comes.*)

"Go on," Mr. DeWine says. "It's a fire or something. Go outside."

So they go, April practically dragging Richardson, the two of them replaced by five more and three more after that, and here charge a handful more, all of them with crab legs and flying arms, the last kid—Tyson, his orator!—missing a shoe. This is like the end of a period but at fast-forward and without the grab-ass and ha-ha-ha, students appearing from everywhere. One girl he's never seen before—she resembles Marisa Tomei, but chunkier—runs by him screaming "John" over and over. "You can't do this," another girl is saying. "It's just not fair." That's all. Just those two sentences, like a chant, the same sentences he will shortly find himself saying. But right now here are more kids bearing down on him, the short fellow—Fishboy, is it?— with the shiny Penn State jacket tripping and knocking two look-alikes down with him, all of them having the devil of a time getting up off the floor. And, shit, here are those goofy noises again, but louder this time.

"You seen Ms. Petty?" He's collared a boy lugging a bass fiddle, the instrument bigger in all dimensions than he is.

"Who?"

Mr. DeWine pulls the kid to the side. Down the hall, the litter is incredible. Books. Purses. Backpacks. Baseball caps. A blouse is there, too. And a pair of coveralls. Christ, what were all the fire drills for? He expects zoo life next. A giraffe would not surprise him one whit.

"Ms. Petty?" he begins. "She teaches junior calculus."

"I don't take that till next year, sir."

So Mr. DeWine asks the next kid—a geek from student council possibly; he has that squeaky look about him. Another *no*. And another, this one from the dorkier end of the food chain. Nothing but *no, no, no* until, interestingly, there's no one left to ask, the hall having become as still as deepest space. Which means that, despite the jan-gling of the alarms and sirens woo-wooing in the distance, Mr. DeWine can hear, with phenomenally stunning clarity, what he dares not believe is gunfire.

(*That moment? When he at last apprehends how monstrously dim-witted he is? When he learns how far up his ass his head has been? Friends, it's now. Right now.*)

"No," he says, as much to the brickwork as to himself.

But there it is again. A shot. Like a cannon, he thinks. Shit.

You'd think he would run now, wouldn't you? You'd bet that, know-ing what he knows, he'd turn the other way, scram for the doors he came in through. You'd think, because he's read the papers and watched CNN and has heard about those psycho punks in Arkansas and Colorado, and because he possesses the same instinct for self-preservation we all have, that he'd know what to do. At the very least, his body would react independently, right? His muscles, his fist of a heart.

But he does not move. No, Mr. DeWine—get this—sits, leans against the wall, the real mystery to fret over. It's a fire, he tells himself, not the last of his wishful thinking. He's no hero, that's not in dispute. And violence? Christ, the only fistfight he had was—when?—maybe in junior high, in the days when they had junior high. Instead, he tells himself again that the smoke in the air, bitter and grainy, is from a fire. Faulty wiring probably. Or some butt-wipe setting off M-8os in the restroom. But, all along, Francis Michael DeWine has known better. It's just like TV, friends. How sad. You go to a movie, a bona fide shoot-'em-up, and it's boom-boom-boom, just like now. Gangsters, terrorists, invaders from another galaxy—God, they're all in the library. It's astounding, really. His lungs have gone slack, the air in here too thin. The knee is seriously hurting now, the throbbing like a tom-tom. Skiing. What a dumb-ass sport.

"They didn't work."

Someone—a boy of wicked angles and rattles and marvelous heat—has sat down next to him.

"FAT MAN and Little Boy," the kid is saying. "I must've fucked up the timers."

The kid seems to wobble under a halo of fireflies, blinking lights, and a buzz constant as ocean noise.

"Are you John?" Mr. DeWine says. "A girl was asking after you."

"Whiskey," the boy says, his voice not at all the snarl a villain should have.

The fire emergency sprinklers have come on now, a fierce shower drenching the hall, the walls slick with running water, the floor shiny like a postcard of a river from a world where the outside is weirdly in.

"You can't do this," Mr. DeWine says.

Oh, but he can, says the boy.

"It's not fair. Really."

Time has unraveled. Yesterday, Frank DeWine was a Cub Scout

stealing Life Savers from the Stop-N-Go. Only a month ago did his voice change. He was born with a full beard and a three-pack-a-day habit.

"You cold, Mr. DeWine? You're shivering."

Yes. So cold. Between his ears, a glacier has ground through the center of him, the fissures and folds of his brain jammed with ice.

"You want to say anything?"

"Like last words?" Mr. DeWine asks.

Whiskey nods. He takes no particular pleasure in this scene. Business is being conducted, that's all. The "therefore" and "whereunto" pages of the contract. The paragraphs in which the who's who and the what's what become the *quid pro quo* and the hickory-dickory-dock.

"I'd like to say something about my father," Mr. DeWine begins, though for several breaths he can't think of what exactly he might mean. "He had big hands, like paddles."

Again Whiskey nods. Mr. DeWine is being a good sport. Not like some you could name. Not like, oh, Bethany with her forgive-us-our-trespasses bullshit.

"I don't think he ever struck me in anger," Mr. DeWine is saying.

"My dad, too," Whiskey says. "He just sends me to my room, or takes away the car."

Whiskey has raised the assault pistol and placed it tenderly against the vein pulsing at Mr. DeWine's temple. The boy has an interest, keen but thoroughly professional, in this moment. He wonders what we will make of his own last words, those typed on the page folded in his shirt pocket, after he, at the muzzle velocity of 1,230 feet per second, has transformed himself into liquid and light, meat and whitest bone.

"Anything else?"

Yes, Francis DeWine thinks. Yes, there is.

REVOLUTIONARIES

LONG BEFORE HE turned radical and disappeared into that "underground" we once upon a time used to hear so much about—and much before he showed up in my life again—Jimmy Spalding and I were best friends.

As kids we swam the flumes, the irrigation canal that passes over a railroad trestle where my father's farm—now my own—backs up to the levee for the Rio Grande River north of Las Cruces. At Alameda Junior High, the only middle school in what was then a town of ten thousand, we cocaptained our bowling team, the Flying Aces, one of whose trophies I still have in a closet somewhere. In the ninth grade, we climbed C Mountain, dragging my mutt, Sneaker, along, and from a cliff thousands of feet higher than any bush in our desert, we turned our backs on what we knew was Hicksville to watch clouds churn our way from the Wonderland we'd heard California was.

"Going out there," Jimmy said. "Soon as I get my driver's license. You and me, pal. Do the whole scene, the beach trip."

In those days we aimed to be surfers. Or astronauts. Or truckers. We had the healthy fantasy life of all teenagers—a dream life composed of open space and money and women from the pages of *Nugget* and *Gent* magazines. We smoked cigarettes and talked tough and brought other guys—Jay Bullard and Mark Runyan—into a club that became part Three Musketeers, part Three Stooges. We'd watch *The Bowery Boys* at Jimmy's house, in the rec room his father had built after they bought the American Linen Supply firm. We joined the wrestling team, me at 136, Jimmy at 144. One month we read everything by Leon Uris—especially *Battle Cry,* which, when I've looked at it since, seems nothing like the WWII Sherwood Forest that I remember. We saw *Psycho* at the State Theater and a week later read *Last Exit to Brooklyn,* which Jimmy declared was art with all the gland left in.

"I'm meant to do something," Jimmy would say. "I got a real relationship with destiny."

Then, the summer after we graduated, in '66, as if one of us had died, we stopped being friends. I went for a national thespian conference at the University of Indiana, stayed on for a course in the drama I still enjoy, and did not hear from him for two months.

"How come you didn't answer my letters?" I said in August. "I called three or four times, too. Your dad said he didn't know where you were."

"Been on the move, man." He shrugged. "San Francisco, Telegraph Hill, the VDC—the whole works."

He was standing inside his door, more in shadow than out.

"It's all coming together," he was saying. "Rock 'n' roll, the race thing, Vietnam. It's a process, Buddy. Medgar Evers, Reverend King, Bob Dylan."

I had planned to tell him about the kid I'd met at IU, Morgan Maxwell, whose father was a VP with Kemper insurance. Morg had said that maybe the company plane would take us all—Jimmy too, I'd insisted—to the Rose Bowl that winter.

"No can do," Jimmy said. "I got priorities now."

Sunlight was flying off a thousand surfaces, dizzying and sharp.

"I'll come back tomorrow," I told him. "We'll see a movie, go up to the club."

"Better not," he said. "I'm real busy. Got many things to do."

"After school starts, then?"

We were going to the local college, New Mexico State University, a deal we'd agreed to the September before.

"Yeah," he said. "That could be a real possibility."

I was trying to keep my mouth shut and back up at the same time. This wasn't Jimmy, I was thinking. This wasn't anybody I knew at all.

"Listen, man," he said, "I'll call you, okay? I got to straighten some things out first, serious head stuff."

So that fall we left for what I know now are two different worlds: me to that future opened up by Econ 102, Range Management, and the *The Principles of Organic Chemistry* by Petry and Wallace; Jimmy to the fractured present revealed to him by the *Evergreen Review,* Alan Watts, Jim Morrison and the Doors. I'd spot him every now and then, a figure moving alone and always upstream against the seven thousand shitkickers and jocks and sorority girls we undergraduates were. In front of Corbett Center one time, I saw him handing out leaflets—a broadside from Senator George McGovern of South Dakota: "Who really appointed us God for people elsewhere around the world?"

"Long time," I told him. "How's it going?"

"Great," he said. "Got work to do, my man. Minds to change, hearts to heal."

He had a pile of dead-baby pictures—napalmed, he said—and a smile that had little to do with making B's in Intro to Sociology.

"You really believe this stuff, don't you?"

"Abso-goddamn-lutely," he said. "You ought to join us, Buddy. We have no rules and everybody sleeps late."

Walking around us as if we both had the plague were kids who wanted to be doctors or mechanical engineers or state lawmakers or teachers—plain college kids who, I hoped, would one day be my friends and neighbors.

"Sorry," I told him. "If I knew what to do, I'd do it, honest."

"Man," Jimmy was saying, "you're young, you can be like me. I got it knocked, Buddy. I say what I want, smoke a little dope, it's paradise."

That October I heard that Jimmy intended to march on the Pentagon with Joan Baez. I learned, too, that he'd burned his draft card to send the ashes to General Hershey. In April of '68, before Johnson ended the bombing in North Vietnam, I found an essay, "Liberation from the Affluent Society," clipped under the windshield wiper of my truck. "Read this shit, man," an attached note said. "Essential knowledge herein. Dig the part on mechanisms of manipulation and repression." He'd signed his initials inside a peace symbol. "It's like the man said," Jimmy had scrawled, " 'Rise up and abandon the creeping meatball.' "

That summer I worked for my father—chopping cotton, running the cultivator, odd jobs—and spent my free time at the country club. I didn't see Jimmy until I ran into him outside Young Hall, the English building, the next semester.

"What're you taking?" he wondered.

"Lit survey," I said. "Keats, Byron, those guys."

"I approve," he said. "The revolutionaries, first-rate. Broaden the mind, let the light shine in."

His hair hung long now, braided in the back, and watching his face was very hard work. He was pale, too, as if he'd spent three months in a closed room.

"I talked to your dad a couple times," I said. "He said you'd disappeared."

"Big rally next month," Jimmy said. "You ought to show up. We'll get stoned, do miracles outrageous. It'll be highly provocative."

I thought about my own father, particularly the happy noises he made about Nixon, and what Mr. Agnew was calling "an effete corps of impudent snobs." Plus I had a girlfriend, Mary Jane Byrd, a Chi Omega who would one day be my wife for several years and part of the reason I'm telling this.

"I got classes," I said. "Maybe I'll watch."

He nodded, and I felt old—less his pal than his enemy.

"I like the hat," he said. "You're going to make one hell of a cowboy, Buddy."

For three straight weeks his name was in the *Round-Up,* the student newspaper. He even made the *Sun News,* the local daily. He was quoted often and with what seemed like considerable care. He called for upheaval and anarchy, a repudiation of mindless affluence. He mentioned H. Rap Brown and the SDS, as well as what Fidel Castro was said to have accomplished.

"You know this guy, don't you?" Mary Jane said to me once.

She'd worked a year in Up With People and had a cheerful disposition I couldn't get enough of. What's more, she planned to be a TV newscaster and I wanted to be around when the world saw how beautiful she was.

"Well," she said, "I think he's an idiot."

I was there that Friday, part of the curious who watched nearly two dozen students and faculty and lonely townsfolk march across the steps of the administration building. They were what motley is: Waving signs, they shouted, "Hell, no, we won't go!" and Jimmy led them in a speech that used language like "oppression" and "imperialism" and "colonialism"—all the words and habits of mind, he has since told me, we have to learn anew every time there is murder and public suffering in an acre of the world we own.

"We want ROTC off campus," he hollered once. "We want Bob Hope off TV and Frank Sinatra out of the movies." He waved his hands. "We want classes in nudity."

Toward the end—before the campus cops and four state policemen broke it up by dragging Jimmy off—he delivered a rambling, singsongy declaration that mentioned Abe Maslow, Aldous Huxley, Carl Rogers, D. T. Suzuki—names that passed over me like clouds. They were the dead or the living, or the never-were. I wanted him to talk—if that's all this was—about being afraid, about what dead William Wordsworth's verse skills had to do with anything, and about what I was supposed to be doing in five or ten years. But he went on— "We're discussing human worth here!"—his hair flyaway, his T-shirt too small and covered with buttons, his cheeks painted like an Apache's, ignoring the hecklers who said he was queer, or chickenshit, or a commie.

"And now," he announced, "in keeping with the theatrical theme of today's lesson, I will piss on this wall."

Instantly, a state policeman, a sergeant named Krebs who is now the road superintendent for our Dona Ana County, burst out of the door behind Jimmy, and the scene was like two minutes of Walter

Cronkite's evening news: words were exchanged, an official arm snatched Jimmy by the neck, and a second later he was spread-eagled on the pavement, facedown, blood oozing from one ear.

"We'll surround this place," Jimmy was shouting. "We'll be holy men, chanting and beating drums, and this place will rise into the air. At three hundred feet all the evil spirits will fall out!"

Every time I play this moment in my memory, I see myself interfering—honorably and fearlessly; I am strong, in this dream world I construct, and I am angry. I act righteously, like Superman or one loudmouth world-beater Jimmy believed in. I do not stand, as I did, beside my girlfriend, Mary Jane Byrd, and shake, breathing hard. I do not watch my friend yanked away, one arm twisted behind his back.

"I hate this sort of thing," Mary Jane Byrd said. "Whenever I hear about it, I just close my eyes and pretend."

A couple of hours later, I visited him in a private room on the second floor of Memorial General Hospital.

"Your dad told me where to find you," I said.

He was sitting up in bed, wearing a hospital nightgown, a knot of gauze around his head, one eye swollen shut in a pulp of blue and yellow flesh. The room had eight shades of white and the half-dozen hairs on his chin made him look feeble, stupid.

"Big man, my father," Jimmy was saying. "Pulled some strings, I gather. Asked me if I was concerned about my reputation, about a job. Man, I don't want a fucking job."

In a chair beneath the wall-mounted TV sat a girl I'd never seen before. She was dark as an Indian, plus fleshy in a way that made you think about sex first.

"That's Carla," Jimmy said. "We're sort of going together. It's antirevolutionary, I guess, very retrograde. I see us having lots of babies."

She made a point of ignoring the hello I offered.

"Gonna run some errands," Carla said, getting up. "I'll catch you later."

"Classic bohemian," Jimmy said after she left. "She's from Parsippany, New Jersey. Came down here to molest ag students and be an agitator. We have a real spiritual thing."

Out the window I could see traffic on Water Street. Directly across stood the Papen Building, an improbable ten-story bank and office tower whose basement Jimmy and I had explored when it was going up years before. We'd been in its vault, all its secret rooms.

"Some scene, huh?" Jimmy said. "Man, what a rush the violence is. They wanted to rip my face off, 3-D Apocalypse. I was quoting Che Guevara in the cop car."

We were going to break, I was thinking. There was nothing between us anymore—not music we liked, not stories, not anything to think about.

"You lost a tooth," I told him.

He smiled. "I like the hole. Has symbolic value."

We used to fish for carp in the backwater pools of the Rio Grande. Carrying pointed bamboo or cottonwood branches, we'd sprint up and down, slapping the water and howling. I was thinking of that and where we used to hide the Pall Mall cigarettes we'd swiped from my father.

"You ever try LSD?" Jimmy asked.

In my mind, I was already out the door, putting between us then all the time and distance I feel now about these events.

"I'm really disappointed in you," he said. "You'd be so much more interesting as a leftist."

For James Edward Spalding, I now understand, violence as a way of life started the day the citizens of Rush Springs, Oklahoma, voted to outlaw public dancing. "That was the last damn straw," he'd said. "After I heard that, I knew I wasn't dealing with the rational. I was into Oz."

While I was being graduated and married (plus joining Kiwanis and our country club), and managing the farm and doing musicals like *Guys And Dolls* and *The Music Man* at our community theater in La Mesilla, Jimmy was drifting outward and sinking, moving—so he admitted three days ago—underground, marching and protesting, going to jail, learning about machine pistols and pipe bombs that can be concocted from kerosene and guano. In fifteen years, while I was buying this and that, and planting onions and then lettuce and then chilies, and watching the world zoom by in a haze, Jimmy was going deeper and further and quieter. In the fifteen years between that day in the hospital and the night be appeared in my kitchen, while he was building a foot-thick file in the National Security Agency and whirling unpredictably under America, I was losing my dad to pancreatic cancer and my mom to the plain old grief, and divorcing and waking up every month, or year, to drink Old Grand Dad and marvel at the quiet loneliness I was living in.

"There's no movement anymore," he confessed that night. "Just freelancers. We wander, my friend. That's what I do: I drift and live off my anger."

I'd been at the men's locker room at the country club playing stud poker, and when I got home, something in the air—"the big mystery that is the twentieth century," Jimmy would say—told me I was not alone. My hair stood up on the back of my neck, I prepared myself to beat the holy Jesus out of the dipstick who was trying to rob me, and then I saw him drinking coffee at my breakfast table, and right away, in all the beating organs I have, I was pleased he was here.

"Hope you don't mind," he said. "I made myself at home. We old-time hippies consume a lot of caffeine. Keeps the edges sharp. Gotta stay one jump ahead of the bad guys."

"How'd you get in?"

His was Br'er Rabbit's goofy grin.

"Magic. Hocus-pocus from the criminal elements, plus an American Express credit card."

He looked like a banker at a bowling alley: a good taxpayer's haircut and black horn-rimmed glasses that gave me the impression he had something to lose. He was gray at the temples and too tan for the March we'd had.

"Who mashed your nose?"

It was bent like those you've seen in *The Godfather* movies.

"Plastic surgery," he said. "Had a mole removed, too. Very hush-hush."

He'd been gone and now he was back, and for an hour he explained how he'd come here. Until the surgery, he'd used a wig he'd bought at the Max Factor School for Makeup in Hollywood.

He'd taken classes at Kansas State University. He'd been a pen pal with the IRA's James McCann. He'd met Kunstler, written for *Overthrow* magazine, one time walked into the Rahway Penitentiary in New Jersey, been hooked up with the Peace and Freedom Party. The names came and went: Las Vegas, Habana, Chicago, Sulphur Springs in Florida. He'd even bunked at an SLA house owned by Donald DeFreeze.

"That man did a thousand push-ups a day," Jimmy said. "He was once cornered by a cop with a police dog. Field Marshal Cinque was real pleasant until he snapped that dog's neck."

I asked a farm boy's question about Patty Hearst. Something was up. As in the old days, we'd get to it in a minute, or an hour.

"Nice lady," he said. "Not the sort to get nervous in a crowd."

He'd spent one summer in St. Thomas, learned to scuba dive, and he entertained the idea of becoming a deep-water laborer for Shell Oil in the North Sea. He'd attended a rock festival in Puerto Rico. "Saw Black Sabbath on Easter Sunday," he said. "A bad scene—knife fights, too hot, rapes, no medics. That's when I knew it had turned serious."

I was thinking of my own life—bacon and eggs, the price of dry fertilizer, the Agriculture Department Block runs, where my mind went when the sun went down. Jimmy was right: Life was serious, and I had the two slipped disks and one tiny ulcer to prove it.

"Met Dr. Spock once," Jimmy was saying. "He did a physical for my daughter, Ruthie. That man makes a mean banana daiquiri."

"You're married.

"Exactly," he said. "This is a very straight, nearly Republican child I have. She's a champ, not like us at all."

A name came to me from the long-ago days: "Carla."

He nodded and I had time enough to study this man who, I would learn, remains of real interest to the FBI for such activities as bank robbery, interstate flight to avoid prosecution, possession of explosives, assault, resisting arrest—a thousand antisocial incidents that make fascinating reading in the Water Street Post Office. A kid, I told myself. A wife.

"What're you doing here, Jimmy?"

The silence went on enough to be important.

"Actually, I'm not going to be here long—you don't need to know where I'm going—but I need a favor."

I was concentrating on my coffee cup—how hot it was, how old. It had elephants in different positions that looked like sex, a gift from Mary Jane Byrd, and was meant to be the first funny thing we'd see in the morning.

"I'm meeting Carla," he said. "She and Ruth are driving over here from Tucson."

"That's where they live?"

"It doesn't matter where they live, Buddy. We do this reunion bit pretty frequently, a sentiment thing. I thought you wouldn't mind."

I took note of what is heard hereabouts at two in the morning: the wind, a wall clock, my mostly paid-for house taking its own pulse, the Fletchers' three-legged shepherd in their onion field.

"There's something else, isn't there?"

"We'll be out by daybreak," he said. "Maybe a little later."

Eight at the latest, I told him. My loan officer, Victor Fears, from the Citizen's Bank was coming out at nine. I had a pile of debt and, at the moment, a dozen payment books to prove it.

"Right on, Buddy," Jimmy said. "I knew I could count on you."

"I'm doing a lot of dumb stuff lately."

He stood at the stove now, and it was nothing to see him as he was at fifteen—too skinny through the chest, full of jokes about what a smooth operator he was.

"You're like me, man," he was saying. "I stole all my ideas from the Lone Ranger—goodness against evil and injustice. And never shoot to kill."

An hour later we sat in my Buick station wagon outside his old house on Amador Street so he could teach me about the property fetish that underlies genocidal war. His old house stood dark (his dad had died two years earlier), almost concealed by new landscaping, and Jimmy was telling me that it—the olden times, the hard rain, the winds Bob Dylan sang about—was coming back.

"Nicaragua," he said. "Salvador, people in the streets."

I had mentioned what Mary Jane Byrd said men were—which had to do with not looking around yourself carefully and being pigheaded in matters of the heart.

"What's it feel like?" I asked.

He was looking at his hands as if they held a surprise for him.

"The violence," I said. "What's it like?"

"You get used to it," he said. "You abstract, invent stories."

In Jimmy's old house lived the Whittiers, a family I'd met twice and now seemed connected to by something deeper than happenstance or the running forward of our lives.

"First time," he said, "I wet my pants. The rush was incredible, just movement and light and voices. Then everybody—the citizens, Ma and Pa Kettle—everybody does what you say. It's hard to understate a feeling like that."

His words were piling up like stones.

"It used to be fun, a party."

"And now?"

He shrugged.

"Now it's work, a job." He had a cigarette going. "Sometimes I have to remind myself what it's for, who the enemy is."

The silence had shape and substance. Between us was not space but time, what the years had made. We had been brought together again—yes, like magic—but between us, as between planets, was only space we might holler across.

"I get tired," he was saying. "Sometimes I don't know who I am."

I knew that feeling, I thought.

"A fugitive's brain is filled with data," he was saying. "A hundred names, numbers, lots of ID. Revolution requires a first-class memory."

He told me he'd been L. Manning Vines, from Sioux City, Iowa; blood type O; born August 13, 1948. And Archie Felts from Atlanta, whose father was Ira, whose mother was Velma, who had brothers named Bert and Maxwell. The invented past piled up: a hundred jobs, a deck of Social Security cards, made-up work records, biographies borrowed from *Seize the Day* and *The Old Curiosity Shop*, surnames from *The Guinness Book of World Records*. Everything was faked: whole families imagined, breathed into life for an interview, a license check. "I got a whole population in my head," he said. Family trees that stretched back to England and France and goddamn Holland, a story that put him in one place and not another, mirages he inhabited for an hour, a month, a bus ride. Part of him belonged to an Elks Club in Missouri, another to a YMCA Big Brothers program in Columbus, Ohio. He was a fifth-grade teacher, a bricklayer in Union City. A part of him—a part as impossible as men on Mars—owed money; a part had stock in BioGen.

"I've even been you," he said. "For two days a long time ago, I was Joe Benson Neville, Jr. You were a mean son of a bitch then, Buddy, but you were exceedingly happy."

I understood, then, why he was really here: as if it had already happened, as if I'd already read the newspapers or watched the six o'clock broadcast from KTSM in El Paso, I could see the smoke, the confusion, a person like me going whichaway in a daze.

"Where?" I said.

"Close," he said. "Very close."

I took a second, attended to the thud my heart made and how my breathing worked.

"Nobody'll get hurt, right?" I asked. "This is important to me."

A car drove by and his face filled up with light—a new nose, shapes from a geometer's mind, what emotion is.

"A few hours from now," he began, "an invented PFC creature named Blocker from Peoria, Illinois, will strike a blow for the Great Blah-Blah-Blah. It will be dramatic, telegenic, but very modest in terms of property loss. It's the eighties, man, blood isn't the issue anymore."

I had the car started. We could go now, I thought. Or we could still be here when the sun came up. I had the sensation that I was outside, perhaps in the room of Jimmy's old house, where the Whittiers now slept, watching. My ex-wife came to mind, Mary Jane Byrd, and the long-limbed Chevrolet dealer she'd taken up with. I felt fifteen years roll up and unfurl, leading me back in a rush.

"Let's go home," I said.

.   .   .

Near four A.M. a car came up my dirt road from Highway 85, a four-door Ford so plain I thought I'd seen it everywhere. "Carla," Jimmy said. He'd been pacing for the last hour, quiet and deliberate, field-stripping his smokes. I'd asked him once about the ditty bag he'd dropped beside me on the steps. It was GI stuff, olive drab, official. "Tools of the trade," he'd said. "I'm a True Believer, sad to say." Now he walked over, his face blank, a sober man with an earnest mission, and picked up the bag.

"We'll be back in two hours," he said. "Three at the outside. Ruthie'll stay here."

Behind the wheel sat Carla, my garage light too bright in her eyes. I was thinking about my dog, Sneaker, which had been run over, and what Carla might say about that. Behind her sat another. Ruthie. The passenger door opened. All right, I was thinking. Okay. And then Jimmy was inside, his Everyman's Ford accelerating quietly toward the highway.

"You must be Mr. X," the girl said. "Daddy's real secretive about these things, so don't tell me your name, okay?"

Something dry and small, possibly bone-like, broke free inside me.

"I'm Ruth," she said, extending her hand. "I had a name from the revolution, Little Star, but Carla says public schools aren't ready for a whole lot of poetry yet."

She was fourteen or so, and too much like a nighttime teenager to be looked at straight on—the windblown hair that is said to be popular nowadays and eye makeup that maybe covers up the inner life.

"I take it you know what they're up to," I said.

"I'm in the ninth grade," she said, "I stay in my room, or hang out with kids I know. I don't know anything."

We watched their taillights go south on the highway until a semi with its brights on passed us too fast going the other way.

"So what's on our agenda?" she wondered.

In an hour—after a breakfast I made and the dishes she washed—we sang "Pink Shoe Laces" by Dody Stevens, "Great Balls of Fire" by Jerry Lee Lewis, "If I Didn't Care" by Connie Francis, "Good Golly, Miss Molly" and "No Other Arms, No Other Lips"—songs I had been collecting ever since my father died and the house became mine. I don't know how we got from *A* to *Z*—from knowing about terror to knowing what old-time music says about love—but in one hour the big world vanished and we took up residence in the smaller world of broken hearts and expensive 45s. Once she learned the lyrics, Ruthie was terrific, unafraid to throw open the mouth and just yowl when the feeling hit. She even insisted I play the bongos Mary Jane Byrd had bought years ago; and I, exhilarated and cut free for a time, banged away like a dervish, until Ruthie said, between records falling on my turntable, that she couldn't wait to get out, go away.

"I have it all planned," she said. "After I graduate, I'm going to Iowa maybe—a real small college."

On the record player, the King, Elvis Presley, was telling us about his blue suede shoes.

"They don't know, do they?"

She shook her head. "I get these quizzes at home. They make me read the *Nation* and *Commonweal* and *Mother Jones*. I'm supposed to save the world, they say. Go to Berkeley. Be there when the shitstorm comes again. They started taking me on these trips last year."

She was going to cry.

"You want me to turn them in, don't you?"

"Daddy said you wouldn't. Said you were a cool guy."

I took in the character of my living room: the La-Z-Boy I sleep in, the Motorola TV I watch too much of, the Woolworth's guitar I sometimes play when I need Willie Nelson's view of things.

"What'd Carla say?"

"She said you were retrograde, completely co-opted. That's the way she talks. Said you were bourgeoisie, no balls."

My heart did a strange turn, a twist on its thick root.

"Maybe she's right," I said.

So we waited. We sat on the steps where her father and I had waited, and watched the new day come up—a day that would be hot and clear all the way to heaven. I had my eyes on the Organ Mountains to the east—the San Augustin Pass, near where they'd tested the Apollo rockets—jagged purple spears of bare rock behind which, if my guess was correct, Jimmy and Carla would now be doing their business at the MAR site in the desert missile range. I'd driven past it many times—on my way to ski in Cloudcroft, or to picnic at the national monument at White Sands—a bubble of glass a thousand yards north of the two-lane highway, miles and miles of unguarded flatland around it; inside, from what I'd heard, was a radar arrangement that offered a view of the skies from California to Alabama. It was an eye that missed nothing from above, and I wondered who had built such a thing and who would care if a bomb went off near it.

"I'm not going to say anything," I told Ruthie.

She was sitting beside me, a school bag between her legs.

"That's okay," she answered. "I'll do it someday."

I wondered what Mary Jane Byrd might have said about this, and I didn't know. I thought of my golfing pals—Arch Stewart and Ray Berger and Coke Johnson—and I thought about the twenty-six states I'd visited and the Italian food I prefer and the lamebrain way I go about finances, and I didn't know. And then Jimmy and Carla returned and Ruthie stood up to shake my hand.

"Maybe Montana," she said. "Maybe that's where I'll go."

"Yes," I said. "Good luck."

And next Jimmy was coming toward me and it was time to say goodbye to him, too.

"Don't come back," I said. Carla was in the back of the car, maybe asleep.

"You're pissed," he said.

I was practically inside him now, as close to him as that name of mine he'd used way back when. He had dropped away from me years ago, and now I was dropping away from him.

"I don't want to hear from you ever again, do you understand?" I had made a fist and held it under his chin, out of sight of his family. "I weigh a hundred and ninety pounds, Jimmy Spalding, I work every day out here with my hands, and I expect I could really hurt you."

His eyes widened slowly, by degrees, and only an instant passed before he understood.

"This is sad, isn't it?" he said.

Here it was that I noticed his teeth. It was hard to tell which one had been knocked out, they were so shiny and even. He was that guy on TV who sells cars or land in Texas.

"My friend," I said, "this is downright pitiful."

In *The Music Man,* my favorite musical, we learn there is trouble in River City. There is trouble and it is fixed by brass and ooom-pah-pah and spirited marching and by what chemicals are released in the brain when folks find themselves caught up in the big parade. I had that on my mind when Jimmy left when I set about to vacuum and dust and wipe away any evidence that he'd come through my house. I took an inventory of myself—the growing potbelly Johnny Carson laughs at, and the bad right knee Dr. Weems says he'd like to fix one day—and with the record player going loud as thunder I had my house all to myself, and feelings I believe in.

I thought of Victor Fears, who was coming to loan me money, and Janet Miller, who is a Mesilla Park jeweler I sometimes sleep with. And then, the Shirelles singing to me about how it was between boys and girls, I thought of Mary Jane Byrd—what flower she smelled like and how she could roll over in a way that made nighttime beautiful.

"Oh, Lord," I said to myself and the walls. Maybe she would be up by now, I thought. And maybe she'd like to hear from someone—a terrible me—that she'd once known.

SWEET CHEEKS

for EKA

IN THE END, all she had was, well, the whatnots: doodads as odd and silly and, to use her daddy's phrase, downright unnecessary as tits on a teacup, whatchamacallits useless and excessive enough to offend a soul as merry and rich as Old King Cole. To her, it was "stuff," no more sensible to have than was a bikini at the North damn Pole. But afterward—-after he'd moved to Dallas, and July had turned into November, and there was scarcely an *A, B* or *C* about him she did not dream of—she found herself unable to junk any of it—which, as she told the plenty in Las Cruces who listened, was the problem, wasn't it?

She'd met him, the lawyer, at the Southside Johnny concert at the Pan Am Center at NMSU, and later, when they knew each other by first name and she could see he wasn't just a spiffed-up cowboy with spit for brains, he took her to El Patio, a bar in Old Mesilla, and, what with his talk about wrongful employer discharge and antitrust (plus an entire chorus of "It's Not Unusual" he could hum the Tom Jones of), he succeeded in more or less sweeping her right off her too-damn-big feet.

At first he didn't spend the night. He'd call her at the bank, Frank Papen's ten-story eyesore on Main Street across from the Loretto

Shopping Center, and say how about the greyhound races in Juarez. Or dinner at the Coronado Country Club in El Paso. Or let's go up to Picacho Hills and play ourselves some golf. And she'd go, him the sort who watched his language and used his turn signals and was at pains to say "Excuse me" every time he went to the gents'. They'd bet the dogs, or eat high on the hog, or play nine holes of the most agitated golf in the desert, then he'd drive to her house on Calle del Sol, the three-bedroom piece of cardboard her old man had bought her after she graduated from ENMU in Portales.

They'd sit around watching Letterman or Leno and whatever shoot-'em-up TNT had on cable, maybe do a little reefer she kept in her nightstand, trade shots or just drink straight from the bottle, then they'd make love, as shy and solicitous and eager-beaver as what the word *naughty* tells us. But he never stayed over. You'd hear him in the A.M., clattering in the bathroom, getting into his pants, humming sha-la-la's from the Beatles half of history, and next he'd be at her ear, saying, Goodnight, Cheeks. Or Babycakes. Or Sweet Chips. Crapola that there ought to be a law against using with an honest-to-goodness grown-up.

By Halloween, the stuff had started coming in. The Turdriffics first, no kidding. Miniature soccer and football players made out of, get this, sanitized horse manure.

"Whoa," she said. "What the devil?"

But he raised his finger to his lips, storybook and sweet-as-you-please: "Shhhhh."

Next arrived the leather ashtray. After that a plaster-of-Paris frog in polka-dot panties and brassiere. An argyle sock to fit King Kong. The USS *Constitution* in a bottle. Ex Libris bookplates. Then, yup, books: *The Redneck Way of Knowledge,* which was blank, and a pound of Nostradamus gobbledygook that should have been. A Beefeater gin refrigerator magnet. Sea monkeys. Ash from Mount St. Helens. Alvin and the Chipmunks reciting Hamlet, that section about being and not.

"What on earth?" she said. "What the heck?"

And each time, his face lit by that smile the white-collar teach the blue- in Disneyland, he'd say it was for fun. Gags to cheer everybody up. Laughter, medicine, all that jazz.

A week later he'd told her he loved her. Gosh: All those words, and without the singsong that gooey is. And she, caught off guard by the sixty-pound concrete candlestick sitting at her feet, asked him, please, pretty-please, to repeat himself. He got down on one knee, à la Valentino, clasped his hands across his chest, his an expression that shot right to the core of her.

"No kidding," he said.

Around them—on the floor, against the walls, chockablock on the shelves he'd nailed up one weekend—were six months of UPS and parcel post: a game of Twister, a crackpot's idea of the Eiffel Tower in toothpicks, a Bayer aspirin the size of a chafing dish, every color Pez candy in the universe, a papier-mâché Roman Coliseum, and here came those words again—and again and again, as remarkable as a blizzard in Panama. Wait, she told herself, and tried to. Wait. But she got only to three-Mississippi before she yanked him up by the necktie, her heart thudding in her throat, saying that, gosh Almighty, she loved him, too.

She really, really did.

Still the stuff came—each the each that special is. A wrought-iron Liberace. Three "Money Back Guaranteed" pennies from heaven. A state-of-Alabama-approved electric chair (batteries not included), an old-timey hat box that said DO NOT OPEN: CURSE IN EFFECT and an ooh-la-la nightgown that in block letters warned moms and dads everywhere to KEEP OUT OF REACH OF CHILDREN—itself an hour's worth of ha-ha-ha. And she supposed the stuff would be coming still if, of course, he hadn't told her in July that he'd taken a new job. In Texas.

She was sitting and he wasn't; then he was and she'd found the other dozens of places in the room to lean against. She felt like a juggler, tossing one apple—or a chain saw—beyond her limit—an absurd image.

It was an opportunity, he said. The chance of a you-know-what. Dewey & Howes was the yamma-yamma-yamma: After a moment she didn't know what he was saying, only that, eyes fixed to the left of him or to the right or on what was reported to be a certified hairball from a certified Montana polled Hereford, she was saying yes, the do-or-die parts of her insides cracking or instantaneously drying up.

Yes, she did understand.

Yes, they would stay in touch.

Yes, this was rotten luck.

Yes, no reason this had to change anything. There was, after all, Trailways and American Airlines and her own Buick LeSabre. Yes, yes, yes—a hiss that, for all the difference it made, you could have heard in Zululand.

They made love that night, their last. They mumbled "pardon me" a lot. And "sorry." And damn near tried to keep their give-and-take free of any chitchat that had an *L* or an *O* or a *V* or an *E* in it—trying, it seemed already, to reach each other across time and distance, plus whatever other dimensions heartache could be measured by.

As before he got up early and, courtesy of a Ronald Reagan night-light, he tiptoed around the bedroom, pulling on his loafers, tucking his shirt in, zipping his trousers. A minute later he stood in the bathroom, combing the hair he was proud of, brushing his teeth, gargling, and making the other sounds it was not possible to ignore—those ten or ten million notes the Rolling Stones had once upon a time used to assert that things were bad and might not get better. Then, appearing like a ghost beside her, he bent to her ear, the smell of him as hopeful and promising as the money she was around day after day after day.

"Goodnight, Oodles," he said.

The first man after that was a polo player from that Hurd rich-boy bunch up the Hondo Valley near Ruidoso, a so-and-so as subtle in courtship as a thunderclap. Next was an Aggie assistant basketball coach, Irk Something Something: On the dance floor of the Roadrunner Lounge and to the wah-wah of Uncle Roy and the Red Creek Wranglers, he didn't even make it to the bridge of "Loving on Back Streets" before he was whispering sweet blah-blah-blahs about Helen of Troy and Cleopatra, anybody from any age with the right chromosomes. So, while she waited for the tabs and slots of herself to fit together correctly, there wasn't anybody.

Away from work, she felt lost. She didn't stop at, say, My Brother's Place. No Cork 'n' Bottle. One time she went into Ikard's Furniture across the street, but without him—the lawyer—it wasn't the same. She didn't know, for example, what the dickens could be done with a settee. So she went home. Watched Sam Donaldson pick on some undersecretary of whatever. She made it about a third into *The Name of the Rose,* always quitting where what's-his-name, you know, found about the thousandth croaked monk. Jeepers, what a life, ratty and cockeyed and dull. She watched ESPN, the International Barefoot Skiing Championships, and then switched the channel to yell the questions at the boneheads on *Jeopardy.*

Sure, she and the lawyer talked, fairly often at first. He called her—what?—Sweetums or Honey Bunch, bragged about the Simon Legrees he'd saved a dozen good guys from, asked when she was coming for a visit.

"Six Flags," he said. "The Texas Schoolbook Depository."

That was his word, *visit,* as if she were one of his Lambda Chi brothers, as if he weren't the only person she'd ever, ever, ever wrenched herself inside out for. He didn't mean to be cruel, she knew, but there it was anyway—miles and miles of dirt and weeds and a big blank sky between what was and what most assuredly was not. It was a form of fate, she decided, forces as manifest as the Elvis Presley piggy bank on her bureau. Sometimes the bear this, sometimes the bear that—wasn't that how love went? Yin for an hour, yang for two.

No, she assured him, she wasn't mad.

No, not upset.

No, not at all.

And suddenly he was gone, in regard to love nothing to listen to except the crackle and buzz that hanging up sounds like.

One day she tried to get rid of his stuff, the goodies. In the kitchen, she sought to imagine the world without sixty percent of the doohickeys piled on her dinette table. Without the clamshell lamp. Without Christ on a Crutch. Without that glow-in-the-dark Thumbelina or Tinkerbell that some Taiwanese Wong Ho had snazzed up with a Scarlett O'Hara hoop skirt and a rhinestone wand.

From the utility room she dragged out a box, but, after coming oh-so-close to just plopping into it whatever she grabbed first, she thought *what the hell* and started wrapping each piece in newspaper—the dribble glass, the New Guinea witch doctor's shrunken head—as if, like in the poem, so much depended on the relation of one object to another, and that to yet another, until all objects—this plastic piece of lunacy and that—were related exactly as, well, fate had intended.

An hour whooshed by. Down the street, the ice-cream truck was playing its chimes, "Popeye the Sailor Man." An Uncle Sam know-it-all had come on NPR to say who was losing in Latvia, Estonia, among poor Baltic bastards everywhere. Another voice, this also sleepy and full of private schooling, repeated gossip about—who?—Johannes Brahms maybe. Christ. She poured a drink, Johnnie Walker, poked at a ham-salad sandwich, and then she found herself, chin on her hand, wondering what the dickens she was going to do. She had a box. It was full. Now what?

From the phone book she scribbled down the numbers of the DAV, the Salvation Army, the Military Order of the Purple Heart, and she was only two digits from a tax-deductible donation when she realized, as much with her heart as with her head, that by the weekend she could be telling a do-gooder named Tito or Floyd that what he had lugged to his truck was a genuine imitation-body-part chess set: toes, ears, eyeballs—the works. A token of affection.

That Friday she went out with the service manager for Lackey Chevrolet-Toyota. It was November, time not to be damaged any-more.

Grow up, she had scolded the self in the mirror. Pull the shoulders back. Put on a happy face.

They drove to the Double Eagle, where she ate, she had to admit, like a pig. Gulf shrimp the size of a fat man's fingers. Chicken stuffed, rolled, dipped, and every other cooking verb from France. In the lounge, knee-to-knee in chairs so low you needed help to climb out, they had cocktails: a bourbon for him, for her a green thing with a paper parasol. He was her age, twenty-eight, and divorced but not nearly ruined from it. He was a Libra to her Cancer—the two of them, they agreed, as suitably matched as any with houses and cusps and sun-sign mumbo jumbo.

At her doorstep, she thought to invite him in—God, she did not want to call it a nightcap—but she wondered how to explain the, you know, stuff. The coasters from Triassic-period limestone. The shopping bag of Wacky Wall Walkers: The s-t-u-double-f.

It was late, he said. Big day tomorrow, Saturday, he had to go.

She started counting again—one-Mississippi, two—numbers enough to say or do anything that could be said or done in her condition. She imagined she was already in bed alone, staring at the two-person sombrero on the wall. She remembered the dreams she'd had—how weird they were, and the cold, the way they seemed to afflict a look-alike named Mary Jo.

He'd call in the morning, he said. Okay?

She considered his eyes, which weren't a whit like the lawyer's; and his hands-on-hips way of keeping his tummy in.

Why not? she said. That would be terrific.

And then, the second after she jiggled her key in the lock, he kissed her as she hadn't been kissed since high school, lips too mashed to be anything but meaningful.

She tried to love him after this. Boy, did she.

At the bank, a mortgage application from a Greene or a Mendoza spread on the desk like gigantic playing cards, she'd think of the ways her service manager was good to her. He liked slow-dancing—the Conversation, the Quarter-Waltz—and even knew the "alibi," a ballroom trick for getting out of a corner. He could boil Italian, he said, a joke. Raised a Baptist, he didn't know what he was now (here his hands flew all over the place, like crazed birds), but he believed in something, if only the whole being greater than the sum of its widespread parts. He'd played football for the Aggies, but, not altogether engaged by the biology and American lit and Tuesday-Thursday sociology he sat through, he quit. He knew about flowers: zinnias, azaleas, the herb family. When he was going to be late, he called. He didn't nag her about smoking, and, best of all, that first night he actually entered her house, the night they slept together, he didn't utter one evil thing about the knickknacks she was the full-time mistress of.

"Neat" was what he exclaimed. He couldn't believe it. Wow. He picked up the itty-bitty Hong Kong rickshaw, studied it as thoroughly as painstakingly pointless handiwork can be studied.

"Will you look at this," he said. He touched the Popsicle-stick bird-cage, the .44 Magnum cigarette lighter, the Texas jackalope. "Geez."

It was clear, she thought, that he loved her—that his, too, was a world tilted and loose and loud—and she wished she could see inside him (as she could see inside her anatomically correct man doll) and thus find out what his organs were doing. His thumping heart. Those pink, wet wrinkles of the brain.

She took his hand, smelled on it the work he did, and steered him toward the bedroom. She would learn something, she hoped, and when they were undressed, his outfit more neatly hung than hers, she did.

"The lawyer," she began.

Her service manager was holding her—his name was Bobby and he was blond, even his movie star mustache—and here she was, hers the tone best used for "true" and "false" in school, telling about a guy, the lawyer, who'd filled her up and set her spinning; a man who'd given her eight "because's" for every event, good or bad, under high heaven.

She described a trip to White Sands—the national monument, not the missile range—and how the sun worked in that flat, wasted world, and what common animals the clouds were, plus who said what when, and why time went bang-bang-bang. She told Bobby about the after-noon the lawyer shampooed her hair, the nerves he'd struck.

Her service manager was holding her—his name, yes, was Robert Ray Dunbar and he could sew a coat button, he supposed, and spoke enough Mayfield High School Español to be understood in jail—and here she was, harebrained as any mad scientist she'd heard of, talking about, as it has been talked about to her, asset-based financing, as well as which Japanese sedan to buy and why. She told him about window-shopping with the lawyer, in particular sighing over a bed big as a wrestling mat and how scared or dumbstruck he'd been, as if humbled by what could be accomplished in that faraway corner or this. The lawyer hailed from Nebraska, she said. A Cornhusker. His parents were Ellen and Russell. He'd had a mutt named Moe, after the Stooge. He threw right-handed, hated brussels sprouts, read Stephen King and anything *Time* magazine said was funny. Salsa made his nose run. In eighth-grade shop he'd planed a mahogany table, kissed his first girl the night Jimmy Carter campaigned in Omaha—what else?

She was shaking. She had taken everything out, she believed, hook by hasp by hinge by nail, and now she was herself a million-zillion thingamajigs, each vital and tiny and dumb, and she guessed she had only four-three-two minutes to find them there and there and there and so make herself whole again.

"What else?" she said. "What?"

Her service manager held her—his name, Lordy, was Bobby, like a kid, a charter member of the Vic Tanny Health Club on the bypass— and here she was, watching her arms tremble and ordering herself, for crying out loud, to pay attention: There was much in life to know and maybe life enough to know it.

"It's all right," he was whispering. "Truly."

Then, not with all his might, he squeezed her, this decent Bobby person, and she grew curious to learn what he might say, or do, if he discovered that beneath him now, wriggling and moaning "ah-ah-ah," was not her at all but only the bone and hair and flesh of a fool using her name.

Each day, she thought, became a wall between herself and the lawyer. Each day a wall. She tried new food—Thai and Jewish—and this too became part of a wall. So did the clothes she bought: the too expensive espadrilles, a blouse a red she'd never seen before, underwear as wicked as she could stand without snickering. The wall, she told herself. She subscribed to *Southwest Art* and, more foolish business, to the *Sporting News*, aiming to lose herself in the mysteries unique to batting averages and Remington Indians on the warpath. She and Bobby went to the community theater at the old State movie house on the downtown mall, what had once been as bleak and windswept and jerkwater a main street as any she could conceive of, and, sitting in the front row, she willed herself into that September-remember world of

The Fantasticks or into what woe-is-me drama eight bucks had bought. Another day. Another wall.

One weekend—was it already May?—they went to Albuquerque, driving almost without saying a word, nature racing past at sixty, sometimes seventy, miles per hour, Bobby's pickup as quiet as a capsule in deepest space. He had something to tell her, he announced when they reached the Holiday Inn. She didn't have to listen, he said, but he was going to speak his mind anyway.

She regarded herself and this place. There were no windup toys, no herky-jerky contraptions that chattered and squeaked and went snap-crackle-pop. There was a bed, not seriously meant to live with, and a too-high table and a too-hard chair and a Motorola color TV, plus carpet that must've been the ugly brown that easing cleaning is— but no felt cloth duck appliqué flyswatter. No coffee mug with elephants on it playing basketball. No four-leaf clover hunting hat for Bullwinkle the moose.

Instantly she knew what Bobby was hemming and hawing about, the exact words he'd use, what the entire unfair, stupid me-me-me sentence would be. Even if he took a half hour, even if he stood on his head (which he could), it would start with "I" and end a billion years later with "you."

"Don't," she said.

He snatched up her suitcase, set it down, moved it twice more, then told her "Fine," his expression sideways and not simple as one-plus-one anymore, and then—bless him—he said anew what a grand old time they'd have that night.

In July, she took her vacation, which, except for a weekend at her daddy's cotton farm outside Portales, she spent at home. In the afternoons, content with himself and everything else under the sun, Bobby came over, usually with a six-pack of Bud Light, one with a bottle of Cuervo Gold that they quit before they reached the bottom of. Bobby fixed the grease trap in the kitchen sink. He barbecued, his a secret sauce with one part peanut butter. They went roller-skating, did the hokey-pokey with nearly one hundred other folks thrilled to be falling down. Oh, it was summer, the valley hot as those drugstore joke postcard scenes of hell, the sky too far up to be real or blue. She lay on her stomach in the backyard, her pillow a Scrooge McDuck beach towel, her bathing suit a two-piece she hadn't worn since college.

"Bobby," she said.

Two giant steps away, he was on his knees, painting an Adirondack chair he'd thought would be cheap to send away for, and immediately she didn't know why she'd called his name or what, if anything, might blurt out of her. He was wearing Bike athletic shorts, splotched green from the bucket at his feet.

"Bobby Dunbar," she said, at last sure what was going to be said next.

She had been thinking about the heat—the dry, close, mean kind this world was—and now his head came up, cocked, his hair so white you wondered how he got here to Planet Earth.

"Yes," he said. Not *yeah*, not *huh*, not *what*. Yes.

So, given what was what and who who, she wondered the only wonder she could: "Are you happy?"

He looked—wasn't this goofy?—high and low, as if he'd lost his wallet, and said at last, as she knew he would, "Sure"—an answer that came with a smile and shrug. "What about you?"

A neighbor dog was barking, Rex, somewhere a door slammed too hard, and way off Mikey-Mikey-Mikey was being hollered for.

"Yes," she said. "I guess I am."

And in a moment, the center of her still as night, she actually was. Happy. She had a thought, too fast to catch up to; then another, this the one to hold. In her bathroom, above the toothbrush holder, was a Siamese cat clock, its tick-tocks eyes that blinked each second. So was she really happy? On her dresser sat a wooden, hobnailed boot pencil holder. Was she? In her guest lavatory hung Esperanto wallpaper. Yes, she was.

Still on her stomach, she watched Bobby painting—swish, swish, swish. Here was a man who couldn't whistle, who loved Fernando Valenzuela and every other Los Angeles Dodger, who was allergic to mustard. Here he was.

Eyes closed now, she was concentrating, a picture in her mind of gizmos tightened and arranged and sorted and swept clean away, of a room empty as the horizon, of surfaces shined and sterile and hard; of herself, strong and honest as a nickel, letting go of at least a year of stored-up laughter. And then the vision was gone—poof—and she had not jumped up squealing to give this man the hug of his very own life.

July. September. Thanksgiving. Happy New Year. This is how her year went—in chunks, in spasms. She'd roll over in bed and a month would be gone. She'd stub her toe and look up to see Lincoln's birthday on the calendar. One night she kissed Bobby, and March, its raw wind and sometime frost, disappeared. April became an afternoon, May a day with no junk mail, June a doorbell going bong-bong-bong.

Soon it was July, and she knew, every cell and tissue and blessed thump-thump of her knew, that he'd call. The lawyer. She arranged to be home as often as possible. She had a project, she told Robert Ray Dunbar, busywork from the bank.

"A merger," she told him. "Don't worry," she said. She needed a month, that was all. Everything was fine between them, she insisted. She used her daddy's word: "Hunky-dory."

He seemed doubtful, scratched his neck, looked near and far for help. "You sure?"

She smiled, smooched him as a mother might. "Of course, what's not to be sure of?"

You could see his brain work, the clever gears and cogs of it.

"I'm getting a speedboat," he said. They'd go waterskiing at Elephant Butte, okay?

After he'd driven away, after he'd honked bye-bye, she shut the door to wait. He wouldn't call tonight. The lawyer. Her phone was a Coke can, but it wouldn't ring. Not tonight. She just flat-out knew. It wouldn't ring until between him there and her here, as between the moon and Mars, there was nothing, not even an idea.

So, patiently and deliberately, she began taking down the walls. Those many, many days. That western novel she'd chuckled to the rootin'-tootin' end of. That kit to knit with. That color of hair she now had. A bottle of crème de menthe had to go out, as did a spider plant. Her Volkswagen wristwatch had to be set, her Tiny Alice tea service polished.

Oh, he'd call, bet your bottom dollar. And the conversation, sigh-filled and helter-skelter with why's and wherefore's, would rattle on for hours. I love you, he'd say, words never said before anywhere, any-time, words meant to stand for everything you could make or wish for. I miss you, he'd declare, and she would feel in him the holes and hollows she felt in herself—the backward time ran, the topsy-turvy. Again he'd say it. Again. The food of it, the warmth. The phone, its innards composed of wires and solder and miracles. A breath from her, deep as deep goes. Hello, she'd say.

"Honey pie," he'd start, "is that you?"

THE ELDEST OF THINGS

MOZER'S FIRST DEALER was a Latino named Spoon who roared up Chester out of Hough each Thursday in a vintage black-over-white Mercury so sweetly tuned it seemed capable of speech—a thunder as throaty and pure, Spoon told him once, as oratory itself. Spoon always parked behind the Church of the Covenant, and Mozer would appear a little after noon, just before his class in the Romantics. The dialogue and actions never changed: Spoon would say "Man!" and "Madre!" and "Don't be sneaking up like that, hombre!" and Mozer would slip himself into that auto slowly and with great ceremony, its interior so full of red plush and shiny leathers it could have been the giant steel shoe of Satan himself. Spoon always had the radio tuned to JMO, or another spade station, his head, with its fertile hairdo, bobbing to a rhythm Spoon identified as equal parts funk and blood-stuff, the bass in the door speakers so heavy it seemed to pound on Mozer's leg, maybe make a bruise and leave a welt.

Spoon dealt primo toot, iced and crystal, white enough to be a starlet's thigh, which he presented to Mozer in a glassine packet, rolling his Juarez eyeballs heavenward, saying the blow in question was either

Chilean or direct from the Golden Triangle, strong enough to bend iron or set off train noises in the deep, primitive corners of your brain pan. Mozer always did a sample, which was protocol, the first snort bitter and laden enough to send him in search of words like *churl* and *hunch*. Then he paid, in old bills, Spoon the superstitious sort who thought of new money the way the Huns thought of achievement in bronze. They'd say adios, Spoon still caught up in the throes of thump and new music.

"You be careful," Spoon would say. "Maybe one day you don't want no more nose, okay? Maybe you go loco, want to be a bird or flashy gangster."

The woman came into Mozer's life during that one semester he was calling Coleridge and Keats "tangents of lust" and "the milk-spurned bards of indecent closure," a pair like Mutt and Jeff, one full of limp and midnight oil, the other a dingus on the upside of the perilous peak that was a wintry but heartening time of versifiers. The coke, he figured, made him blabber that way: the several lines before class each Tuesday and Thursday that spun him into the lecture hall in a state he accepted as wired and supreme, all about him afflicted and cast low. Exercises in wonder, his lessons were breathless accounts of perfection and the mysteries that attend knowledge, which invariably ended with him throwing off his sport coat, or climbing onto his chair, and shaking his fists as if he were leaving this life for fable and legend.

Elaine Winston was a Miltonist, a first-year assistant professor with an office on the first floor, and, as he learned happily, herself mad with learning. His hair slicked back, he went to her one day, followed her into her office after seeing in her face what he was convinced was scepter-love and, well, theophany.

"Miss Winston," he said, his voice full of his Louisiana upbringing, "looky here."

Yet, before she could sit, even before she could say hello, Mozer placed on her desk a vial of fluff Spoon said could launch you into Deityville by way of your own biles and ferments. It was Colombian rock, Spoon had said, mayhap as old as the earth itself, on account of it had evil in it, which led to an expanded view of the universe, which led in ultimate terms to a consideration of shit like Hierarchy and Ultimacy itself. Mondo heavy stuff. Made you want to bark, to perform a foulness with your fingers. Took the contemplation right out of the daily business of finding and keeping.

Both of them agreed later that it was no surprise that immediately, her hands steady with purpose, she opened the vial and, with the patience of a DEA assassin, laid out two thin but exact lines. After all, she told Mozer, she'd read the literature and had been to the movies; plus, she'd watched TV and, in her UC–Santa Barbara days, had tried root and downers and something which a now-lost boyfriend had described as Laotian, a melted fungus which you waved before your lips and lugged with you into Old Night—which was what Mozer yearned to hear, so, as he locked the door and switched off the light and unzipped her teacher's skirt, he was saying the Lady—the toot, the snow—was, like themselves, the outmost work of Nature, much beyond havoc and spoil and that they, Elaine Winston and himself, Richard E. Mozer (of Tulane and the University of Texas-Austin), would soon be passing beyond tumult and din for the uplifting horizons of organized beauties and that composite body in which incorruptible matter predominates, love.

For months after this, through a Cleveland winter frigid and piled with ice and into a glorious spring, Mozer's lectures were magic and biology both—hour-long sessions even the student newspaper, the *Observer*, in an unsigned editorial, called bifurcated and multifarious, "the eldest of things." One period Dr. Mozer spent on Shelley's "Music, When Soft Voices Die," spotting in its eight lines neither the beloved nor the quick, but privation and deficiency—in his mind the vision of a serpent with hips leading a legion of duteous and knee-crooking knaves. When he grabbed the chalk and dashed to the board to scrawl figures of analysis, he looked like a caveman, his face beleaguered, as if he'd embraced each and every one of his rascally needs. He told Elaine Winston, and she him, that they were entering a time of gulf and effulgence and pouring forth—a time washed by the waters of Abana and Pharpar, a time of fawn, renegade, and hapless wight! During another class period, when he was to be addressing the horned moon and Mr. E. K. Chambers's *A Sheaf of Studies,* he tenderly fixed his head against the bosom of Mindy Griffith, a South Philadelphia sophomore COSI major, and claimed to hear, through her sweater and blouse and brassiere, not the heart but the steady, fairyland tromp-tromp of Mr. Wordsworth's footsteps in the Rydale woods.

"No bramble," he whispered. "No evergreen, no palm."

Then, holding her by the shoulders, he said there was in her courage and outlawry, even the wonted face renewed.

That March, when he should have been concerned that Elaine Winston was speaking of warmth and beachfronts and heavy palm trees, he began telling his classes about his family, offering his vision of child-rearing and where woe comes from. And one day, after taking a richness from Spoon that was said to have come from the very ash, honest, of the rood itself, he informed his class, while his organs beat like a Sousa drum corps, that he'd had no youth at all, that he had vaulted across the decades, from gamete to scholar, without benefit of the swerve and downwardness of adolescence; and that, were he to wed, it would be to a woman whose face had something in it of friskiness and of thorn.

That afternoon, drinking Pepsi under a young maple in front of Gund Hall, Mozer told Elaine Winston of the goody Spoon had promised him: a mixture likened to the tears of a lost people—the Goths, say—cocaine cut with the subsoil those NASA technicians at Lewis Research Center were bringing back from Uranus, stuff that made fire of water, and earth of air. Lord, he said, it was itself love. Which was the gift, he told Professor Winston, he most wanted to give her, conveying this wish by licking her hands and mentioning conglobed atoms and seminal forms and female divinity.

"No," she said. "I can't."

He imagined them on the flaming ramparts of the world, him crafty and gaunt, her light incarnate.

"I'm sorry," she said. "It's impossible."

He mentioned glimmer, heart-baking rays, splendor.

"Please," she sobbed, "no more."

It was love, he said, and were she coke, he would now be at her toes, she that blessed white rail that stretched to infinity, she that orbit of song and purity; he was ready, he insisted, for transcendence.

It was then, while he kissed her cheeks and eyes and forehead, that she confessed she'd taken another job. In Florida. She would be leaving at the end of the term.

For his next appointment, Mozer went flying toward Spoon's Mercury like a hawk with serpent wings, his topcoat flapping, his ski cap pulled shut over his ears. He believed that his innards, all link and hook and snap of them, were frozen, rattling like bolts in a bucket. He was sobbing, too, and even before he flung himself into the car, he was well into the latest chapter of his life, that unlightsome and diminished part, that part of yoke and aery gloom. Mozer saw himself in the upper waters of this world, drowning. He gagged and something inside—his spleen, he thought, or junked heart!—banged hard against his breastbone.

While Spoon studied him, Mozer spoke of the circumfluous liquids, the calm upon which the World is built, the metaphorical jasper, the unmixed fire, the goo and slop, the pneuma of the Stoics. He told Spoon about Elaine Winston's decision and the wreck he was because of it; and, watching students gingerly tread the ice-slickened sidewalks near the building next to him, he speculated on the nature of man, the hylomorphic principle, multiple and gross, of substantial composition into the material world. He spoke of the *Fons Vitae* of Avencebrol. The *Hokmah.* The *Yod* and the mysterious *AWIR.* Before running out of breath, he said that he was dumped, mashed, crazed, wrung out, wracked, and no more good for this world than war.

For a second, while those on Spoon's radio sang to them of high-heeled sneakers and wig hats, neither spoke. Then, like a hungry man sitting down to a thirty-dollar T-bone, Spoon said, "Doc, don't worry. I have just the thing."

And from nowhere—or the next world, Mozer thought later, or the world after that—appeared several grams of doody cut fine as morning mist. It was a weight, Spoon assured him as he left the car, that in minutes would strip away the pain and lay bare the shiny, cartilaginous root of himself, his spring and heavy, greased wheel.

During April, Mozer got used to the idea Elaine Winston was leaving by rededicating himself to his work. It was, he would say later, his period of plucking up and casting out, a time of victual and wound. He scratched out a paper on "So We'll Go No More A Roving" for the MMLA section on Byron for the St. Louis meeting, a paper he delivered with such a sorcerer's fury that it appeared to many in the Marriott suite that, at a mention of laurel and myrtle, he might burst into flame. He mumbled about "features of intelligent genera" and marched into class wearing a rag around his ears, saying he was pity and Dido's pyre, that heavy-headed carouser who was the sin of apotheosis given tendon and hackle.

In one class, rolling on a circuit made smooth and gleaming by two lines of what Spoon claimed was flake chipped from Eden's first tree, Dr. Mozer forged a lecture that linked, in a moment quiet enough to have come from death, the Ens, the hinder parts of God's essence, and the "houmoousian," the latter of which his pupils were to conceive of not as the Father and Son and the Holy Ghost, but as Larry, Curly, and Moe—the modern Wise Men of burlesque and pain. It was an insight, Mozer noticed, that left eager Mindy Griffith limp with hope.

The following Tuesday, in the parking lot of the Church of the Covenant, the sky dark with soot, Mozer told Spoon he wanted stuff that said "smote" and "wither," that would his soul and bounteous fortune consecrate.

"An ounce," he said.

Spoon, in a yellow fedora that could have come from a Mickey Spillane book, nodded gravely. "You feeling low, Doc?" he wondered.

Mozer said that he and Elaine—for old times' sake, really, one final fling—were taking a room in the Shoreway Holiday Inn during finals. He used the words *mode* and *issue*.

"I can dig it," Spoon said, and in an instant, as if it had materialized from the black world, Spoon was placing on the seat between them a Baggie that contained a substance that, to Mozer's mind, seemed, apart from its glow and density, to be alive. "No mas," Spoon was saying. "As of today, I am out of business."

He was going back to Mexico, he allowed, where an acquaintance, a big-hearted *caballero* like himself, was in league with an hombre who knew a figure who had a contact with the so-called, which might develop, given ingenuity and gorge, into *resplandor,* radiance. There was much *dinero* to be made, he said. A man in the grip of an idea, he said, could go anywhere in his life.

The world tilted a little for Mozer, the sky crumbling into a hole in the horizon.

"What about me?" he said. There was music in the car, of course, metals and whines—the chorus of a thousand banshees and madmen. "I thought we had an understanding," he said. "*Amigos,* no?"

Spoon was making smacking noises. He said not to worry, *El Profes-sor* was *muy especial,* he was being turned over to a gent—"like a colleague, man"—who, in Mozer's moment of need, would appear, bearing some Lady that was virtually coeternal with the Father Himself.

As he would reveal to his next dealer, the Suit, and the one to follow him, and the one to follow him, his week with Elaine Winston, now-departed assistant professor, was lived in a place unapproached through necessity and chance. It was part manifestation, he said, part similitude. A haven hewn from hardiment and hazard. "There were no hard feelings," he would say. "No guilt."

The first two days, they lived off room-service chicken and wine and a varlet's concoction which, Elaine swore, made you use the terms *hath* and *ye.* It turned thought to deed, and that to a thing which uttered in complex/compound sentences. If anything, Mozer would declare for years, they both grew more luscious: She was the bringing forth and the shining unto; he, decree and ascent. He sprinkled lines on her breasts and thighs, and once he entered the whooshing, ornamented, fibrous, and unsettled chambers of her heart, as she sang to him of the whip and the cradle, the prattling bush and the fetching metabole. Later, he laid a trail which led over a dresser, across the floor, and to the coffee table before climbing a chair, following the curtain folds and ending, it seemed, at the mouth of a warm cave, the first principle of things—"the junction," he hollered, "of form and meaning!" In his joy, he became ape and first man, a being of lope and skinned knuckle and savage mien.

After the third day, and until they left for the airport, they didn't again use the phone or open the drapes. One time, after not speaking for an hour, he went to her as he imagined Keats had gone to his Grecian Urn, muttering about the dales of Arcady, plus pipes and haunting timbrels. She was lamentation, he told her. He looked into her ear, discovering a spot to put everything—his smoking brain stem, the shame and prize of himself, that ragged wind in his chest. An hour later, he found himself yelling about the cataract and trodden weed. She—no, not she alone, but Eve and Sweet Betsy from Pike and Mother Hubbard and Little Red Riding Hood—she was garland and seashore and silk. She was, he decided, swarm populous and writ itself—chaste but messy writ—like a message from the soul.

"In me, there's the rose," Elaine Winston announced. "And ire. And compass. And kirtled Sovereign."

Collapsed against the bathroom door, Mozer applauded. He was seeing everything from beginning to end—from bang in the dark, through swamp and savannah and bustling boulevard, to bang in the dark. And then she stood at the end of the bed, its sheets a snarl of white, her breasts heavy and dark, her head so far away it seemed to scrape the ceiling.

There was in her, she vowed, alimental recompense and humid exhalation.

She was quoting, he knew.

A progeny of light, she was saying. And recess of miracle. And supernal expanse.

When she finally pitched back onto the bed, exhausted, she was talking about optic emanation and preparation and the all-embracing, without which there could never be any, yes, privilege.

In the next hour he knew, even without his watch, that it was time to go, that days five and six had passed. What had come to him, he decided, was understanding, and it came when, feeding from a line that seemed composed of socket and hook and perfect mortise, he looked up and realized that her flesh had vanished and what remained—what he slurped and bit and sucked, and what shouted to him of void and fathom and nitre—was not Elaine Winston, Miltonist, but his own love, brawling damp and full of fear. His love was gnash and twisted limb and lips of dew. It was text and high estate and supped wonders—a clamor of sally and retreat: unsorted, turbid, clip-winged and no more noble than a donkey in ferkin and wig. Most of all, he saw himself as a Mongol, pounding across a cedarn cover—that land of S. T. Coleridge!—hot for the maid that was passion: a chase which would take, he concluded, forever.

Mozer's second dealer, the Suit, was an insurance lawyer who toiled downtown and did not care, as Spoon had, about music or shiny vehi-cles. He was a Yale grad who, as promised, wanted to discuss life and the meaning thereof, who would arrange a meeting in the men's room on the eighth floor of the Statler Office Tower on Euclid; and who would, before laying on Mozer crystal the size of a heavyweight's fist, address the context of the blow, its bewitching history and its humble provenance. One time it was Mao-informed stuff, advanced but cryp-tic, scrutable only to those who knew of the universal hubbub and the mutiny of the spirit. Another time the toot came from a slyboot, Lucretian kingdom and had to it much blindness folly. On another occasion, the stuff was Hebrew, tartareous and cold.

At the meeting before the start of the fall semester, when Elaine Winston had been gone for almost three months, the Suit quietly locked the washroom door and plucked from his jacket pocket an envelope which held what the Suit said was sublimity itself, rumored to have been harvested from the soaked deltas of Mars—misrule made elemental.

"Jesus," the Suit said, placing the item on the counter.

It appeared to be vibrating, as if it had breath and muscle. They peered at it awhile.

Mozer said something about awe—the scalloped rim of the universe. The Suit nodded.

Mozer said something about firmaments—the quaint auguries of nightswains.

The Suit nodded.

Mozer said something about glories, and when the Suit wondered what the Professor was going to do with this modern miracle, a light flickered on in Mozer's memory. His brain shivered and quaked, its fissures and folds darkening.

He had one idea, then a second—both electric and comely, as if he were a mathematician, a scholar versed in the joys of a problem and its meet solution. There was, it seemed, a machine's click in his forehead, and he beheld, the Suit still at his elbow, the crooked and croupy in himself limp away into blackness. He took a deep breath—the first in months, he believed—and he heard, as if with a castaway's ears, a shout and a call, human noise after eons of silence.

He was thinking about Mindy Griffith, that sophomore from Philadelphia, that one whose major in communications science had taught her, doubtlessly, the subtle but potent differences between talk and speech; yes, that fetching, unsafe creature who'd nearly fled her desk that noontime when he'd read from the *Biographia* of shag and rack and the dim, wicked hunter. Oh, he knew now what he would do, all right. And he knew, too, that while one might say that Mozer was a pretty slimy motherfucker, at thirty-five, to hustle the innocent, another might say that he was one hell of a fine person, confident as a gambler, with the courage of a Columbus, to share, to shepherd someone into that new world of love, that enchanted province of paradise and dread.

THE END OF GRIEF

THE WORST THING, in many ways the only thing, I heard about when I was growing up in the late fifties and early sixties concerned the horrible death of my father's brother, my uncle Gideon, on the Bataan Death March in April of 1942, an event that for those of you who, like me, were absorbed by the pictures and news reports of the Vietnam War must now seem as peculiarly dated as the times of knights-errant and fire-breathing dragons.

"Remember this," my father would say when I was small. "We human beings are capable of some real nasty behavior."

Every family has its own history of heartache, its private record of betrayal or misfortune; but when I was a youngster—and probably because we lived so far out of the way, in Deming, New Mexico, in a desert white and scorched and flat as one hell I've heard described— I believed, stupidly, that this infamy, a march of seventy-eight thousand native and American troops on a no-account Philippine peninsula, had touched everyone in our own safe world. From my mother, before she became a drunkard who would be carried off one day to live quietly and ever after in a private hospital in Roswell, and before she and Daddy divorced, I had learned about the other tragedies we Bakers and Hopcrafts (her people) had suffered: bankruptcies, disasters associated with weather or automobiles, paper fortunes that blew away like leaves, a drowning, a stillbirth, a black sheep or two. Yet if my mother could look backward for centuries, to the first of my ancestors who settled in the American Southwest in the early 1800s, my father, smart, too, and just as familiar with our personal lore, could see only from the beginning of the Second World War to what was its mortal end for the young man I am said to be the spitting image of—my uncle.

Now, at thirty-seven, I remember clearly how Daddy, in his odd fashion, used to wish me goodnight with stories from a past that was no more important to me personally than money is to a rock. When I was in the third grade, he'd tell me—sitting at the foot of my bed, smoking a Lucky Strike, an ashtray balanced on his knee—about the diseases the men in II Corps, and my uncle, suffered: dysentery, beriberi, night blindness, hookworm, diarrhea, mysterious swellings. When I was in the fourth grade, a time when I thought only about Little League baseball or swimming meets at the Mimbres Valley Country Club, he was taking me into his office, the newest outbuilding on our ranch, to show me his Department of the Army maps and geological surveys.

"They marched from here," he'd say, pointing to a crosshatching of lines identified as Balanga, "on the East Road to Lubao on Route Seven." His finger would trace the route, sometimes a path of gravel and packed dirt. "They would go from Capas by train and walk the next nine miles to Camp O'Donnell."

Yes, these were the names I heard through grammar school and into junior high: Bagac, and Orion, the Marvilles Mountains, the island of Luzon, Manila Bay. In the year of my first kiss (with Jane Templeton at an FFA fair in our National Guard armory), he forced me to memorize the titles and honors of the Japanese commander, Lieutenant General Masaharu Homma, and several of his officers, including Colonel Nakayama and Colonel Takatsu. While my friends Dub Spedding and Bobby Hover were collecting memorabilia about Ted Williams and Hammering Hank Aaron, I was reading *Back from the Living Dead,* by Major Bert Bank. My father had sent to Alabama for it, had read it so thoroughly that the pages became creased and soiled and clotted with his notes, and by God I was going to read it, too, just as I would read, when he was finished, books like *Zone of Emptiness,* by Hiroshio Noma, and the documents published by the Allied Translator and Interpreter Section (ATIS), General Headquarters, Southwest Pacific Area. Once, when I was a sophomore at Deming High School, brainy enough to be on the debate team and beefy enough to play varsity Wildcat football, he even gave me a quiz.

"Before the surrender itself," he began, "what were our soldiers eating?"

We sat in his office, its many shelves laden with charts and papers and file folders, his desk a clutter of books and writing materials. On one wall hung a pair of khaki trousers and an Imperial Army battle sword; on another, a partial order of battle.

"Who surrendered, by the way?"

"General King," I answered, a name I knew as well as my own. "On April ninth, approximately fourteen hundred hours."

The room was full of smoke already, and, owing to the glare from the floor lamp behind him, he seemed not so much my father as an old, sly stranger—a wizard, I thought, or an Indian medicine man—whose tests I had to pass in order to live as an adult.

"The food, son," he said, "the meat first."

I recited the list: carabao, pack mule, lizard, dog, and monkey, even the meat and eggs from pythons.

"How much did black-market cigarettes cost?"

"Five dollars," I said. "Regularly they were five cents a pack."

He shook his head. "It kept changing," he told me. "Remember the situation: One day a certain price, the next day another. This is vital."

On it went. Name the military hospitals and the officers in charge. How close was Corregidor? Why wouldn't Major General Jones take off his sunglasses? Who was the commander of the 65th Brigade of the Japanese Fourteenth Army? What American college had he attended? Describe the symptoms of malaria. What is Article 3, Chapter 1 of the Japanese Army regulations for handling prisoners of war? Translate *Bushido. Rikutatsu.*

At eleven I stopped him. We'd been at it for two hours. "I got to study," I said. "Physics."

He was shuffling documents, and I wanted to be elsewhere. In my room, I thought. In dreamland. Anywhere.

"Okay," he said. "Tomorrow we'll try something else."

I was at the door when he called me back.

"One more question," he said. "Why wasn't I in the war?"

A wind had come up, from the south and warm as breath. Tomorrow, while we classified soldiers according to sector and probable cause of death, we would have rain.

"Married," I told him.

He was rubbing his forehead, looking into space.

"What else?"

"Medical deferment," I said. "Punctured eardrum, flat feet, pulmonary stenosis."

This sort of exchange worsened as I grew older and, in his mind at least, came to resemble more clearly his brother. We had the same forehead, he'd insist, pitching me yet another curled, yellowed photograph he filed in his fireproof cabinets. We had the same hair, too, coarse as thread and more brown than blond. The same watery hazel eyes. Our cheek structures were virtually identical, high and pointed. We even had, my father claimed, comparable habits of mind. We liked puzzles. Within reason, we took risks: embraced speed, high places, darkness. We hated bullies, dishonesty in our friends. We were nimble, alert, sensitive to climate changes. Gideon had traveled—Palm Springs and Chicago—and so would I. He preferred tall women, so mine, inevitably, would be tall. We were readers but not sissies. When I graduated, Daddy took me out to his office, made me sit, and told me to open the box on his desk.

"It's a present," he said. "You'll like it."

It was a gold Longines, a wristwatch I wear still, and I realized immediately that Daddy had wrapped it himself, maybe a dozen times before he was satisfied.

"Look at the inscription." He leaned across his desk, pointed.

Still in my cap and gown, the tassel tickling my neck, I could hear my mother calling us to the dinner table. The ceremony had been over for an hour.

"Read it," my father told me.

Engraved on the back in small Gothic letters was this: "Gideon Alan Baker. Graduation: 16 June 1940. From his loving brother, Lyman.

"Gideon left it here before he enlisted," Daddy said. "He thought somebody might steal it."

I said thanks and stood to shake hands as I had been taught, firmly and with the palm full.

"You take care of that," he said, coming around his desk; and then I understood, more in my bones than in my brain, that he was smiling as he had smiled in 1940. To his mind, the hand he was holding, long-fingered and too soft, was less mine than his brother's; for him this was an instant of joy he had rescued, as boldly as if it were a person, from a past black and permanent as death itself.

"Gid liked expensive jewelry," Daddy said. "You will, too.

We would break eventually, my father and I, but for three years, while I was at the University of New Mexico, we continued our strange collaboration/review of Bataan, and torture, and my uncle. Within the week of my arrival, even before freshman orientation concluded, my father began writing me, filling his letters with facts I was to confirm in Zimmerman Library. "Find out," he scrawled, "who was responsible for the massacre of the 91st Filipino Division." A month later, he asked me to see if a Major Pedro L. Felix had been at Fort Benning, Georgia, on or about 12 October 1941.

"What for?" I wrote back.

By return mail I had an answer: "Gid mentions him twice. Maybe they met in the National Rice and Corn Corporation warehouse. I'm trying to establish a connection. This man survived four bayonet wounds, including a gash in the intestine."

Even when he admitted himself to Providence Memorial Hospital, in El Paso, to have his gall bladder removed, Daddy wrote, and I imagine now that he did so between visits from his nurses and doctors or after my mother had fallen asleep in her chair. "I need a complete list of General Parker's II Corps headquarters staff," he said once. "Maybe you could try the War College people for me. They stopped acknowledging my inquiries last August."

Those letters, his penmanship bunched and tinier than you'd expect from a large man, were wrinkled and stained, as if he'd kept them in his pocket like Kleenex, or under his mattress; and rare was the note that would say, as one did, "Disregard previous request, found info elsewhere. Now have names of stationmaster and Lubao political officer."

Near Christmas that year I told him I wouldn't do any more research. "I'm done with this," I wrote. "You can't expect this of me anymore. It's not fair."

Never had I challenged him on any issue—not what vegetables to eat, nor how a young man treats a lady, nothing—so I spent a week waiting to see him pull up in front of my dormitory in his pickup, his face alive with the rage of betrayal. Instead I got another note, this one typed and arranged as if for business: "All's fine here (except Mother, who wants nothing more to do with me). I hope you're getting out some. The big project with me is to find somebody who knew Gid over there. Do your homework. I am proud of you. Love, your Dad."

As it happened—because of the co-op program I entered (I'm an oil engineer now) and because being away from home seemed to have given me license to explore the large world far from here—I didn't get home much. When I did, it was only for a weekend—hardly long enough, I see now, to note the effect this obsession (if that's all it was) had on my mother. She drank, but everybody I knew drank—Dr. Weems, my father's golfing partners at the club, our trust officer, the cowhands working for us. Alcohol was as much a part of home life as laundry or breakfast; and alcoholics, after all, were other, less fortunate people: the poor, the lonely, the ignorant—not one's own mother. If I had been smarter, I might have seen the effect during my senior spring break, when I came down to tell them I was planning to marry Deborah, now my wife, but for years what I most remembered about those two days was the food my dad ate and the five-thousand-dollar check he forced on me.

"Do you know what your father's favorite flower is?" my mother asked that last afternoon. "The bachelor button. You wouldn't expect that, would you?"

If she was drunk, I did not know it. My thoughts concerned getting back to Albuquerque before dark, and the O-Chem midterm I had to take.

"His favorite composer is Mr. Bobby Worth," she said. "You know, 'Tonight We Love.' But he likes Ray Austin, too."

In a housecoat, her hair flyaway and dry-looking, Mother was cleaning the silver, the candelabra and serving dishes, even my baby cup; most of her days were like this, I think, hours that she hoped to fill but never could. Hours that, finally, had shape and color and density. Then she got up, went to the kitchen, and returned with an Army mess kit, metal and cleverly self-contained. It held a scoop of something like papier-mâché.

"Take this out to your father."

He was eating, I would discover, less than six ounces of overboiled rice once a day, the diet my uncle had survived on for two weeks before the surrender.

"It's an experiment," Daddy told me. "Don't worry, I'm not crazy."

The office was as I remembered, jammed floor to ceiling with documents, and I watched, fascinated, as he arranged himself cross-legged on the floor like a Buddha, the metal mess kit under his chin as he ate with his fingers.

"No couches in the bush," he said. "Here, you try it."

He held out, balanced on his fingertips, a lump like wallpaper paste, and without thinking I let him put it in my mouth.

"The strong had to feed the weak," he said. "Carry them, too. Sometimes they carried dead men."

The stuff was gummy, as tasteless as sand, less food than pulp.

"They'd drink from shell craters, once in a while from a stream. A couple pesos got you milk, maybe a turnip."

The rice sat in my mouth like paper. Like ash.

"You want some more?" he asked.

I didn't move, just watched him eat and listened to him describe events nearly twenty-five years old. The violence wasn't all of it, he said. The heat, heavy as wool and thick, contributed, along with the terrain—blackened tree stumps, wallows, rice paddies, dust: a jungle that had become the moon. There was humidity like saddlecloth, and foot sores. Some men ate cane bark. You saw corpses everywhere. In the towns—Lamao, Lubao—the civilians might sneak you a mango. You marched eighteen hours; maybe you got salt, maybe you didn't. Some of the Nips had bikes; you had to run double-time to keep up. You went crazy, entered mirages. You died. In the boxcars, narrow gauge and so low you had to stoop, you were packed so tight that the sweat ran down your legs and left your shoes soggy. If you had shoes.

"I can only eat this mush for about three days," Daddy said. "Then I get the runs."

Had my father experimented in other ways to put himself in my uncle's place? Without either a hat or a shirt, had he taken several long hikes in the desert, trying to re-create the exhaustion and pain Gideon must have felt? Had he emptied the tack box in our horse barn to spend a day inside it, cramped and sweaty and alone? I didn't know, didn't want to know. On the afternoon I am writing about, I was frightened—my heart in my ears, my breath ragged and hot—for it was easy to believe, though he kept telling me otherwise, that he had lost his mind, that he did not know this was 1967, or that he lived in America, or that he was a cattle rancher, not a prisoner of war. It was possible to believe that he, like those victims of religious rapture we read about in the papers, had slipped free of himself by a truly black magic. I thought that here, in the familiar quarters of his office, he heard voices, the wet groans and shouts and nightmare whimpers of men dying around him. Here, I thought, between one window that opened toward the Mimbres Mountains and another that faced the blank, shimmering horizon that was Mexico, he saw captains and sergeants without heads or arms, or privates and majors bloated black and left to rot.

"What's your position on this Vietnam thing?" he asked.

On the floor sat his tin mess kit, clean as if our dog, Alex, had eaten there, and it struck me that I had no position on anything, nothing at all.

"I have a position," Daddy said, "and my position is that you steer clear of it, you understand?"

His eyes remained on me as they had when he began telling me about Gideon—about our skinny-boy thighs, our dumb respect for mechanical contraptions, our rail-stiff spines—but now his eyes were saying, as eyes can, that enough was enough. A brother had died, a son would not.

"They change your classification," he was saying, "you let me know. File for CO, take drugs—I don't care—but you tell them no deal, you hear?"

I heard; yes, I did.

"From now on, you're a Communist," he said. "You're a Russian, a Chinese, anything."

Years later, I learned that he had gone to my draft board the day before, in his belt the Colt pistol he took as protection when he strung barbed wire at our section line. As I heard it, Daddy told Mr. Phinizy Spalding, a lifelong friend and the board's part-time director, that Scooter Baker was not going to die in some cesspool half a world away, that Lyman Baker, Sr., himself would see to it that Scooter showed up in panties and bra if it came to that. "I tell you, Phinizy," Daddy is supposed to have hollered in our post office, "you come after my boy, and I'll shoot his goddamn foot off myself. You know I will." What I heard is that my father, his hand on the pistol grip, stood for several minutes, trembling with anger, not two paces from Mr. Spalding, muttering again and again, as if he would for a year, the one word that seemed to make the most sense in the world he knew: No, no, no.

But he was standing in front of me now, calm as the day itself, and I wanted to say that I was twenty-one. I was in love with a brunette economics major from Grants. I wasn't a registered voter yet. I was a kid, I was stupid.

"You listen to me," he said. "I'm going to give you some money—

a lot of money, buddy—and when the time comes, if it does, you get out, you hear me?"

He was speaking to me, I realized, as he wished he had spoken to Gideon—big brother to little, wise man to dumb.

"You go to Sweden," he told me, his voice full of iron and the working life he loved, "go to Canada, Africa—makes no difference. You just go, you understand?"

We looked at each other, seriously and carefully. He was my father, he expected something of me, and there was a part of me that should know it. From his bent-forward shoulders and his narrowed eyes and the quiver in his cheek, I understood that all this Bataan stuff, the horror stories and the painstaking attention to detail and the grainy, time-worn photographs, had been an expression, unmistakable as slaughter itself, of nothing so much as love and memory and death and my relation among them.

As it turned out, I received a high lottery number when I graduated, so I missed the chance, as my father saw it, to define myself morally, to say what sort of son he'd raised. And in time, I admit, I tried to forget most of this. Deborah and I married, I took a job with Sinclair Oil in Texas for a time, and then, in 1976, just about the month our son Brian was born (he, yes, looks enough like me to look like my uncle, too), I came back here, to Deming, to work for a wildcat gas outfit named Mimbres Drilling, and to help Daddy with the ranch. Though my mother's drinking had led to her removal to Roswell, almost 250 miles away, these were good times: Deborah and I bought the split-level brick house we have, joined the club in our own right, made friends again with those I had grown up with. In the years after he stuffed his check into my shirt pocket and gave me a breath-defeating hug, I tried to believe that my father kept his Bataan studies to himself, more or less. I assumed he still pestered the Defense Department and the Records Division of the National Archives in Washington; but I also assumed—at least until a few years later when he called to tell me to drive out to the ranch to meet somebody—that his studies were no longer so dire, nor so mad. He was a man with a hobby, I had told Deborah, like coin or stamp collecting, or knowing the Latin names of desert plants.

"I want an hour of your time," he told me that night. "Just a little unfinished business."

He was crazy, I thought. He was lonely.

"Please, son. Don't fight me on this."

I have said that we had broken, my father and I, but the break was clean, not spite-filled, and could be fixed to the moment I took his money and left. We had parted, I thought. He had gone one way— backward, toward the past, toward grief—and I had gone another; and we had agreed silently, I thought, that there was an era, begun and ended in violence, that we neither would nor could talk about again.

"You found somebody, didn't you?" I said. "Somebody who knew Gid."

"Yeah," he told me. "An officer."

"After this no more," I told him. I felt slumped inside, as if all there was of link and snap and hook had crashed loose and lay ruined at the pit of me. "I mean it, Daddy."

"Sure," he said. "Just tonight."

The man Daddy wanted me to meet was Colonel Redmon A. Walters, U.S. Army, Ret., who, before serving in Honduras and in the Republic of South Korea, had been in the Philippines. On the march from the West Road to San Fernando he had befriended a twenty-year-old PFC named Baker, Gideon Alan.

"They were in the same regiment," Daddy said, "the Thirty-first Infantry. Both knew Brady."

I guess Daddy already realized that Colonel Walters—"Call me Red," he said, "I'm a civilian now"—had in fact not known any uncle; or, rather, he had known my uncle in the same way you and I know the dead whose ages we are or whose places we see. Yet Red Walters was no liar; he was only a man—like my father—who had felt and heard too much, and to whom truth wasn't a thing of records and graphs and testimony. Truth was the simple elements: light and nerve, fear and hope.

"What kind of a guy was Gid?" Daddy was saying.

Red Walters sat where I usually did, so I leaned against a file cabinet and looked out the window to the part of our toolshed I could see.

"He was tough," Colonel Walters said. "Lots of guys weren't, they caved in right away—but not your brother. He was a son of a bitch, is what he was."

I was hearing them, Red and Daddy, describe an old world they regarded from opposite ends of experience, and I felt nothing. Air was air, earth earth, and way off—in time if not in place—I stood, as alien to this as I would be to affairs in Antarctica.

"Where exactly did you meet him?" Daddy said.

Over his shoulder on a shelf stood a copy of General Homma's personal notes, which had come from the Office of Military History in Tokyo. Near it was the volume General Wainright had submitted to the War Department in 1946, *Report of the USAFFE and USFIP in the Philippine Islands, 1941–1942*. I had read them in another life, it seemed. In another world. With other eyes. With another brain.

"It was in Balanga," Red was saying. "Gid was part of that group in the field beyond the jail."

"Here?" Daddy had pointed to a spot on the map the size of a fingernail. It represented twelve unfenced acres in which thousands of men had been bivouacked during the march.

"Even the Japs didn't know what was up," Red said. "It was pretty confusing."

"I heard it was crazy."

"Filthy," Red Walters said. "No medical facilities, boys dying, flies everywhere. There was a kind of cloud over the place. At night it was incredibly cold."

"He looked pretty bad, I bet."

"We all did," Colonel Walters told us. "Thin like scarecrows, and stupid-looking. Some guys couldn't remember their names. Their units. You just wanted to lie down mostly."

"What about the brutality?"

"You got used to it," he said. "You didn't complain. You shut up."

At this point I realized that Colonel Walters had not met my uncle—the odds against it, and my father's hopes, were too great—but the realization reached me slowly and without real shock, the way bad

news must come to the chronically unlucky. It was old news, really.
Maybe it was the news God sees, our human story told so often that it
has lost its capacity to amaze or to instruct.

"He looked like me, right?" I asked.

At that moment Colonel Walters, gray-haired and now too fleshy
at the neck, came alive for me. I could imagine him as he'd once been,
hollow-eyed and feeble and broken.

"Hard to tell," he said. "He could've been big once, like you."

"He had my face, though?"

"It's been a long time," he said "I don't remember faces much anymore."

He was talking about all of them, I think. Clifford Bluemel, Alf
Weinstein, Lieutenant Henry G. Lee, Reynaldo Perez, Lieutenant
Colonel William E. Chandler, the living and the dead—he was saying
that he had known these and more, including the uncle I look like.
Gideon was that boy there from Springfield, Missouri, and that one
there from Pittsburgh, and that one way over there from Los Angeles;
he was the staff sergeant hiding in the thicket, the noncom collapsed
at the Blue Moon Dance Hall in San Fernando, the captain weeping
in Orani, the one sore or dehydrated or sleeping forever.

And so, after I understood this, I had a glass of whiskey with
Colonel Walters and my father, and tried to be very quiet. They discussed horror and time; they discussed suffering and where the mind
goes during battle and what a creature man is. They used words like
delirium and *ruthless* and *hunger*—a vocabulary that seemed more
appropriate to certain melodramatic books—and then, when the
Johnnie Walker was gone, my daddy asked me to see Mr. Walters to
his car.

"Hope I've been some help," the man said.

His hand was meaty, his grip firm like a gentleman's.

"Yes," Daddy told him. "Invaluable. Thank you very much."

Beside his Ford station wagon, our night black as the cape a witch
wears, I asked Colonel Red Walters how my father had gotten in touch
with him.

"At William Beaumont," he said, "in Fort Bliss."

Twice a year Colonel Walters was driving down from Carlsbad for checkups by the Army doctors.

"There was a note on a bulletin board," he told me. "From your dad. Said he wanted to talk to Bataan survivors who'd known his brother. The name rang a bell, so I came up."

As I watched Red Walters drive down our two-mile dirt road toward the highway, I thought about Dr. Hammond Ellis, our Episcopalian minister, and what he says about burdens—a word, as he uses it, that describes what we carry or put aside in time. We can be this or that, he preaches. Good or bad. Generous or stingy like Scrooge. Upright or craven. In any case, we have the option, gotten from our Creator (or from your own self, if that's what you believe), to change. We can be a drinker one day, a teetotaler the next. We can go from dumb to wise, wrathful to peaceful; we can believe or not, trust or not. Succeed or not. But always we have that choice. So, standing beside my old empty and dark house, I wondered about my father. He could be lunatic now, I thought, or not. Sad, or not.

"Lyman Baker, Junior," I said to myself, "you go in there right now."

I must have sat across from him, in my customary chair, for an hour, watching him—betrayed by the lights in his eyes, and by the way he stubbed out his smokes or tugged at his earlobe—take up his life, piece by piece, his examination of himself as patient and thorough as those given to the livestock that have made him rich. I saw him, I tell you, lift up the burdens Dr. Ellis preaches about, take their measure again, and then, one by one, lay them aside. It was slow, I saw, but it was not painful; and in time he had put aside his boxer's temper and his banker's concern for numbers. He was a man with a plan now, I thought. A before B. Work and play. Then he got up, stretched, rubbed his hands, and a dozen, free breaths came back to me.

"I think I'll cut down on the booze," he said. "That would be a good thing, wouldn't it?"

I thought it was and told him so.

"Maybe I'll visit your mother," he said. "It's been a long time."

That was true, too.

"I'm hungry," he said. "Let's go into town, get us a steak."

He was moving now, putting on the leather jacket Deborah had given him for his sixtieth birthday, so I asked him, "What about this?" I pointed to the books, the charts, the records, the maps—the millions of words and thousands of pictures he knew by heart. I wanted him to sweep them away, I suppose, set the whole mess aflame.

"What about it?" he said. "Just leave it."

I had my hand on a folder, one of thousands that were covered with his notes, and a thought, swift as love, came to me. So this is the end of grief, I thought. Of all his burdens, grief had gone first.

"We'll burn it tomorrow, okay?"

"Sure," he said. "Turn out the light, will you?"

THE FINAL PROOF OF FATE
AND CIRCUMSTANCE

MY FATHER BEGAN his story with death, saying the night was uncommonly dark near El Paso with an uncommon fog, thick and all the more frightful because it was unexpected, like ice or a Ringling parade of elephants tramping across the desert from horizon to horizon, each moody and terribly violent. He was driving on the War Road, two lanes that came up on the south side of what was then White Sands Proving Grounds, narrow and without shoulders, barbed-wire fences alongside, an Emergency Call Box every two miles, on one side the Franklin Mountains, on the other a boundless insult of waste; his car, as I now imagine it, must have been a DeSoto or a Chrysler, heavy with chrome and a grill like a ten-thousand-pound smile, a car carefully polished to a fierce shine, free of road dirts and bug filth, its inside a statement about what a person can do with cheesecloth and patience and affection. "A kind of palace in there," he'd always say. "Hell, I could live out of the back seat."

He was twenty-eight then, he remarked, and he came around that corner, taking that long, stomach-settling dip with authority, driving the next several yards like a man innocent of fret or second thought, gripping that large black steering wheel like a citizen with resolve and the means to achieve it—a man intimate with his several selves, scared of little and tolerant of much. I imagine him sitting high, chin upturned, eyes squinty with attentiveness, face alight with a dozen gleams from the dashboard, humming a measure of, say, "Tonight Is Love" by Ray Austin, singing a word of romance now and then, the merry moments of the music as familiar to him as a certain road sign or oncoming dry arroyo.

"I'd just come from Fort Bliss," he said. "I'd played in a golf tournament that day. Whipped Mr. Tommy Bolt, Jr. Old Automatic, that's me. Show up, take home the big one."

He was full of a thousand human satisfactions, he said—namely, worth and harmonies and renewals. He could hear his clubs rattling in the trunk; he could hear the wind rushing past, warm and dry, and the tires hissing; and he was thinking that it was a dandy world to be from, a world of easy rewards and sharp pleasures; a world, from the vantage point of a victory on the golf course, with shape and sense to it, a world in which a person such as himself—an Army lieutenant such as himself, lean and leaderly—could look forward to the elevated and the utmost, the hindmost for those without muscle or brain enough to spot the gladsome among the smuts; yes, it was an excellent world, sure and large enough for a man with finer features than most, a grown-up man with old but now lost Fort Worth money behind him, and a daddy with political knowledge, and a momma of substance and high habit, and a youth that had had in it such felicities as regular vacations to Miami Beach, plus a six-week course in the correct carving of fowl and fish, plus a boarding school and even enough tragedy, like a sister drowning and the body never recovered, to give a glimpse of, say, woe—which is surely the kind of shape you'd like your own daddy's character to have when he's about to round an insignificant corner in the desert, a Ray Austin lyric on his lips, and kill a man.

It was an accident, of course, the state police noting it was a combination of bad luck—what with the victim standing so that his taillight was obscured—and the elements (meaning, mostly, the fog; but including as well, Daddy said, time and crossed paths and human error and bad judgment and a certain fundamental untidiness). But then, shaken and offended and partly remorseful, my daddy was angry, his ears still ringing with crash noises and the body's private alarms.

"Goddamn," he said, wrestling open a door of his automobile, its interior dusty and strewn with stuffings from the glove box, a Texaco road map still floating in the air like a kite, a rear floor mat folded like a tea towel over the front seat, a thump-thump-thump coming from here and there and there and there. There was light enough for him to see the other vehicle, the quarter moon a dim milky spot, the fog itself swirling and seemingly lit from a thousand directions—half dreamland, half spook house. "There was a smell, too," he told me, his hands fluttering near his face. A smell like scorched rubber and industrial oils, grease and disturbed earth. His trunk had flown open, his clubs—"Spaldings, Tyler, the finest!"—flung about like pick-up sticks. His thoughts, an instant before airy and affirming, were full of soreness and ache; and, for a moment before he climbed back to the road, he watched one of his wheels spinning, on his face the twitches and lines real sorrow makes, that wheel, though useless, still going around and around, its hubcap scratched and dented.

He was aware, he'd say every time he came to this part, of everything—splintered glass and ordinary night sounds and a stiffness deep in his back and a trouser leg torn at the knee and a fruitlike tenderness to his own cheek pulp. "I felt myself good," he said, showing me again how he'd probed and prodded and squeezed, muttering to himself, "Ribs and neck and hips," that old thighbone-hipbone song the foremost thing on his mind. His brain was mostly in his ears, and his heart beat like someone was banging at it with a claw hammer, and there was a weakness in the belly, which in another, less stalwart sort might have been called nausea but which in this man, he told himself as he struggled to the roadway, was nothing less than the true discomfort that occurs when Good Feeling is so swiftly overcome by Bad.

At first he couldn't find the body. He walked up and down the road, both sides, yelling and peering into the fog, all the time growing angrier with himself, remembering the sudden appearance of that other automobile stopped more on the road than off, the panic that mashed him in the chest, the thud, the heart-flop. "I found the car about fifty yards away," he said, his voice full of miracle and distance as if every time he told the story—and, in particular, the parts that lead from bad to worse—it was not he who approached the smashed Chevrolet coupe, but another, an alien, a thing of curiosity and alert eyeballs, somebody naive to the heartbreak humankind could make for itself.

The rear of that Chevy, Daddy said, was well and thoroughly crunched, trunk lid twisted, fenders crumpled, its glowing brake light dangling, both doors sprung open as if whatever had been inside had left in a fluster of arm- and legwork. My daddy paced around that automobile many times, looking inside and underneath and on top and nearabouts, impatient and anxious, then cold and sweaty both. "I was a mess," he said. "I was thinking about Tommy Bolt and the duty officer at the BOQ and my mother and most every little thing." He was crying, too, he admitted, not sniveling and whimpering, but important adult tears that he kept wiping away as he widened his circle around the Chevy, snot dribbling down his chin, because he was wholly afraid that, scurrying through the scrub growth, the mesquite and prickly cactus and tanglesome weeds, he was going to find that body, itself crumpled, hurled into some unlikely and unwelcome position—sitting or doing a handstand against a bush—or that he was going to step on it, find himself frozen with dread, his new GI shoes smack in the middle of an ooze that used to be a chest or happy man's brain. "I kept telling myself Army things," he said one time. "Buck up. Don't be afraid. Do your duty. I told myself to be calm, methodical. Hope for the best, I said."

And so, of course, when he was hoping so hard his teeth hurt and his neck throbbed and his lungs felt like fire, he found it, bounced against a concrete culvert, legs crossed at the ankle, arms folded at the belt, with neither scratch nor bump nor knot nor runny wound, its face a long, scolding discourse on peace or sleep.

"At first I didn't think he was dead," Daddy told me. He scrambled to the body, said *get up*, said *are you hurt*, said *can you talk, wake up, mister*. The man's name turned out to be Valentine ("Can you believe that name, Tyler?" Daddy said, "Morris E. Valentine!") and my daddy put his mouth next to that man's ear canal and hollered and grabbed a hand—"It wasn't at all cold"—and shook it and gave a woman's nasty pinch to Valentine's thigh and listened against the man's nose for breaths or a gurgle, and felt the neck for a pulse. Then, Daddy said, there wasn't anything to do next but peek at Mr. Valentine's eyes, which were open in something like surprise or consternation, and which were as inert and blank and glassy, my daddy said, as two lumps of coal that had lain for ten million years in darkness.

It was then, alone and far from home, that he felt the peacefulness come over him like a shadow on a sunny day—a tranquillity, huge and fitting like (he said) the sort you feel at the end of fine drama when, with all the deeds done and the ruin dealt out fairly, you go off to eat and drink some; yup, he said, just like the end of the War Road itself, a place of dusts and fog and uprooted flora and fuzzy lights where you discover, as the state police did, a live man and a dead one, the first laughing in a frenzy of horror, the second still and as removed from life as you are from your ancestral fishes, his last thought—evidently a serious one—still plain on his dumb, awful face.

He told me this story again today, the two of us sitting in his backyard, partly in the shade of an upright willow, him in a racy Florida shirt and baggy Bermudas, me in a Slammin' Sammy Snead golf hat and swim trunks. It was hooch, he said, that brought out the raconteur in him, Ron Rico being the fittest of liquors for picking over the past.

Lord, he must've gone through a hundred stories this afternoon, all the edge out of his voice, his eyes fixed on the country club's fourteenth fairway which runs behind the house. He told one about my mother meeting Fidel Castro. It was a story, he suggested, that featured comedy in large doses and not a little horridness. It had bellow and running hither and hoopla when none was expected. "Far as I could tell," he said, "Fidel was merely a hairy man with a pistol. Plus rabble-rousers." He told another about Panama and the officers' club and the Geists, Maizie and Al, and a Memphis industrialist named L. "Doc" Purdy. It vas a story that started bad, went some distance in the company of foolishness and youthful hugger-mugger, and ended not with sadness but with mirth. He told about Korea and mooseymaids and sloth and whole families of yellow folk living in squalor, not to mention supply problems and peril and cold and, a time later, of having Mr. Sam Jones of the Boston Celtics in his platoon. "You haven't known beauty," he said, smiling, "till you see that man dribble. Jesus, it was superior, Tyler."

He told one about some reservists in Montana or Idaho, one of those barren, ascetic places, and a training exercise called Operation Hot Foot which involved, as I recall, scrambling this way and that, eyes peeled for the Red Team, a thousand accountants and farm boys and family men in nighttime camouflage; and a nearsighted colonel named Krebs who took my daddy bird-watching. Daddy said that from his position on a bluff he could see people in green scampering and diving and waving in something approaching terror, but that he and Krebs were looking through binoculars for nest or telltale feather, listening intently for warble or tweet or chirp, the colonel doing his best, with nose and lip work, to imitate that genus of fear or hunger or passion a rare flying thing might find appealing. "It was lovely," Daddy said, the two of them putting over two hundred miles on the jeep in search of Gray's Wing-Notch Swallow, or feathered forelimb that had been absent from the planet, Daddy suspected, for an eon. There were trees and buttes and colors from Mr. Disney, an austerity, extreme and eternal, that naturally put you in mind of the Higher Plane.

For another hour he went on, his stories addressing what he called the Fine, events in which the hero, using luck and ignorance, managed to avoid the base and its slick companion, the lewd. I heard about a cousin, A. T. Winans, who had it, let it slip away, and snatched it back when least deserved. I learned the two things any dog knows: Can I eat it, or will it eat me? I learned something about people called the Duke and the Earl and the Count and how Tommy Dorsey looked close up. I was touched—not weepy, as my wife Nadine becomes when I tell her a little about my Kappa Alpha days at UTEP or how I stumbled out looking like a dope when I had gone in feeling like a prince. I was in that cozy place few get to these days, that place where your own father—that figure who whomped you and scolded you and who had nothing civil to say about the New York Yankees or General

Eisenhower, and who expressed himself at length on the subjects of sideburns and fit reading matter and how a gentleman shines his loafers—yes, that place where your own father admits to being a whole hell of a lot like you, which is sometimes confused and often weak; that place, made habitable by age and self-absorption and fatigue, that says much about those heretofore pantywaist emotions like pity and fear.

Then, about four o'clock, while the two of us stood against his cinder-block fence, watching a fivesome of country club ladies drag their carts up the fairway, the sun hot enough to satisfy even William Wordsworth, Daddy announced he had a new story, one which he'd fussed over in his brain a million times but one which, on account of this or that or another thing, he'd never told anyone. Not my momma Ellen. Not my uncle Matthew. Not his sisters, Faith and Caroline. His hand held on my forearm, squeezing hard, and I could see by his eyes, which were watery and inflamed by something I now know as determination, and by his wrinkled, dark forehead and by his knotted neck muscles—by all these things, I knew this story would feature neither the fanciful nor the foreign, neither bird nor military mess-up, nor escapade, nor enterprise in melancholy; it would be, I suspected as he stared at me as though I were no more related to him than that brick or that rabbit-shaped cloud, about mystery, about the strange union of innocence and loss which sometimes passes for wisdom, and about the downward trend of human desires. There was to be a moral, too; and it was to be, like most morals, obvious and tragic.

This was to be, I should know, another death story, this related to Valentine's the way one flower—a jonquil, for instance—is related to another, like a morning glory, the differences between them apparent, certain, and important; and the story was to feature a man named X, Daddy said; a man, I realized instantly, who was my father himself, slipped loose of the story now by time and memory and fortunate circumstance. X was married now, I was told, to an upstanding woman and he had equally fine children, among them a youth near my own age, but X had been married before and it would serve no purpose, I was to know, for the current to know about the former, the past being—my daddy said—a thing of regret and diminishment. I understood, I said, understanding further that this woman—my daddy's first wife!—was going to die again as she had died before.

She was a Frenchwoman, Daddy said, name of Annette D'Kopman, and X met her in September 1952 at the Fourth Army Golf Tournament in San Antonio, their meeting the result of happenstance and X's first-round victory over the professional you now recognize as Mr. Orville Moody. "X was thirty-one then," Daddy said, filling his glass with more rum, "the kind of guy who took his celebrating seriously." I listened closely, trying to pick out those notes in his voice you might call mournful or misty. There were none, I'm pleased to say, just a voice heavy with curiosity. "This Annette person was a guest of some fancy-pants," my daddy was saying, and when X saw her, he suspected it was love. I knew that emotion, I thought, it having been produced in me the first time I saw Nadine. I recalled it as a steady knocking in the heart spot, as well as a brain troubled with a dozen thoughts. This Annette, my daddy said, was not particularly gorgeous, but she had, according to X, knuckles that he described as wondrous, plus delicate arches and close pores and deep sockets and a method of getting from oven to freezer with style enough to make you choke or ache in several of the bigger muscles you use to breathe or pray. So, Daddy said, X and Annette were married the next week, the attraction being mutual, a Mexican JP saying plenty, for twenty dollars, about protection and trust and parting after an extended life of satisfactions, among the latter being health, robust offspring, and the daily pleasures unique to cohabitation.

As he talked, my daddy's face had hope in it, and some pride, as though he were with her again, thirty years from the present moil, squabbling again (as he said), about food with unlikely and unfamiliar vegetables it, or ways of tending to the demands of the fallen flesh. X and Annette lived at Fort Sam Houston, he the supply officer for the second detachment, she a gift to dash home to. "It wasn't all happy times," Daddy was saying, there being shares of blue spirits and hurt feelings and misunderstandings as nasty as any X had since had with his present wife. "There was drinking," my daddy said, "and once X smacked her." Still, there was hugging and driving to Corpus Christi and evenings with folks at the officers' club and swimming. I imagined them together and, watching him now slumped in his chair, the sun a burning disk over his shoulder, I saw them as an earlier version of Nadine and me: ordinary as dollar bills and doing well to keep a healthful distance from things depraved and hurtful. The lust part, he said, wore off, of course, the thing left behind being close enough to please even the picky and stupid. Then she died.

I remember thinking that this was the hard part, the part wherein X was entitled to go crazy and do a hundred destructive acts, maybe grow miserly and sullen, utter an ugly phrase or two. Certainly drink immoderately. I was wrong, Daddy said. For it was a death so unexpected, like one in a fairy tale, that there was only time for the wet howl a dog makes and seventy hours of sweaty, dreamless sleep. "X didn't feel rack or nothing," Daddy said. "Not empty, not needful, nor abused by any dark forces." X was a blank—shock, a physician called it—more rock than mortal beset with any of the mundane hardships. "X did his job," Daddy said, "gave his orders, went and came, went and came." X watched TV, his favorite being Garry Moore's *I've Got a Secret*, read a little in the lives of others, ate at normal hours, looked as determined as your typical citizen, one in whom there was now a scorched, tender spot commonly associated with sentiment and hope. Colonel Buck Wade concluded the funeral arrangements—civilian, of course—talking patiently with X, offering a shoulder and experience and pith. "X kept wondering when he'd grieve," Daddy said. Everyone looked for the signs: an outburst of the shameful sort, a tactless remark, a weariness in the eyes and carriage. But there was only numbness, as if X were no more sentient than a clock or Annette herself.

"Now comes the sad part," my daddy said, which was not the ceremony, X having been an Episcopalian, or the burial, because X never got that far. Oh, there was a service, X in his pressed blues, brass catching the light like sparkles, the minister, a Dr. Doyle Patten, trying through the drift and bent of learnedness itself to put the finest face on a vulgar event, reading one phrase about deeds and forgiveness and another about the afterworld and its steady tempers, each statement swollen with a succor or a joy, words so impossible with knowledge and acceptance that X sat rigid, his back braced against a pew, his pals unable to see anything in his eyes except emptiness. No, the sadness didn't come then—not with prayer, not with the sniffling of someone to X's left, not at the sight of the casket itself toted outside. The sadness came, my daddy said, in the company of the driver of the family car in which X rode alone.

"The driver was a kid," Daddy told me, "twenty, maybe younger, name of Monroe." Whose face, I learned, had through it a thousand conflicting thoughts—of delight and of money and of nooky and of swelter like today's. Monroe, I was to know, was the squatty sort, the kind who's always touchy about his height, with eyeballs that didn't say anything about his inner life, as well as chewed nails and a thin tie and the wrong brown shoes for a business otherwise associated with black, plus an ugly spot on his neck that could have been a pimple or ingrown hair. "Stop," X said, and Monroe stared at him in the mirror. "What—?" Monroe was startled. "I said stop." They were halfway to the grave site, funeral coach in front, a line of cars with lights on in back. "Stop here. Do it now." X was pointing to a row of storefronts on Picacho Street—laundry, a barber's, a Zale's jewelry.

My daddy said he didn't know why Monroe so quickly obeyed X, but I realize now that Monroe was just responding to that tone in my father's voice that tells you to leave off what you're doing—be it playing canasta, eating Oreos with your mouth open, or mumbling in the crisis moments of *Gunsmoke*—and take up politeness and order and respectfulness. It's a note that encourages you toward the best, the most responsible in yourself, and it has in it a hint of the nasty consequences that await if you do not. So the Cadillac pulled over, Monroe babbling "uh-uh-uh," and X jumped out, saying, "Thank you, Monroe, you may go on now."

It was here that I got stuck trying to explain it to Nadine, trying to show that funeral coach already up the street, Monroe having a difficult time getting his car in gear while behind him, stopped, a line of headlamps stretched well back, a few doors opening, the folks nearest startled and wild-eyed and looking to each other for help, and X, his hat set aright, already was beginning a march down the sidewalk, heels clicking, shoulders squared, a figure of precision and care and true strength. I told Nadine, as my daddy told me, about the cars creeping past, someone calling out, Colonel Buck Wade stopping and ordering, then shouting for X to get in. X didn't hear, Daddy said. Wade was laughable, his mouth working in panic, an arm waving, his own wife tugging at his sleeve, himself almost as improbable as that peculiar bird my daddy and another colonel had spent a day hunting years ago.

"X didn't know where he was going," Daddy said. To be true, he was feeling the sunlight and the heavy air and hearing, as if with another's ears, honks and shouts, but X said he felt moved and, yes, driven, being drawn away from something, not forward to another. The sadness lay on him then, my daddy said; and this afternoon, I saw it again in his face, a condition as permanent as the shape of your lips or your natural tendency to be silly. X went into an ice-cream parlor, and here I see him facing a glass-fronted counter of Tutti-Frutti and Chocolate and Pineapple Sherbet, and behind it a teenage girl with no more on her mind than how to serve this one, then another and another until she could go home. X ordered Vanilla, Daddy said, eating by the spoonful, deliberately and abstractedly, as if the rest of his life—a long thing he felt he deserved—depended on this moment. It was the best ice cream X ever ate, Daddy said, and for three cones he thought of nothing, not bleakness, not happiness, not shape, not beauty, not thwarts, not common distress—not anything the bootless brain turns toward out of tribulation.

It was then, my daddy said, that X realized something—about the counter-girl, the ice cream itself, Colonel Buck Wade, even the children and the new wife he would have one day, and the hundreds of years still to pass—and this insight came to X with such force and speed that he felt light-headed and partially blind, the walls tipping and closing in on him, the floor rising and spinning, a mountain of sundae crashing over his shoulders and neck; he was going to pass out, X knew, and he wondered what others might say, knowing that his final thought—like Mr. Valentine's in one story—was long and complex and featured, among its parts, a scene of hope followed by another of misfortune and doom.

When Nadine asked me an hour ago what the moral was, I said, "Everything is fragile." We were in the kitchen, drinking Buckhorn, she in her pj's; and I tried, though some overthrown by drink and a little breathless, to explain, setting the scene and rambling, mentioning ancient times and sorrow and pride in another. It was bad. I put everything in—the manner of sitting, how the air smelled when Daddy went inside, the gesture that had significance, what my own flesh was doing. But I was wrong. Completely wrong. For I left out the part where I, sunburned but shivering, wandered through X's house, one instant feeling weepy, another feeling foolish and much aged.

The part I left out shows me going into his kitchen, reading the note my momma wrote when she went to Dallas to visit my aunt Dolly; and it shows me standing in every room, alien in that place as a sneak-thief, handling their bric-a-brac and Daddy's tarnished golf trophies, sitting on the edge of the sofa or the green, shiny lounger, in the guest bathroom opening the medicine cabinet, curiosity in me as strong as the lesser states of mind. It's the episode that has all the truth in it—and what I'll tell Nadine in the morning. I'll describe how I finally entered Daddy's room and stood over his bed, listening to him snore, the covers clenched at his chest, saying to myself, as he had long ago, *headbone* and *chinbone*, *legbone* and *armbone*. Yes, when I tell it, I'll put in the part wherein a fellow such as me invites a fellow such as him out to do a thing—I'm not sure what—that involves effort and sacrifice and leads, in an hour or a day, to that throb and swell fellows such as you call triumph.

THE TALK
TALKED BETWEEN WORMS

1.

According to the tapes, my father, then about as run-of-the-mill a man as Joe Blow himself, didn't want to see the thing. Not a damn bit, he says. But there it came anyhow, roaring in hard and tumbly from the west with a comet's fiery tail, and then ka-BOOM—enough bang to rock Chaves County left and right like a quake.

This was summer 1947, almost nothing to see but weeds and hummocks and desert all the way to the red clay of Texas in the east, and my father, Totenham Gregory Hamsey, gentleman cowboy, was out there. Riding his pickup bouncy like on the fence line, he was hunting for the gaps in the barbed wire that several yearlings had escaped through, when it—the UFO—went boom to the east of him. Maybe like your own self—certainly like me in a similarly serious moment—he was dumbstruck. His blood ran thick and bubbly in his chest, his mouth opening and closing on thinnest air. Something from the clouds had tumbled earthward, and nobody had seen it but a twenty-nine-year-old red-haired rancher with thirty dollars in his pocket and the current issue of the *Saturday Evening Post* on the seat beside him.

His truck had stalled on him, another mystery he lived to tell about, so presently he gave up on it and hopped onto the hood to study the scattered fires and the long, raggedy trench the Martians— or whatever the hell they were—had made when they quit their element for ours. First he thought it was a plane, a top-secret jet out of Roswell Army Air Field, or a V2 rocket gone haywire from White Sands, which gave him, naturally, to expect company—more planes maybe, or soldiers with rifles to shoo him out of there. These were the days of Communists, he says on the tapes: sour-minded hordes from Korea and the Soviet Union that even Governor Whitman had warned you to expect on the doorstep of city hall itself. One hour went by that way—Tot Hamsey, rich man's youngest son, saying to himself what he'd say to others if they, in pairs or in a mob, were to rumble over that hill yonder and want their busted contraption back. But none did. Not for that hour anyway. Nor for the several that followed. Nothing arrived but a turkey buzzard, wings glossy and black as crude oil, which gave everything the once-over—the smoking debris, the perplexed human being, the prickly flora all about—before, screeching in disappointment, it wheeled west for better pickings.

That's when Tot Hamsey, my father, gave his Ford a second chance. Climbed back in the cab, spoke an angry sentence in the direction of the starter button, and breathed deeply with relief when its six cylinders clattered to life—as welcome a noise to hear under those circumstances as is conversation from the lady you love. He could go back to town, he figured. Thirty-five miles. Find Sheriff Johnny Freel. Maybe Cheek Watson, the dumbbell deputy. Tell them the whole story—the sky a menace of streaky orange and yellow, the howl coming at him over his shoulder, the boom, and afterward soil and rock pitched up everywhere. Be done with it then. Bring the bigwigs back here, sure. Possibly hang around to gab with whatever colonel or general showed up to get his property back. Still get home in time for supper.

But Tot Hamsey was a curious man—a habit of character, my

mother once said, you like to see in those you're to spend a lifetime with—and he was curious now, more curious than hungry or tired or wary-witted, and so he put himself in gear to drive slowly down a sandy draw and up an easy rise until he had nowhere to turn but into the raw and burned-up acreage this part of New Mexico would ever after be famous for.

Everywhere was space-age junk, various foils and joints and milled metals as peculiar to him as maybe we are to critters. All the way to more sizable hills a half mile east, the landscape had been split and gouged—the handiwork, it appeared, of a giant from Homer or the Holy Bible racing toward sunrise and dragging a plow behind. Fires flickered near and far, and Tot Hamsey, father of one, could imagine that these were the cooking fires of an army heedless enough to make war against God. The sky had gone mostly dark, several stars twinkling, but no moon to make out specifics by. Just dark upon dark, and sky upon sky, and one innocent bystander in a Stetson from the El Paso Hat Company tying a bandanna over his mouth and nose to keep from breathing so much vile smoke.

The silence was likewise odd, somehow cold and leaden, another thing to spook you in the night. He thought he'd hear wildlife, certainly. Coyotes in a pack. The sheep from Albert Tulk's place. But nothing, not even a dry wind to sweep noises here from civilization, which gave him to believe that all he'd known had vanished from the empire of man. His daddy's banks. His mother Vanetta and his two brothers. Mac Brazeall, his own hired hand. His wife, who was my mother Corrine, and me as well, only a toddler. Even the town of Roswell and all others he'd suffered the bother to visit.

He turned himself on his heels, eyes fixed on the collapsed horizon, a full circle. Panic had begun to rise in Mr. Hamsey, him a Christian reared to believe in peril and the calamitous end of everything. It did seem possible, he thought. All of modern life, now gone. Streets he knew. The Liberty Bar, Brother Bill Toomey's radio station, his grammar school on Hardesty Road and the crotchety marms that taught there. Every bit of it, great and small. The president of the United States, not to mention those muckety-mucks who ruled the world beyond. Maybe even the vast world itself. Which was probably all rubble and flame and smoke and which, as he thought about it, meant, Lord Almighty, that maybe Tot Hamsey was the last of whatever was—the last man in the last place on the last day with the last mind to think of last things on Planet Earth.

You can go out there your own self, if you wish. Just visit the UFO Museum. Not the classy outfit across from the courthouse near Denny's, but the low-rent enterprise way south on Main Street, past the Levi's plant and Mrs. Blake's House of Christmas. The man there is Boyd Pickett, to matters of heaven and earth what, say, the Devil is to truth and fruit from a tree. For ten dollars a head, he'll drive you out there in his Crown Victoria—it's private property, he'll tell you, him with a sweetheart lease arrangement—and show you the sights such as they currently are. For five more dollars, he'll dangle a Tyco model flying saucer on #10 fishing filament behind you and snap you a full-color Polaroid suitable for framing, which means—ha-ha-ha— you with a moron's grin and hovering over your shoulder physical evidence of a superior intelligence, which you are encouraged to show to your faithless friends and neighbors in, oh, Timbuktu or wherever it is you tote your own heavy bale.

For $8.50 you can have the as-told-to story between covers: how in July of 1947, one Mac Brazeall, ramrod for the Bar H spread out of Corona, heard a boom bigger than thunder and, as dutiful a Democrat as Harry Truman himself, went out to investigate; how he found what he found, which was wreckage and scalded rock and scorched grama grass, and how he took a piece of the former to Sheriff Johnny Freel, who viewed the affair with skepticism until Mac Brazeall, patriot and full-time redneck, crumpled a square of metal in his hands and put it on the table, whereupon, like an instance of infernal hocus-pocus, it sprung back into its original shape; and how Sheriff Freel, heart plugged in his throat, got on the phone to his Army counterpart at the air base; and how, in the hours that passed, much ordnance was mobilized and dispatched, and heads were scratched and oaths sworn; and how by, quote, dawn's early light, you could look at the front page of the *Daily Record* and see there a picture of jug-eared Mac Brazeall, smug as a gambler atop a pyramid of loot, taking credit for a historical fact that had begun when my father, Tot Hamsey, heard the air whip and crack and, as if in a nightmare, witnessed his paid-for real estate turn to fire and ruin in front of him.

I've been out there a few times, the first with Cece Phillips (now my ex-wife) when we were hot for each other and stupid with youth. This was summer 1964, me only fresh out of high school and not yet in possession of the tapes my father, once a doctor-certified crazy man, would one day oblige me to listen to. Ignorant is what I'm trying to say, just a boy, like his long-gone daddy, unaware that what lay before him was a land of miracles terrifying but necessary to behold; just a boy fumbling at his girlfriend's underclothes while everywhere, invisible above, eyes might have been looking down.

That night the moon was up, golden as a supper plate from the table of King Midas himself. In the back seat of my mother's Chevrolet we had gone around and around for a time, Cece Phillips and me, breathless and eager-beaver, nothing there or there or there outdoors but sagebrush and the shapely shadows hills make. We must've seemed like wrestlers, I'm thinking now. Clinch, paw, and part. Look this way and that, not much coming out of our mouths but breath and syllables a whole lot like "eeeff" and "ooohh." Cece said she couldn't—not now anyways, not in this creepy place. And I, an hour of lukewarm Coors beer my inspiration, said she could. Which gave us, for a little while, something else to talk about before it became clear she would.

Not much to report here. Nothing mushy-gushy, anyway, from romance books or love songs. Just how time seemed to me to pass. One second and then another, like links on a chain that one day has to end. This is who we were: Reilly Hamsey, beefy enough to be of part-time use to the Coyotes' coach for football; and Cece Phillips, hair in the suave beehive style of the stewardess she intended to be. We had music from KOMA out of Oklahoma City, and no school tomorrow or anytime until fall when we were to take up college life at New Mexico State University in Las Cruces. This was us: bone and heat and movement, as we had been at the drive-in or in my mother's rec room when she was away at work. Just us, youngsters who knew how to say "sir" and "ma'am" and "thank you" and be the seen-not-heard types adults are tickled silly to brag about.

Then this was over, and I was out-of-doors.

Was anything wrong, Cece wanted to know, and for a second I believed there wasn't.

"I'm gonna take a leak," I told her, and moseyed away to find a bush to stand behind.

A pall had fallen over me, I think now. A curtain had come down, or a wall gone up. Something that, as I stood with my back to the car and Cece, I could feel as plainly as I only moments before had felt the buckles and bows of Ms. Phillips herself.

Behind me, Cece was singing with the Lovin' Spoonful, hers a voice vigorous enough to be admired by Baptists, and I, for the first time, was doing some serious thinking about her. About the muscles she had, and the dances she was unashamed to do at the Pit Stop or in the gym. She could stick-shift fast as I and knew as much as many about engines, those farm-related and not. She was tall, which appealed, and loose in the legs, swift as a sprinter.

"Don't go too far," she was saying. "We got to go pretty soon."

Thinking about her. Then me. Then, oddly, my dog Red and how the fur bristled on his rump when the unexpected rapped at our front door on Missouri Street. Then my still-pretty mother and the colonel from the Institute she was dating, him with a posture rigid as plank flooring. Then, inevitably, my father, Tot Hamsey.

"Darn you, Reilly Jay," she hollered out. "You tore my skirt."

I imagined my father exactly as my mother had once described him: in front of the TV in the dayroom of his ward, his long face empty of everything but shock and sadness, his eyes glassy as marbles, the sense that in his head were only sparks and such thoughts as are thought by birds.

"You all right?" Cece called. "Reilly, you hear me?"

I was done with thinking then. I had reached a conclusion about Cece and me, one I was surer and surer of the closer I came to the car.

"Reilly," she said, "what's wrong with your face?"

We were doomed, I was thinking, the fact of it suddenly no more surprising than is the news that it's hot in hell. We would go to college, that was clear. Cece, I guessed, would become pregnant. Yours truly would graduate and work for, say, Sinclair Oil in Midland and Odessa or thereabouts. More years would then roll over us, a tidal wave washing through our lives as one had smashed through my parents' own. Eventually, I would find myself back here in Roswell—exactly, friends, as it has come to pass—and very likely I would be alone. As alone, according to the story, as my father had been the night he, years and years before, learned what he learned when the sun was down in this weird place and there was nothing else to do but heave himself into madness.

"I'm fine," I told her. "Put your clothes on."

Tot Hamsey finds the body in this part. The extraterrestrial. Finds it, listens to it, watches it expire. Then, having wandered a considerable distance away, he leans himself against the crumbling bank of an arroyo and, sprocket by spool by spring, feels his own simple self come plumb apart. The very him of him disassembled, which are his own words on one cassette. His boyhood, which was largely carefree and conducted out-of-doors. His school years, which go as they came, autumn by autumn. His playing basketball. He had popped an eardrum by diving in the wrong place at the Bottomless Lakes, and that went, as did the courtship of several town girls, including Corrine Rains, who became his wife and my mother, as well as his years at the Nazarene College in Idaho. He put aside—"very carefully," he says on the tapes, likening himself to a whirligig of cogs and levers and wheels—all he'd done and thought about doing. About being for two whole days the property of Uncle Sam, and the tubby doctor who discovered that Tot Hamsey was one inch shorter on the left side. About working carpentry with his brother Ben at the German POW camp south of town. About being another man's boss, and knowledge to have through the hands. About me even, the tiny look-alike of him. For almost an hour, until he heard the sputter of Mac Brazeall's flatbed well east of him, he sat there. He was only mass and weight, one more creature to take up space in the world, more or less the man I visited in 1981, the year after I came back to this corner of America—a man who regarded you as though he expected you to reach behind your head to yank off your face and thus reveal yourself as a monster, too.

For a time, so he says on one tape, he didn't do much of anything that July night in 1947. Sound had returned to the world, it seemed. He could hear the cows he'd been searching for bawling in the hard darkness south of him. He was in and out of the debris field now—back and forth, back and forth—the smell of char and ravaged earth sometimes strong enough to gag him, so he kept the Ford moving. Every now and then, slowing to roll down the window, he hollered into the blackness. If it was a plane from the Army base, then, shoot, maybe somebody had bailed out before or otherwise survived the crash. He might even know the pilot or those the pilot knew. But no answer ever came back. Not at point X or the other points, near and far, he found interesting. So for a while he didn't stop at all, fearing that if he did leave his truck he might find only a torn-off part of somebody—a leg maybe, or a familiar head rolled up into some creosote bush—and that was nothing at all Tot Hamsey cared to find by himself. You could be scared, yes. But you didn't have to be foolish. Instead, you would just stay in the cab of your nearly new Ford pickup and if, courtesy of your headlights, something should appear, well, you would just have to see that, wouldn't you, and thereafter make up your own mind about what smart thing to do next.

He's hearing the voice now, he says on the cassette. He's been hearing it for a while, he thinks. Not a voice exactly, but chatter akin to static—like communication you might imagine from Shangri-la or a risen and busy Atlantis. Bursts of it. Ancient as Eden or new as tomorrow. The language of fish, maybe. Or what the trees confide in each other.

"Trees," he says on the tapes, his own voice a whisper you would not want to hear more than once after sundown. "Vipers. And bugs. And rocks. The talk talked between worms."

He's stopped the truck now. But he's not jumpy anymore—not at all. This could be a dream, he thinks, him still at home with Corrine and nothing but work in the sunshine to look forward to. He thinks about his friends, Straightleg Harry Peterson and Sonny Fitzpatrick, and the pheasant they'll hunt come winter. He thinks about his daddy's deacon, Martin Willis, whose porch he's promised to fix on Saturday.

It's a dream, he tells himself, feeling himself move left and right in it, nothing to keep him from falling over the edge. It's a dream, water a medium to stand upon and wings everywhere to wear. It's a dream, yes, time a rope to hang from and you on a root in the clouds.

It's a dream, Tot Hamsey says on the tape, but then it is not— never has been—and there he is at last, staring into the face of one sign and terrible wonder.

The books describe it as tiny, like a fourth-grader, with a head like a bowling ball on a stick. *The Roswell Incident* by Charles Berlitz and Bill Moore. *UFO Crash at Roswell* by those smart-alecks from England. They all say that it—the spaceman my father found—was hairless, skin gray as ash, its eyes big as a prizefighter's fists. Something you could lug for a mile or two, easy. They're wrong. The thing had skin pink as a newborn's with hands like claws. You could see into it, my father says on the tapes. See its fluids pumping, an ooze that could be blood or sparkly liquids or goo there aren't yet names for. And probably it could see into you. At least that's the way it seemed to him—it with a Chinaman's eyes that didn't close and no ears and nothing but sloppy wet holes the size of peach pits to breathe through.

"Touch," the thing said. The static was gone, English in its place— more phenomena we're told that Uncle Sam has an interest in keeping hush-hush. "Don't be afraid."

My father looked around, no help on the horizon. He'd been given an order, it seemed, and there appeared to be no good reason not to obey it. So his hand went out, as if they knew each other and had been summoned hereabouts to do common business. It was like touching a snake, he says. Or the deepest thing from the deepest blue sea.

"Help them," the thing said—another sentence you probably find silly to believe—and only a moment passed before my father noticed the three others nearby.

They were dead. That was easy to tell. Like oversize dolls that have lost their air—a sight downright sad to see but one Tot Hamsey told himself he could forget provided he now had nothing else awful to know and thereafter nothing more to remember.

"Wait," the thing told him. "Sit."

Ten paces away the pickup was still running at idle, headlights on but aimed elsewhere, and my father imagined himself able enough to walk toward it.

In an hour he could be home. He would eat supper, play with his boy, and listen to the radio. Corrine was making apricot jam, so he would sample it. He would take a bath, hot as he could tolerate. And then shave, using the razor his father had given him for Christmas. He could shine his lace-up shoes, read a true story in the *Reader's Digest,* or tell Reilly more about Huck and Tom and Nigger Jim.

Sonny Fitzpatrick wanted him to help put the plumbing in a bungalow being built by the road to Artesia, so he could puzzle over that—the supplies he'd need and what to charge Sonny's father for the hours involved. He'd been good at math. At geometry and angles to draw. He'd been better at literature, the go-getters and backsliders that books told about. He was only twenty-nine. A husband and a father. Much remained to be done in life.

But this, he thought. This was like dying. Like watching a horrible storm bear down on you from heaven. Nowhere at all to hide from the ordained end of you.

"Listen," the thing said, and Tot Hamsey was powerless not to.

My mother has told me that he came home around sunrise. He'd been gone overnight before, so that hadn't worried her. Sometimes he had a two-man project to do—a new windmill to get up or a stock tank that needed to be mucked out—so she had slept that night, me in my crib in the other bedroom, imagining him holed up in a rickety outbuilding in the badlands, eating biscuits hard as stones and listening to that blowhard Mac Brazeall say how it was in moldy-oldy times. She was not surprised when she heard the truck, or when she looked out the window to see him standing at the gate to the yard. He would do that

on occasion, she thought. Collect himself for a minute. Slap the dust
from his jeans or shake out his slicker and scrape his boots clean if it
had rained. Then he'd come in, say howdy to Reilly, maybe swing him
around a time or two, and over breakfast thereafter tell what could be
told about doings in the hardscrabble way west of them.

But for a long time, too long to be no account, he didn't move.
He had a finger on the gatepost and it seemed he was taking its
pulse. Behind the curtain, my mother watched, her own self as still
as he. He'd lost his hat, evidently, and half of his face, like a clown's,
seemed red as war paint. She wasn't scared, she said to me more
than once. Not yet. This was her husband, a decent man top to bottom, and she had known him since the third grade. She'd seen him
dance and, drunk on whiskey, play the piano with his elbows. He
could sit a horse well and had a concern for the small gestures of
courtesy that are now and then necessary to use between folks. So
there was nothing to be frightened of, not even when he came in the
front door and she could see that his eyes had turned small and hard,
like nail heads.

Whatever wound in him was wound too tight, she thought. Whatever spun, now spinning too fast.

After that, she says, events happened very quickly. He gathered up
several tablets and disappeared into his workshop, a pole barn he'd
built himself back behind the clothesline. She put his breakfast out—
bacon from Milt Morris's slaughterhouse and eggs she'd put a little
Tabasco in—but in an hour it was still outside the door. She could hear
him in there, a man with a hammer and saw, something being built.
Or something coming apart. She took me to the Hawkinses' house so
I could play with their boy Michael. At noon he was still in the shop,
the door shut.

"Tot," she said. "You hungry for lunch?"

She could hear him, she thought. Like the fevered scraping and
scratching of a rodent in a wall.

Later, the afternoon worn white with sunlight, she told him Sonny
Fitzpatrick was on the phone.

"He wants you there first thing in the morning, okay?"

She tried the door then, but something was blocking it, and she could only see a little through the space: Tot Hamsey's back bent to a task on the table in front of him.

"Tot?" she said.

He turned then, eyes hooded, nothing in his expression to suggest that he knew her from anybody else who'd once upon a time crossed his narrow path—a look, she said later, that froze the innermost part of her. The vein or the nerve that was like wire at her very center.

"I'll tell him you'll be there," she said.

After she picked me up at the Hawkinses' house, she tried the door again. This time it didn't move, so she went to the window. He was still at the bench, a leather apron on, passing a piece of metal back and forth in his big hands. She could see now that the door had been blocked by his table saw, a machine that had taken both him and her to move four months before. Exasperated, she rapped on the window.

"Supper in an hour," she said.

But he didn't come out for that. Nor for the serial on the radio. Nor for my bath, or for the story time that was supposed to follow. At the back door, she stood to watch the workshop. The lights were on, but he'd put a cover over the window. A sheet possibly.

This time she knocked harder. His supper dishes were still on the step. Untouched. "You've got to eat something," she called. "Tot Hamsey?"

A moment later, she'd said his name again. And again. She thought he was just on the other side of the door, maybe his face, like her own, against the wood, the two of them—except for the pine boards—cheek to cheek. He was huffing, she thought. As if he'd raced a mile to be there. As if he had more miles to go.

"Oh, honey," she sighed.

It was the same the next day, she has said. And the day after that. No evidence that he'd come out of the workshop. Only the slightest sign that he'd eaten. Once she thought to call his father, Milt Hamsey, but he was the meddlesome type, quick to condemn, slow to forgive. A holier-than-thou sort with a walleye and hair in his ears and no patience whatsoever with the ordinary back and forth of lived life. Too much anger in him. Like a spike in the heart.

No, she thought. Tot was only fretful about something. Or working an idea to a point. Besides, it was nobody's business what went on
in Tot and Corrine Hamsey's house.

On the fourth day, she got the newspaper from the box by the
fence line near the road. Whiskered Mac Brazeall was in it, a picture
of his idiotic self on the front page, with his cockamamie story about
the flying saucer parts he'd found off the Elko trail leading into the
Jornada. Other articles about bogeymen in the skies above Canada
and Kansas and all over the West. The base was involved, she read.
Soldiers and officials from the government everywhere. Maybe spies.
Just about the most far-fetched thing she'd ever heard of.

At the step to the workshop, she asked Tot if he knew anything
about this. "You were out there," she said. "That's where you were,
right?"

Tot Hamsey came toward the door then. She heard the table saw
being shoved aside. He would look like a hermit, she believed. Ravaged and blighted. Then he was in front of her, not a giant step away,
and she thought briefly that he'd had his heart ripped right out of him.

"What's it say?" he asked, his first words in nearly one hundred
hours.

"You coming out?" she wondered.

He had that look still. Murder in him maybe. Or fear. "Give it
here," he said.

Now she was scared, a part of her already edging back toward the
house. The room behind him, though ordered as her own kitchen, was
cold as an icebox, the smell of it stale, like what you might find if you
opened a trunk from another century. She told herself not to gasp.

"This has to stop," she said.

"It will," he told her. He was reading the paper now, his lips moving as if he were chewing up the words.

"When?" she said, but the door was already closing.

They had reached an understanding, she decided. She was not to
trouble him anymore. She had her own self and me to tend to. If anybody called—Sonny again, for example, or nosy Norris Proctor or
Tommy Tyree from the Elks Club, anybody wanting anything from citizen Hamsey—she was to make up an excuse. A broken leg, maybe.

The summer flu. A lie, anyway, he and she could one day laugh about. In turn, she was to get about her own business. She would have to call her dad for money, but that was okay. He owned two hardware stores and was rich enough for three families.

She was to wait, she thought. A hole had opened in her life, hers now the job to see what creature crawled free from it.

He possessed treasure, he says on the tapes. Not the pirate kind. Not wealth, but secrets. "My name is Totenham Gregory Hamsey," he scribbled on the first page of the tablet I would one day find. "I was born in 1918, on March the 13th. My mother says I was a sweet child." For page after page, he goes on that way, his handwriting like a million spiders seen from above. He'd seen a human die, he wrote, and had watched another, me, being birthed. He knew a U.S. senator and had shaken the hand of Roy Rogers. In Espanola, he'd ridden a Brahman bull and had taken a trolley in Juarez, Mexico. "I look good in swim trunks," he says on one page, "and have a membership at the Roswell Country Club. I am no golfer, though." He knows bridge and canasta and can juggle five apples. Jazz music he doesn't like, but he'll listen once to whatever you put on the record player.

"I have knowledge," he writes, and by page twenty-six he has started to give it. Pictures of how it is where they live. Their tribe names and what they do in space. The beliefs of them, their many conquests. They are us, he says, but for the accidents of where and when we are.

On the fifth day, according to the tapes in his file cabinets, he goes into the house. He doesn't know where his wife and child are. Nor does he much care. They could be strangers, people at a wayside: They're going one way, he another.

Beside the couch in the living room, he finds the stack of newspapers—the Army everywhere and Sheriff Johnny Freel looking boneheaded. It's a weather balloon, my father reads. A rawinsonde, a new design, a balloon big as a building in New York City. A colonel from Fort Worth has confirmed this to all who thought the opposite. The intelligence officer from the base, Jesse Marcel himself, has put minds at rest. Mac Brazeall, cowpuncher, was mistaken, wrong as wrong could be. Not spacemen after all. Not Communists, either. Just Uncle Sam measuring winds aloft. All is well again.

He feels sorry for them, my father says. They have small minds. They are insects.

For the next hour, he busies himself with practical matters. He gets out his good suit. For the journey. He showers, shaves, and brushes his teeth. He eats, for fuel only. He settles his affairs. "I am not coming back," he writes to my mother in a note he'll put on the dining room table. "You are young. You can be good to someone else."

Outside, the landscape fascinates. Dry and cracked and endless. Storm clouds boiling up in the distance. They are there. His friends.

"Reilly," he writes to me in the same note, "study. Know your sentences and your sums. Do not give offense to your elders. Keep yourself clean. We move. We ascend. We vanish."

Carefully, he dresses. It is important, he thinks, that he look presentable. He wears cuff links, stuffs a handkerchief in his coat pocket. In the mirror, he sees a man of virtuous aspect—hair nicely combed, shoulders squared, tie in a handsome Windsor knot. He hears himself breathing, amused that he still needs our air.

On the phone, he asks for Charlie Spiller personally. "I need a taxi," he says. "In one hour."

He imagines Charlie Spiller on the other end of the line. A man with a fake leg. A lodge brother. Another creepy-crawly thing from a vulgar kingdom.

"One hour," he says. "Exactly."

He's at the end of something, clearly. All that can be done has been done. He is not here. Not really. The past has closed behind him. He's gone through a door, a seam. There is no point in looking back.

On the dresser in the bedroom, he leaves his wallet and his Longines wristwatch. For a little while, sadly, he will need money. To pay Charlie. To pay for the Greyhound bus. To eat a sandwich along the way. He will not need his driver's license. Nor other papers. He is not anybody to know. None of us is. We are wind and dirt and ash. We are weight that falls, flesh that burns. We are oil and mud. We are slow and cannot run. We are blind and do not see. We are echo and shadow and mist.

At the workshop, he checks the padlock. Inside, beneath the floorboards, in a pit he has dug, are his secrets. His papers wrapped in oilcloth. In the box are the metals. The mesh-like panels. The tiny I-beams. Dials and switches and wires. His keepsakes from the future.

He turns once to look at the house. He imagines his thoughts like laundry on a line. All is well.

"This is not lunacy," he says on the tapes I would find. "I'm a man who's died and come back, is all."

At the dirt road by the fence line is the place he needs to be in a minute. Charlie Spiller drives a Dodge, a big car to go places in. Charlie Spiller cackles like a crone and can take direction. He can tell a joke and crack his knuckles, tricks to perform in the places he goes. Charlie Spiller: Another human to forget about.

From his pocket, my father takes his keys and throws them as far as he can into the desert. He straightens his tie, shoots his cuffs, and buttons his suit coat.

If it is sunny, he does not know. If raining, he cannot feel it. Instead, he has a place to be and a passel of desire to be there. He speaks to his feet, to his legs and hips, to the obedient muscles in each.

The voices. They've returned. The stones have messages for him. The cactus. The furniture he's leaving behind. Much is being revealed. Of sovereigns and viceroys. Of sand and of rocks. Listen. You can hear them. Like water. Like lava a mile beneath your feet.

"I had knowledge," he says. "My name was Tot Hamsey. All was well."

2.

IN 1980, for all the reasons unique to modern times (boredom, mainly, plus anger and some sickness at the pickiness of us), Cece Phillips and I went bust. She got the house in Odessa, not to mention custody of Nora Jane (like her mother, a specimen of womanhood sharp-tongued and fast to laugh at dim-wittedness), and I came back here, to Roswell. The city liked well enough what it read on paper and

so put me to work in the engineering department where I compute
the numbers relevant to curbs and gutters and how you get streets to
drain. Besides the physical, you should know, much had changed
about me. I'd sworn off anything stronger than Pepsi and did not use
a credit card and had learned to play handball at the YMCA on Washington Avenue. In the mayor's office next door, I met a Clerical II,
Sharon Sweeny, and spent enough agreeable hours with her at the
movies and the like to think, in boy-girl matters of moon and June at
least, that two and two equaled more than the four you'd expect. I ate
square meals, cleaned up my apartment regularly, and kept my p's and
q's in the order they're notorious for.

Then, in 1981, the curious son of a curious man, I went to visit my
father.

"You're Reilly," he said, his first words to me in decades.

"I am," I said, mine to him.

He was living in, quote, a residential facility, meaning that if you've
got enough money, you can break bread in what looks like a combination hospital and resort motel with a bunch of harmless drunks and
narcotics addicts and taxpayers who need to scrub their hands thirty
times before they can dress in the morning. He'd been there since
early in 1954, after my grandfather—who is himself dead now—found
him up at the New Mexico State Hospital in Las Vegas and drew up
papers that said, as papers from rich men can, that T. G. Hamsey
could live at the Sunset Manor here until the day arrived to put him
in the family plot in the cemetery on Pennsylvania Street.

I didn't recognize him. Umpteen-umpteens had gone by, and I was
looking for the stringbean adult in the snapshots my mother had given
me. He was collapsed, if you must know. Time had come down cruel
on him, the way it will on all of us. Plus he was over sixty years old.

"Do you have a cigarette?" he said.

We were standing in a lobby-like affair, couches and end tables
with lamps on them, the windows beyond us giving onto a view of
Kmart and Dairy Queen and all else crummy the block had become.

I'd quit, I told him.

"Perhaps next time," he said.

He was a stranger, as unknown to me as I am to the Queen of England. He was just a man, I was telling myself, one I shared no more than cell matter with.

"Are you scared, Reilly?"

That wasn't the word, I told him. Not scared.

"What is the word, then, son?"

I didn't know. Honest.

"I'm something you've heard of, right? I'm a river to visit. A monument somebody wrote about. Maybe a city to go to."

We had sat, him in an armchair that seemed too small, me catty-corner on a leather couch so slick you could slide off. I wanted to leave, I'll admit. It was my lunch hour, and I thought of myself at El Popo's, eating Mexican food with my friends, little more to fret about than what paper needed to be pushed in the afternoon and which shoot-'em-up Sharon Sweeny and I could munch popcorn in front of that night at the Fiesta.

"I knew you'd come," he said.

It was hot outside, the heat shimmering up in waves from the asphalt parking lot, but I yearned to be out there in it, striding toward my car.

"Just didn't know when," he said. "You're a Hamsey."

True enough, I thought. Cece Phillips had once told me that I was about as predictable as time itself.

"How is she?" he asked. "Your mother."

She was in Albuquerque now, I said. She'd married again—not the colonel from NMMI when I was in high school, but the man after the man after the man after him.

"That's good," he said. "She used to come by, you know."

"A long time ago," I said.

That was right, he said. A long time ago, she used to visit with him, in this very room, tell him how it was with his parents and his brothers. With herself. With even their growing-up son.

"You didn't say much," I told him. "That's what Mother says."

He cast me a look then—equal parts disappointment and confusion. "That's not how I remember it."

He seemed fragile and delicate, not a man who once upon a time could heft a hay bale or hog-tie a calf. He was neither the snapshots

I'd seen nor the stories I'd heard. He was just a human being the government counts every ten years.

"I'm tired," he said.

He was dismissing me, so I stood.

"Shall we shake hands?" he asked.

I had no reason not to, so we did, his the full and firm squeeze of a candidate for Congress.

"You'll come back?" he said.

I had been raised to be polite, I was thinking. Plus this had only cost me minutes, of which I had a zillion.

"Next Friday," I said.

Nodding, he let my hand go then, and I turned. This was my father, crackpot. Loony-bird. This was Totenham Gregory Hamsey. And I, suddenly thick-jointed and light-headed and not breathing very well, was his son.

"Reilly," he called.

I had reached the door, only a few feet between his life and my own.

"Don't forget those smokes, okay?"

He was a man who'd survived a disaster, I thought. A fall from a ship or a tumble down the side of a mountain. He'd walked through a jungle or maybe had himself washed miles and miles away by a flash flood. Buried alive or lost on Antarctica, sucked up in a tornado or raised by wolves—he was as much a figure out of a fairy tale as he was a man whose scribblings on the subjects of time and space and visitors I would eventually read often enough to memorize whole sections. Yes, he had horror in his head, events and visions and dreams like layers of sediment, but that day he only wanted cigarettes. So, the next week, I brought them.

"Luckies," he said, smelling the carton. "A good choice."

"A guess," I said. "I didn't know you smoked."

"I have seniority," he told me. "I do what I like."

This time we didn't sit in the lobby. We went to his room, and walking down the corridor he pointed at various doors. "Estelle Barnes," he said at one. "A dingbat. Nice woman, but thinks she's a ballet dancer. Sad." At another, he said, "Marcus Stillwell. Barks a lot.

Sounds like a fox terrier." It was like that all the way: people said to weep or babble or to seek instruction and wisdom from their house-pets—our own selves, I told Sharon Sweeny that night, except for chance and dread and bubbles in the brain.

At his own door, he jiggled the knob. "Locks," he said. "I'm the king of the hill here."

It was like an apartment—a class-A kitchen, a sitting room, a siz-able bath, a bedroom—the fussed-over living quarters of a tenant whose only bad habit is watching the clock.

"You like?" he asked.

I'd thought it would different, I told him. Smaller.

He looked around then, as if this were the first time that he him-self had seen the place. "Yeah," he said. "Me, too."

I almost asked him then. I really did. I almost asked what you would, which is Why and What and Why again. But, owing to what I guess is the me of me—which has nothing to do with the pounds and inches of you nor the face you're born with—I didn't. I was only a vis-itor; he, just an old fellow with a dozen file cabinets and maybe a thou-sand books to call his pals.

"You turned out okay," he said.

I had, I thought. I really had.

"You know," he began, "I've seen you a couple of times before." He was sitting across from me, his head tilted, a cigarette held to his lips. "Come here," he said, rising and beckoning me to his window. "Over there."

Outside, nearly a hundred yards away, stood the back of a 7-Eleven. Beyond that ran the highway to Clovis—the Cactus Motel and the Wilson Brothers' Feed and Seed. The sight wasn't much to whoop over, just buildings and dirt and three roads I had once calculated the code-meeting dimensions of.

"You had a city car," he said, gazing afar as though I were out there now. "You wore a tie. And cowboy boots."

He was right. Eight months earlier I'd been with a survey crew—storm drains and new concrete guttering—and now I was standing here, seeing what he'd seen.

"You have your mother's walk," he said.

Cars were going up that street, and I remembered being out there, once or twice turning to look at where I stood now, once or twice one wet winter day thinking I knew somebody in that building. My father.

"You're a boss, I take it."

Sort of, I told him. There was a wisenheimer, Phelps Boykin, I reported to.

He was still staring straight ahead, and as if by magic I imagined I was inside his head, feeling time snag and ravel up, the present overwhelmed by the past. He was at my shoulder, me close enough to smell him, and he was leaning forward, nose almost to the glass. His hand had come up, small and speckled with liver spots, my own hand in twenty or thirty more years, and it seemed, having recognized something out there, he was going to wave hello.

"You know what I'd like?" he said.

That hand, unmoving and open and pale, was still up, and, my own hand twitching at my side, I had no idea what he'd like.

"An ice cream," he said. "I'd like a dish of vanilla ice cream."

The tapes don't say a lot about the state hospital in Las Vegas, a ragtag collection of brick buildings—one of them, maximum security, surrounded by barbed wire atop chain-link high enough to fence out giraffes, and each with a view of the boring flatlands you have to traipse across to get out of the Land of Enchantment. All I came to know is that Charlie Spiller drove Totenham G. Hamsey to the Greyhound bus station, where the latter bought his ticket and got aboard with nothing in his hands but air and heat, him in a seat all to himself. He says he stood at the hospital's door until they took him in. Says he marched up to the receptionist's desk and told that wig-wearing woman that he knew exactly where he belonged, that he could see into the knobs and fissures of her soul, that she was like we all are, which is puny and whiny and weak—just spines with blabbing meat at the top.

She was goggle-eyed, he says, and looked up and down for the joke. Says he stripped to his undershorts and shoes then, to show her that he meant business, and uttered not another peep until a director, a fussbudget with an eyebrow like a caterpillar and hair like a thatched roof, escorted him into an office for a man-to-man chat, whereupon time—"of which," he says, "there is too goddamn much"—went zoom, zoom, zoom, and the past snapped away from him like a kite from a string in a hurricane.

I'm not sure I believe any of this, though I like the idea of a Hamsey semi-naked in a public place. Still, given what I know—from the tapes, from the papers in the boxes and files in his apartment, from two visits to his hidey-hole at the farm—all he said seems as straightforward as breakfast. Given the givens, especially how I turn out in this story, I sometimes see him chalk-faced, his teeth gritted, outerwear at his feet, no light or noise in his world except that rising up in him from memory, nothing but gravity to keep him earthbound, only ordinary years between him and eternity.

When he was alive—when I was visiting on Fridays and taking him to the Sonic for a chili-cheeseburger or out with Sharon Sweeny and me to the Bottomless Lakes for a cookout—he didn't talk much about such matters. Talked instead about the Texas Rangers, whose games he listened to on KBIM, and about the mayor's father, Hob Lucero, a man he'd busted broncos with, and what it's like to tango and box waltz with someone named Flo, and how to tell if your cantaloupe is ripe or which nail to use when you're pounding up wallboard.

He was a Republican, he said one week. Which meant to him gold bullion and gushing smokestacks and cars you hired a wetback to polish twice a month.

Then, a week later, he asked me about NORAD—what I knew of it.

"What?" I said. I was preoccupied by a loud difference of opinion I'd had with Phelps Boykin earlier that morning.

"The Marine Corps has a metallurgy lab in Hagerstown, Maryland," he said.

He was mainly talking to himself, I thought. Didn't make a whit of difference who sat in the seat beside him.

"They're liars," he said. "Lowdown pencil pushers who wouldn't know the truth if it bit them on the hindmost."

Here it was I left off thinking about crabby Phelps Boykin, supervisor, and took up the subject of cracked Totenham Hamsey, father. It was a moment, I think now, as dramatic in its circumstances as maybe gunfire might be to you in yours.

"Del Rio, Texas," he announced. "December 1950. A colonel—one Robert Willingham—reports an object flying at high speed. Crashes. He finds a piece of metal, honeycombed. Had a lot of carbon in it. Cutting torch wouldn't melt the damn thing."

He put a Lucky to his lips, took a puff, held it for seven beats of my crosswise heart.

"There's more," he said. "A whole lot more."

We were parked off McGaffey Road, southwest of town, the two of us eating burritos in a city car. Across the prairie the humps of the Capitan Mountains were the nearest geography between us and another time zone. We'd been doing this for nearly two years, going to Cahoon Park or down to Dexter or up to Six-Mile Hill. Father and son—an hour or two of this or that.

"There's hoaxes," he said, still gazing afar. "Spitsbergen Island off Norway, September 1952. Aztec, New Mexico. March 1948. A yahoo named Silas Newton says there were seventeen hundred scientists out there. You can't imagine some of the goofballs running around."

I was looking at the ground, specifically a slumped area a few yards ahead of us. For a moment it seemed that something grotesque might charge out of it, and me with only a greasy paper bag and a new driver's license to defend myself.

"You don't believe this, do you?"

Clouds roiled off in this distance, shapes that ought to be meaningful to someone like me. "Not really," I said.

"It's like God, isn't it?" he said. "Maybe necromancy. Or fortune-telling."

Sharon Sweeny believed in God, I told him. Which was all right. And Cece Phillips had recently said that our daughter, Nora Jane, believed in ghosts and astrology. But me, I didn't blow much one way or the other.

"That's too bad," he said.

It was about as useful, I told him, as pretending you could fly or see through walls.

"There's a lot like you," he said.

I had started the car, the air-conditioning throwing a fine cold blast on my hot face. "I've got to get back," I said. "There's a man I have to see."

He was sitting up straight now, his the expression teachers get when you mess up, and I realized that two conversations had been taking place, but me with only ears enough for one.

"I could tell you everything," he said at last.

I revved the engine—more cold air, more words in it to worry about.

"I could do that right now, Reilly. All you have to do is give me the go-ahead."

I was thinking furiously. Me with a brain like a Looney Tunes engine, all its clever gears whirling and spitting off sparks. He could tell me. About the third of July in 1947 and all since. About his leaving. About my mother and me, left behind.

"What do you say, son?"

We stood at a crossroads, I believed. In one direction lay the past; in the other, tomorrow and the tomorrows after that. One was mystery and sore hearts and done deeds you couldn't undo; the other, me and a girlfriend and a GMC truck to make payments on.

"No, sir," I told him. "I don't need to know any of that."

Which is how we left it for that month, August, and the next, and those others that passed before he showed up at my office late in May, him in a suit coat and white shirt and handsome string tie. As fashionable as a State Farm agent.

"I walked," he said. He looked flushed, maybe thirsty for an ocean of water, so I asked him if he wanted a fruit juice or an RC from the machine in Drafting.

"You're a messy one, aren't you?" he said, waving at my desk and my table and my cabinets, charts and state-issue reference works piled haphazardly atop each. "Hamseys, so far as I can tell, are not a cluttering people."

"Yes, sir," I said. Clearly, he had something in mind. A surprise to spring on his only child.

"Your mother kept a clean house."

He was right about that, too. So spotless and tidied that one Friday near Easter I'd come home from school after track practice (I threw the shot) and, my house as still as a tomb, I'd thought that my mother, like her husband before her, had also vanished.

"Tell me about her," he said. "The man she married." He was smoking now, flicking his ashes in his cuff, his movements deliberate and precise, as if he had to explain to his shoulder and his elbow and his fingers what to do.

"His name is Barnett," I said. "Mother calls him Hub. He's something at Sandia Labs. Management of some sort."

He took another drag—not much air in here to push the smoke around. "Military?" he asked.

I didn't think so, I said. He was about to retire.

"A big man, I'm guessing. Your mother liked big men."

I hadn't thought about it, I admitted. Hub was about average size, maybe a bit overweight. Had a big laugh, though. Like Santa Claus.

"A man of substance, I take it."

Tot Hamsey was like an adding machine, I thought. This information, then more, eventually the sum he was adding for.

"Is he kind?" my father said.

I guessed so, I told him. Didn't exactly know.

"Corrine never went for coarse types," he said. "Ask Norris Proctor."

It was a name, like many others, I could not attach to a face. Tommy Murphy, Pug Thigpen, Mutt Mantle, Judge Willy Freedlander—these were people I'd only heard of, names no more than jibber-jabber to go in one ear and out the other. Folks either old or gone or dead.

"I don't have any regrets, Reilly. Not a one."

He was gazing at the most impressive of my wall maps, the city's zoning laid out in a patchwork of pink and blue and red and yellow, section after section after section of do's and don't's—where you could manufacture and peddle, where you could only sleep and mow your lawn—a world I probably took too much satisfaction in being a little bit responsible for.

"Project Mogul, they called it," he was saying. "Radar targets—foil, so the story goes—being strung from a balloon."

"Yes, sir," I said. This was his surprise: the there and then that had become the here and now.

"The 509th," he said, "right here in Roswell. Only air group trained to handle and drop atomic bombs."

I felt as I had that Friday afternoon near Easter. With my heart like a fist in my throat, I started to tell him again that I didn't want to know any of that talk.

"Sit down, Reilly," he said. He was speaking to me as he'd once himself been spoken to; so, looking at him as I guess he'd looked at it, I did. "Pay attention, boy. I don't have all day."

I was to wait. To sit here as I had there. I was to be quiet. Above all, I was to concentrate on something—that color photograph, say—and not look away from it until the floor was the floor again, and I would not be falling toward it.

"Project Sign," he was saying, "ATIC in Dayton. Hell, Barry Goldwater's in this. You still with me?"

I was. Me. And the photo. And the floor. And one man of substance.

CUFOS, Erv Dill, Ubatuba in Brazil, 1957, 1968, Nellis Air Force base in Nevada, magnesium, strontium, the Dew Line, *True* magazine, radio intercepts, MUFON, the sky, the Vega Galaxy, the suits they wear, the vapors we are helpless without, the bodies in the desert, the sorry-ass home our rock is, the swoop and swell, the various holes in heaven—all this and more he said, me and the walls his respectful audience. And then, loopy as time to a toad, a half hour had gone by, and he was through looking at the map.

"I'm not crazy, Reilly."

I told Sharon Sweeny later that I was playing a game in my head—*A* is for apple, *B* for ball—me not capable of offering aloud anything neutral yet. I was at *F*—for fog—when he spoke again.

"There's no power, son, no glory. There's nothing—just them and us and the things we walk on. I have proof." Wiping his forehead with a tissue he'd drawn from his trousers, he seemed finished, the back a little straighter, no spit at the corners of the mouth. "Here," he said, another item from his pocket.

I took it. A key ring. Maybe ten keys attached.

"My files," he said.

G, I was thinking. What was G for?

Sharon Sweeny—my sweetie then, my Mrs. now—says the call that Thursday came at about the exact minute Peter Jennings was demonstrating how soggy it was in rain-soaked West Table, Missouri. I have no memory of this; nor have I any recollection of going to the phone and barking "hello" in a manner meant to mean "no" to those interrupting my dinner hour to sell me something.

Sharon Sweeny—as right a wife for me as white is right for rice—reports I said "yes" two times, the latter less loud and certainly with too much s in it.

Next, I've heard, I sat. In the chair by the table I usually pay my bills from. I eased the phone away from my ear, I am told, and regarded it as naked primitives are said to stare at mirrors. I appeared frazzled, my foot tapping as it will when I have eight somethings to say but only one something to say it with. I am told—by Sharon Sweeny, who was between bites and only a few steps away—that I mumbled only one sentence before I hung up, which was "I see," words she thinks must've taken all I had of strength and will to get loose. When I stood, she tells me, it seemed also an act with maximum effort in it.

"Where're you going?" she says she said.

On a hook by the front door hung my jacket, and Sharon Sweeny claims I approached it as though I expected the sleeves to choke me.

"Quik-Mart," I evidently told her. "I'd like a cigarette."

She was frightened, hers truly on the brink of teetering or breaking into a full run. "Who was on the phone?" she asked.

"I haven't smoked in years," it's said I said. "But tonight, just now, I'd like a pack. It's a foul habit, you know. Hard as the dickens to break. I wouldn't wish it on anyone. Not a blessed soul. You believe me, right?"

She had come toward me, I understand, a woman now close enough to see the focus flashing in and out of her man's eyes, him with his chin lifted as though listening for a sound not to be heard twice in a lifetime.

"Reilly?"

So, his own strange news to deliver, Reilly told her: Totenham Hamsey, middle initial G., was dead.

Congestive heart failure, it was, that old man going down at the feet of his dance partner Estelle Barnes, would-be ballerina, still eight or nine bars left of "Woodchoppers' Ball." But, as I say, I remember not an iota of how I came to share this knowledge with my beloved big-boned Clerical II. I do not remember the next day, either, nor the day that replaced it. About the funeral, at the grave site his father had paid for years and years earlier, I recall only a single incident—me and my mother and her husband Hub and a preacher named Wyatt who looked like he was trying out for a community theater musical, plus a handful of residents from the Sunset Manor, accompanied by a nurse who stood as though she had wood screws in her heels, and sunlight pouring down on us like molten metal but me not melted in the middle, and then Sharon Sweeny, my hand held in hers, leaning to my ear to whisper, "Stop humming, sweetheart. I can't hear what the man's saying."

The day after that, I recovered myself, came to—in my father's apartment, me appointed to move his stuff out to somewhere else. His colognes, I think, hastened me back. Frenchy fragrances of vanilla and briar and oily smoke—odd for a fellow never known, so my mother has since said, for other than Vicks or Old Spice. "Sweet smellies," he'd called them that first day he'd showed me around. So there I was, with several packing boxes from city hall, me too big in a bathroom too brightly lit to flatter, feeling myself return, as if to earth itself, inch by inch by inch, until I had no one to lead me about except the familiar blockhead in the mirror and him in need of both a haircut and a professional shave. Mother wanted none of this—not out of meanness, I hold—so Sharon Sweeny had made arrangements with the Salvation Army to take all it had a use for; I was the help, a job I'd apparently said yes to when, after the casket was lowered, that nurse with the sore feet had waddled over to remind me of the workaday consequences of death.

I packed his clothes next, only two sacks of mostly white dress shirts and dark slacks you apparently are urged to buy in lots of ten, plus lace-up shoes—all black—that you could wear for another half century. For reasons owing to sentimentality and the like, or so Sharon Sweeny later insisted, I kept the string tie for myself, it being his neck-wear the last time we'd visited. Then, the kitchen having only food and drink to throw away and not much of either, I went to the living room and, my innards clotted and pebbly and heaped up hard beneath my ribs, stood in front of the steel cabinets I had the keys for.

"My treasure," he'd said four days earlier. "Yours now."

Out the window I noticed the spot where, years before, he'd seen me at work in boots and my own starched white shirt. I imagined him watching me then, as abstract and fixed as my mother had been the morning, years and years before that, when she stood behind her curtains to study him at their gate, nothing in him—I would soon enough learn—but ice and wind and heavy silence.

"You take care, Reilly," he had said in my office, and now, no other chore to distract me, I was.

For company, I had turned the TV on—*General Hospital*, I recall, in which attractive inhabitants from a made-up metropolis were falling in love or scheming diligently against one another. They were named Scorpio and Monica and Laura and Bobbi, and for a moment, it as long as one in war, I desired to be at the center of them: Reilly Jay Hamsey in a fancy Italian suit, his teeth as white as Chiclets, him with lines to orate and a well-groomed crowd happy to hear them.

"In the shop," he had said. "At the farm. That's where."

I was fingering the keys, each no bigger than my thumb. One fit one cabinet, another another, and all I had to do was turn locks clockwise, no real work whatsoever for the hand and wrist of me.

"Under the floorboards, son."

T. G. Hamsey, I was thinking. Son of Milton Hamsey, banker, and Vanetta Fountain Hamsey, homemaker. Brother of Winston Lee, oilman, and Benjamin Wright, bankrupt cattle baron. All deceased. Nothing now but these cabinets and me. In one, only papers and tape recordings; in the other, bone and flesh and blood.

Music had come up from next door, a foot-tappy ditty that for a minute I endeavored to keep the steady beat of.

In the desert that night years ago, Cece Phillips had declared that we—you, me, all the king's men—had been put here on earth for a purpose: "We're meant to be the things we are," she said. It was an idea fine to have, I told her, if you're sitting atop a pile of us and have nothing at all but more whoop-de-do to look forward to. "Fine to have," I'd said, "if you don't have to get up when the alarm says to."

That's what I was thinking when I slipped the key in the lock of the leftmost cabinet. What if you're one Reilly Hamsey, a middle-aged municipal employee with only a remote control to boss around and tomorrow already coming up over England? What if, no matter the wishes you've wished, you've nothing above your shoulders but mush and nothing in your wallet but five dollars and nothing in your pants pockets but Juicy Fruit gum? What if, when your hand turns and the lock clicks open and that first drawer slides out, you're always going to be the you you are, and this will always be the air you breathe, and that will always be the ragged rim of the world you see?

"I hate them," my father had said, teary-eyed. "Look what they've done to me."

On the TV a wedding was taking place, Lance to Marissa, their friends and relations elbow to elbow and beaming, squabbles and woes set for the occasion aside. They were gowned and sequined and fit, no illnesses to afflict, no worries that wouldn't—in one episode or another—disappear, theirs the tragedies you only need a wand to wave away.

"Hey," I said, addressing those Americans from the American Broadcasting Company. "Look what I'm doing here."

3.

THEY HAD crammed it all in his head, he'd said on the tapes. What conveyances to take, the packs of them, their minerals and gases, the councils they sit at, their rectitude in matters moral, their currencies, their contempt for us. They have prisons for their villains, schools for their youngsters. They have nationalities, Chancellors and princes, blood allegiances to fight for. Leaders have risen up among them.

They are disappointed, spite-filled. "They have been to the end of it," he'd said. "Where the days run out. The minutes. Where the fires are."

The fires—one image to have between the ears the day Sharon Sweeny and I parked at the road leading to the farm. The place wasn't much to look at, the city having crept up to the nearby cotton fields, the irrigation canals mostly intact but the fence line in need of expensive repair.

"You still own it?" Sharon asked.

My grandfather had sold it, I told her, maybe five years after. Part of the proceeds had put me through college. The rest my mother had given me for the house in Odessa.

We'd stopped for a Coke on the way out, and she was drinking the last of it now, looking at the tumbledown buildings, while I, like a clerk, was scrambling to sort out my thoughts big to little. "Seems tiny, doesn't it?" I said at last.

"When I visit my parents in Socorro," she began, "I can't believe I ever lived there. I mean, it's like a dollhouse."

The day was bright, the sun as fierce this morning as it would be this afternoon, nothing between it and us but seconds, and I was glad I'd brought a hat.

"You ready?" she asked.

Briefly, before the roof of my stomach caved in, I thought I was. "Give me a moment, okay?"

I'd dreamed about this last night. I'd read his documents, page after page that seemed less scribbled on than shouted at. I'd listened to his tapes, hours and hours of them, and then, Saturday already faint in the east, I'd dreamed. Me. And treasure to find. And strong Sharon Sweeny to help.

"You think she'll like me?" she was saying.

My eye was focused on a tumbleweed snagged on the barbed wire at the gate, my mind on the single reason for not backing out of there. "Who?"

Nora, she said. Nora Jane.

I had forgotten. My daughter, a sophomore at Texas Tech, was coming over for summer break—a chance to meet Sharon Sweeny and maybe later tell her mother, Cece Phillips Hamsey, what good fortune her old man had finally stumbled into—and, Christ, I had forgotten.

"Cece says she likes golf," I said. "Maybe you can take her over to Spring River for a round."

I felt tottery, I tell you, as different from myself as tea is from tin. And before I gave in to the coward in me, I imagined myself standing down the way a bit toward town, me a shitkicker with nothing to do but stroll past that unremarkable couple sitting in the city car at the end of a rutted road leading to one ramshackle house.

"We could leave," I told Sharon Sweeny, which prompted her to lift her eyebrows and take my closest hand.

"No, we couldn't, Reilly."

She was right, but I would require several more moments, thoughts surfacing twelve at a time, to realize that.

"There's money," I said. "Seems he had a lot of it. I found a Norwest bankbook."

That was dandy, she said. And I believed she meant it.

"We could get a house," I told her. "I always wanted a swimming pool."

That was also dandy, vocabulary I now couldn't hear too much of.

"Nora could have her own room. Maybe spend more time with us. A real family."

Her hand tightened on mine, and something sharp and whole and nearly perfect passed between us.

"Reilly," she said. "Start the car."

Like my father, I guess now, I too am excellent at following orders, so I did as told, pleased both by how I kept my hands on the wheel as we rolled up closer and closer and closer, and by the fact that I could look left and right if I wanted to.

"How long's it been abandoned?" she asked.

Didn't know, I told her. Tax records described it as a lease farm, the land owned by a conglomerate out of Lubbock. Mostly silage was being grown. Cotton every now and then.

"It was pretty, I bet."

The night before, yes, I had dreamed about this. One tape, then another. Tot Hamsey's voice raspy and thick and slow, as though it were oozing up through his legs out of the ground itself. Then, my bed ten sizes too small and ten times too lumpy, dreams. Of spacemen. Of smoke. Of one sky rent clean in half.

"It won't be there," she was saying. "The box."

I had braked to a stop beneath a Chinese elm more dead than alive, the uprights for the adjacent wood fence wind-bent in a way not comforting to contemplate.

"You'll see," she said. "It's a delusion. A fantasy."

Half of me wanted her to be right, and it said so.

"He was a nice man," she said. "Just—well, you know."

I did, and said as much—not the worst sentiment, even if wrong, that can go back and forth between beings.

"Let's eat afterwards," she said. "I'm starved." She had her sunglasses on now, her feet on the dash, a paperback mystery in her lap. Her toenails were painted and, time creaking backward inside of me, I believed pink the finest, smartest color ever invented by the finest and smartest of our kind.

"Sweetheart," she said. "Put your hat on."

Which I did. And soon I was out and the trunk was open and shut, and there I was, Sharon Sweeny's garden shovel in hand, already halfway to the square building on the right, nothing but dust to raise with every step, nothing to hear but a fist-like muscle in me going thump-thump-thump.

The padlock was gone, as he'd figured it would be, so I had little trouble tugging that door open, its hinges flaky with rust. This was five months ago now—before I went back a second time for the box—but I still see myself plainly, me smelling the musty smell of it and going in, the darkness striped by sunlight slicing through many seams in the wall, and the scratching of mice or lizards finding holes to hide in. The room was not as he recalled. No jig or band saw. No hammers or clamps or drills hanging in their places on the walls. No work apron on a peg. Just dirt and cobwebs and broken lengths of wood, plus a bench toppled on its side and a huge spool of baling wire and a short block V-6 engine and a far corner stacked with cardboard high as the ceiling.

I felt juvenile, I tell you, this too much like a scavenger hunt for an adult to be doing, and for an instant it seemed likely that I would leave, me suddenly with an appetite, too. In ten minutes, Sharon and I could be at the Kountry Kitchen, only a table and two cups of coffee between us. But then something hooked and serious seemed to twist in me—a gland perhaps, or a not-much-talked-about organ, or whatever in us an obligation looks like—and, the air in that room dense and hot as bathwater, I found myself knocking on the floorboards with the shovel—whack, whack, whack—listening for one hollow whump, me the next Hamsey man to hunt for something in the dark.

Three times I traveled the length of that room—shoving junk out of my path, twice banging my shins, once almost smacking myself in the forehead on a two-by-four hanging from a rafter—before I heard it, and heard it again. Which means you are free to imagine me as I was: unmoving for two or twenty heartbeats, in me not much from the neck up—exactly, years and years before, as my father must've felt in the desert when he rode over that hill and saw what he saw. Then sense began coming back, thread by thread, and I crouched, knees cracking. Sound was again plain from the outside world—a tractor's diesel motor and the corrugated metal roof squeaking and groaning in the wind—but that shovel now weighed at least one thousand ugly pounds, and cold upon cold upon cold was falling through the core of me, light raining down like needles, with darkness there and there in spouts and columns, and no terrors to know but those you can't yet see.

"Oh," I think I said. And thereafter, nothing more to exclaim, I was on my fanny, prying up the first of four boards.

I was thirty-seven years old and thinking of those years placed end to end, which gave me to wonder where they had led and how many more I had, and at last those floorboards were loose and flung aside and at least the easiest of those questions had been answered.

It was like a root cellar, roomy enough for you to lie at the bottom of and throw open your arms.

"Okay," I said, my last sensible remark that hour.

I'd had a vision years before—me and Cece Phillips and the desert at night and how the future would turn out between me and her. This time, on the way to a different car and a different woman, I had none. I had lifted the box, skimmed the bundle of papers wrapped in oil-cloth, put it back, and now—well, I didn't know. Thousands and thousands of days ago, a terrible thing had crashed in my father's life. Today, something equally impossible had landed in mine.

"It wasn't there, was it?" Sharon Sweeny said.

I had put the shovel in the trunk and, brushing the dust off my pants next to her door, I thought of worms. Their wriggly, soft bodies. The talk they talk. "Just a lot of trash," I said.

She was relieved, I could tell, me once again as simple a character as any between the covers of the book in her lap. "What took you so long?"

My father had died, so Estelle Barnes had said, with his face composed, maybe even peaceful, and to my mind came a picture of him curled on the floor at her feet—his eyes blank, his thin lips parted, his hair flyaway and wild. The end of him, the beginning of me.

"What do you think I'd look like with a mustache?" I asked Sharon Sweeny.

"I don't like them droopy," she said. "Makes a fellow appear sinister."

I needed another minute here, I was thinking—time that had to pass before anything else could commence.

"You still hungry?" I asked.

She nodded, a gesture as good to see as are presents under the tree at Christmas, so I started around the car to the driver's seat. I was counting the parts of me—the head I had, the heart—and for the next few steps I had nothing at all to be scared of.

THE HUMAN USE
OF INHUMAN BEINGS

WHAT KAREN MY wife calls my obsession—my angel—first
appeared to me when I was eleven, one of three kids, lifelong pals
virtually, who were digging a cave in the steep bank of an arroyo
about a hundred yards across a cotton field behind my father's
house. It was June, hot as hot gets in southern New Mexico in that
month—dry as ashes, the air like brass against your teeth, the light
as painful to the eye as a whine is sharp to the ear—and we had been
at work since midmorning, shoveling almost nonstop, grunting with
our shirts off like convicts in the hokey movies you can hoot over on
late-night TV.

"A fort," Mickey had called it, but mostly our cave was to be a hide-
out—a refuge, really—where we would smoke the Winston cigarettes
Arch Whitfield stole from his old man while we thumbed the almost
greasy pages of the *Swank* and *Sister* magazines I'd found the week
before under my daddy's living room couch. We were a club, I've told
Karen, and, according to our plan, we aimed to be blood brothers and
camp out there so we could sneak around after dark shooting out
streetlights with fence staples or spying on Mickey's big sister, Ellen

(herself something, it still seems to me, out of pages private and shameful enough to hide).

Around twelve-thirty we stopped to eat the baloney sandwiches and warm Coke I'd brought. Mickey would be dead in about fifteen minutes, but, lying on my side at the mouth of the sizable entrance we'd dug, I couldn't have imagined any event like that. Instead, while Arch and Mickey talked, I was watching the distant cinder block fence that was the back of my parents' property and thinking about how tired I felt, my scrawny arms loose as noodles and blisters already starting on my fingers.

There isn't a lot to know about this moment, nor about those, before the cave collapsed, that followed. In those days, Mickey wanted to be an astronaut (this was about the time John Glenn, so I've since heard, peed in his pants in space), but this day he was talking about the Communists—Reds from Cuba and China and Russia itself—and how, if they invaded in the bloodthirsty swarms Mrs. Sweem, our batty fifth-grade teacher, raved about, then we'd retreat to our cave, three pint-size Musketeers, and wreak havoc on convoys and troop movements with our BB guns and high IQs.

"We'll be guerrillas," he said. "The scourge of the land."

I tried imagining the desert all the way to the Organ Mountains, thirty miles east, filled with trucks and tanks that three chicken-chested grade-schoolers were going to disable with spit wads and bombs made from baking soda and vinegar.

"What about it, Arch?" Mickey asked. "We'll steal, pillage, forage. All we need is a uniform."

Arch said okay—a know-nothing remark from a kid who then only wanted to roam center field for the Dodgers, an ambition that now must seem pretty corny to the alfafa and lettuce farmer he's grown up to be.

"We'll be a militia," Mickey said. "Colonels X, Y, and Z. We'll have to swear to secrecy."

For a minute, we were quiet, in the distance a cloud like a cow going left to right in the disk of sky I could see, and I went back to the thoughts I'd carried out here this morning before it seemed likely that I'd be doing battle with Fidel Castro and Nikita Khrushchev.

My parents wanted to send me to church camp in the mountains up near Santa Fe, which is about six hours by car north from the spot I was then sitting in, and of course I didn't want to go. They weren't religious people, not by a long shot—"Catlick," my daddy always said, "lapsed all the way"; they just wanted me gone for a week, so they could get down to the business (I see now) of cleaning up the disaster of their marriage without having underfoot a nosy student from the honor roll to talk around. So I was thinking about that and about the night before when I'd heard my mother say, "Professor Prescott, you're a pathetic son of a bitch, you know that?" and about the thick and sour silence that followed her remark to my father. In the darkness, her voice had had an edge raw as a razor and, in my bedroom at the end of the hall opposite theirs, I felt the air around me turn cold as nights in Greenland, the thump of my heart the only noise after that to listen to.

While I didn't know exactly what was going on, I knew something profound and permanent had happened in my parents' bedroom. A statement had been made, one ugly sentence after midnight, and thereafter nothing would ever be the same—not in my house, not on the block of houses I could see from my spot on the floor of the cave; not even on the acres and acres of bleached desert I was looking to the very end of when Arch said, "Up and at 'em, you guys, let's hustle here."

I didn't want to move, and I have told Karen that nothing felt so good then as the cool earth against which I lay curled about six feet away from a mouth-like hole of sunshine.

"C'mon," Arch said. "I got to go to the pool at three. My mom will have a fit if I'm late."

"What do you say, Mick?" I asked.

His tennies behind his head for a pillow, he was beside me, his hair flopped over his forehead like wet leaves.

"I've got to go, too," I said. "We're going to the movies."

He looked peaceful, I remember, as composed and unbothered as maybe a Musketeer is supposed to look, nothing between him and happiness but the shovel Arch was pointing at him, and then he said, "Well, I'll be a monkey's uncle," an expression as full of grin and good

cheer then as the night before my mother's had been poisonous and
full of hiss—in any case, not the last words you or I would utter had
we only six to say before place and fortune conspired to snatch us off
into eternity.

I heard it then, like a bark in my ear: *Move.* It was an order whose
consequence was not less than life or death—much like those I
received, seven years later, from the TL I served under in Vietnam—
so I scrambled to my hands and knees and stared at the entrance as
though I expected my father to be out there, his face white with fear.

"Let's go, Mickey," I said, and began to crawl out.

The cave hadn't started to collapse yet—that was only seconds
away—but again the voice came, this time from several directions at
once, not loud but urgent, not panicky but fierce, and until I scrabbled
out and was picking up my own shovel, I thought I'd only heard Arch
Whitfield, Junior Olympic swimmer, being bossy and clowning around
and not Abaddon or Barakiel or Inias or Harbonah. Not any voice
from those weightless and wanton creatures that visit from the Princi-
palities and the Powers I eventually learned about in church camp.

Arch noticed the trouble first.

"Billy," he said to me, his voice cracking.

And then I was looking, too.

At the entrance, a ragged archway tall as the big man I now am, a
little dirt was falling like rain and inside, just before the ceiling itself
let go and crashed down with a hollow and desolate whump, Mickey
Alan Crawford was slowly sitting up to face us, his watery blue eyes
not yet going from amusement to horror, his freckly arms not yet rising to cover his head.

"Guys?" Mickey said. "Guys?"

Clods came first, then slabs of earth like the concrete squares of a
sidewalk, the whole thing sucking back and down on him, and for an
instant—time enough anyway to wish you were as muscle-bound and
honorable as Hercules—you could see him in there, through a
swirling, clotted mist of sand and dirt, not making a word or a squeak,
just his face baffled and eyes shiny as new paint as if, the way it must
be for many, he'd been asked a question that couldn't be answered by
anything less than death itself.

"Oh, no," I said, my own voice failing to hold.

But it was already over, this long-ago accident, and Arch, yelling and waving his arms, was running toward his house and I, coming apart my own self, had fallen to my knees to chop at the pile of dirt, crying and sniveling "Shit, shit, shit" until Arch was racing back—his mother, frantic and screechy with grief, trailing behind in her polka-dot swimsuit—and me still clawing and scratching at the dirt, finding nothing and nothing again, my fingers black with dirt, my own chest heaving as if I, too, were underground and fighting upward through the cold and the fear, the whole of the earth having landed hard on my head.

And then, as I've told Karen too often, the voice came again, as detached as those you nowadays hear from your car when the door is ajar, telling me to stop, enough had been done, stop, and I could see that it was coming from a man, substantial as a ditch rider, standing on the bank above me, not twinkly as angels are in Hollywood but ho-hum as a common cowboy. He was shaking his head as if, apart from this hour's mortal business, his was a job as pleasant to undertake as is the eating of cherry pie on Sunday.

"That's enough, Billy," he said. "Lie down, son. Help is coming. Rest."

They sometimes arrive in hosts, these celestials—guardian or not, patron or otherwise. Egyptians had them, as did the Irish. For the Gnostics, they were the Cosmocrators. Small birds have them, as do tame animals. There's an angel for patience, as there is one for hope and another for, yes, insomnia. Like an army, there is a chain of command, Cherubim atop Thrones, Virtues above Powers. I have no idea how they move, what conveyance they take up and down to arrive here from the gold-paved and food-filled heaven that is their usual home. That's why they're angels, I guess, because they inhabit a dimension we only have oooohhhs and aaaahhhs to describe.

Notwithstanding what Karen now says, I am not a nut about this. Honest. I've just come to know, as my daddy might have said, a thing or three. Remember, please, that seeing Mickey buried at the cemetery three days later didn't make me crazy, either. I was calm, is all, even-minded as an umpire. "Shock" is what my daddy said when he took me up to St. Paul's camp the next week.

"It's a defense mechanism," he said, twice patting my knee when it probably seemed to him that I was on the verge of tears or trembling. "Time heals all wounds," he said, another cliché, and I turned to him then, barely able to hear because the top was down on his Ford Fairlane convertible.

I was thinking that I should tell him—about the voice, about the whiskery gent who had stood over me for a moment and touched my forehead, his fingers icy as well water, before, like a genie, he disappeared.

"You'll be okay," my father said, and, easing back from the brink of something terrible and sad, I sat straight ahead in my seat to see the landscape fly by.

"Dad?" I began.

I could feel him glance my way, and I think now that he was looking at me as he very likely had the night after my mother cussed him: He had come to my room and, lit from behind by the bathroom light, he'd stood in my doorway, skinny as a nail, something about his posture suggesting caution and fear and deepest regret.

"There's swimming," he was saying. "And horseback riding. Softball. Craft stuff—the works."

For a mile or so, while he told me how I'd spend my week, I watched the scrub and jagged mountains, all purples and grays and greens that don't mean anything. And I think that if I am a little like a machine, as Karen sometimes says I am, then it started here when, through one dip then another, around one turn and another, I felt the valves and gates of me close tight.

"What was it you wanted to say?" my father asked.

In those days, he was a chemistry professor at NMSU, with special interest in anisotropic crystals, so I knew—more with my heart than with any other organ that knows things, knew as my grown daughter Dede claims she knows stuff—that, as a practical man, one whose faith lay in the periodic table and what in his lab he could cook up in beakers and dishes, he would only be puzzled, then alarmed, if I, in his new car at sixty-five miles an hour on a road he could probably recite the exact molecular composition of, started talking about visitors and light and sound that came from above.

"It was nothing," I told him. "Never mind."

He gulped, as you would were your own unsettled self saved by silence.

"This'll be a good week," he said. "I promise."

You would think, would you not, that I should have seen an angel or two in Vietnam, where much was murdered and maimed, a place with an honest-to-goodness need for the human use of inhuman beings. After all, as Mickey Crawford had predicted, I was fighting Communists, sneaking around with a rifle and a higher cause to serve. But I did not—not once—though it did seem, during basic training at Fort Bliss in El Paso, that one was present if only unrevealed.

This was in my fifth week there, me just one of thousands who were that year turned into men from the boys we'd earlier been, and perhaps fifty of us had been trucked a ways into the badlands east of the Franklin Mountains to learn how to survive a ville some gung-ho full bird had constructed. That morning, we sat in bleachers while below us, bobbing and weaving behind a lectern, a sergeant yelled at us about being watchful and something-something to the nth degree. Behind him stood this odd collection of buildings—mostly sticks and the like, good tinder if you had a Zippo and a punk's sense of humor— the whole of it fenced (exactly as such turned out to be way across the ocean blue). It was booby-trapped, he said. CS gas and punji stakes, not to mention pits filled with human excrement that you would fall into, sure as sunrise, if you were too damn bumble-minded to pay attention.

For an hour he went on in this manner, alerting us to trip wires and demonstrating how our adversary, the wily Mr. Charlie, could rig up an explosive—from, hell, no more than a seemingly discarded C ration can, ladies!—that would blow your leg into the next rice paddy. Or blind you. Or cause you misery for the rest of your piss-poor life. I was enthralled, I admit, eager to learn what might save my skin; and I was also semi-distracted, wondering about whatever gland or gene it was that had caused me, several days after graduation, to have presented myself at Uncle Sam's recruiting office, my only credentials a record of A minuses and sufficient leaping ability to be second off the bench for the Las Cruces High School basketball Bulldogs.

As it had been the day Mickey and Arch and I dug our cave, it was hot, the sun blazing down and the sky so blue it looked phony. We had been divided into rifle teams, Able to Foxtrot, and soon enough one team was instructed to go into that mock village to make it safe for me and mine in green. I knew a few of the boys in the first squad, all of them with nicknames having something to do with body parts or point of national origin—kids named Tex or Ears or Fats—and I was real disappointed to see each of them, one after another, not get much beyond the gate before they were "killed" or otherwise made fools of.

A minute later, another team went in, hot to trot but stealthy as cats. Still, there were more surprises—holes out of which rose the out-raged enemy, walls that were false and places for cutthroats to hide, grenades that went boom when you flung open a door for a look-see. I was scared, I have to tell you, my heart slamming left and right—more scared, it would turn out, than I was months later when I landed in the place this wasn't the actual of, and I remember watching Swamp Thing and Doc disappear in a cloud of harmless smoke that meant, except for the months and miles they were lucky not to have lived and traveled yet, they were ruined forever. Truth to tell, I felt as I did that day our fort began to crumble, my lungs filling with air too dense with light and thorns and threads to breathe. Half of me wanted to turn and go running headlong into the desert, me shedding my pants and shirt quick as my muscles would permit. My other half, that percentage that was angry and pent up, wanted to charge up to our red-faced sergeant to tell him to stop and send us home. But I didn't. I was stuck, is all, rooted to the earth in a line, and then a voice could be heard behind me.

"Jumping Jesus," it said, amazed.

In the fake village, Tiny and Gator were inspecting a well that, according to our teed-off noncom, led to a tunnel that led to a room that was a hive of make-believe troops, and I remember turning to the voice behind me, expecting the expectable. I wanted to be out of there, and I was hoping it was an angel to make it so.

His name would turn out to be Brownie—a name no more unusual than Red or Bucky or Fender—but when I turned to him, I didn't see anything ordinary. Instead, I saw a creature aglow with blues and yellows and oranges—the effects, I think now, of too much sweat in the eyes and too much need in the chest.

"Looky there," he was saying.

Behind me, so I gathered, others of us were learning the lessons you learn when you are smashed to smithereens, but I was concentrating on Brownie, and then he had stopped staring over my shoulder, his weapon at rest in his arms, to take a peek into my eyes (which may have seemed to be spinning as wildly as those that mad scientists have).

"What's with you?" he said.

I did not know. I had seen an angel years ago, I could have told him. Maybe he was another.

"Wha—?" he said, backing off a step, and I was wondering what had turned his face dark with confusion. Then I saw it: My hand had come up, one finger extended and moving toward him. Behind me, the sergeant was calling for Foxtrot, me and this fellow among them, but neither of us had budged. My hand was still edging forward, my index finger coming ever closer to his midmost button. I intended to see if he was real. I was going to poke him, maybe pat him down head to toe, and you could see him see that in me. You could see him, real name Brownfield Woodward, study me across the inches that separated us, his eyes narrowed and his mouth tight as the hole to paradise. Time was moving very slowly here, as it does when you can't sleep, and I remember thinking what a sparkle I myself would make when my finger passed through the twinkle he was. I expected I might burn up or be thoroughly electrified, that I might shoot up into the sky or be atomized into the dust pixies are said to sprinkle.

But I had already done it, made contact, and nothing had happened. I was touching his shirt, a patch of sweat below his breastbone, and nothing had come of our connection. Not a buzz, not any flash of fire that I had read about or thought to predict. He was human matter, like me, and I had proved it. And so, once more able to huff and puff like the Big Bad Wolf, I turned away from that trooper, thoughts settling in me like sand.

Our sergeant was beckoning, and I found myself moving, one step and another, time smooth as butter and me still a victim of it. I was sharp enough to see what imperiled me and careful enough to tiptoe around it, and then this, too, was over—as were the next and the next and the next I have lived to brood about.

I chose to tell it, my story about the angel, only once—to Karen the day I asked her to marry me when we were students at the University of Arizona. This was the same year my parents finally divorced and my father sold his house to move into the Town and Country Apartments up behind Apodaca Park, the baseball fields where I had played Little and Pony Leagues, and something—maybe the goo I am, or the goo I will one day be—had moved me to confess to her that the angels that had appeared to Hippolytus in the second century A.D. were so tall that, well, their feet were fourteen miles long.

"Imagine it," I was saying. "Over ten thousand came down on Mount Sinai when Moses was given the laws. In Islam, they—"

"Billy Ray Prescott," she said, "what are you talking about?"

I took a breath, felt the links of me stiffen and clang.

Beside me, Karen was fussing with her purse, and for a moment I yearned to be small enough to fit inside it. Just me and her comb and her makeup—stuff she'd have forever.

There was a time, I told her, when I knew everything that could be known about angels. Their origin and duties. Their relationship in that hierarchy that leads to God. How they got their names. Even their personalities as such were revealed in the books and pictures I had studied in the library or, when I was eleven, in the reading room at St. Paul's.

"I'm not religious," I told her that day.

She nodded, not clearly convinced. She knew me as a Mr. Clean type (yup, I was one of those early bald fellows with a neck like a fire-plug), older than the frat boys and jocks who'd chased her, plus a guy with thirteen months of in-country slaughter I had put as far behind me as memory and geography would allow.

"I'm a Libra," I told her.

She knew that, she reminded me, exasperated as she nowadays gets when cause takes a half hour to make effect. Still, I had a speech to make then, and, yes, I was going to speak it.

"I believe in justice and balance," I told her. "I'm a hard worker, don't smoke, do my own laundry, like a clean house. Karen, I know how to fix a car. I pick up after myself."

As if I had said I was related to Little Miss Muffet—or were warning her about, say, the Communists massing to charge over the ridge behind us—she was focusing on me hard, her eyes dark as pea gravel, exactly the look I received last week when I told her about the second visit of my angel.

"Billy," she said, "are you sick? Here, let me feel your forehead."

I considered my situation then, the kids in T-shirts and shorts walking past, and for an instant I pictured me as she must've: a mostly well-mannered communications major, virtually on bended knee, yakking for all practical purposes about spacemen or plants that had mastered French.

"Mickey Crawford," I said presently. "1962."

She was leaning back a little—body language, they say. "What are you talking about?"

Something was ticking in me like a bomb, so I told her: the cave. The angel. The sky gone white as old bone. The sun like ice. The ambulance bumping across the stubbly field. That crowd of neighbors, all struck quiet and hangdog. Arch holding his mother's hand as if he expected a chasm, maybe stinky with smoke and brimstone itself, to yawn open beneath him. And my father.

"An angel?" she said, her body still doing most of the talking.

"My dad told me I could go home," I said.

She looked patient—part schoolmarm, part traffic cop.

"He picked me up," I told her. "Held me in his arms all the way back to the house. Patted me on the back. Smoothed my hair. Whispered to me all the way."

A kid was going by us now, too close on a bicycle, and until he disappeared around the faraway corner of MLB #67—about as long as it had taken my father to lug me across the field years before—I watched, my blood pumping three ways at once in my brain.

"Billy, you're scaring me."

Whatever was ticking in me had stopped, and I had not burst into pieces or toppled over in a heap.

"Miss Needham," I said at last, "I need you desperately. Let's be man and wife, okay?"

She smiled then, in a manner that seemed to involve her shoulders and a goodly percentage of her torso, and in that first minute after she said "yes," I understood I was obliged to put aside, like gewgaws and trivia you've outgrown, all I knew about Thrones and Dominations, those swift and heedless beings who get here by magic and stay around to make us mean.

"You wait here, Billy," she said. "I'll get you a Coke."

The fall after we married, Karen and I moved to El Paso, where I'd gotten a job as an associate writer for the *Live at 5:30* program at KTSM TV; and then, soon enough and fortunately, I became assistant producer, then day-of-show producer, then assignment editor for news and executive producer, rising through time, one rung then another—first the guy who does the field interview about the new tiger at the zoo, then the guy who oversees the live broadcast of what the zookeeper can say to well-barbered talent named Doreen or Chad, then the guy who orders the guy to do all that; and finally your hero became the guy who's supervising nearly five dozen other humans whose days are spent thinking up two-minute stories about rock 'n' roll grannies or talking lawn mowers to share with the half million Americans with color TV in my corner of the desert.

Rising and rising, I say, until William Prescott, Jr., had mostly forgotten all the goofy secrets and peculiar wisdom he'd discovered in the days and years after the stringbean-like corpse of Colonel X, ravaged and limp and blue in the lips, was dragged out of its grave.

The NAB meeting was in Dallas this year, that confab where shows like *A Current Affair* or reruns of the *Mod Squad* are bought and sold, and where celebrities like Montel Williams and Regis Philbin show up to shake your hand for having rented them five evenings a week from the KingWorld syndicate.

It was the last day and I had gone up to my room off the hospitality suite the station had booked in the Westin Galleria, which is that next century of hotel from whose westward windows you can see jets climbing and falling like dragonflies from D/FW. I was tired, too full of what was being sold that day—yammer and video about a public that seemed crabbed or confused and bent in the brain, programs about pistol-packing priests or vegetables in the shape of public monuments, the whole of it served up by blabbermouths who seemed to have been concocted out of the fancy fluids and rare gases my father, before his retirement, had fussed over like a wizard. It was late, the only other person in the suite my son-in-law, Mike, who, as my assistant and a Southern Cal MBA, was along to keep track of the dollars and cents we were spending to bring to West Texas information about, oh, a cheese that caused cancer and the Arkansas moonshiner who was a new father at age seventy-six.

"Long day," Mike said. His tie loosened, collar undone, loafers kicked off, he looked like he'd reached a place in his calculations where numbers had personalities unstable enough to cause fistfights on either side of the decimal point.

"The longest," I told him.

I wasn't really paying attention. Dede, my daughter and his wife, was expecting their first child—a boy, it's turned out to be, named after yours truly—so I was preoccupied with that and with the thought, given the gut I'd seen in the mirror that morning, that I needed to lose about twenty pounds.

"Champagne, boss?" he said, pointing to the table.

The suite looked like the mess a circus leaves behind, but there were still a couple of untouched bottles and, bushwhacked by fatigue, I felt thirsty enough to drink them, plus whatever else bitter and fizzy that room service could send up in a hour.

"Don't mind if I do," I said, realizing—also with a start—that I wanted to be drunk and that, like shows about witches from Wisconsin and dogs that do long division (Corgis, I think, a snappy, prissy breed), this would be yet one more odd development I'd end up telling Karen about when I got home the next afternoon.

For an hour, we shot the breeze, Mike and me, told tales out of school—who was a crabapple, or a lazybones, or a bottom feeder nobody in management would be sad to say so long to. I told a couple of stories about my youth and Vietnam, and Mike, wistful as what the word *swain* suggests, told a really sweet version of how he'd fallen in love with my baby girl.

Once, moved by the hour and the confidences, I thought to say something about angels—their fine-spun hair, the clatter some are said to make when they land, the ghastly wail others shriek in the ears of those whose hearts tend toward evil—but Mike was telling an SC story about football, a tale that went as much backward as not (like this one you yourself are hearing), so I just treated myself to another swallow of Cold Duck and said "Uh-huh" in agreement until the punch line came to make me chuckle.

By the second bottle, we'd taken up the bigger world—Saddam and the like—all the woe-washed men and women who didn't seem to have enough virtue or good sense or ordinary compassion. I was feeling fine, clean inside and able to go back and forth in my brain without losing myself between mind and mouth. But a moment later, when Mike said he was going back to his own room, I knew I'd succeeded in getting tipsy, the physical universe a landscape of carpet and armchairs I'd have to crawl through to find my bed.

"You okay, Billy?" Mike said.

I expect I looked bleary, or partially paralyzed.

"You think anything's out there?" I asked, making a gesture meant to include to all phenomena out-of-doors and wandering unattached overhead.

"You mean like UFOs?" he said.

I meant spirits, ghosts, and whatever. Trolls, maybe. Demons and devils and gnomes. The whole shebang.

"The whole shebang," he said, clearly choosing his words very carefully and comically glancing left and right to see if we were alone.

"Seems possible to me," I told him.

He was standing now, his sleeves rolled down, his belt tightened a notch or two—the actions of a normal man at the end of a normal night.

"It does?" he said.

I had eight thoughts, then eighty, several of which had to do with drinking and the truths you find doing it.

"Sure," I said, and then, helpless to do much else, I stumbled through a spit-filled paragraph that had in it observations about little green men and hobgoblins from the netherworlds, plus wolf men and vampires and whatever else that might explain the miracles of earth and wind and fire.

"What about bleeding statues," I said, "that kind of thing?"

"I don't think about it," he said. "Honest."

I didn't think that possible and made the mistake of saying so.

"I'm not a complicated guy, boss," he said. "I just turn the mind off."

Mike looked wind-whipped, his face the color of old cardboard— just the way I'd look, I fear, if he admitted that he had a tail or scales instead of skin—so, feeling the winds whistling in me, I just chuckled to say I was kidding. I was being dumb as a doughnut, and it was time to stop.

"Sorry," I told him. "Too much Geraldo Rivera, I guess."

His was a smile not less than three-quarters full of relief, broad as a piano keyboard.

"Maybe you ought to take a vacation, boss. You and Karen go somewhere."

And so, after he'd shut the door behind him, I rolled leftward and found the floor I'd been looking for.

In bed, I didn't seem myself. The radio was going, an oldies station, and I did my best to keep the melody to "Lonely Teardrops" by Jackie Wilson and that grapevine song by Marvin Gaye, tune after tune that seemed to connect the me's I was in yesteryears to the middle-aged me I am now. Helpless as a log in a flood, I was being driven back into the past, before long finding myself sitting on my suitcase at the beginning of the bladed road leading out of St. Paul's church camp, feeling my lungs fill with simple gladness when my daddy rolled up in his Ford Fairlane to take me home.

Next, stranger memories assaulted me: my daddy hunched over the toilet bowl in his bathroom, moaning and clutching his arms—in the midst of a heart attack he would survive—and my mother standing over him, her expression sidelong and smug as a tyrant, saying, "It's just the Monday morning blues, Billy, you go on to school." And this: one trooper from Hotel Company, a kid named Heber from the 1/26, licking a photograph at LZ Thelma in MR II. And this, too: my mother marrying a cattle rancher from the Hondo Valley, the pair of them perfect as magazine models selling wine from faraway places. I wasn't weepy, just beset, a part of me frightened as a kid in a haunted house, another part wrought up enough to have to find a way—boy, is this spooky—to make myself heard in the night.

So I sang. The shoo-bops and the do-wah-diddies that are the nonsense you make when you are, as I was, foggy-minded and utterly innocent of the real words. And then, before my angel again appeared, I was asleep, still fully dressed, in a land, as I've heard it described, of dreamy dreams, where time pools and stretches, where events come to you like clips from a thousand crummy movies; a land where you are yourself a floaty thing that can move without benefit of motors or muscle and where, before you have any other way of knowing it, it is revealed to you that in this valley of et ceteras nothing is holding you up but want and ignorance and luck.

He had not changed, my angel. Unremarkable as a shopper at a bus stop, he looked as he had that day Mickey Crawford suffocated, and for a moment, before I went down and around and the night broke into shards around me, I wondered what he'd been doing over the years between then and now.

"It's not Dede?" I said, hope and fear only two of the motivations for my question.

It was not, he said.

In the quiet, I was watching him as I believe he was watching me, creatures at the opposite ends of time. In that special voice of his, like an echo coming to your ear down a mile-long pipe, he'd arrived to warn—or prepare, or teach, or help; hell, I don't know—and for an instant, after I'd risen to sit upright and leave my bed, I feared I might still be asleep and thus doomed to turn around and so see myself lying infant-like in the middle of a king-size bed, my wrinkled suit coat up around my shoulders like a shield, but my body so brilliantly lit up that I could count the bones through my skin.

"Don't be scared, Billy," he said.

I didn't think I was, but my hands had flown up, palsied-like and grabbing at air.

"It's not Karen," he said.

Then, as if I had been conked about the ear, I knew.

Perhaps I had known the moment he had touched my toe to fetch me back to the conscious world, or maybe he had sprinkled me with dust or whatever awful powder their terrible tribe uses for the spells they cast. In any event, like a TV show—maybe like a TV show I myself was in this place to buy—I was now seeing my father in his apartment, at the stove frying the minute steaks he liked, the instant before his heart seized up and he slumped to the floor. He was smiling, my father was, his grin as fixed a feature of his face as his eye color and unlobed ears—a smile as lopsided as it had been that day, years and years ago, when he'd said goodbye to me at St. Paul's and arranged himself again behind the wheel of that spiffy Fairlane he loved. He didn't look old now, I thought. Not wizened or shrunken or ruined. Just frailer, thinner, and less nimble—what I'll be when the sun goes down in 2025.

It was hitting him now, the shivers of his battered heart, and for a moment, before the floor came up to him hard and fast, he looked befuddled—like Mickey Alan Crawford the instant before the cave slammed down—as if, his eyes going flat and empty like candle wax, he was seeing death bear down on him, its approach sudden, infinite, and wrong.

"It was quick," my angel said.

They separate the sheep from the goats, I was thinking. The wheat from the tares. Our angels do not age, nor do they fall ill. They may not reproduce, neither may they marry. They become visible, so I'd once read, by choice, and to some—the daft, the hopeful, the condemned—they have appeared with wings and hands, or full of eyes and encompassed by wheels within wheels. As I've told Karen, one book claims they are the oil of joy for our mourning. They are not. That book, like so many, is lying.

"Go away," I told him.

"You'll be all right?" he asked.

It had returned, that giant's fist closing around my insides: I had heard other sentences after dark—these, like my mother's one night long ago, frightful enough to change the way the world is seen—and, air upon air upon air underneath me, I thought I had stepped off the cliff of the planet itself. All I had were the facts of me—my height, the Cadillac I drive, how clumsy I am at tennis, how loudly I can laugh when the joke is harmless and blue—those details that are the sum of you when you have but one last lesson to learn in life.

When I opened my eyes, he was gone.

It was well past midnight, my floor quiet, in the distance the wail of sirens growing fainter. Karen was up now, I knew. She had received a call from the manager of my father's apartment building—I had seen that, too, one of a thousand images pulsing in my head—and she was searching in her bedstand for the number of the phone I was sitting next to. In twelve hours, I could be home. In another sixty, I could be standing graveside. But now I was here, a lamp on, the room cold as February, waiting for a bell, so that, my ears still thumping with the impossible beating of wings, I could pick up the phone and say, "I know."

THE VALLEY OF SIN

NEITHER DEMING'S BEST golfer nor its worst, Mr. Dillon Ripley was, as the six thousand of us in these deserts now realize, its most ardent, having taken to the sport as those in the big world we read about have taken to drink or to narcotics. Almost daily, you'd see him on the practice tee—elbows, knees, and rump in riot—his fat man's swing a torment of expectation and gloom. With him would be Allie Martin, our resident professional, and together, hip to hip, faces shaded against the fierce sunlight we're famous for, hair flying in breezes, they'd stare down the range, as if out there, waiting as destiny is said to wait, stood neither riches nor simple happiness, but Ripley himself, slender and tanned and strong as iron, a hero wise and blessed as are those from blind Homer.

On the weekends, noon to dusk, he'd be accompanied by his wife, Jimmie. He had bought her the spiked shoes and loose cardigans of the classic linkster, and he tried teaching her, as he was being taught, how to grip the club, what "break" was, and what enchantments came to mind when the ball soared, as it ought to, or plopped into the cup on its last revolution. Golf, he told her, was bliss and bane. Holding her by the shoulders, as earnest about this as others are about religion, he would say that golf was like love itself. He used words like *passion* and *weal*. He mentioned old terms for the equipment: mashie, niblick, and spoon. He knew everything about the game, its lore and minutiae, and his weekday playing partners—Watts Gunn, Phinizy Spalding, and Poot Taylor—had often heard him remark that one day now, when he'd squared his affairs at the Farmers and Merchants Bank, where he was a vice president (Loan Department), he, Jimmie, and the two children would vacation in Scotland, specifically near the Old Course at St. Andrews, home of the Royal and Ancient Golf Club. He imagined himself, he told his partners, among the ridges and hillocks, cheerful at the sight of meadow grasses and sheltered dunes, knolls and hollows and whins as dear to him as money is to some. So profound was his affection for the sport that once, at the fourteenth tee, already set over his ball, scarcely any traffic at all on the gravel service road which paralleled the fairway, he announced— a week before Jimmie ran off with Allie Martin—that he knew what best tested the kind we are: It was not death or travail or such woe as you find in newspapers; it was the hazards of unmown fescue and bent grass, or a sand wedge misplayed from a bunker known as the Valley of Sin.

It happened in May, the Sunday before Armed Forces Day. We suspect that Dillon was too involved in his forthcoming round to notice that Jimmie, erect as a hat model, brighter in the eye and cheek, leggier, seemed nervous or rather too beautiful that morning. Dressed in his so-called Cuban outfit (red NuTonics, pink slacks, black polka-dot shirt), he felt superior. Eating as if starved, he told his oldest boy, the teenager Brian, that today was an anniversary of sorts: on this day in A.D. 508, Dillon claimed, King Clovis had established Paris, formerly Lutetia, as the Frankish capital, following his vanquishing of the Visigoths.

"So what?" the boy grumbled.

There was evidence—Dillon had the boy by the ears now, smiling like a clown—that golf, which may have been suggested by the Dutch game kolven, was already being played in Scotland.

"Oh," the boy said, "great."

To the youngest girl, Marcia, Dillon described the ancient burns and thickets that were extant when our forebears—smaller, hairier, ruder—ruled a world flat as a cookie sheet.

"Jeez, Dad," she said, shaking her head. "You know some awful dumb stuff."

Looking as if he'd slept for a century, Dillon arrived at the first tee before noon. He did not use a cart, instead hiring as his caddy Tommy Steward, a Wildcat football player thought to be the most wayward AA right tackle in Luna County, New Mexico; and through the front nine, which he played well if not stylishly, Mr. Dillon Ripley had the stride of a general, as well as the amused expression of a citizen worth ninety thousand dollars a year.

"I feel young," he told Phinizy Spalding.

He recounted an anecdote about his Lambda Chi days at SMU, a boozy, melancholy escapade about women, which was embarrassing enough to be true; then, at lunch in the clubhouse, he revealed that this July he and the family would be visiting the British Open. He mentioned Watson, Nicklaus, and Trevino, plus such legends as Old Tom Morris and the vaunted Harry Vardon. He mentioned Strath Bunker and Hill Bunker—the Scylla and Charybdis of the 172-yard par-three eleventh. And, after buying them all, including Tommy Steward, a Bloody Mary, he marched his foursome to the tenth hole, quoting Sir Guy Campbell on "the thick, close-growing, hard-wearing sward that is such a feature of true links turf wherever it is found."

Hard for us it is to know our fate—or grace or, for that matter, our doom—when it appears. For some, it has a hue; for others, a sound. For Dillon Ripley, as for most, it had a face and a name and it swept by him—on the fourteenth fairway, of course—at upward of forty miles per hour, a silver '79 Volvo sedan.

"Hey," Tommy Steward said, waving his chunky tackle's fist, "ain't that Allie?"

Yonder, gaining speed, its horn whining, the car flew toward them, dust boiling up in the wake. Dillon, his wood balanced against his leg, was washing his Maxfli, watching the Volvo swerve. Light glinted from the windshield like sparks. It looked as if, though you couldn't be sure, there were two people inside, the passenger lifeless as sculpture, the other thrashing to and fro as if overcome with ecstasy. For a time, Dillon's foursome had a single organ of understanding: They looked and shrugged and opened their hands to say that, well, what'd you expect? This was old Allie Martin, Mr. Cut-up.

Tommy said, "Is he drunk or what?"

Poot Taylor recalls he had no thoughts at all, just the notion, felt like ice in the heart, that something—our planet, its moon, the hithermost stars—was awry.

Watts Gunn believed he smelled rain in the west, where clouds had built into a pavilion high as heaven, and he wondered if the windows in his Monte Carlo were closed.

Next to Dillon, Phinizy Spalding, a fast driver himself, was thinking of chaos, and a question came to mind regarding babble and sloth. He saw, as well, a pall falling between him and the future.

And then, when the Volvo came abreast, horn blaring, and throwing up road filth behind, Tommy Steward hollered, "Hey, Mr. Ripley, ain't that your—?"

Zooming past, looking headlong, was Jimmie, indifferent as truth, her shoulders pearly, luminous, and bare.

"Lordy," Tommy said, aghast, "she's naked!"

There was a noise, choked but awful as thunder, and when our linksters turned around, stricken Dillon was in collapse, his lips a disheartening shade of blue.

After three weeks in the Mimbres Valley Hospital, his heart mended with diet and drugs, Dillon Ripley returned home. His instructions from Dr. Weems said to avoid difficult physical activity. No lifting, for example. Walking was fine. But no golf. Not yet. A housekeeper, Mrs. Fernandez, who lived on Iron Street, had been hired to tend to the children; and, though few saw him, the rumor was that Mr. Ripley was well, reading his chief diversion, not mournful. Many spouses, we were learning, had been abandoned by their mates, and Mr. Ripley was being as stalwart about his condition as, say, the fish is about its. Life was a jungle, it was said in the clubhouse, and we, its upright creatures, were no more noble or charmed than thinking worm or sentient mud. Hereabouts, in fact, heartache was compared to history; both had to do with time and inevitable sadness. Many people, moreover, accepted the view offered by Dr. Tippit at St. Luke's Presbyterian—a view which held that ours was a fallen orb, burdensome indeed, but bound to improve, to yield itself to the wish of an enlightened master. Yesterday, it was argued, man was only an ape; today he was more upstanding, to be sure, but hardly far enough from the trees he'd sprung from.

That winter, Dillon Ripley attended the Christmas and New Year's parties at the club, turning a cha-cha-cha with Millie Gunn and doing a modified twist with Grace Spalding. He looked hale, thinner by thirty-five pounds, and everyone wondered when we'd again see him at the practice tee, his spine stiff as a sentry's, his powerful and collected gaze fixed on the horizon.

"Soon, soon," he answered.

Though no one said as much, people were still keenly interested in Jimmie and Allie. Poot Taylor had heard they lived in Florida, Allie trying to qualify for his A card so he could compete on the satellite tour. Dr. Weems understood they were in Honduras, Allie in a field which included all manner of felon and vagabond duffer. Watts Gunn thought they had fled to Cincinnati, as Jimmie supposedly had a younger sister there. If Dillon knew, he wasn't saying. Instead, he danced—the Cleveland chicken, the rumba, a naughty knee-knocking mambo Jackie Gleason would have envied—and proposed a champagne toast to what his daddy had called fortune.

"Which, as I understand it," he began, smiling at us whom he had known all his life, "is part pluck, part guile, and part sense of humor. Happy New Year!"

In February, the month Dillon put his house on the market, Tito Garza, who handled the night watering at the club, found the flagsticks on the tenth and eleventh holes twisted into impossible shapes—one, it was said, an idea of horror made steel, the other a loop a drunk might make falling down, the nylon flags themselves scorched. We had the sense, felt like an icy current of air, that something parlous, of claw and cold blood, perhaps, had invaded our course, its vast mind consumed by a single thought of rage.

Three weeks later, we Sunday linksters began finding note cards stuffed into the cups on several holes on the backside. Each card was margin to margin with handwriting so fine and peculiar it looked like crewelwork practiced by a lost race of tiny, nearly invisible people. Under the magnifying glass Mr. R. L. Crum kept in the men's locker, you could tell the writing was either complex as knowledge itself or witless as mumbo-jumbo. "The world is almost rotten," read one. Another: "We are a breed in need of fasting and prayer." On a third: "Porpozec ciebie nie prosze dorzanin."

His face blotchy with passion, Abel Alwoody, who'd been to Vietnam, insisted it was all gook to him and called forth for us a vision composed of fire and ash. Judge Sanders suggested it was a prank, probably from the Motley brothers, whose shed adjacent to the twelfth hole he had recently condemned.

"Hold on a second," Garland Steeples said. The air in that locker was close, heavy as wool. Steeples was the high school counselor and it was clear he was bringing to our mystery his professional training in the human arts of hope and fear. He pointed to several words, "want," "venery," "vice," and a phrase, "the downward arc of time." His face, particularly around the eyes, was dark as winter. It was a moment to which the word *ruin* might apply. "What I see is this," he began.

He was speaking of misrule and Bolsheviks when we began edging away.

Through April and May, a season glorious in our arid clime, there were no disturbances, other than several late-night calls to Yogi Jones, the new pro, who felt he was listening either to a ghost or to a very arch infant. Then, the first week of summer, near midnight one Wednesday, when he was necking with Eve Spalding, Phinizy's daughter, on the fourteenth green, Tommy Steward, fuzzy-minded on red-dirt marijuana, thought he spied a figure, possibly human, darting amid the cottonwood trees. There was a new moon, pouring light down like milk, and the high wispy clouds that mean a wind is up from Mexico. While he held Eve, he spotted it again, loping like a low beast but wearing the togs of a sportsman, and his heart shot to his throat like a rodent, all claws and climbing hard. Words came to mind: *flank, cranium,* and *haunch.*

"Eeeeeffff," he groaned. "Aaarrgghh."

Even from a distance, the thing appeared murderous, a creature of carnage and outrage like those scale-heavy, horned, thick-shouldered figures he knew about from nightmare. In an instant, tumbling Eve aside, he was dashing in a dozen directions at once, shirttails flapping.

"What's the matter?" Eve was saying, almost frightened herself. She had her blouse open, her breasts—like Jimmie's, months earlier—firm and white.

Tommy sputtered: "Naaaaaa, naaaaa."

His arms, as if jointless, whipped the air. He felt he was breathing sand. A thousand ideas came to him, none concerning humans. And then, in a way more swift than flight itself, the thing, wretched as a savage, leaped in front of him, not ten giant steps away. It was in skins, yes, and dirty as orphans you see in French movies. One fist was shaking overhead, and in the other, like a cudgel, hung a golf club heavy with sod.

"Goddamn," Tommy was yelling, "Jesus H. Christ!"

Noise was everywhere—roars wrathful and morbid both. The ground had begun to tilt, and Tommy, dry-mouthed and trembling, felt he was staring at the hindmost of our nature, its blind pink eyes, its teeth wet as a dog's. Then, dragging and pushing and carrying Eve, Tommy was gone, running elsewhere—anywhere!—in a fury, too addled to scream.

That month, until too bored to continue, Poot Taylor and Watts Gunn, riding in an electric golf cart, patrolled the country club at night, each armed with a .22. The night the lookout ended, someone sneaked onto the ninth green and, using a shovel (later found in a mesquite bush), dug several pits, the deepest in that spot from which the great Willie Newsome had once sunk a chip for the Invitational Championship. In the morning, signs were discovered. They had the theme of heartwork and dealt with such concepts as travesty and blight. "Pray and your life will be better," one read. "We are base," another said, "and nothing can be done."

In August, Mr. Dillon Ripley sold his house and moved his family twenty miles farther south in the desert, to Hatchita, where, as we understand it, there is no sport at all save hunting and where the winds, infernal and constant, blow as if from a land whose lord is dark and always angry.

THE VIEW OF ME FROM MARS

A WEEK BEFORE I became a father, which now seems like the long ago and far away fairy tales happen in, I read a father-child story that went straight at the surprise one truth between children and parents is. It was called "Mirrors," and had an end, to the twenty-three-year-old would-be know-it-all I was, that literally threw me back in my chair—an end, sad somehow and wise, which held that it is now and then necessary for the child, in ways mysterious with love, to forgive the parent.

In "Mirrors" the child was a girl, though it could have been a boy just as easily, whose father—a decent man, we have to believe—takes her to the sideshow tent at a one-horse and one-elephant circus in the flatlands of Iowa or Nebraska or Kansas. She's seven or eight at this time, and—as we have all begged for toys or experiences it can be, I see now, our misfortune to receive—she begs and begs to see the snake charmer and the tattooed lady, the giant and the dwarf. He gives in, the girl decides much later, because of his decency; or he gives in, as my own father might say, because he's too much a milk-and-cookies sort of fool to understand that in that smelly, ill-lit tent is knowledge it is a parent's duty often to deny or to avoid. It is a good moment, I tell you, this moment when they pay their quarters and go in, one person full of pride, the other sucking on cotton candy, the sad end of them still pages and pages away.

In that tent—a whole hour, I think—walking from little stage to little stage, the girl is awestruck and puzzled and, well, breath-taken, full of questions about where these people, these creatures, live and what they do when they're not standing in front of a bunch of hayseeds and would it be possible to get a face, a tattoo, printed on her knee. "Can I touch?" she asks. "Do they talk?" A spotlight comes on, blue and harsh, and nearby, in a swirl of cigarette smoke and field dust, are two little people, Mr. and Mrs. Tiny, gussied up like a commodore and his society bride; another light snaps on, yellow this time and ten paces away, and there stands a man—"A boy," the barker tells us, "only eighteen and still growing!"—who's already nine feet tall, his arms long as shovels, nothing in his face about his own parents or what he wants to be at twenty-five. These are clichés, my smart wife, Ellen Kay, tells me ("Sounds too artsy-fartsy," her exact words were when I read the thing to her), but in the story I remember, these are the exhibitions girl and man pass by—the girl Christmas-Eve impatient, the man nervous—before they come to the main display, which is, in "Mirrors," a young woman, beautiful and smooth as china, who has no arms and no legs.

The father, complaining that he's grubby-feeling and hot, wants to get out, but his daughter, her heart hammering in her ears, can't move. As never before, she's conscious of her own hands and feet, the wonders they are. She's aware of smells—breath and oil and two-dollar cologne—and of sounds, a gasp here, a whisper there, exclamations that have in them ache and horror and fear. "C'mon," the father says, taking her elbow. But onstage, business-like as a banker, the woman—"The Human Torso," the barker announces, "smart like the dickens"—is drinking water, the glass clamped against her neck by her shoulder; is putting on lipstick; is writing her name with a brush between her teeth; is, Lordy, about to type—with her chin maybe—a letter to a Spec 4 with the Army in Korea, her boyfriend.

Outside, the midway glittering and crowded with Iowans going crosswise, the girl, more fascinated than frightened (though the fright is coming), asks how that was done. The father has an Old Gold out now, and the narrator—seven or eight but on the verge of learning that will stay with her until seventy or eighty—realizes he's stalling. He's embarrassed, maybe sick. He says "Howdy" to a deadbeat he'd never otherwise talk to. He says he's hungry, how about a hot dog, some buttered popcorn? He's cold, he says, too cold for September. "How?" she says again, pulling at his sleeve a little and watching his face go stiff and loose in a way that has her saying to herself, "I am not scared. No, I am not." And then he says what the narrator realizes will be his answer— sometimes comic, often not—for all thereafter that astounds or baffles and will not be known: "Mirrors, it's done with mirrors."

There's a pause here, I remember, six sentences that tell what the weather is like and how, here and there, light bulbs are missing and what the girl's favorite subjects are in school. *What?* she thinks to ask, but doesn't. "It's an illusion," he says, his voice squeaky the way it gets when he talks about money they don't have much of. "A trick, like magic." Part of her—the part that can say the sum of two plus two, and that *A* is for Apple, *B* is for Boy—knows that mirrors have nothing to do with what she's seen; another part—this the half of her that will remember this incident forever and ever—knows that her father, now as strange to her as the giant and the dwarf, is lying.

His hand is working up and down, and his expression says, as lips and eyes and cheeks will, that he's sorry, he didn't mean for her to see that, she's so young. Something is trembling inside her, a muscle or a bone. One-Mississippi, she says to herself. Two-Mississippi. Over there sits a hound dog wearing a hat and somewhere a shout is going up that says somebody won a Kewpie doll or a stuffed monkey, and up ahead, creaking and clanking, the Tilt-A-Whirl is full of people spinning around and around goggle-eyed. Her father has a smile not connected to his eyes—another lie—and his hand out to be held, and going by them is a fat lady who lives on Jefferson Street and a man with a limp who lives on Spruce. Her father seems too hairy to her now, and maybe not sharp-minded enough, with a nose too long and knobby. She tells herself what she is, which is a good dancer and smart about which side the fork goes on and who gets introduced first when strangers meet; and what she is not, which is strong enough to do pull-ups and watchful about who goes where and why. She is learning something, she thinks. There is being good, she thinks. And there is not. There is the truth, she thinks. And there is not.

And so, in the climax of what I read years and years ago, she says, her hands sticky and her dress white as Hollywood daylight, "Yes, mirrors, I thought so"—words that, years and years ago, said all I thought possible about lies and love and how forgiveness works.

In this story, which is true and only two days old and also about forgiveness, I am the father to be read about and the child is my son, Stuart Eliot Polk, Jr. (called "Pudge" in and out of the family); he's a semi-fat golfer—"linksman," he insists the proper term is—and an honor student who will at the end of this summer go off to college and so cease to be a citizen in the sideshow tent my house here in El Paso now clearly is. Yes, forgiveness—particularly ironic in that, since my graduation years ago from Perkins Seminary at SMU, it has been my job to say, day after day after day, the noises that are "It will get better" and "We all make mistakes" to a thousand Methodists who aim to be themselves forgiven and sent home happy. There is no "freak" here, except the ordinary one I am, and no storybook midway, except my modern kitchen and its odd come and go.

I am an adulterer—an old-fashioned word, sure, but the only one appropriate to the ancient sin it identifies; and my lover—a modern word not so full of terror and guilt and judgment as another—was, until two days ago, Terri Ann Mackey, a rich, three-times-married former Zeta Tau Alpha Texas girl who might one day make headlines for the dramatic hair she has or the way she can sing Conway Twitty tunes. In every way likable and loud and free-minded, she has, in the last four years, met me anywhere and everywhere—in the Marriott and Hilton hotels, in the Cavern of Music in Juarez, even at a preachers' retreat at the Inn of the Mountain Gods in Ruidoso in southern New Mexico's piney forests. Dressed up in this or that outfit she sent away for or got on a trip to Dallas, she has, to my delight and education, pretended to be naughty as what we imagine the Swedish are or nice as Snow White; she has pretended, in a hundred rented rooms, to be everything I thought my wife was not—daring and wicked, heedless as a tyrant. Shameful to say, it seems we have always been here, in this bright desert cow town, now far-flung and fifty percent tickytacky, drinking wine and fornicating and then hustling home to deceive people we were wed to. Shameful to say, it seems we have always been playing the eyes' version of footsy—her in pink and cactus yellow in a pew in the middle of St. Paul's, me in the pulpit sermonizing about parables and Jesus and what welfare we owe the lost and poor and beaten down.

"Yes," my wife, Ellen Kay, would answer when I told her I was at the Stanton Street Racquet Club playing handball with a UTEP management professor named Pete Walker. "Go change," she'd say, herself lovely and schoolgirl-trim as that woman I'd collapsed atop a half hour before. "I phoned," she'd say, "Mrs. Denbo said you were out." Yes, I'd tell her. I was in the choir room, hunting organ music that would inspire and not be hokey; I was in the library, looking up what the Puritan Mathers had written about witchcraft and gobbledygook we are better off without; I was taking a drive in my Mercedes, the better to clear my head so I could get to the drafting of a speech for the Rotarians, or the LULAC Club of Ysleta, or the Downtown Optimists. "You work too hard," she'd say, "let's go to Acapulco this year." And I'd head to my big bedroom, the men I am, the public one amazed by his private self—the first absolutely in love with a blond continental-history major he'd courted at the University of Texas in 1967; the second still frazzled by what, in the afternoon, is made from deceit and bed noise and indecency. And until two days ago, it was possible to believe that I knew which was which, what what.

"Where were you?" Ellen Kay said, making (though too violently, I think now) the tuna casserole I like enough to eat twice a year. "I called everywhere," she said. "It was as if you didn't exist."

Upset, her hair spilling out of the French roll she prefers, she said more, two or three paragraphs whose theme was my peculiar behavior and the sly way I had lately and what time I was supposed to be somewhere and yet was not; and suddenly, taking note of the thump-thump my heart made and how one cloud in the east looked like a bell,

I stood at the sink, steadily drinking glass after glass of water, trying to put some miles between me and her suspicions. Terri Ann Mackey Cruz Robinson Cross was all over me, my hands and my thighs and my face; and, a giant step away, my wife was asking where I'd been.

"You were going to call," Ellen Kay said. "You had an appointment, a meeting." I had one thought, which was about the bricked-up middle of me, and another, which was about how like TV this situation was. "I talked to Bill Watson at the bank," she said. "He hasn't seen you for a week, ten days. I called—"

Her wayward husband had a moment then, familiar to all cheaters and sorry folks, when he thought he'd tell the truth; a moment, before fear hit him and he got a 3-D vision of the cheap world he'd have to live in, when he thought to make plain the creature he was and the no-account stage he stood upon.

"I was at the golf course," I said, "watching Pudge. They have a match tomorrow."

The oven was closed, the refrigerator opened.

"Which course?" she said.

Forks and knives had been brought out, made a pile of.

"Coronado Hills," I said. "Pudge is hitting the ball pretty good."

She went past me a dozen times, carrying the plates and the bread and the fruit bowl, and I tried to meet her eyes and so not give away the corrupt inside of me. I thought of several Latin words—*bellum* and *versus* and *fatum*—and the Highland Park classroom I learned them in.

"All right," she said, though by the dark notes in her voice it was clear she was going to ask Pudge if he'd seen me there, by the green I'd claimed to have stood next to, applauding the expert wedge shot I'd seen with my very own eyes.

As in the former story of illusions and the mess they make crashing down, there is a pause here, one of two; and you are to imagine now how herky-jerky time moved in our house when Pudge drove up and came in and said howdy and washed his hands as he'd been a million times told. You are to imagine, too, the dinner we picked at and our small talk about school and American government and what money does. While time went up and down, I thought about Pudge the way evil comic book Martians are said to think about us: I was curious to know how I'd be affected by what, in a minute or an hour, would come from the mouth of an earthling who, so far as I knew, had never looked much beyond himself to see the insignificant dust ball he stood upon. I saw him as his own girlfriend, Traci Dixon, must: polite, fussy as a nun, soft-spoken about everything except golf and how it is, truly, a full-fledged sport.

Part of me—that eye and ear which would make an excellent witness at an auto wreck or similar calamity—flew up to one high corner of the room, like a ghost or an angel, and wondered what could be said about these three people who sat there and there and there. They were Democrats who, in a blue moon, liked what Bush did; they had Allstate insurance and bankbooks and stacks of paper that said where they were in the world and what business they conducted with it; they played Scrabble and Clue and chose to watch the news Dan Rather read. The wife, who once upon a time could run fast enough to be useful in flag football, now used all her energy to keep mostly white-collar rednecks from using the words *nigger* and *spic* in her company; the son, who had once wanted to be an astronaut or a Houston brain surgeon, now aimed to be the only Ph.D. in computer science to win the Masters at Augusta, Georgia; and the father—well, what was there to say about a supposedly learned man for whom the spitting image of God, Who was up and yonder and everywhere, was his own father, a bent-over and gin-soaked cattle rancher in Midland, Texas?

I hovered in that corner, distant and disinterested, and then Ellen Kay spoke to Pudge, and I came rushing back, dumb and helpless as anything human that falls from a great height.

"Daddy says you had a good round this afternoon," Ellen Kay began. "You had an especially nice wedge shot, he says."

She was being sneaky, which my own sneaky self admired, and Pudge quit the work his chewing was, a little confusion in his round, smart face. He was processing, that machine between his ears crunching data that in no way could ever be, and for the fifteen seconds we made eye contact I wanted him to put aside reason and logic and algebra and see me with his guts and heart. On his lip he had a crumb that, if you didn't tell him, would stay until kingdom come; I wanted him to stop blinking and wrinkling his forehead like a first-year theater student. The air was heavy in that room, the light coming from eight directions at once, and I wanted to remind him of our trip last January to the Phoenix Open and that too-scholarly talk we'd had about the often mixed-up relations between men and women. I had an image of me throwing a ball to him, and of him catching it. I had an image of him learning to drive a stick shift, and of him so carefully mowing our lawn. Oddly, I thought about fishing, which I hate, and bowling, which I am silly at, and then Ellen Kay, putting detergent in the dishwasher, asked him again about events that had never happened, and I took a deep breath I expected to hold until the horror stopped.

Here is that second pause I spoke of—that moment, before time lurches forward again, when the eye needs to look elsewhere to see what is ruined, what not. Pudge now knew I was lying. His eyes went here and there, to the clock above my shoulder, to his mother's overwatered geranium on the windowsill, to his mostly empty plate. He was learning something about me—and about himself, too. Like his made-up counterpart in "Mirrors," he was seeing that I, his father, was afraid and weak and damaged; and like the invented daddy in that story I read, a daddy whose interior life we were not permitted to see, I wanted my own child, however numbed or shocked, to forgive me for the tilt the world now stood at, to say I was not responsible for the sad magic trick our common back-and-forth really is.

"Tell her," I said. I had in mind a story he could confirm—the Coke we shared in the clubhouse, a corny joke that was heard, and the help I tried to be with his short game—a story that had nowhere in it, two days ago, a father cold and alone and small.

THE WAY SIN IS SAID IN
WONDERLAND

1.

THE FIRST TIME they met, Eddie pulled out the pistol. A Soviet
Makarov nine-millimeter automatic with rust spots on the barrel and
a faded red star on the black plastic handgrip. This was '72, the summer before the bailout from Saigon, the occasion a welcome-home
barbecue for Bobby, her husband, and his buddy from MR II up near
Con Tien.

"This is I-Beam," Bobby said. "Short for IBM, he's smart."

Turned out he almost had a degree in physics from the University of Houston, but Carol Ann didn't know that yet; she only knew
that he was a wiry so-and-so, slope-shouldered and skinny as a file
but surprisingly soft-spoken, as if all Uncle Sam had asked him to do
during his hitch was to sit atop a jungle roost drinking skim milk and
nodding hunky-dory to the dignitaries making merry on the prome-
nade below.

"A pleasure," he said, and then nothing: just the two of them, the
afternoon August sun a huge orange behind his head, while Bobby

hurried away to say howdy to the new people coming through the gate into the backyard. "Eddie," he said, "L-for-Lonnie Heber."

She got her name out then, Carol Ann Spears, surprised by the mealy mouthful it was, and what she did, a teacher at Zia Elementary near Pecan Acres south of town, and then she realized that her hand was still locked in his—a cold thing big as a paddle—and it crossed her mind when she again engaged his dark eyes that here was a fellow with secrets you might need a whole lot more than *open sesame* to find out.

Throughout the afternoon, she watched him. He took a chair near Bobby and didn't say much. Let Bobby do the bullshitting. "Should I tell 'em about the S-2?" Bobby said once, and Carol Ann discovered Eddie Heber staring at her, grinning this time as if the two of them— he and she—had made a connection the grits and white bread folk between them wouldn't comprehend if you wrote it down and drew pictures of the sort her second-graders whooped over.

"Sure, help yourself," Eddie said, and Bobby was off, his an escapade that seemed to take as long to tell about as it did to live through.

She picked up a little—the LT, the boonie rats, the LURPs, Sam the Sham—before she went back to her conversation with Rhonda Whitaker and Ellen Dowling. Rhonda's boy, Jerry, was deficient in history, plus being a cut-up in class. Still, a minute later, she could feel him again, Eddie Heber. A smile with too much tooth in it. A face so alive it required concentration to watch. Spooky. He looked like a fugitive that had raced all night through prickers and brambles to get here.

That's the way it went until dusk. A volleyball game started, girls against guys, and every time she jumped or chased the ball when it rolled over to the Hoovers' fence, he was watching, this funny little fucker from Albuquerque. She felt naked, like a specimen, like the hamsters in the cage in the science corner of her classroom—just a piece of business for his amusement—so after the third time she had to bend over in front of him, her shorts squeezing up her thighs, she thought she'd just march right up to him, get in his face, tell she didn't appreciate his—what?—his leering, and he could just smack his lips somewhere else, she didn't care what had happened in Vietnam.

But when she spun around, he was gone. His chair had a half dozen empties beside it.

"C'mon," Bobby was saying, wanting the ball. "Let's go, Carol Ann. Everybody's waiting."

Then she saw him talking to Ellen Dowling by the keg, and he seemed bigger, more muscular, less bowed and clutched-up, a whole other order of human being—like something born in midair and half an idea that wouldn't make sense until you were eighty or eight thousand.

The Millers, Hank and that airhead of his, Carla, went home first. About nine. After that, folks started drifting out in twos and threes— the Krafts, Mr. Preston who owned the hardware store where Bobby, having flunked out of State, had worked after his reclassification to 1-A. "Welcome home, short stuff," they said. "Glad you're back." Then the Fosters took Rhonda home—she'd squabbled with George, her creepy husband, and he'd left with a couple of Bobby's old Bulldog teammates from Las Cruces High. About eleven, Margie and Louis Delgado said adios. Carol Ann was tired. Bobby had been home two days, and all he wanted to do was screw. Wanted her to take it from behind, wanted to do it with the lights on, like they were on a stage. And all he'd talked about was this Eddie Heber. This primo buddy of his. Coming down from the Duke City for the cookout. "Me and Eddie," Bobby had said, "we were tight." Tight—a word Bobby had wound up his whole face to say.

She'd taken three personal days, gotten the sub herself—Mrs. Feldman—done the lesson plans, made the slaw and the potato salad, called all the guests, and now, watching Bobby scuttle back and forth like a dog between bones, she was beat, hollow as an echo. It wouldn't make any difference to Bobby: He'd want her any way. He was feeling good—loosey-goosey, he called it. Wouldn't be spit to him that his buddy, Eddie L-for-Lonnie Heber, would be snoring on the couch in the living room. You could hear through the walls in this place—that's what the builder was famous for, ticky-tack and walls you could poke your pinkie through—but Bobby wouldn't care. He'd want to party. To shake his tailfeathers. His phrase. Then, like the blackest of black magic, her thoughts flying whichaway, Eddie was beside her, light-footed enough to be a ghost, his lips almost against her ear, his whisper a knot she couldn't find the beginning to.

"What?" she asked. Outside, Bobby was bear-hugging Sammy Vaughn and then playing grab-ass with Sammy's ex-wife Alice. Somewhere a car door slammed and somebody—Harry Hartger, another of Bobby's old bosses—was singing a Joe Cocker tune he didn't have the recklessness for, and here came Eddie Heber again—at the other ear this time—smelling of beer and charcoal and English Leather, his the voice the devil might have if it popped up in your living room near midnight to watch you tidy up. "What?" she said.

"I said you're probably a heartbreaker, right?"

The pistol came out then. He reached under his shirt, a Hawaiian eyesore he later said he'd bought as a joke.

"I know you," he said, half his face closed, the other half open like a closet door. "I know your hair, the size of your shoe."

For a moment, Carol Ann thought it was a squirt gun or maybe a cap pistol—a toy remarkable and cunning as theories about lived life on Mars—and then, clearly, it wasn't, and when he pulled back the slide and it seemed entirely possible that a round had been chambered, she could see that whatever was in him had turned around at least three whole times.

"You were a Zeta girl," he said. "Pledge chairman."

His jaw was slowly working, a sheen of sweat at his temples, his eyes beer-glazed and starting to go red at the corners, his breathing quick and labored as if he were thinking about sex or had done the impossible—like carry the ocean to her in his arms all the way from California without spilling a drop.

"Over there," he was saying, "I saw your picture a million times. Made Bobby get me a copy."

Later—after she and Bobby had divorced, after Eddie had reentered her life—she remembered this moment for what didn't happen. She did not panic. She remembered turning toward him, not increasing by much the arm's length between them, just swiveling as if on a pivot. A man, marvelous as a maniac from a movie, was standing in front of her. He seemed shiny and slick, more a figure sprung from a dream than from any crossroads on earth. He had something in his hand—a gift, possibly—but her own hand was coming up to decline it. She remembered being clear-minded, her thoughts as shaped and ordered as pearls on a string, and after she gently pushed the gun aside she advanced on him, feeling his heat as she got closer, stopping at the point where, if her breasts were to brush his shirtfront, he might vanish like a soap bubble.

"I made up stories," he was saying. "You were wearing a dress, a white one. The boys at LZ Thelma loved that story."

Outside, Bobby was still messing around. Tonight he would want her, sloppy and rough and over in a wink. After that, she would sleep, scrunched over to the edge of the bed, the ex-PFC sprawled beside her about as easy to rouse as a log. It would be morning after that, and him starved for her anew.

"Where'd you get the gun?" she asked.

Firebase Maggie, he said. Belonged to a dink.

She was almost his height and close enough now to see he had excellent teeth, white and straight, not yellow and fang-like as she'd feared. It seemed a tunnel had opened onto a distant and severe light.

"You kill him?" she wondered.

"Found it," he said. "A dozer dug it up when some concertina wire was being strung at the perimeter."

She was nowhere now, she thought. She had stepped through a gap—a seam, a tear—and tumbled into a world as deformed as dreamland itself. She had slipped through in an instant, quick as a wish, but she was not alone.

"You trying to scare me?" she said. "Or just piss me off?"

He seemed to ruminate then, something in his face gone to tilt, and it occured to her that he might be suffering a fever. What was it they could get over there? Dengue or beri-beri or malaria.

"I'm drunk," he said, but unslurred in a manner that gave her to understand he was sober as a surgeon.

"You sneaked up on me," she said. "That's not very sporting, Mr. Heber."

The other half of his face had come open now, as if a strong wind were blowing from his insides out.

"You get in the habit," he said. "It's like smoking."

Here it was, then—for reasons she understood she would need no less than a lifetime to comprehend—that she kissed him, tenderly at first and with her eyes open, him staring at her, too, but little in his expression to say that he hadn't expected their love affair to begin this way, not even when, before she let go, she bit his lip. Hard.

"I bet you're a son of a bitch, too," she said.

In 1986 they met again. It would turn out that he had been married as well, had three kids, all boys, who lived in Redondo Beach with their mother. He had been sliding, he would say. Drifting, coming undone—pick a word. Worked in aerospace for a while. LTV in Dallas. A computer company in San Antonio. Then—boom—a layoff. Squabbles. Fights. Tears like a river. Two days in jail in Houston. Worked the offshore rigs for a time. Next a breakdown. Total. Bugs on the walls, the night sweats. Visions. Voices from the TV. It was the booze. It was want and venery.

She hadn't heard him come in. At her desk, school over for an hour, she was marking a spelling test. A-l-l-i-g-a-t-o-r. R-e-p-t-i-l-e. The cold-blooded family you were wise to step over or avoid altogether. She was thinking about her boyfriend after Bobby Spears, a slim-hipped rancher up the valley who raised polled herefords. He liked to race motocross in the hills near Picacho Peak. Did impressions—Nixon, Porky Pig, Johnny Carson. Then, as if he'd materialized with a poof from a flashpot and a blast of horns from the biggest of the big bands, Eddie Heber was in the back of her room, sitting at Tiffany Garcia's desk, a cigarette going, his eyes flat again and dispassionate as math, and part of her seemed to have gone from wet to dry without any heat in between.

"If you're looking—" she began, but he was already shaking his head. He'd found what he was looking for.

When he said her name, something caught in her chest—a bone, a clot of tissue—and the air sucked out of the room. She would have known him anywhere: A light, weird and cold as a glacier, seemed to come off his skin. He was too pale, too much of everything lonely and still and sad. His hair was long now, past his shoulders, as sleek and beautiful as a matinee Apache, longer than her own; and except for that, he seemed not to have been gone long at all, only minutes, as if he'd just stepped out to use the toilet. But when he rose, she could see that maybe his face had come off and had been put back in pieces, the features loose on his skull, parts from different puzzles of the same scene.

"You can't smoke in here," she said. "Mr. Probert has a cow if anyone smokes in the building."

She was apologizing, she realized, and suddenly felt too big for her clothes, her life too small for anything unrelated to Eddie Heber.

"You want to go for a ride?" he said.

But when he sat near her, another desk scooted up close, she understood they wouldn't be leaving for a few minutes yet. He seemed to be composing himself, pulling himself into a shape she wouldn't be frightened by. She was stunned by his size. He was bigger now—weights, she would learn; he'd done sixteen months in Parchman, in Arkansas, a fourth-degree assault—and she thought about him without his shirt, without any clothes whatsoever, between them only light and air and time.

He'd gone off the deep end, he said. It wasn't a Vietnam issue. It was human. The wires too tight. The wheels spinning too hard. The twentieth century—all loop-de-loop and greed and the low road of scoundrels. Now he had a lawn and yard service. Greensweep. Been in town for over a year. Rented a house on Espina, up near the armory.

He had shoved the words in her head. That's what she thought later, that he had not spoken at all—not using the old-fashioned organs of speech, at least—and that somehow it had become time for her own short story.

"Bobby Spears," she began.

He nodded gravely. "A girlfriend. You got fucked over."

Carol Ann caught herself looking at his cigarette, its smoke like a cloud with curls and a beard. Eddie Heber knew. Everything.

"Me and Bobby had had drinks about ten months ago," he was saying. "At the El Patio bar in old Mesilla. Bobby Spears is a rock. He never changes."

"That was a long time ago," she said. "I'm better now."

In the silence, she could hear him breathing again, like that night over a decade before. His breath was language itself, she thought. It told you who and why, gave you information about the way you could behave, what you could expect. It wasn't complicated, just queer as reflections in a funhouse. Talk to be talked in the afterlife.

"Where's the gun?" she asked. She had to get that settled.

He stubbed out his smoke on the bottom of his boot. His hands were coarse, the fingers long and thick as hot dogs, the nails oddly well manicured. Plus, he had a tattoo now, a dragon on his forearm—"Jail-house art," he would say eventually.

"Threw it away," he told her. He'd stepped out on the chopper platform—this was at Texaco 31—and pitched the weapon into the Gulf of Mexico.

She had stood, the flutter of her heart the only thing about this encounter that didn't surprise her.

"I want that ride now," she said.

Before they went to his place, he drove south on I-10, almost down to Anthony, then turned back north on old 85, the two-lane nearer the mostly muddy Rio Grande. Time seemed to have stopped, the air thick with heat, sunlight scattered everywhere in splinters and spikes.

He'd been crazed, he said. An affliction. Once he hadn't been able to use his hands. They'd been hooves. Mallets. Whole days had passed when he couldn't talk. He'd seen a doctor. Another. He was angry, he told them. Genuinely and profoundly teed off. The world had failed him. He tried vitamins, yelling in the woods—the works. The world got fuzzy at the edges. Cynthia split. She hadn't needed a lawyer because he'd given her everything—the Ford, the house, even the Oreos in his lunch bucket.

It was late now, the sky west of her, toward Deming, rich with blood and streaky clouds with yellow undersides, everything too high and too filmy, and she thought she'd just awakened from a hard, terrible sleep—a sleep with too many people in it, too much jibber-jabber, and too much peril to be alone in—and the first person who'd appeared to her upon waking was this man next to her, the one saying that he hadn't made love to a woman in three years, maybe a little more. The pinching under heart had started again, but Carol Ann found she had a place in her head where she could arrange herself against him.

In his driveway he hurried around to her door and held out his hand—a gentleman. Touching him was like touching a circuit only God could flick the switch for—God, or another entity said to be lavish with lightning and brimstone. And while he guided her up the sidewalk, she wondered how she would explain this peculiar turn of events to her colleagues, particularly Ruthie Evans, her best friend; or to her students when Eddie began picking her up in the parking lot; or even to Bobby Spears himself should she bump into him in the Food Mart.

She was once Carol Ann Mobley, she told herself. Her mother was Rilla, to honor an ancient relative in Texas; her daddy was Bill but called Cuddy by the cowboys who worked the ranch. She had other thoughts, all impossible to collect: A wind, vicious as an argument, had come up to spread them willy-nilly. She believed she had asked him a question—"That night, what were you talking to Ellen Dowling about?"—and she believed he had answered—"You," he was thought to have said, "you and me"—but he was fumbling with his keys and all she could do was wait for the ground to quit shaking.

She seemed to recognize his house, the marvelous clutter inside. Afterward, she felt she'd suffered a vision, the present undone year by year by year until she was a child, a girl who was yet to grow up and go to college and meet a boy named Bobby who would bring into her life a man named Eddie who would unlock a door to a future she could barely walk through.

She was counting now—the world's snowflakes, the Sahara's grains of sand—putting between herself and whatever was coming next numbers she hoped one day to get to the end of. Eddie Heber had sat her down, swept several magazines off the sofa, *People*, the *Statesman*, a much-thumbed paperback *Webster's*, and he put a club soda in her hand; he was talking to her, one word—love—coming at her again and again, his voice the last ton of a twenty-ton day. It was a replay, she believed. She had already done it: She'd already peeled off her clothes and urged him down on top of her. She'd already felt him, fretful and needy and clumsy but cool as wax, move her this way and that, her hips rising, her fingers on the knobs of his spine and on his shoulders and on his knees, the strangled noise he made trying to hold himself back, her hands not strong enough for his head, her legs hooked behind his heels, the carpet scratching her back, boxes and crates and motor parts the only items to look at except for a face empty as a hoop.

Then it was over, the replay, and she was still dressed, out of numbers to count and soda to drink, and she had asked him if he was going to be bad for her.

He hoped not, he said. But one never knew.

"One?"

"A turn of phrase," he said. "Nothing personal."

She was studying his living room, a corner of the kitchen, the hall. Back there was the bedroom, she guessed. One would have to rise, one would have to walk. A path led through the books, the unbalanced-looking piles of them, the titles as much about rocks and trees as they were about stuff you had to know to survive what daylight revealed. Somehow, one would have to put oneself on that path, past the laundry in a heap, past the speaker cabinets and the snapshots that had spilled out of a grocery sack.

Robert Spears, she thought. That was a man she had known, as were Karen Needham's brother and Tim Whitmire. J. T. Something-something, a mechanic with a scar across his nose. Another who'd imagined himself Jerry Lee Lewis, a date as dull as was water wet. A decision had been reached, she realized. Later, these were the rooms she remembered when she wondered where she had abandoned herself. There: by the cushions. There: by the wobbly-looking table in a corner. There: near the end of a path to another door to pass through.

Now she was moving, her joints loose and oily, and Eddie had fallen in behind her, saying please excuse the mess. He was sorry. He'd intended to do more.

"That's all right," Carol Ann told him.

She had given pieces of herself away—a piece to every man she'd ever loved—and now, like coins and like words and like threads, they were all coming back.

2.

HE TOOK HER dreams first, little by little, the weight of them and their meaning. She dreamed of her daddy's ranch outside Clovis, the land wind-whitened and parched, and he took that. Eddie Heber. In junior high she had been a cheerleader, the Falcons, green and white pleated skirts with an appliqué megaphone stitched on the sweater. He took that, asking her to cheer for him, and applauded vigorously when she returned to bed. She'd broken her arm—her left—in a fall from a borrowed bike in front of her church. He grabbed that, and St. Andrew's itself, as well as the summer camp she went to in the mountains near Ruidoso. Her first snowman, her crush on Davy Crockett, the *Ed Sullivan Show* when she listened to the Beatles ask to hold her hand—he took those, and many times that first week she awakened with a start, her ears ringing, the sweat cold on her forehead, the sheets a tangle around her legs, and feared to see everything he'd taken suspended near the ceiling like stars to be wished upon.

Other times she found him staring at her. Or a part of her. Her ankle. The mole on her shoulder. A shaving nick on her knee. It was like being watched by a plant. Once she found him with a penlight, bent to her chest in wicked concentration. "Don't move," he said. Nothing else in the room was visible, as if beyond the light was only blackness void as space. The sheet around his shoulders, he smelled like well water and Marlboros, rusty and stale. "Ssshhh," he said. He held her lipstick, a red so blue in this light that it looked like ink. "You're beautiful," he said, the word as much made from iron and silver as from air and tongue and teeth.

He drew on her then, around her nipple, his mouth set hard as knob as if this were work that required precision and monk-like patience, a version of top secret science practiced underground. A moment later, he kissed her there, his lips soft as hair. A jolt surged through her, static sizzling up her spine. She wanted to say *no* as much as she wanted to say *yes*. She was in her skin. And out. Close and far. He would ruin her, she thought. He would take her apart hook by hasp by hinge and put her back together haphazardly and jury-rigged, the outside in, the private public as her face. Morning was coming, hazy and already squawky with birds in the tree outside their window, and she knew she'd soon find him on his back, his lips smeared and swollen and red.

For days—when she wasn't at school and when he wasn't mowing lawns or hauling yard trash—they talked. It developed that he could cook. "Baked fruit curry," he said once, showing her with a flourish the cherries and the pineappples and the peach halves. "Dilly bread," he said another time. "Eggplant casserole." They were announcements, these dishes. Declarations as formal as those that bigwigs got when they entered a ballroom to fanfare. In return, she told him about her wedding to Bobby Spears, the justice of the peace who'd performed the ceremony in the living room of her daddy's house, Bobby's haircut a whitewall like that he would get a year later from Uncle Sam. Her sorority sister, Deedee Harrison, had played the piano, "Cherish" by the Association. Her dress had come from Juarez, her own design of lace and satin and pearl buttons up the back. She had a lot to say, she felt, and exactly the right person to hear the whole of it. He drank— Bicardi, George Dickel, Buckhorn beer—and she talked. He cooked—chocolate cream roll, tamale ring—and she told about her cousins, Julie and Becky Sims, and how her mother danced the Hully Gully and the first time seeing her father without his dentures, until the string of her had unwound and gone slack and she understood, less with her mind than with the worn muscle of her heart, that Eddie Heber was crazy.

"My boys," he said one evening. Eric and Willie and Eddie, Junior. They were like him—agile as waterbugs and pesky, in and out of everything. They could cook, too. He'd learned it in the service— that's what he'd been, a chef, his MOS. An E-4 with a soup spoon. Cooked for the brass in Hotel Company with the 1/26. Petit Fours, Salmon mousse, lemon meringue pie—as at home in a pantry as was Picasso in a garret in gay Paree. Working for Uncle Sugar was like working at the Hilton Inn. The ruling class billeted in Airstream trailers, played golf on a three-hole course the Seabees had hacked out of the bush.

"Could've been Mexico," he said. "Puerta godamn Vallarta."

Still in his workshirt, the sleeves rolled to the elbow, he was making almond macaroons. After school, she'd spent the afternoon searching for rosewater, three teaspoons of it, and now he was putting the recipe together—the egg whites, the superfine sugar, the flour, the blanched nuts—moving between the baking sheet and his bottle of Black Jack on the counter. He'd become handsome, she thought. His hair was still long, tied back in a ponytail, his face now brown as a Mexican's, and she remembered that night, years and years before, when he was skinnier, drawn and wasted like a castaway, a man with a pistol and the hooded, melancholy eyes of a vagrant. He had not been trying to scare her, she thought. Not really. Even then, he had been in love. Love could make you do anything, maybe howl or drive in a circle. Love might even involve guns.

Vietnam, he was saying. Best time of his life. Fucking aces high. Like *Bandstand* without the dress code. All the brutal business in the highlands or the delta never got anywhere near him. Steppenwolf on the eight-track, Budweiser in the fridge. Direct phone link with the World. Tried to ring up Bob Dylan one night, tell the guy he was full of it. No answers were blowing in the freaking wind. Hell, nothing blew over there. By comparison, R&R was a major disappointment. Couldn't wait to get back in the bush and rustle up some Knickerbocker fritters for X-mas.

"That's not what Bobby said," she told him.

"Bobby," he said. He could've been referring to a tree he'd trimmed. "Bobby was a clerk. During the day, he typed COM/SIT reports, hustled the commissary files."

For a minute, she refused to believe it, a Polaroid of Bobby in camouflage coming to mind.

"He bought the outfit in Hong Kong," Eddie told her. "On Nathan Street. I got a suit, looked like the lost member of the Temptations."

In the next hour—humbug pie, with raisins and molasses—he showed her more of himself. He'd been a liar, he confessed. In high school. At Houston. Sophomore year, for example, he'd told a girlfriend that his parents were dead. Marge and Gene. In a car wreck near Portales. They were alive, he said. Retired. They liked to ski—

Sandia, Angel Fire over near Taos, up in Utah. His dad had worked for the Air Force, an engineer. His mom—

A question was coming, she realized. When he was finished, however long the current monologue took, however roundabout the getting there, he would ask her something—about them, certainly, but also about the vegetation and the land and the humans they were upon it—and she would have to get an answer out without stuttering like an idiot who'd only learned English the week before.

"Fix me a drink?" she asked.

He made her a Cuba Libre—too sweet, she would recall—and he told her about Cynthia.

"Maiden name Lanier," he said. "From Galveston, a bone fide heiress. Oil. A million cousins and uncles, mostly in Louisiana. A gruesome people. All named Tippy or Foot or Beebum."

"You hit her," she said.

The next second, she would remember, was the longest she ever lived through.

"Once," he said. "During a spell."

Another second came, it, too, filled with pins and points.

Afterward, he said, Cynthia had sicced a mob of close relations on him. Spent a week in Baylor Medical.

The sun had gone down a while ago and the kitchen, except for the light glaring over the stove, had become gloomy and choked with cigarette smoke. He was almost to the end of himself, she decided. All the bounce had left his voice, the ends of his sentences coming in whispers. Only dribs and drabs were reaching her: Fort Smith, Arkansas. A Starvin' Marvin. Light that turned the skin yellow as mustard. The walls wobbling. Behind the register, a female redneck, sullen as a snake. A quarrel about change. About the magazine rack. About the swirl the universe made going down the drain at his feet. Glass shattering, Pepsi bottles rolling like bowling pins. An arm, his own, sweeping along the service counter. The *Globe*. Castro playing voodoo with Kennedy's brain. Finally, a fist, his own. No more redneck Betty Boop standing up. Just, when the cops arrived, Edward L-for-Lonnie Heber sitting splay-legged in an aisle gobbling brown sugar from the bag.

"Eddie," she said.

She had his attention now, like being looked at by every peasant in China.

"Don't be crazy anymore, okay?"

"It's my temperament," he said. "I take offense."

He had put food in front of her—a wedge of pie and a macaroon, both cool—and she tried to eat a little. The light was in her eyes, still harsh as a screech, so she made him turn it off. She was thinking about her job—the numbers and shapes and science she was employed to pass on to the children that the neighborhood sent her. They liked geography, these kids. Tanika had chosen Zanzibar; Ellen Foley, Egypt. Cotton came from one place, copper from another. Everyone had a country to be responsible for—the tribes that rampaged the hinterlands, the chiefs who rose up to lead them, what they ate in their own huts and hovels, and what they loved first in a fight. That was the world, she thought. Ice at one corner, hot sand at another. That was the world, a patchwork you memorized for a test. That was the world—a spin of fire and smoke and wind and sweets to eat in the dark.

"Carol Ann," Eddie was saying.

He'd found her hand, and she, her heart a racket in her ears, could tell that his question was coming now—would she move in with him?—but she had her answer ready, the words of it as simple as those the lucky say in war.

After Valentine's Day, two weeks of living with him, she thought of the gun—Eddie's Makarov, scraped up from a field the LT had ordered cleared for horseshoes. She'd had a cold—the sniffles, chills occasionally—so she stayed home, faked a seal-like cough for Mr. Probert, then lay in bed all morning being serious with Donahue and Sally. At eleven, Jerry Springer came on—"Centerfold Sisters," the girls blond and top-heavy and humorless as nuns—so at the commercial she shuffled into the kitchen for a cup of Red Zinger. She was at the cupboard when she realized it was still here: the pistol.

Eddie hoarded, nothing decrepit enough or useless enough or suf-

ficiently broken to throw away. Everything, she realized, had come
with him: clothes, notes he'd scribbled to himself, a stack of *Times
Heralds* from Dallas, shoes he'd scuffed the heels from, books he'd
quit, letters and bills and cards from the kids. He'd made his way to
her, she thought, gathering scraps and scraps of paper along the way—
another trail—and, if she wanted, she could track backward through
his life, the piles and mounds of it, until she came upon him at, say,
fifteen—or five, or twenty—and could see him there, crumpled in
his hand the first thing that marked the path he was to travel
through time.

In what had become his reading room—the third bedroom,
already tiny and now cramped as an attic with cassettes and periodicals and accordion files—she sat in his chair, the footstool in front of
it laden with catalogues and maps of places he'd, so far as she knew,
never been to, places like France and mountainous Tibet, as remote
and strange as lands you found in pop-up books about fairies and gyp-
sies and high-hatted wizards.

For a time, she toyed with the switch to the floor lamp. On and off.
A cone of light over her shoulder, then a wash of morning as gray as
the paint on warehouses. He'd stuck foil on all the windows. A bulletin
board dominated one wall, his customers scheduled in a grid that went
till the new century. She was pleased to see that he'd planned to be
busy through 1999—the year, according to Mr. Probert, that Jesus,
willful and heedless as a spendthrift, was returning to boil the mess
man was. She imagined Eddie then, over fifty, still lean as pricey meat,
that figure beside him maybe her own aged self in a dress too fussy
with snaps and buckles and bows to be anything but science fiction.

Eddie was an optimist, she decided. Every morning, he made
lists—prune Mrs. Grissom's firebush, take down the shed at the Sam-
ples' house, get insecticide from the Mesilla Valley Garden Center—
and he drove away in his pickup knowing what lead to what and it to
another until, at sundown, he could come back to this room to draw
another X in his calendar. An X for then, an X for now. X's enough for
the future—maybe for jealous Jesus Himself—and whatever sob-
filled hours came after that.

She sighed when she looked at the metal file cabinet underneath the grid. That's where it was, she thought. The gun. For a moment, laughter from the TV reaching her even here, she wondered what he would say if he knew that she had opened a drawer, the top one, all squeaky and warped, and found it there, the barrel rust-flecked as she remembered, a web of cracks running up the grip on one side. She was curious about how his face would work, the chewing movements at his temples, if he knew that she'd held the pistol, absently rubbing the faded red star, studying the peculiar markings near the trigger guard, before she put it back—that squeak again—and went to see, as she was doing now, what opinions the bosomy Miss Septembers had regarding certain monkeyshines between girls and boys.

Once upon a time, she thought, Eddie had had a secret. Now she had one.

The end of February. March out like a lamb. Easter. He was fine for those months. May flowers. Then June and he arrived for the class party on the last day straight from work—a new home he was land-scaping in Telshor Hills, another big shot with a wallet like a loaf of bread. He ate a square of the spice sheet cake he'd baked the night before, drank Kool-Aid, even wore a party hat when Cheryl Lynn Baker—the Miss Priss in the third row—pointed out the rules. Parties and hats went together like salt and pepper. Afterward, when she was cleaning up, he told her she could relax.

"It doesn't happen the way you think," he announced. "It's gradual."

He was sitting at her desk, smoking with deliberation, flicking ashes onto a paper plate.

Other rules, she guessed. Out the window, she could see some older kids—sixth-graders, maybe Ruthie Evans's kids—gathered around the tetherball pole. It seemed probable that a fight would start out there. Or a powwow.

"It builds," he told her. "Something goes haywire. The waters rise."

In the hall, a bell was dinging: three-fifteen. School had ended, officially.

"You're warning me," she said, a question. The first of many. Like rules.

His shirt stained with sweat, a line of grit on his brow from his headband, he looked like a warrior who'd scrambled out of the hills for food.

"I fill up," he was saying. "It spills."

Outside, the sixth-graders were wandering off in pairs or alone. Mr. Probert was out there, she assumed, persnickity and loud as a drum. He looked like a man who'd removed his own sense of humor with a chain saw.

"You'll tell me when?" she asked.

Reaching for a fallen column of Dixie cups, he had stood, not hurriedly.

"I'll clean up," he said. "I'll tell you when."

For the Fourth of July, he took three days for them to visit her folks in Clovis. Since she'd left for college, her father had put in a pool, so he and Eddie sat under the awning on the cool deck drinking Pearl Light while she floated on a rubber raft near the diving board. Every now and then, she could hear them chuckling softly, then her daddy teasing her mother who wouldn't leave the porch for the sun. "That water's cold as scissors," she said once. The light here was different—thinner somehow, less wrathful than in the desert—the landscape grassier, not so hardpan but without tooth-like mountains at the horizon to show you how far you had to go.

On the Fourth itself, they watched the fireworks from the city twelve miles south, miniature bursts of gold and green, like showers of foil, the sounds of the explosions arriving well after she'd seen the glitter against a sky black as the cape a witch wears.

"Incoming," Eddie remarked once, before taking her hand to let her know he was fooling. It had been like this in Vietnam, he told her father. A swimming pool, a porterhouse steak for each trooper, and a Air Force light show far, far away.

That night, after her parents had gone to bed, Carol Ann wished Eddie sweet dreams at the door to the guest bedroom where he was to sleep.

"They don't know," he said. "About us, I mean."

She couldn't see much of his face, just eerie glints from his cheek and nose. She hoped he was smiling.

"They're old-fashioned," she said. "Mother would be upset."

His hand came up then, out of the darkness, and reached into the cup of her swimsuit to hold her breast. He was dry, nothing in his touch to suggest that she was more to him than wood and nails and strings to pull.

"You didn't tell me you had a nickname," he said. "Squeaky."

Larangytis, she said. In grade school. It was, well, embarrassing. Sounded more like a frog than a mouse.

"You had a horse, too," he said. "Skeeter. It threw you out by the corral."

His hand was still there, unmoving. He could have been wearing a leather glove, and for a second she thought to go in the room with him, that she would shrug off her top and lie beside him until whatever was kicking at his heart ran out of anger.

"I like your parents," he told her. "They're stand-up people. You don't get much of that nowadays."

He had stopped smiling, she supposed. You could hear the earnestness in his voice, the sour note it was. She guessed he was thinking about the heroes he rooted for in the books he bought— books whose covers were all about doom and distress and deeds wrought by righteousness. In those books, standing up was a virtue. So far as she understood, the vices included hypocrisy and backstabbing. In Eddie's books, the characters suffered no fools. They rose up, indignant as children, and let fly with arrows and poleaxes and lances.

"Eddie?" she said.

His hand had moved, like a claw. Down the hall, her father was coughing, a wheeze without any charm to it. She had been Squeaky once, she thought. She been a Mobley, then a Spears. Now what? What were you in the dark? *One.* That had been Eddie's word months and months ago. What were you when the gears slipped or ground or disengaged completely?

"It's happening," he said.

She nodded.

"Forewarned is forearmed."

3.

IN EARLY AUGUST, he stopped cooking. For several days he ate only peanut butter from the jar, then macaroni and cheese. He stared at the TV, yelled abuse at the prettified newsfolk NBC had hired to educate him.

"You could see a doctor," she told him one evening.

Only as a last resort, he said. It was like breathing through a soaked washcloth. They wrenched open your skull, dropped a torch in there, wriggled their fingers in the slop.

His hand was shaking in a fashion she suspected he was unaware of. It got better as you got older, he'd told her on the drive back from Clovis. He was getting older all the time.

"You're proud, aren't you?"

He smiled at her then, the whole of his face engaged in the effort.

"I am the King of Pride," he said. "The absolute fucking monarch."

On Thursday, the day his letter to the editor appeared in the *Sun-News*, he was working for Judge Sanders, putting in a rock and cactus garden, so she drove over to park at the corner, far enough away to be inconspicuous. She'd seen the list—ocotillo, monkey flower, brittlebrush, gravel from an arroyo behind A Mountain—his handwriting square and tight, as if written with a chisel.

They'd made love the night before—he only to her, she believed, but she to eight or nine of him. One of him had been feverish, another chilled enough to get goose bumps. One laughed, another whistled from the foot of the bed and lunged at her like a tiger, his head wagging heavily, his eyes wide as nickels. The one in the refuge of the corner, knees to his chest, was not the one who rose from it, slow and shaggy-seeming. She hadn't been horrified, she thought now, recalling the steady thump of her heart. The lovemaking itself had been tedious: a matter of tabs and slots and deliberate movement. Eddie had been dry weight, all bone and ash—flesh that rocked back and forth regularly as clockwork. Once he sang along with his boom box— Patsy Cline, she remembered—but his voice had run out long before the music did, and when she lifted his face to look at him, she discovered that he was gone, the shell of him slick and unfeeling as glass.

"It's like a landslide," he said. "Imagine a mountain crashing down on your head."

He was a shade, she'd thought. Insubstantial as an ghost. And for a time, astride him, trying to make him hard, she believed he was trying, in a way twisted with love, to protect her from the knowledge that life was not glorious and purposeful and prodigious with reward. They were a kind, he and she, dragged upright by time but too stupid to follow the generally forward direction thought best to go.

"Help me, Eddie," she said. "Please, help me."

He was trying, he said.

Again, she asked, but this time he said nothing, so she leaned into him, his smell at once tangy and greasy, salt and lemon and soap, her face against his neck, her lips to his ear, saying the word *love* with as much bite as she imagined a dictator might say the word *kill*.

Much later—after she'd gone away, after he'd come back to himself—she realized that this was the first time she'd told him she loved him, but it was a sentence she remembered cleaving to, like a monotonous beat, for one minute, then two, as pure and aggrieved the last time said as it was the first. The covers in a heap at the foot of the bed, she grew cold as she spoke, the *I* of her pressed into the *you* of him, not knowing what she hoped to prove, then knowing—from his witless moans, from his hand stroking the small of her back—that she had everything to prove: He would be worse before he was better—yes, she understood that—but he had to know, even in the worst of it, that she loved him.

So she kept saying it, a speech delivered into his neck and shoulder, to his cheeks and his forehead as she kissed him, into his chin after he smoothed back her hair, to his lips until he'd stopped trembling and she was quiet and it seemed that nothing—least of all sentiments having to do with the soul of her—had been said at all, until they reached a point in the night when he drew her to his chest to tell her to listen closely to the clatter and bang in him that were his various demons.

"I'm scared, Eddie," she said.

So was he, he told her. He was helpless.

On one wall several shadows were at play from the flickering candlelight, none of them meaningful or part of love.

"Tell me about the picture," she said. "The one Bobby made for you."

It was her spring formal, he said. She looked like ice cream to him. The only cool thing in the world. The LT, a West Point grad, had said Eddie's affection for it bordered on the inordinate.

"That was wrong," Eddie said. "My affection was as ordinate as the day is long."

Scarcely an inch apart, they lay side by side. Like an old couple, she thought. A modern schoolmarm and the King of Pride. She thought of her parents—Rilla and Cuddy—lying, probably like this, as distant from her as she seemed to be from Eddie. Once, when she was seven, she'd watched them nap, and she had tried, standing at the door to their bedroom, to imagine their dreams, wondering at last if, where in them it was dark and breezy and broad as heaven, they dreamed themselves lying each by each, inert and almost breathless, no one but Carol Ann to beckon them back to the wakeful world.

"Let's go to sleep, Eddie," she'd said.

Yes, he said, an answer with too much hiss in it.

"I love you," she'd said.

And he'd said it, too, the terrible simplicity of it all she could remember between then and now, between Eddie looking as if his arms would fly off in agony and Eddie now bustling back and forth in the sun at Judge Sanders's house.

In her lap, she had the *Sun-News* open to the letters page. It was mid-August, school to start in three weeks, and already some lame-brains were writing to complain about a teachers' strike Carol Ann didn't think would actually happen. At home, reading his letter had frightened her, but here, only a half block from him, she tried again, saying aloud the first paragraph—it seemed as long as her forearm— until her eyes came free of the page and she could see that Eddie was stock-still at the door to his pickup, his head tipped back, the sky blank and almost white behind him. Edward L. Heber, the letter-writer, was not lunatic. Edward L. Heber was angry. Things are out of whack, he'd written. Collapsed and ruined. There is hunger. And ignorance. And false piety. And—but she'd stopped again, Eddie with a broom now, leaning on it and again gazing upward.

He was a moralist, she decided. Maybe that was good. A hopey thing with wings.

For another twenty minutes she watched him work, the yardage between them filled only with heat shimmering up from the asphalt. Load after load, he was shoveling out gravel, carrying it to a pile near the walk leading to the judge's front door. Clearly, this was how he managed—one simple undertaking at a time, scoop, walk, dump—his manner calculated and efficient, as if he could do this, happily and well, until he found himself at the bottom of a pit, alone at last with the one stone that had made him furious. She tried to conceive of the inside of his head—the fountain of sparks in there, the rattle—but a second later she realized he had stopped, in midstride almost, as fixed as a scarecrow.

"What're you doing here?" he said.

Still carrying the shovel, he had taken only a half minute to reach her—she'd timed it. Amazingly, he had not dropped even one pebble.

"I don't know," she said. "I should be over at school, but—" She shrugged. What with the union yakking about the strike, she didn't see any profit in fixing up her classroom if in a week she was going to be walking a picket line and generally making a spectacle of herself. "I thought we could go out to dinner tonight," she said. "Maybe a movie after."

It was blabber. What she really wanted to do was grab his sleeve, make him leave the shovel here, the truck there, and get in the car with her. They would sit for a while, another lovelorn couple in paradise. She would hold his hand—or he, hers—the afternoon would wear on, dusk would arrive, then twilight, then night itself full of random twinkles or a moon on the wane.

"I made a call," he said. "This morning."

Before she understood completely what he'd done, she sought to rewind time, yank the cord of it back so that he was not here, beside her window. She yearned to be young again, the ideas of love and loyalty as alien to her as were orchids to Eskimos.

"Bobby Spears," she said, a statement of fact, like the number of bushels in a peck.

The shovel jerked now, a handful of gravel spilling.

"He's got an extra room," Eddie said. "You'll be safe there."

Her lungs filled then—a gasp, nearly—and she feared Eddie would be turning now, going away, back to his work, back to the truck, back to the thirty-two steps between it and the mountain he had contrived to erect in the front yard of a retired Federal Court judge. He was trying to protect her again. Maybe that was good, too.

"Don't be mad, Carol Ann," he said. "I don't know anybody else."

"What about the girlfriend?" she asked.

They were married, Eddie told her. The girl—Sally or Sarah; he wasn't sure—was pregnant. Bobby was different now.

"This seemed like a smart idea, Eddie?"

He looked beleaguered, a beast run to ground by hounds and horses.

"I only had one card left," he said. "I played it."

On the seat next to her, the paper was still open, the rage and sorrow of this man not anything any citizen would remember tomorrow, or the days to follow. Elsewhere were articles about mayhem and conniving and the snapped-off ends of hope. We are craven, Eddie had declared to his neighbors, and to his neighbors' neighbors, and to anyone else who could read left to right. We must mend. Now.

"How long?" Carol Ann wondered.

He didn't know, he said. Six weeks maybe, more or less. It'd been quite a while since the last episode.

She thought about the night before, watching him sleep, the peace it had seemed to bring him, then her own sleep, nothing but wire in her dreams—fists of it, huge coils sprung and flyaway and mangled— then awake and seeing him frozen in the hall, the light a streak in front of him, his face shriven and collapsed, a scary amount of time going by before he shivered to life again and stumbled toward her.

"I'll give you a month," she said. "I couldn't last any longer."

Okay, he said, little in the word to indicate it had any meaning for him.

"I gotta go back to work, Carol Ann."

"Okay," she said, her turn not to mean too much.

He moved then, the shovel a counterweight to keep him from falling over in a heap. His tattoo had come into view, crude and obviously unfinished, the handiwork of a B&E offender named Pease. Sometimes Eddie wore a bandage to cover it. He was ashamed, he'd told her long ago. A dragon, he'd sneered. How fucking pathetic.

"Eddie," she called.

More gravel fell.

"What'd you see last night?" she asked. "In the hall."

He told her then, but she believed she hadn't heard correctly, so she asked him to repeat himself—"Fire," he said, the way sin is said in wonderland. And while he walked away, she thought she could see it, too, the yellow and red of it roaring up and up, and the terrifying wind of it overtaking everything in front of her—the trees, these houses, the telephone poles, shrubs, Eddie's truck, at last Eddie himself—until all that remained was rubble scorched black as a nightmare.

4.

SHE GUESSED that he cracked—caved in completely—her second week on the picket line in front of her school. She had not gone to Bobby's house—"It would be too complicated," she'd told Sally, Bobby's pretty wife; instead, she rented a furnished efficiency in a fourplex Mr. Probert owned up the valley toward Hot Springs, a place where she learned, the instant the door shut behind her, that a day could have too many hours in it, an hour too many minutes, time as mixed and fluid and dreadful as heartsickness itself. She woke too early, she discovered. Stayed up too late, darkness a thing that seemed to have texture and depth.

The first few days, she didn't eat much, once almost fainting on the line, so each morning thereafter before her shift, she made breakfast—a bowl of Cheerios, wheat toast and jelly, a glass of grapefruit juice—and sat in front of it with the promise to herself that she would do this—and the next chore, plus whatever ought to follow—and then, for one creaky revolution of the planet at least, she would not have to do it again. Often as she ate, she wondered what Eddie was doing, the idea of him so urgent and so virile that sometimes he seemed to appear across from her, his hair gleaming, his face soaking up most of the light she needed to see by.

Several times she called, his machine clicking on to say he was not in. He'd bought a gag tape—the voices of Daffy Duck and Bogart and Ronald Reagan—and twice, aiming to be cheerful, she left messages in the style of Marilyn Monroe and Yosemite Sam. The last time she told him the gossip she was hearing—Rae Nell Tipton was divorcing Archie, the slime; Mavis Rugely had a goiter—but she quickly ran out of silly news and, the tape whirring like a breeze, she suspected he was squatting near the phone, his own cigarette going, a comforter over his shoulders to keep him from coldness no one else in Dona Ana County could feel.

"Go to bed, Eddie," she said softly. "Put the beer down, honey. You need rest."

She imagined him shuffling back to the bedroom, all the lights on so he could see the winged creatures in the night that had swooped down to scold him.

"Lie down," she told him, and when she assumed he was settled, the covers bunched to his neck, she began to talk to him again, hers the voice she used at school when it was time for nap and dreams fine as mist. They would go places, she promised him. Canada. Niagara Falls. Florida. If he wanted, he could invite his kids. They'd rent a van, maybe a Winnebago, and in the summers they'd drive all over America. She'd camped a lot, she reminded him. She knew the forest. Plus, she liked to climb, the steeper the better, get to the peak of a mountain and shout into the valley you'd left. "I'm a good sport," she said, listening closely. He wasn't asleep, she thought. He remained alert there, still suspicious, his gaze as watchful as a stray dog ready to run.

"It's okay, sweetheart," she said, and took enough breath to start again on the list of vistas to visit and adventures to share.

The next day, she thought she saw his truck a ways down the block from the sidewalk she marched up and down on, but she couldn't be sure: Kirby Holmes, the loudmouth from the classroom next to hers, was telling another of his Cajun jokes—a singsongy anecdote with too many wishy-washy characters in it and about nothing life-or-death that could actually happen between men and women. She became distracted—Kirby was jumping around and making her look here and there—and suddenly what might have been Eddie Heber, maybe standing beside his pickup, his wave constant and spiritless, was only emptiness, just a street that went up and up and finally over a hill, a curve going on and on into the sterile and wild desert.

He had cracked—she knew it—so that night she drove over to his house. "Oh, Eddie," she sighed, as much exasperated as frightened. All the lights were on—inside and out, as far as she could tell—the place a glow she figured the cops might worry over. After she used her key to get in, she suppressed the impulse to turn around, to close up the house again, and disappear.

"Eddie," she called.

A tornado had torn through here, it seemed, and she wondered where in the litter of tipped-over furniture and strewn paper and crumpled clothes she would find him.

"It's me, baby," she said, then again and again until she tired of the echo.

Cautiously, she picked her way through the living room, magazines like stepping-stones laid out by a child. He'd been drinking Coors, she noticed, at least a case of empty cans stacked in a lopsided pyramid beside his chair, and for a moment she presumed to smell him, the sand he brought home in his jeans, oil and gasoline from his mowers, the sticky goop that trees left on his shirt. In the next moment, she made a lot of noise—coughing, slamming the door—the hopeful half of her certain that he would rush out of the bedroom now, or the bathroom, and lead her somewhere by the hand as he had the first time she'd come here; but she could see the holes in the plasterboard, the hammer plunged in a gash near the kitchen entry—dozens and dozens of holes, precise and in a pattern that she suspected would remain awful even from over a mile away—and she knew that Edward Lonnie Heber had lost his ability, miraculous as love itself, to appear in her life out of thin air.

In the kitchen, she found the knife on the counter, its blade crusty with dried blood. Next to it was a smeared handprint—three fingers and the heel of his palm. Another smudge. And a third, droplets spattered against the backsplash and on the floor tile leading to the hall. Her heart in her throat like a rat, all claws and confusion, she told herself to calm down—"An accident," she insisted and, after another moment to believe it, insisted it again—and followed the splatters to the bathroom, where the sink was splotched with prints and speckles of blood, the medicine cabinet door hanging open. He'd had an accident, she thought. He'd gotten out iodine, Mercurochrome, and Curad bandages, the box of adhesive tape ripped apart as if he'd attacked it with his teeth. From the tub she picked up a towel matted with more blood. He had been crazy. And bleeding. And bending over here to—what?

Sitting on the edge of the tub, she was thinking hard about not thinking even one little bit. "Be calm," she told herself.

Later, when he came home and she could see that he'd tried to slice out the tattoo on his arm, she told him that she'd run throughout the house then, out of thoughts to think, at once furious and miserable. Numb and trembling, she opened every door, even the closets, a part of her convinced that he'd fled into one and that she'd find him curled on the floor, unconscious in a nest of shoes and workboots, only the body of him left to holler at or pound on.

She went into the backyard, she told him, into the utility room at back of the carport, that she'd looked behind the stockade fence he'd built to hide the garbage cans from the street. She told him what her heart was doing, the ragged riot it was, and how quickly she'd run out of breath and that she'd stubbed her toe in his study when she'd seen that his X's had stopped, all of them; and that she'd only sat when she played back his messages, hearing voice after metalic voice, men and women alike—some fretful, a few downright offensive—asking where the hell he was or would he come on Wednesday; and then came her own voice, whispery and strained, at the instant she spotted his note to her on his wall calendar, a little girl's voice almost that asked him to call her, to say he was all right, that she missed him, even as she read his note once, then twice, then a third time before the sentences, clearly too ordinary to be only about him and her, made sense: "It's bad," he'd written. "I'm checking myself in. Don't know how long. I knew you'd come."

Somewhere a car horn was blasting. It seemed endless, noisy as news from hell.

I can wait, she told herself.

In the morning, she called Ruthie. She had not slept, she thought, though she did remember bolting up rigid and saucer-eyed three or four times from a dense and muddled state akin to sleep. She had been dropping down a hole, the bottom hurtling up silently to catch her.

"I'm going to have to skip my shift," she said.

"No problem," Ruthie said. "You'll miss Rae Nell's celebration, though. The ice-cream man's supposed to come by, union treat."

Ruthie went on—harmless chitchat about Rae Nell's separation, plus Mr. Probert's scowling at the pickets from his office window—but Carol Ann could not listen.

Dawn had come up sparkling and sharp, the destruction around her plain to even the most innocent eye. She was being evaluated, she felt, and the image of a big book—an old-timey ledger of a book, sizable enough for the paws of Goliath of Gath himself—had come into view. A hand seemed poised over a newly turned page, ready to begin the burdensome process of recording about her what had been true and not.

"It could be a while," she said. "You shouldn't count on me."

"You sick, Carol Ann?" Ruthie asked. "You sound pukey."

She considered what Eddie had left her, a whole year to keep her occupied. She had been drunk, she felt, all life's elements—the mineral included—beautifully sensible now that the fog had cleared between her ears. She would clean, she had decided.

"Personal business," she said. "Eddie says howdy."

After the first room, she developed a rhythm, trying to empty her mind to keep from crawling into bed and tugging the spread over her head for a year. Still, there were times—too many times, she would remember—when she found herself stopped, her eyes fixed on a wall or a doorway, the next thing to patch or to polish too much like the last. In the bathroom, she kept finding blood everywhere, as if he'd stood in the center of the room spinning, his arm outstretched, drops flying in a spray. She imagined him under the light fixture, weeping and turning and beating his arm against the sink, his head full of squawks and howls and hoots and groans, blood in streaks and splatters.

While she worked, she played his boom box—the Rascals, Simon and Garfunkel—keeping the music low so she would hear the phone when it rang. In the evening, she exercised with the barbell she'd uncovered in the storeroom by the Weber grill, and toward midnight, after her shower, she wrote letters on the portable Olivetti Eddie used for his monthly statements. "Dear Bobby," she typed, congratulating him on his marriage, on what a lively wife Sally seemed to be, and wishing him good fortune with his new baby. In too many pages, she explained their life together. They had been young, she wrote him. Babies themselves. They couldn't know what might make them joyful. Then she stopped, nothing between her brain and the keyboard but hands that seemed strange as boots on cows. In the background, the Everly Brothers were warning a bird dog to stay away from their quail; that bird dog was to leave their lovey-dove alone. "You were once a good man," she wrote. "You can be so again."

The next letter went to Eddie's kids, in care of their mother. "I am Carol Ann Mobley," she began. "I used to be a teacher." They were children, she remembered, the oldest—Eric, the towhead—no more than a seventh-grader, so she put down only those features of her character that they wouldn't be disappointed to discover on their own. "I am a Democrat," she wrote. "Except squash, I like most vegetables. I love your father very much. I oppose disloyalty and cheating. Maybe next summer we can meet, go to Yellowstone." She saw them in the wilderness, like pioneers, self-sufficient and content to feast upon the bounty nature provided. They had a house hewn from timbers Eddie had harvested. They bathed in streams, walked the hills and dales they owned. In the evening, after dinner, they stood in a circle, holding hands and looking upward to whatever eye was looking down.

That evening the last letter went to Milton E. Probert, Principal: "I quit," she wrote, adding the word respectfully above her signature before crossing it out. Respect had become irrelevant. As had duty and work life and civility, all the notions which made the past the past.

"Don't give the children to Kirby Holmes," she printed on the envelope after she sealed it. "He's a jerk and a show-off."

·   ·   ·

His call came later in September while she was wishing for rain, a sooty sky of it, a grade of weather from the meaner verses of the Bible.

"It's you," she said. The letter the night before—"The last of the last," she'd told herself—had been to her parents. I am getting married, she'd written. The man you met last summer. He's sick now, but he'll be well soon. Expect us for Christmas. "Where are you?"

The VA unit, he said. William Beaumont Hospital at Fort Bliss.

"That's in El Paso," she said. "I know that."

His reply was toneless, impersonal as a suit, as if he'd been taught to talk by spacemen.

"I could drive down," she said. "A visit."

She didn't know how, but she could tell he was shaking his head, and after a few seconds it came, his *no*. He was in tough shape, he admitted. They'd given him stuff, the medics. Drugs. His face had puffed up. "I looked like a pumpkin," he said. A moment passed—time like a maze dark and big enough to lose your way in—before she realized he'd made a joke.

"I called your customers," she told him. "You're in California, they think, a family emergency. Most of them understood."

She had more to say—that, in fact, she'd mown several lawns herself, that she'd learned how to run the weed-whacker, that she'd even cut down an upright willow with black-leaf disease. Many, many days had passed, she wanted him to know, and she was a quick study, but he was talking again, words coming to her as if they'd come to him down a wire from heaven, punctuation a courtesy only necessary to the crawling ugly order of beasts, little to suggest she wasn't listening to an angel, infernal as a machine, that could only chatter at top speed.

"Slow down, baby," she said.

Here it was then that he told her he'd cut his hair.

"It's a butch," he said. "I look in the mirror, there's a ghoul."

She remembered him as he'd been when they met—years and years ago. An eon, it seemed. There had been people—ghouls themselves, no doubt. Games had been played. She could remember laughter, throaty and barking. Arms and legs and hips and corners to round, shouts that became hoots, the music of horns, all brassy and clanging like sheets of metal, and always his eyes fixed on her, no matter where she was. It was like thinking about the age of dinosaurs and bogs, the world too wet and smoky and hot to support any animals except those pea-brained and ponderous, a time of bruise-like skies and churning, molten seas when humankind was not yet even mud.

"I'm forty-one," he said. "Christ, I'm supposed to live another thirty years."

Something had ended, she realized. Something new had begun.

"Eddie," she said, "what were you doing? Before you came to school that day—all those months before you took me home?"

His answer had no consequence, she thought. They had it, the pistol. It was Russian, she recalled. Mar-something. Or Mak-. In that drawer, the screechy battered drawer. She'd held it earlier that day, light as a book you could read in an hour. It had once been Eddie's, now it seemed to be hers. Whatever. It was there—useful or not.

"I was following you," he was saying. "There are probably laws against that now, right?"

"I-Beam was mustering his courage," she suggested, his nickname from that other era.

By the same instinct of heart and happenstance that earlier she had known he was shaking his head *no*, she believed now that he was nodding *yes*, and for a second she imagined following herself as he had. Carol Ann in pursuit of Carol Ann. Seeing how crummy and humdrum her life had been. Pointing to the ruts she'd worn in the world, the lines she would not cross. But Eddie had mustered his courage, he'd caught up with her. Courage. That was all it had taken.

"When I was little," she told him, "I wanted to be someone else."

He knew the feeling, he said. Another joke without much ha-ha in it.

"A girl you read about in a magazine," she said. "With red hair. A ballerina. I could make her up and be her, Eddie. My voice changed. I had green eyes and could speak the most fluent French. Her name was Sabrina."

Her liked it, he said. Sounded exotic.

Sitting at the kitchen table, the phone like a weight against her ear, she understood she had only a fixed amount of conversation left. Only a dozen words—possibly fewer—none of them less precious than gold or rare jewels from the vault of Ali Baba himself. In the background she heard hospital noises, goblins and wraiths and specters on the loose, and Eddie's breathing in the foreground like waves washing rocks. Only a few more words, she thought, then she could lie in the tub, the water to her chin, perhaps a glass of wine handy, and not know how the next minute would turn out.

"Come home, baby," she said. "Sabrina says come home."

THE WHO, THE WHAT, AND THE WHY

for Leif and Susan, Eric and Jesse

ONLY SIXTEEN MONTHS after our daughter's death from, improbable as it may seem in the nowadays and hereabouts, mononucleosis, I began breaking into my own house, as expert a sneak thief as if I had taken to the trade as a toddler.

The first time, I burst out of sleep as if dragging myself up from the deep end of our swimming pool, breathless and arm-weary, a man—if you'd seen him splashing and kicking—who clearly had not been exercising for pleasure. It was two A.M., dark as dark gets in fairy tales, and I remember that from one state of being to the other, from sleep to wakefulness, I carried nothing, as if whatever I'd stumbled upon in my dreams—the who and the what and the why—had broken free of me, as gone from me as was our daughter, Harriet.

I remember slipping out of bed, my wife, Becky Sue, as imperturbable as a mannequin. It was Thursday, which meant in the spring this takes place that she had school tomorrow (two dozen fifth-graders whose job it was to learn from her some long division and when to use *who* and *whom*); for me, as I went downstairs in my robe, this day meant that only hours from now I'd drive down the valley to the airport and fly to Dallas to find myself, more hours later, in a studio, its walls acoustically perfect, saying, for enough money to buy a Toyota truck, what is scrumptious about Fritos corn chips.

I am, you see, a "voice," meaning that if you have been watching TV at all or listening to the radio in markets served by what ad agencies in Dallas or Phoenix or sometimes L.A. can accomplish, then you have heard me, in the "warm and fuzzy" tones I am hired for, say what is written in regard to United Airlines, or Buick LeSabres, or the symphony of Columbus, Ohio. But on the morning I am now telling you about, I was only and thoroughly me—Robert "Bobby" Patterson, a once-upon-a-time Rice University political science major, a U.S. Army reject (bad feet and a heart murmur), a husband for nearly two decades—the kind of guy who at too many liquor-fueled parties over the years has tried the back flips and handsprings people probably hoot about at the Olympics.

I rose, I have since said to my wife, as if I'd heard a voice calling, and wandered a time, not disoriented entirely but in fact a little slack-minded, as if part of me—the parts, scientists say, that still belong to reptiles or what we share with even less-scaly scraps of life—was putting off for a time what it knew it had to do, the way you put off the cauliflower till you've finished the baked potato. In my office, a big room with lots of shelves and plenty of space to build the model airplanes I like, I sat at my desk, fiddling with the light switch on my lamp. My insides, I say, were not knotted or otherwise distressed, but I was, well, anxious, a man either early for a date or, like the White Rabbit, very, very late. Then I was up, out my sliding glass doors, and around the cool deck, the pool waters undisturbed, our corner of the desert here in El Paso as clean-smelling as wind and emptiness can combine to be. Behind me reared one hump of the Franklin Mountains, atop which are nothing except radio antennae that go blink-blink-blink, and below me, down the curvy gravel road we own, sat the big homes that belong to the Coronado Country Club, where I sometimes go to take a drink in the men's locker with the far-flung neighbors I have up here (men like Forry Bell and Tubby Walker, who wonder good-naturedly how it is I can make so much money and usually not have anything productive to do before eleven in the morning or after two in the afternoon).

It's funny, I believe now, but you can think many things when you are dressed in your pajamas and slippers and you are walking over terrain that awfully much resembles the moon and there are hostile creatures that live mainly in the dark and don't much like whatever it is we are too near wherever it is they hide. So I was thinking about that— snakes and rabid coyotes and lizards whose unexpected lefts and rights can make you piss your pants—and I was thinking, too, about an affair I'd once had with a flyweight redhead who could yodel and could herself go unexpectedly left and right with visible vigor; and about a conquistador treasure said to be buried in the Organ Mountains north of here, and about what it must be like to leap out of an airplane with nothing to save you but a sack on your back made from silk and rope, not to mention considerable good faith in the fellow who'd packed it. And then—this is the genuinely spooky stuff—I was not thinking any longer.

I was, in fact, not even me, not Bobby Patterson at all: as transformed as Jekyll was to Hyde, I was one Tom H-for-Harding Butters, a felon, a man with three ex-wives, a Harley-Davidson tattoo on his forearm, and passing ability to pluck the guitar country-style. I had drunk poison, the goo that chronic grief is, and I had become Tom Butters— from Cobb County in Georgia, I think—an eleventh-grade dropout who was nevertheless able to add and subtract enough to know when he was being effectively diddled—and I was strolling up a road in the hills west of El Paso, muttering, "Well, well, easy pickings tonight."

So it was that Tom Butters went easily into your hero's almost-paid-for house (through a sliding glass door that some dumb ass must've left unlocked) and thereupon helped himself to what Becky Sue Patterson, the wife, later held was trash the criminal element was most welcome to: namely, a thirty-second-scale model of a USAF Flying Fortress and a gag jewelry box with half a Wilson golf ball glued to the top, plus an armful of books having to do with Wild West gunslingers and perhaps sixty dollars in pesos from a jam jar on her husband's desk. All in all, Becky Sue would say in the morning (and later to the police that State Farm insisted upon), it wasn't so much the "valuables" as it was the weirdness of the whole shebang—the way she'd arisen before the alarm and without disturbing her snoring husband, and how she found everything strangely out of order: a couch moved, the refrigerator open, pictures re-hung, the heat lamp glowing in the guest bath, Bobby's new pitch-ing wedge on the glass coffee table in the living room, all the Tanya Tucker tapes rearranged.

Sure, I had a memory of this, but not firsthand. I felt I'd seen Tom Butters in a movie, not necessarily a fine one, either, and while Becky Sue stormed around that morning, saying "Jesus H." and "Can you believe this?" I went around, too, also as openmouthed and astounded as my offended wife, remembering this or that about Tom Butters. I remembered Tom Butters going into my office and playing with the doohickeys he found there, and how stupidly depressed he was to dis-cover that the only items worth taking—computer and TV and VCR, for example—you'd need a truck and certainly another villain to get away with. I remembered how he slumped in the easy chair my mother had given me for my fortieth birthday, his feet put up exactly as I do mine, and how he wished for three fingers of Seagram's red-eye to sip while he made up his mind. Tom Butters was thinking about a song he liked, a sighin'-dyin'-cryin' tune that mentioned hope and wings, and what he ought to be doing in life and what sort of Nashville cowboy star he'd be; then he roused himself, semi-burdened by the goofy curios he had my sense of humor for, and thought to mosey around this house for twenty minutes, pretending he lived up here in the foothills with distant neighbors you'd have to use a bullhorn to get the full attention of.

And then this ended, the movie my memory was, and I, entirely myself, told Becky Sue to do what had to be done, law-wise, and that I'd call from Dallas that night. I was standing in my kitchen, some-thing in me rattling like a marble in a tin cup, and I was promising myself—just as I have promised here to tell the truth and nothing but—that I wouldn't think again about Tom Butters, or who in me he was, until much, much later, until I'd told you and you and you out there, in take after take after take, what it is about, oh, Whey, Gum Arabic, Malic Acid and Disodium Inosinate that Kellogg's claims is such a cotton-picking delight to eat with bananas for breakfast.

.   .   .

I know you're probably skeptical about the daughter business, about how likely it is to die from a disease you get from kissing or running yourself down. But, I say to you now, it is possible in America for someone—let's say, for argument's sake and without personalizing overmuch, a child—to feel bad, and then worse, and finally rotten in a way that will require machines and catheters and not enough dollars in the world to fix, and that all your high school pals will find themselves in a Presbyterian church listening to J. S. Bach's "Sheep May Safely Graze" and attending to what can be learned from Old Testament lessons out of Ecclesiastes. Notwithstanding your nice manners and how gifted you are at the piano, or the color of your favorite horse, it is possible—hell, I have Autopsy #A88–216 to prove it—to get Epstein-Barr virus and to have your immune system so degraded that you acquire, against whatever odds doctors earn a living from, acute interstitial pneumonia, and thereafter find yourself the victim of "purulent exudates" and "pelvic venous plexis"; and soon enough you become a child who will in twenty days curl up and turn yellow and finally go somewhere, according to the beeping hardware over your bed in ICU, where the numbers are all zero and the lines all flat.

It is likewise possible for that child's father to go flat-out crazy eventually and, from the life he'd led or the dreams he'd dreamed, become as many someone elses as China has Chinamen. The second time I was Hector Walls (aka: Herkie, Harold, Hank), with a bum leg and three-page list of felony arrests plus a health-nut parole officer who was really fussy about the cigarettes I smoked. As Tom Butters had, I went in the sliding glass door by the pool, rested in Bobby Patterson's leather chair, and, once I got my night vision, fed myself a plateful of chicken salad from the Amana. I had a girlfriend named Peggy (whose do-what-I-say face came to me two or three times while I crept throughout this place), plus a pound dog named Cannibal that I had no problem at all seeing in residence here. As Bobby Patterson reconstructs it now, Herkie Walls must've spent several hours on the first floor, turning over cushions, peeking behind paintings (maybe for a wall safe, I don't know), lying for a time on the bed in the guest room, and leaving dirt from his work boots on the quilt Becky's granny had made her for a wedding present. And then it was morning, sharp and bright and blue as poster paint: Becky was up first and yelling at her lazybones husband to get out of bed and see this.

Herkie, it turned out, was a vandal, and, sad to say, when I beheld what he'd wrought, I was for a minute scared, my heart banging in my ears. Something was being asked of me, I thought. Something drastic, or heroic. So I tried to tell Becky, as she stood aghast in our living room, that, well, I had the feeling I'd seen this before.

"Oh, Bobby," she scolded, "just shut the hell up."

I took a minute with myself, thought of my organs, the chunks and hunks and slabs of them, whirling in a pool under my heart.

As before, I had no real memory of this, just a prickliness akin to déjà vu or other sensations I suppose there are fancy foreign phrases for, but by then Becky Sue was cursing, asking *what on earth* in the direction of our curtains, which had been torn, and of the junky clutter that was once expensive, even fine Mexican pottery. Hers was behavior that scared me, too, and so it was easy—as easy as reciting lines strangers have written down for you—just to keep quiet and make my way to the phone to complain to an ear at the other end of the line that the Pattersons, Bobby and Becky Sue, had been again robbed and maybe a little bit terrorized.

That day I had no obligations, no product or service to be sincere about, so I followed the police around and watched Becky kick at the mess Herkie Walls had made—the broken this; the smashed that. I was trying to be generally helpful, plus not too much amazed when tracks were discovered that went uphill a ways and at last disappeared where the ground turned to rock.

Only one time did I think to confess what I knew, and that was when the police were gone and Becky Sue was saying for me to call Rosalita, our cleaning lady, and then to call Carl Preston, her principal, to make apologies for being late: I was looking at the screen to our front door, how an X had been slashed in it, and, suddenly, when I opened my mouth (my eyes squeezed shut as they do when it is your job on earth to concentrate and nothing more), knowing Becky Sue had stopped on the stairs to hear me, I "saw," as if on film, Herkie Walls go out the door and wheel around to face me.

Instantly, day became night—Becky Sue not on the stairs but still in dreamland, all that had happened yet to be discovered—and there was your narrator as Herkie Walls, me awake to myself, ours the evil eyes truly bad guys see the world through, ours the grin thoughtless ravaging can make. Something inside tore free and, like a boulder, went tumbling and crashing downward toward the bottom of me.

"What?" Becky Sue said.

Apparently I had spoken, or blurted "uh" with shock, but I waved my arm to say it was nothing, and a part of me in the here and now watched a part of me in the then and there go limping slowly into the darkness.

For a time after this, no one in me came to burgle at night. Summer rolled around with many parties to go to and many artworthy sunsets to shout about. Becky Sue was taking a course at UTEP—recertification credit, I think, more words and handouts about, hell, playground management or what to do when a third-grader tells you to take a flying fuck—and I flew off every week or so to this recording studio or that to utter for hours and hours sometimes what would only be twenty or thirty seconds in actual airtime. That summer, I was doing lots of characters. "Be a grit," the producer would say, and for a morning I was, a hayseed's hayseed, a clodhopper in bib overalls with mud between his toes. One day I was a PM, as British and merry-old as kidney pie; the next, as Swiss as chocolate. This was fun for me, I tell you, to put to work an imagination I didn't often use and then use it to urge you to fly to St. Croix or to buy your love seat from the White House on Pisano Street.

Becky Sue and I were in good spirits, time putting between us and one hideous memory many new and better ones: We were going away from Harriet, going forward, while behind, like a stretch of road you are relieved to see the last of, there remained only no-account markers—a fight you shouldn't have had, a drunk you shouldn't have been—to say what had befallen you way back when. Except for moments the words for which always began "Remember when," Becky Sue had recovered, and I, too, was mostly whole, only a little bit like a crybaby when I was alone for too long or when I had to go into Harriet's room to find in the closet something we'd stored there. Still, this was a good summer, filled with folks like Forry Bell and his wife, Marty, who sold me stocks that did right well (as promised), and a vacation we took to the Yucatán Peninsula to see how it was when, as the foolish song goes, the world was young. We were like youngsters ourselves, Becky and I, courting ourselves anew, bathing often enough to be conspicuous, phoning at odd hours to say one or the other was missed, and making love in the way Tubby Walker claims is mostly funny bone, kneecap, and satin sheet.

And then they came back, our nighttime visitors, the legion of men I was and was and was. Unlike Herkie Walls, they were not cruel but peculiar, even sad, taking a cookie or watching TV. They were named Tunch and Philly Dog and A.T., and they arrived from such places as Wyoming and Yorba Linda, California, men who had once been fine but were now not. They ate with our silverware or helped themselves to my blue jeans and sometimes wrote a note with my typewriter to say thank you.

More than once, after it became clear that really no danger was involved, Becky Sue volunteered to stay downstairs, to keep watch.

"I'm going to catch one of these jokers," she said, "find out what the deal is."

The first time, I woke to find her fully clothed on the living room couch, a pot of coffee handy, curled asleep with a flashlight held to her chest, on an end table a birthday cake, in the center of it a candle you'd use in a blackout. Another morning, all her shoes, high-heeled and not, were lined up in front of her, like soldiers on parade, and another time our laundry was folded and sorted and set in stacks to be put away.

"Jumping Jesus," she said, laughing about it, this as much a joke to her as what passes for humor in the headlines. "Jumping damn Jesus."

And, of course, through it all we told nobody, as there didn't seem any way to explain, short of theories too bizarre and hokey to be believed, that Becky Sue and Bobby were, well, being trespassed upon by ghosts or hoboes or whatevers that liked to spirit away with them such goodies as golf tees, Tupperware jugs, and every copy of *House and Garden* magazine.

In September, when Becky Sue had to go back to school, it fell to me to stay up nights, to keep watch. I felt foolish, like a chicken in a bikini, but I was a good boy and, having been told what to do, I did it. So every night after Leno, after a kiss or two, and if I didn't have a morning appointment or work that required a plane trip, I'd stay up, arrange myself in my study, acclimate myself to the night, and become reacquainted with the sounds that come up after the sun goes down. But they didn't come, the men I was. Not a one. At first I was relieved, content to have myself back as myself, but then, owing to restlessness and ordinary fear, I was lonely, even sore for companionship, a little bit angry that I—so I backasswardly reasoned it—had been abandoned. I felt bony and broken off and too clumsy for the indoors, a man composed of coat hangers and galvanized roofing nails. And then he returned, Herkie Walls.

I had been standing at the door, blue-hearted and somehow mournful, and when I said as much to my backyard, he was there again, in a T-shirt and jean jacket, already angry and mean-minded.

"Howdy, partner," he said, his smile too toothy to be life-lifting, and, half of me wandering off and drying up, I stepped aside to make way for him.

He was me, all right, a man with my hair gone whichaway and no concern at all for posture, a me as I might have turned out, a me with no wife or pals or dead daughter to dwell on.

It's an unsettling feeling to be in- and outside yourself at the same time, but—and one reason this story's being told—I was, Bobby watching Herkie, Herkie going headlong about his business. This time he went upstairs, in a manner that suggested he'd had lots of practice since last he was in my house, and I followed, not at all surprised that he headed straight for our bedroom, the door open, only my wife in there and whatever heaven she was dreaming of.

For a minute or two, he stood at the foot of our bed, his expression sidelong and cocked, like a dog that has heard something far off and perplexing, and then he touched her, his finger to her foot, and I understood he was thinking clearly about what a choice item she was and how, if he pulled back the covers, which he did, he could study her in her nightie and maybe know fifteen or twenty things about himself and what he'd returned for.

Breathing shallow, his face twenty percent improved by shadows, he didn't move, just peered and peered, something about this woman vital to him, and then she stirred, mumbled "What?" still mostly sleep-soaked, and Herkie, his voice mine, said "That's okay, baby" and not another thing until, in the hall, I put a hand to his shoulder and told him *no*.

He was about to go into Harriet's room, and so we had a moment then, me and me. Time was spreading, I could tell, running out of groove, my house a jumble of angles and corners and nooks to hurt yourself on, and I was overtaken with the need to speak in a hurry, three words at once almost, to say that there was nothing in that room that he'd want, not a thing, the valuables and mementos given away to friends or donated, even the clothes gone to be useful elsewhere.

He seemed confused, maybe split inside himself, and so in a stran-gled whisper I tried to tell him how it was and how I just wanted to be left alone by him and others like him, those who were the sour and vicious and lowlife in me.

"Go away," I told him, the center of me frozen to a point, "just go the hell away."

But he didn't move, the son of a bitch.

A little time went by. And, in the drip-drip way time can, some more. We were there, eyeball to eyeball, Herkie and Bobby, a fellow and his counterpart, and then an alarm was going off too loud, and I had nothing but sunrise to face.

"Slow the dickens down, son," my father used to tell me, an instruc-tion easy to give when you're, as he is at sixty-six, rich and civil and have several girlfriends to coddle. But it was instruction I saw the wis-dom of after that encounter with Herkie Walls, instruction I seemed to take so completely to heart that by the time I ran into Tom H-for-Harding Butters in Harriet's room nearly a month later, I was almost at a complete stop, inert as a stone and only a little bit more sentient.

Tom was clearly sad, ruminative, and thrown back on himself, and so was I, this being the anniversary of Harriet's death and thus an occasion which calls for much recollection though very little chitchat.

I had awakened, I have told Becky Sue, not with a start but neverthe-less all at once, coming to life after midnight the way you see runners cross the finish line, exhausted and absolutely through with them-selves and normal stuff.

As before, I had gone outdoors, seemed to spin around three or four times, and then returned, approaching Bobby Patterson's house the way you see people go up to doors they expect to be shooed away from. This was the end, I guessed, and nothing to do but have it.

Time had not been kind to Tom Butters: He'd had, as it is put in the fat novels I like, reversals—a sweetheart lost or too smart for him, not enough money to go when beckoned, some work he was too proud to do well—and right now, in memory, I see him collapsed on my daughter's bed, too lanky for the thing, really, his hands behind his head, eyes open to what the ceiling might reveal. Plainly, he felt hol-low that night, somehow less than the three that one and one and one come to, and for a time he was bitterly amused by the idea of himself as a contraption with not much to do except eat and drink and repeat the penny-ante hopes he had. He was dreaming about going some-where—the South Seas, Timbuktu, Oz—and then he was not, know-ing there was nowhere to go that was not itself already too much like this place and time. He did wonder, however, why this room was so—well, *emptified* was his word, sterile and cell-like, perfect for thinking as it turned out but at the same time a room that nearly leached your thoughts right out of your head and left you too breath-defeated to argue about it.

At this point in the movie of me that I told Becky Sue about, Tom Butters heard a noise and got up to find it, indifferent to the creaks the bedsprings made. In the center of the room, he turned his head a little but often, and got himself straight with east and west. A party was going on somewhere, he believed, and if the noise kept up, he'd find it soon enough and so make some sense out of the whoops and ho-ho-ho's reaching him across the dry, windswept hinterlands.

At Harriet's window, the one from which she used to yell down to us at the pool, the Tom Butters in me stood gazing, near then far, adjusting his field of vision, making notes to himself about what was and what wasn't. He was singing another song, this one echoey and

twang-filled and heart-thumping, and then he wasn't: What had sharp-
ened into view were two men under an extremely bright yard light
about a hundred yards away—the Forry Bell and Tubby Walker that
Tom did not know—smacking golf balls into the desert.

They were happy men, all right, a bit under the influence but more
like animals in their joy than like humans who should know better, and
so for the next half hour Tom watched them, as pleased with them as
they were with themselves, the picture of grown men being juvenile
and heedless under a lamplight, a sight as good for Tom's insides as
water is for thirst. They whacked and flailed and swatted, sometimes
stumbling about to get their balance, and Tom Butters could see that
though they weren't good or even remotely athletic, they were indeed
enthusiastic, not mindful at all regarding any of the do's and don't's
daylight seemed too full of. They were average as dirt, he decided, just
more blessed by happenstance, and so there didn't seem to be any reason—not one, at least, that couldn't be wished away or laughed right
in the fat face of—for him not to join them.

"Go on over there, boy," he told himself, and then waited for his
legs to work.

He was having a debate with himself, clearly, taking up this idea
and that, weighing what had weight in him and what didn't. He
scratched his chin, brooded seriously over himself. He'd get a haircut,
he was thinking. Maybe do four or five thousand sit-ups. Later get a
tuba and learn to toot it. Then, nodding affirmatively and putting
down the ticky-tack he'd arranged to steal (a map of the North Pole
and a shoehorn and a shamrock suspended in glass), he whirled
around fast, eager to get going and not mooning over himself any
longer, and—poof!—it was only me again in the world.

Just like that, like presto and abracadabra, it was me throwing on
my robe and slippers, heading toward the garage for a bucket of balls
and my three-iron. They were forever gone, these men I was, and I,
hollering happily, was charging out the door, aiming to wake West
Texas with the noise in my heart.

WHAT *Y* WAS

BEFORE I DROPPED out—got kicked out, actually, another story for another time—I had a course in college about The Movie. That's the way I remember it in the catalogue. Capitals *T* and *M*. Like it was The C(rucifixtion) or The D(epression), instead of a chance to see a lot of foreign T(its) and A(ss) and know, at the end of it, how to smoke a cig-arette through your ears.

The first day, the professor—a blowhard, I thought, the sort who's all hat and no cattle—drew a picture of a bent-over pyramid, or a lean-to, on the blackboard. "Inciting incident," he said; with great flair, he pointed to the leg of the upslope. "Then rising action." His pointer was going up now, about forty of us wondering what this critter had had for breakfast. "Then climax," he said, pointer at the tip-top. "Then falling action." Down we went, gaining speed, like falling off a sky-scraper. "Then reversal." A nasty crook in the trail, it looked like. "And denouement." What my father would say was "all she wrote," which is where, I used to hope, the ruinous are ruined, and the good go yon-der into the sunset.

Yup, I was the happy ending type. Me, I rooted for the sodbuster to get the dance-hall dolly (or vice versa), the dog to come home after a long adventure in the hinterlands, the mother to rise whole and happy from her deathbed in the hospital. Now, however, I'm, well, a falling action guy, which is that moment, to use my ex-wife's phrase, just after the feathers have hit the fan. You know what I'm talking about—that instant following what my long-gone professor called the "showdown." The dust ain't quite settled, the bad guy lies still twitching in the dirt, and there's one more piece of business, itself dire or nearly life-and-death, that Yancy, our older and wiser hero, needs and has the goddamn wherewithal to do. Lordy, something about that moment just makes me hum. The worst has happened, the best ain't far away, and you can see the moral to all this back-and-forth coming at you like a high school band up Main Street.

Let me give you a for instance. Imagine a couple, man and wife. Somebody—har-de-har-har—like me maybe, and like my ex-wife, Corrine. They're in the early forties, married since the Stone Age. Two kids, both boys, both in high school. What else? They're in their second house, mortgaged up the wazoo. He's what we hereabouts in the desert call a "land man," which is that person who goes out to find the heir, or the heir's heir, to property that bigwigs at Texaco or the Shell Oil Company want the mineral rights to; the wife, she's a kindergarten teacher, a whiz with papier-mâché and building blocks. They're Protestants, as half-assed in this as they are in politics. They both look pretty good still, the pot they're going to—we all go to pot eventually, right?—maybe a dozen years away. Only about thirty-five percent of their habits are bad. He likes Oso Negro rum a little too much. She laughs out loud at the TV. He smokes (more initials: LSMFT), and she has a puff or two when she's feeling frisky. Normal folks, no? Just like your own damn self were you suddenly plucked out of your own life and made to go from A to Z for an hour and a half after the lights go out.

The thing is, though, the guy's a peckerwood. Can't keep it in his pants. Nohow, no way. For example, he's over in El Paso or in the badlands outside Hagerman or up near Tatum—hellfire, could be anywhere there's gas and crude oil to be accounted for—and sees a woman in the lounge of the Holiday Inn. Before you know it, he's sweet-talking. One drink. Another. A little hootchy-kootchy on the

dance floor. He's a conversationalist, is what he is. Another lost art.
Quick with a ha-ha-ha, quicker with his Visa card. One thing leads to
another—ain't this always the way, right?—and around midnight you
can hear hoopla and heavy breathing coming from room 311 overlooking the pool. It's not love, mind you. It's just rooting and rutting and
dipping the wick. It's the animal parts of us, is all. The gland running
off with the brain. Something about a strange woman in her panties
and lacy bra that, till sunrise at least, puts our hero two or three steps
closer to paradise.

Then one day he comes home and he can tell that his wife knows.
Not the particulars—not yet anyway—just the headlines.

Naturally, he tries to make conversation. Tells how it was in Carlsbad. The son of the son of the son he found living in the rusted car-
cass of a '68 Ford Econoline van behind the El Burro Bar. A drunk
now worth nearly fifteen thousand dollars on account of acreage his
daddy's daddy owned in the wasteland.

"Took me six days," he says to her. "A record."

She doesn't say much. No need to, he thinks. The girl's name was
Beth Ann, or Christine, or Suzi; and she was a clerk at the Bureau of
Records in Dexter, or the secretary to the mayor of Clovis, or herself
away from home and feeding herself out of somebody else's checkbook. All that's important is that the wife knows. You can smell the
betrayal in the air.

"What's for supper?" he asks.

She tells him, and then more time passes. Tick-tock, tick-tock.
Links on a chain that one day has to end.

The thing I like about this whole business is how unexpected it is.
No showdown at all. They've had the fight, just without the words and
the tossed dishes. Now they're citizens of some weird country, is what
they are. They've had the tragedy—fire, flood, or famine—and, like all
folks putting two with two, they've accepted the inevitability of four.
It's all math, friends. Us just numbers, with ding-dongs attached.

So the evening goes on. The sons come home from soccer practice
or whatever, the supper gets eaten, Tom Brokaw has a half hour of
horror to share with them as Americans.

The husband doesn't say much himself. He feels peaceful. The end is nigh, so he just lets himself rise, that moment I like coming to him in an hour or two.

The wife? Hell, I don't know about her. Not a lick. She ain't perfect—none of us is—but she's a fine thing nonetheless. You'd want her as a neighbor, I'm sure. She can keep a confidence, for example. Or give you a lift to Walgreen's if your car's on the blink. Most of all, she's got patience—maybe the way Midas had gold. Which probably explains why she stayed with this dipstick for so long. I could speculate, but I won't. I'm about as good at guessing as a snake is at driving a tractor. She must've known all along, though. About Betty and Millie and whoever else there was to know about. Then something in her, the very her of her, went pop. Or snap. Or bang. Pick a noise, friends. That's the sound of you going dry and cold inside.

So it's eight P.M. now. Then nine. Time and more time piling up. Their sons are in their rooms. Homework and the like.

God knows what my old professor would make of this period. He liked the artsy-fartsy stuff. Lots of camera angles and insufficient light to work by. Music, too. He loved the ooeey-gooey crapola in the background, said it was part of, quote, the vocabulary. Me, I just like thinking. Ruminating, my daddy called it. Which is X, then Z, and you trying to figure out what Y was.

It's ten o'clock, then ten-fifteen.

"You want something to drink?" the wife says.

Good God, she's a civil creature, no? So he says sure, this to-and-fro more than twenty percent marvelous to him.

In a moment, she's back, Cuba Libres for the two of them and something else unexpected to say.

"So you found the guy?"

Indeed, he did, and says so, yet another rung on the ladder toward the moment when the villain takes it between the eyes.

"Went to every bar on Rogers Street," he says. "You wouldn't believe the losers in those joints. He'd been living out of that van for years. A regular hobo. Stunk to high heaven."

Outside, a fierce wind has come up, a lot of real estate from Arizona now moving its way from the west. He's got a full day tomorrow, records to search in city hall and a golf game at the Institute course in the afternoon. It's a good life, he's thinking. A full wallet, a new car to drive, and at least thirty more years to live high on the hog. He ain't a bastard, not really. The race has been run, friends, and he's at the end of it.

"What'd you do today?" he says.

There's a light in her eyes he hasn't seen before, and for an instant he believes that she's going to yell at him now.

"You being polite?" she says.

He is, and says so, the first of about ten million other words to go back and forth between them.

"The usual," she says, and up another rung we go. Chit from him. Chat from her. Dialogue, in short. She's serious, as is he, but it's like code they're talking, the stuff between the lines—the silences—more important than anything you might pay cash money to overhear. It's common, is what it is. He sips his drink, she hers. Sip, sip, and sip. A throat is cleared. Another. Rung upon rung upon rung.

"So this is it," she says at last.

This is the closest they've ever been, he thinks.

"Yes," he says.

His answer seems to take about five minutes to reach her, then it does and he can see it register. The end of them. But for the paperwork and the dollars and clothes to move out, the very end of them.

"I'm tired," she says. "I'm going to bed."

In case you weren't paying attention, that was it. The showdown. A real modern one, from what I can tell. Not much whoop-de-do. Not a lot of, er, vocabulary to help you know what's what. Then the part I like. Which is falling and one more surprise to know.

For a long time, he sits where he is. He's not stricken, or otherwise bent in the heart. He's content, I've decided. Like a fat man after a big meal. For the first time, maybe, he's at peace. No more lies to tell. No more secrets to keep. Amazing, man. Abso-goddamn-lutely amazing.

In the bathroom, he brushes his teeth. The woman's name was

Selma, a student out at the ENMU branch, boobs big as cantaloupes; or Mary Jo, a clerk for the Mode O'Day at the mall near the Wal-Mart; or Something Something Fitzgerald, hair red as fire and a singing voice like LeAnn Rimes. They were other countries, he thinks. Persia and Sweden and Shangri-la itself. They were tongues and lips and backsides new as dreamland. Lordy.

She's not asleep, but makes no sound when he gets in bed beside her. It's a big world, friends, and he's in it, one of many lying on his back, the next day rising up clear from Never-Neverland. He feels clean, pure. Open him up and you'll find only light inside.

Then she says what she says and his little movie takes a turn for the worse.

"I'm cold."

He could get a blanket, he says.

Friends, I'd give anything to be in her head at this moment. I'd like to know where the thought starts, in what muscle or cell or itty-bitty nerve. First, the thought. Then the goo to go with it. Then the brain to say it.

"Let's make love," she says.

Now it's his turn to have an idea.

"You sure?" he says.

She laughs, another happenstance to think about later, and says she's surer about this than she has been about anything for ten years.

"It won't mean anything," he says.

Of course it won't, she says. Nothing does.

But, good God, it does. It's reversal, is what it is. Because, praise Jesus, she's the newest pretty maid. She's that one from Ruidoso, the track groupie; and that one, the UPS driver, who lives on Missouri Avenue. She's the blonde with the green high heels and the one who barks when she gets on top. She's new. He's in the room of a woman he only met an hour ago. She's not from here. Hell, she's from Mexico or Mars. Oh, she's just new all over. New shoulders. New fanny. The newest woman to come into a life that only a minute before even my old wind-bag professor would have known was going steadily toward the weepy music and the who-was-who.

WHEN OUR DREAM WORLD FINDS US, AND THESE HARD TIMES ARE GONE

for John Vincent McCue

Every time Garland told the story (which, according to CPL Zookie Limmer, was singular and strange enough to be Foe itself), he gave it a new title, his favorites being those with sweep and miracle. With the 18th ARVN in MR3, it was "A Change in Luck This Way Comes," after what Garland called its tone of comfort in a world of predicament and baleful taints. Near Tay Ninh, in April, while the Bad Guys were conducting a lethal undertaking you know now as "human waves," Garland called it "Let My Beloved Come into This Garden," on account of its endearing puzzlements. In May, it was known as "To Any End Any Road May Run," and without interruption from CBUs or any Air America spookiness, its telling took less than fifteen minutes—from woman's arrival to her lonesome departure.

Onan Motley, a Utah hillbilly on loan to the TAOR for his Canary Island cigars and La Dolce Vita sunglasses, heard it as a "Love Story of Splendor," and he clearly remembered the words *vagrant* and *impossible,* not to mention the way Garland's face took on that weird, unlived-in look, as if in the ages between event and memory he'd lost the gist of it himself. In June, before Oogie Pringle rotated out, Gar-

333

land, in exchange for a Motorola TV, repeated it to a DAO officer as "Bus Stop," but the man couldn't be sure, having heard that month many tales of infliction and hostility, plus a few of what he called "flimsy human means."

After a time, though, everybody knew it as Garland H. Steeples's story—"The Girl of My Dreams"—a thing he told maybe a thousand times in 1968, always reminding folks how he was stuck in this little town named Deming, New Mexico, at the Greyhound station, almost halfway between L.A. (which he was leaving because of some personal difficulty he'd rather not go into) and Dallas (which he thought he might visit on account of a sister named Mrs. Darlene Neff and the absolutely rich idea of prairie life and that seldom-heard discouraging word). "I was going to get a job," he told Howdy Holmes, a man who looked like a Jack Nicklaus caddy. "Live me the good life," he said. "I'll improve some, too." He had his mind on a car, a LeSabre, a vehicle with substance and sleek Detroit styling, something worthy of his finer habits—which were, primarily, common sense, a wolf's smug smile and the ability to put aside vulgar needs. "I see me living in a bachelor pad," he told everybody, "maybe with a waterbed. Get me some art, too."

Anyway, Garland would say, having established who's who and what's what, into this bus station walked this woman—here his eyes would get like matched moons—with hair like wet bark. "I was struck," he told Lamont Wilson. "I'd been on the road twenty hours or so, I was a little tired, had nothing to eat but two Snickers bars and a bag of Chee•tos, and when I see her, she's like food, you know, a basic, a staple." It took a half hour for them to meet formally, Garland's brain curing like ham. "I kept imagining her in my place," he said, seeing her in frilly nighties, pedal pushers, maybe a pair of Tijuana toreador pants, black and bawdy. She was Asian, not homey with the lingo, but, waving his arms, using his fingers with patience, and pointing, he learned she was eighteen—"My own age," he said once, "how's that for luck?"—and came from a place called either the Iron Triangle or the Ia Drang Valley, a place like Mars where nobody wore underpants and they hummed all the time. She was going to be a rock 'n' roll star—"I got name all pick out," she said, "the Innocent, okay?"—but right now she was working for Jesus.

"Christ plenty damn big," she said. "Save villains, then go show biz. Meet Elvis Presley."

They sat for a long time, the only two in the place—a place, according to Short Time Safety Moe, more *Twilight Zone* than teenage heaven, a place of swirls and murks. Garland told the girl about his daddy Royce, who was a diesel mechanic for JLS Truck Service, and his stepmomma Tracy June, who wasn't anything yet but had her eyes peeled for opportunity, and his younger sister, Roylene, who was maybe going to do ballet if she stopped growing and was now writing a term paper on the bronchial tree.

"She liked me," Garland told a spade Marine named Philly Dog. "I couldn't shut up. She was smiling and saying how cool Jesus had been to me, and I was blabbing about everything on account of how I was nervous and she was so fine and I was lonely and maybe she was, too."

He told her he had a thousand talents—among them posture and respect—and his favorite subjects at Monroe High School had been geometry and the kind of history in which those above are flattened by those below, but he hadn't graduated because of this aforementioned dispute with Mr. Strojan, his health teacher. Garland said he was a Taurus, which meant he was an ace in the steadfastness department but handicapped by shortcomings in the area of temper.

"Me, too!" she said. "Blow up fast like despot."

"I got the wanderlust," Garland added, showing her on a map so well creased it looked like human skin that he'd been to Warrenton, Oregon ("Man, that place is a drag," he said, "fish city, the smell will make you cry"), and Las Vegas ("Won me fifty bucks there in a IHOP slot!"), and a thousand Arizona towns all alike with dust and mean faces and speed traps. In Texas, he said, he wanted to go to the place where Kennedy got killed, then visit the Alamo, walk in the footsteps of Davy Crockett and that inventive Bowie fellow.

"Oh, big damn steps," she said.

She had a laugh, he told the boys near the Perfume River, like, well, *liquid*, free and refreshing, the kind that Little Red Riding Hood might have were she real and in the company of an eager-beaver like himself. He told Chunk Odom, a Spec 5 in charge of the liquor-ration files at the Dak To commissary, that she had skin like expensive paper, creamy and close-pored—an epidermis so tight and pure it put you in mind of Philosophy and Achievement. There was a smell about her, too, Garland said. Roses, maybe, or something with vitamins in it. Spanky Morris, with the 7th in Delta Company near Cheo Rheo, heard she had these impossible sandals and toes, to use Garland's words, of delight and true daintitude. From the grunts in Darlac Province, you would've thought she was part princess, even related to several of the Mings themselves. The Hungarian ICCS delegation mentioned her in one of their communiqués.

"After a while, "Garland said, "I asked her where she was going."

She showed him her ticket.

"Wyoming?" he said, shocked. "What's in Wyoming?"

She said something about heathen and made private sounds Garland took to be divinely derived.

"I was hoping she'd come with me," he told a door-gunner on a Psyops sound ship once. "I said I could be a fine companion—talk, entertain when necessary, good at conserving money."

But she said no, sir. Wyoming. Then rocking and rolling. Say hi, Sam the Sham and the Pharaohs. Say hi, James Brown. Throw off powers of darkness. Take up the light and shake self's tail feathers.

Garland told a captured NVA regular that her name was Hoang Minh, something with tinkle and good feeling in it, but that she was going by Mary for the time being; and one time in '69, after Garland was gone, the name surfaced in a COM/SIT report of a radio intercept out of Duc Lap. Another time a CIA clerk found her name in an REF on one of the prisoners in the snow-white interrogation rooms in Saigon. The report said she and Garland spent the whole afternoon talking, she in speech that had lilt but no sense to it, he in the hopeful language of a kid starved for company.

"It was love," Garland told his CO once. This was in a tight spot near the Do Long Bridge, all about them people going insane or passing through the flame into hell. "Honest," he said, "I felt my heart move. I'm sitting there, grinning, feeling the fittest, and then—

crunch!—that thing just flops over." It was like combat itself, only full of release and ease instead of the pent-up. His fluids turned warm, he said, and his outlook became as generous as a Rockefeller's. "I had thoughts, too," he said. "I'm sure she could read them in my face."

They ate cheeseburgers next door at the 70–80 Truck Stop and watched the sun go down ("That was the best sunset I ever saw," he told Archie Coy, "everything since has been a disappointment!"), then she showed him a song she was writing, one which featured melancholy and trouble in the form of human thwarts but which finished with a chorus of do-do-do's that put you in mind, say, of truth and what the human tribe deserved. "It was about me," he said to Archie. "There was a guy in it who was tall, which I am, and big with his spirit."

Then, at night, they the only customers in the station, she slept. "Put her head on my shoulder," he said. "Can you believe her breathing?" he said, not the Vietnam huff 'n' puff of panic and wet fear, but like the strings of her nerves had loosened. "My arm was around her," he said once to an I Corps dipstick named Mayhew who didn't believe any of it. "She was tired, you could tell." Then Garland, himself overcome and deeply satisfied, fell asleep.

"I had this dream I was on the bus, the last seat back by the Portosan." It was an old bus, he said, from the forties or thereabouts, shaped like a bullet traveling backward and so high you could look into the faces of passing truckers. Everybody was smoking, he said, Camels, Lucky Strikes (a guy from the Delta heard it was Pall Malls or one of those sissy smokes, like Viceroy). Outside of El Paso, this woman got on, maybe three hundred pounds, with plenty of sweat. She swayed all the way to the back, lugging a ratty suitcase, hunting a seat, and Garland knew that he was going to get up, be polite, let her have his. Which he did. She was mean-looking, he said, like maybe her mood had permanently shifted to the anger side of feeling. Like she was unwholesomeness itself breathed into life by Want and Envy.

In his dream, she was chewing Red Man, her teeth slicked like a dog's. So, he stood beside the toilet, people squeezing by to relieve themselves, him growing headachy from the road noise and smoke thick enough to drown in and the odors of dozens in close, heavy heat.

It was horrible, he told an Ohio draftee at LZ Thelma, standing for hundreds of miles, a colicky baby crying up front, the driver once yelling at some guy to take his feet off the chair, and that huge woman pawing through her clothes. "You didn't want to look in that suitcase," he told everybody. "It was shameful."

The miles rolled on and he could see nothing outside except heat shimmers and red dust from the flatlands and once a scrawny horse rubbing against a bent-over telephone pole. "It was a nightmare, what it was," he said, like Vietnam itself, everlasting and tawdry. His legs cramped and he felt greasy, his hair having lost all its youthful flair, soreness had come over him like a big net. And, after a time, he was crying himself, his diaphragm tight like a drumhead, out of breath from the bane of it all, face muscles tense and twitching, unable to stop drooling, wishing he was back somewhere in a bus station, say, with a pure beauty resting on his shoulder, being close to the life-affirming.

"And when I woke up," he said, "I was."

(This was Pee Wee King's favorite part, where Garland H. Steeples jerked awake, his face spotted with sweat, expression full of alarm and despair. Pee Wee had heard the story during some 105 shelling out of II Corps and when Garland had come to this part, all the jungle out-rage stopped at once—all manner of bat, bird, monkey, and crawling things going without screech or howl or intelligent chirp. "It put you on the approach to something," Pee Wee told his girlfriend years later. He said he heard a million things that night, that instant: the breath-ing of rootwork and fruit sweating, perhaps the tick-tock of Uncle Ho's famous Longines wristwatch.)

"I slept again, of course," Garland said. But this time when he opened his eyes, she was walking toward a bus. For a moment, he couldn't feel anything, neither air from the open door, nor tremble, nor plastic seat he was leaning against. A second later, in the fumes and the light coming at him from the floor and ceiling and dirty win-dows, a feeling hit him with a thump, fiery nerve wheels spinning in his brain. "I was hoping she'd turn around," he told an A Camp non-com. "Maybe wave, maybe come back and hug my neck. Something."

But she kept going, knapsack over her shoulder, disappearing at last onto that bus, that vehicle lurching onto the highway as if the driver were withered and vile in his interiors. "It was like it didn't happen at all," he said, as if it were a poor man's wish constructed in the imagination from the common materials of need. "The end was like in the movies," Garland said. "When people get off the phone, they don't say goodbye or anything. They just hang up."

Oh, he could admit later, it was a thrilling moment, fraught and prodigious, "The experience was like finding out you were adopted," he said, "or a switched baby." (Once, he told a Can Tho medic, there was a certain nose resemblance between himself and Mr. Henry Cabot Lodge; a certain aspect to the eye region, also.) But, mainly, he believed his was a story about luck, about being in the right place and so on, from which he developed a supremely abstruse theory involving intersecting planes and profane holiness and advanced species to be found only in special literatures, and featuring a lot of parlez-vous about numbers and where vigors come from, and how one climbs on and off another, and nameless but sanctified residues, and the inevitable convergence which was supposed to take place when raunch gave way to uplift and heartwork became the point of all human endeavor.

She was the girl of his dreams, all right, and on the day he shipped out, neither to be seen nor heard from again, he claimed he was entering a new period in life, one of identifiable comforts and delicious viands, a thing of appetites and the means to satisfy them. He said bye-bye that day to fifty guys, shaking hands and kissing on the cheeks, finally moving toward the transport so loose and so free that it appeared to several men, among them Dorcey Eugene Wingo, that Garland, falling away from the current fracas like meat from a bone, was about to take up residence in the pearly palaces of dreamland itself, him a charter citizen of an empire supported only by wish and marvel, and a near miss with love.

After he left, you heard the story often and from unlikely sorts. It was told by "Black Luigi," and appeared in the chitty-chat of GVN, the Mission, and the Corsican Mafia. Edward Landsdale himself, pouring tea and whiskey in his Saigon villa, told a Special Forces spook that it was bogus, a narrative that ducked evil in favor of the big lie of fantasy. You heard it in the old headquarters of the Deuxième Bureau from a drunken Cat contractor from Des Plaines. It was heard in a New Life Village once, all the fremitus gone from it. You heard it embellished or picked clean. Were the story a human being, someone said, it would wear short-shorts and read French. Once, O. T. Winans, a Roy Acuff look-alike from Houston, heard the yarn from a Seabee who'd heard it from an engineer in the 11th who'd heard it from those at the V-ring near CoRoc Ridge where it had been picked up by those sneaking over the Laotian border. O.T. said the story had then only hair and knobby elbow, all the hormonal elements removed, the meeting itself taking place in some rotted gook paradise, Garland no more than that oft-cited boy meeting that familiar girl and doing a thing which involved exertion and gristle that went squeak-squeak-squeak. Sometimes Garland wasn't in it at all, his place being taken by those with an eye on the Furthermore; and sometimes he was so stripped away or made over he could be, in the same telling, tall and short, full of swank or a man with a patch over one eye and a mission cribbed from the next generation of comic book. In the Philippines, the story took an hour to tell; and once, in a place of casual death, it took many days, several of its lines muffled in the boom-boom-boom of incoming.

Then it came back to the World. Zookie Limmer told it to his momma, the story now a property with a dozen heads and enough episodes for Metro, Goldwyn, and Mayer themselves. Ellen Morris, Spanky's wife, told him to shut up after she heard, for the fifth time, that part wherein the couple performs a serious clinch, all the time making fitful animal utterances; and Archie Coy got fired from his position as assistant manager at a Kroger's for putting it on the PA, his voice full of howl and cosmic flutter when he did the imitation of the hero's love-bloated heart and the way his muscles began snapping when the woman, now fully defined and moving aboard a sleepy-time wave of chiffon, drifted out-of-doors and into her fiery and splendid conveyance, a chorus of celestials making an adenoidal noise of rise and virtue.

The story was told last, it appears, by Onan Motley in the Mile 49

Bar outside of Tatum, New Mexico, to a barfly named Bonnie Suggs who kept saying, as they drove to her place in the Vista Trailer Park, "Is that so?" or "You're fooling, Onan, ain't you?" He was drunk, wine having soaked even the slightest of his molecules, but he said "No, siree, lady," lingering over many moments, those with texture and depth, just as he later lingered over Bonnie's tight tummy and welcoming thighs, grabbing her tangle of hair and holding on—through the gloomy sections, especially—trying to put himself in the place Garland was, a discrete and illuminated landscape of wanting love and having it.

Onan went slowly over the details of the station, spending nearly an hour on the pinball machine, which was called Invaders and offered endless rewards based upon reflex and greed. He showed Bonnie where the litter was, how the fluorescent light highlighted all the scuffs and pits in the floor tile, where the No-Pest Strip hung and what the old codger behind the counter did with his tongue when asked a tough question. Onan made the sounds of passing trucks, from horn to mushy air brakes, illustrating how close the road was and describing bird life and who came or went and how they looked in dress or work shirt or, once, in a wash-'n'-wear suit by J. C. Penney. Then the story was over, and the two of them lay in sheet and sweat, Onan swollen with pride and thanks, almost feeling for an instant or two the shining presence of Garland himself—at that moment which may have been the high point of an entire life—underscoring the moral which he said every time his story had: a moral which was complex and finicky and a thing as fundamental as shelter, a moral, you know, which resisted all words save those which trafficked in fortune and love.

X

LONG AGO NOW—but still as vital a chapter of my moral history as my first kiss (with Jane Templeton at the FFA marriage booth in the National Guard armory) or my first love affair (with Leonna Allen, now an LPN in Lubbock, Texas)—I saw my daddy, Hobey Don Baker, Sr., do something that, until recently, was no more important to me than marriage is to mermaids. In an event even now still well known to the six thousand of us who live here in Deming, New Mexico, my father struck a man and then walked from the sixteenth green of our Mimbres Valley Country Club to the men's locker, where he destroyed two dozen sets of golf clubs, an act he carried out with the patience you need nowadays to paint by numbers or deal with lawyers from our government.

I was seventeen then, a recent graduate of our high school (where I now teach mathematics and coach JV football), and on the afternoon in question I had been sitting at the edge of the club pool, baking myself in the summer sunshine pale people write home about. I was thinking—as I suspect all youth does—about the wonder I would become. I had a girlfriend, Pammy Jo (my wife now), a '57 Ford Fairlane 500 (yellow over black), and the knowledge that what lay before me seemed less future than fate—which is what happens when you are raised apart from the big world of horror and cross-heartedness; yet, at the moment I'd glimpsed the prize I would be—and the way it is in the storybooks I read—disaster struck: Rushing up behind me, my mother ordered me to grab my shirt and thongs and to hurry out to the sixteenth green, our road hole, to see what the hell my daddy was fussing about.

"He's just chased Dottie Hightower off the course," she said. "Listen, you can hear him."

You couldn't hear him, really, just see him: a figure, six hundred yards distant, dressed in white slacks, a white sport shirt, and a floppy bucket hat to cover his bald spot—an outfit you expect to find on Las Vegas gangsters named Cheech.

"I don't hear anything," I said.

"He's out there being crazy again," she declared. "He's cussing out everybody."

We stepped closer to the chain-link fence surrounding the pool, and, my mother leaning forward like a sentinel, we listened.

"You hear it?" she said. "That was language in reference to smut."

I'd heard nothing but Dub Spedding's belly-flop and an unappetizing description of what Grace Hanger said she'd eaten for dinner last night. Daddy was stomping now, turning left and right, and waving his arms. In pain perhaps, he snatched his hat off, slammed it to the turf to charge at it the way he attacked the lawn mower when it would not start.

"Look at that," Mother said.

Daddy was standing in front of Butch Ikard, who still sells us our Chevrolets, and Yogi Jones, our golf pro, and pointing at Mr. Jimmy Sellers, who was sitting in his golf cart and having a beer.

"He's just missed a putt, that's all," I said. "Maybe it cost him fifty dollars."

But then, by the way she drew her beach towel around her and how her face went dark, I knew that what was going on out there had nothing to do with money.

"Maybe he's sick," I said.

His talk was vile, about creatures and how we are them.

"Hear that?" she howled. "That was the word *wantonness*."

I could hear birds, nearby traffic, and suddenly, like gunfire in a church, I heard my father. He was speaking about the world, all right—how it had become an awful place, part zoo, part asylum. We were spine only, he was saying. With filth attached. We were muck, is what we were. Tissues and melts and sweats. His voice was sharp the way it became when the Luna County Democratic Party, which he was the chairman of, did something that made the Republicans look selfless.

"You get him right now," Mother said, shoving me onward.

At the pool nobody had moved: The Melcher sisters, old and also rich, were frozen; even the kids in the baby pool—the ones still in diapers, the toddlers—had stopped splashing and now stood as if they'd instantly grown very, very old.

"What do you want me to do?" I said.

This was a man who, in teaching me to box, had mashed my nose and introduced me to the noisy afterworld of unconsciousness; and now he was out there, pitching his clubs into the sky and ranting.

"Hobey Don, Jr.," my mother said, leading me by the elbow to the gate, "don't be so damned lamebrained."

I do not know now, twenty-five years later, what had ravaged my father's self-control, what had seized him as surely as devils are said to have clutched those ancient, fugitive Puritans we descend from. I can tell you that he was well known for his temper; and, by way of illustration, I can point to the time he broke up Mother's dinner party for Woody and Helen Knapp by storming into our dining room, his cheeks red and blue with anger, in one fist the end of a trail of toilet paper that stretched—we soon learned—through the living room, over the petrified-wood coffee table my Aunt Dolly had picked up at an Arizona Runnin' Indian, down the hall, beside the phone stand which had belonged to my Granny Floyd, and into the guest lavatory.

"Elaine," he hollered, "you come with me right now."

Mother had stopped chewing her green beans.

"Woody," he said, "you and Helen, too. I want you to see this."

Daddy stood next to me, waving that flowery tissue like a football pennant.

"And you, too, young man."

What was wrong was that Mother (or Mrs. Levisay who house-cleaned Tuesday and Saturday) had put the roll on the holder back-ward so it dispensed from the front, not from behind as it goddamn ought. We were a sight: the nearly five hundred pounds that were the Knapps squeezed into our bathroom with Mother and me; Daddy ordering us up close so we could see—and goddamn well remember for the rest of our miserable, imperfect lives—that there was one way, and one way only, sensible as God intended, for bathroom tissue, or anything else, to be installed.

"You wouldn't drive a car backwards, would you?" He was talking to Mr. Knapp (napkin still tucked under his chin!), who looked as hopeless and lost as any stranger can be in a bathroom. "And Helen there, she wouldn't eat soup with a fork, would she?"

I could smell us: Mother's White Shoulders perfume, what the Pine Sol had left, the sweat Mr. Knapp is given to when he isn't sitting still.

"Things have a purpose," my daddy was saying—shouting, actu-ally—and pointing at the john itself. "Man, creature, invention—the whole kit 'n' kaboodle."

Toilet paper was flying now, shooting overhead like streamers at a Wildcat basketball game. Mrs. Knapp, her shoulders and head draped by enough tissue to make a turban, was looking for a way out, slapping the walls, pawing blindly, and yelping in a squeak Mother said had been picked up at the Beaumont School for Girls in El Paso, "Woody, help me. Help me, now."

"Remember," my father was saying, "purpose." He had arranged himself on the closed toilet seat. "This may seem small to you, but, good Lord, you let the little things get away, next thing you know the big things have fallen apart. Toilet tissue one minute, maybe govern-ment the next."

Another time, while I was doing the dishes—just had the glassware left, in fact—he wandered past me, whistling the tune he always used when the world worked right ("I'm an Old Cowhand"), and flung open the refrigerator. It was nearly seven, I guess, and he was about to have his after-dinner rum concoction. I was thinking about little—the TV I'd watch or that History Club essay I had to write for Mrs. Tipton. And then I heard him: "Eeeeffff."

The freezer door went bang, and instantly he was at my elbow, breathing in a panic, hunched over and peering into my dishwater as if what lay at the bottom were sin itself.

"What the hell are you doing?" he hollered.

I went loose in the knees and he swept me out of the way.

"How many times I got to tell you," he boomed, "glasses first, water's hottest and cleanest—then the flatware, plates, serving dishes. Save your goddamn saucepans for last!"

I was watching the world turn black and trying to remember how to defend myself.

"Here, I'll show you."

And he did. Not only did he rewash all the dishes, but he also— now muttering about the loss of common sense—opened every cabinet, drawer, and cupboard we have so he could spend the next five hours washing, in water so hot we were in danger of steam burn, every item in the house associated with preparing, serving, and consuming food. Chafing dish, tureen, pressure cooker, double boiler, candy dish, meat thermometer, basting brush, strainer, lobster hammer—everything disappeared into his soapy water.

"Scrub," he said. "Hard." He was going at one dish as if it were covered with ink. "Rinse," he said. "Hot, dammit."

A minute later he sent me to the utility room for the flimsy TV trays we own, and then he stopped. Every flat surface in the kitchen— the countertop, the tops of the freezer and the stove, the kitchen table itself, the trays—was piled high with our plates and such.

"See," he howled at last, "you see how it's done?"

There he stood, arms glistening, shirt soaked, trousers damp to the knees. His eyeballs were the brightest, maddest points of reference in the entire universe; and, yes, I did see.

He even blew up one time in Korea, going off the way shotguns do, loud and spreading. Mother told me that one day, unhappy with his duties as the I Corps supply officer, he appeared at the residence of his CO, plucked his major's insignia from his shoulders, threw them at the feet of that startled officer.

"Pick those up, mister," he said.

The man looked flabbergasted, so my father said that, owing to shoddiness in the world at large and the preeminence in that cold, alien place of such vices as sloth, avarice, gluttony, backstabbing, and other high crimes he'd remember later, he was quitting—which he could do, he reminded that man, on account of his nonregular Army status as a reserve officer and his relation to my Uncle Lawrence, then a six-term congressman from the Fourth District of New Mexico.

"Colonel," my daddy is reported to have declared, "this is squalor, disease, violence, and hunger, and I will have no part of it."

So he had blown up in the past and would blow up many, many times after the day I am concerned with here. He would go crazy when my cousin Delia drowned at Elephant Butte and when the Beatles appeared on *The Ed Sullivan Show.* Later, he exploded when Billy Summer won the club championship with a chip shot that bounced off the old white head of A. T. Seely. He blew up when Governor George Corley Wallace used the word *nigger* on national TV, and he beat our first RCA color set with my Little League Louisville Slugger when Lyndon Johnson, jug-eared and homely as dirt, showed America his surgery scars. As he aged, my father bellowed like a tyrant when Dr. Needham told him his gallbladder had to come out, and he raged like a cyclops at the lineman from El Paso Electric who tried to string a low-voltage line across a corner of our ranch. When he was fifty, he was hollering about calumny and false piety; at sixty, about the vulgar dimwits loose in the land; at seventy, about the excesses of those from the hindmost reaches of our species. Even a week before he died— which was three years ago, at seventy-four—he lay in his hospital bed, virtually screaming at his night nurse about the dreamland that citizens lived in. "This is a world of ignorance and waste," he hollered, "no bridge at all over the sea which is our foreordained doom!"

Yes, he had blown up before and would blow up again, so on the day I trudged across our flatland fairways, I assumed he was loco this time because, say, he'd caught Butch cheating. Or that Yogi Jones had spoken unkindly about Hebrews. Or that Jimmy Sellers, whom he seemed most mad at, had gypped him on the Ramada Inn they were partners in.

I have told Pammy Jo many times that mine was the most curious eight-minute walk I will ever take. I have read that in so-called extreme moments—those that Mother associates with the words *peril* and *dire*—we humans are capable of otherwise impossible physical activity. In emergencies, we can hoist automobiles, vault like Olympians, run at leopard-like speeds. So it was with my father. As I drew nearer, my flip-flops making that silly slapping noise, Daddy spun, bounced as if on springs, whirled, hopped, and kicked the air. He threw his ball onto the service road. He windmilled his arms, stomped, spit on the putter he'd jammed like a stake into the heart of the green. He even dashed in a zigzag that from above might have looked like the scribbling Arabs have. I was reminded of the cartoon creatures I see on Saturday-morning TV, those who race over the edge of a cliff to hang unnaturally in the air for several seconds, their expressions passing from joy to worry to true horror. And then I realized—almost, I am convinced, at the same moment he did—that my father was going to roar headlong at Mr. Sellers, stop in a way that would jar the innards, and coldcock that man.

"No," I croaked, and when Daddy left off his tirade about murkiness in the moral parts and the rupture that was our modern era, something tiny and dry broke free in my chest. To my knowledge, he'd never struck a man in anger before, but as he went at it now, like an honorable citizen with a single unbecoming task to do in life, I could see that violence—if that's all this was—was as natural to him as fear is common to us all.

"James Edward Sellers," he was shouting, "I am going to tear out your black heart."

I reached the green just as Mr. Sellers, fingering his split lip, was picking himself up.

"Let's go," Daddy said, using a smile and a voice I never care again to see and hear. He seemed composed, as if he'd survived the worst in himself and was now looking forward to an eternity of deserved pleasures. "Grab my bag, son," he said. Nearby, Mr. Ikard and Yogi Jones had the faces you find on those who witness such calamity as auto wrecks: gray and why-filled.

"Where you going?" I asked.

He pointed: the clubhouse. "Now," he said. "This minute."

I hustled about, picking up his clubs, finding his two-iron beyond the sand trap behind the willow tree. This was over, I figured. He had been the nincompoop my mother said sometimes he was, and now he could be again that fairly handsome elder who read books like *Historia Romania* and the biographies of dead clerics. He would, I believed, march into the clubhouse, collect himself over a mixed drink, and then reappear—as he had done several times before—at the door to the men's locker. Into the caddy master's hand Daddy would place a written apology so abject with repentance and so slyly organized that when it was read over the PA, perhaps by Jimmy Sellers himself, those lounging around the pool and walking the links, as well as those in the showers or in the snack bar or in the upstairs dining room, would hush their chitchat, listen as librarians can, and afterward break into that applause which greets genuinely good news.

At the men's locker, I found the door locked. Twenty people had wedged themselves into the narrow, dim hallway; with amusement, I thought that, as he had done with Woody and Helen Knapp, Daddy had herded them here, mad and delighted, to show them the proper way to fold a bath towel or how a gentleman shines his wingtip shoes or what tie to wear with red.

"That was the trash can," Mr. Hightower said behind me. We had heard the banging and clatter that metal makes when it is drop-kicked.

Elvis Peacock was shaking his head. "Could have been the towel rack. Or that automatic hand-dryer."

You heard the crash and whang of doors slamming and a two-minute screech that Mr. Phinizy Spalding identified as the wooden rack of linen hooks that ran from the showers to the ball washers.

Patient as preachers, they listened and I listened to them. A jerky scraping was Dr. Weems's easy chair being dragged. Pounded. And, at last, splintered.

"What was that?" someone said.

We'd heard a deafening rattle, like gravel on a tin roof.

"Pocket change," Herb Swetman told us. "He's broken into the cigarette machine."

A glass shattered, Judge Sanders's starting pistol went off, and it was time for me to knock on the door.

"I got your clubs," I said.

He was moving, spikes clicking and scratching like claws. I had the thought that this wasn't my father at all but the boogeyman all children hear about. It was nothing to believe that what now stopped behind the door, still as the stuff inside a grave, was the scaly, hot-eyed, murder-filled monster who, over the years, was supposed to leap out of closets or flop down from trees to slay youngsters for the crimes they sometimes dream of.

"What do you want me to do with them?"

I was speaking directly into the MEMBERS ONLY sign, feeling as awkward and self-conscious as I would one day feel asking Pammy Jo to marry me. Crowded behind were Frank Redman and T. Moncure Yourtees, our assistant city manager. Behind them stood the Clute brothers, Mickey and Sam, both looking as interested in this as their Pope is in carnality. Last in line, silhouetted in the doorway, stood Mr. Jimmy Sellers himself. A muscle had popped in my neck and for a time it was impossible to breathe.

"You all right?" I asked. "Mother is real upset."

Here, then, hushed as Dr. Hammond Ellis says will be the day-break of doom, my daddy, his face clearly pressed against the door-jamb, told me he had something special in mind. I recognized his voice as the one he'd used ten years before when, drunk and sore-hearted with nostalgia, he had sat on the end of my bed to tell me how his brother, my Uncle Alton (who was alleged to be as handsome as Cary Grant and Rock Hudson combined) had died in the Battle of the Bulge in WWII; it was a story of deprivation, of fortitude in the face of overwhelming sadness, and of what we human brothers—in our German incarnation this time—are capable of in a world slipped free of grace.

"What do you want me to do?" I asked.

"You listen carefully," he whispered.

"Yes, sir." He was my father and I was being polite.

He said, "I want you to break those clubs, you hear?"

The news traveled down the line behind me and returned before my mind turned completely practical: "How will you know?"

Mr. Phinizy Spalding had lit a cigar, the smoke just reaching me.

"Junior," Daddy was saying, "I am your parent and you will do what I say." He could have been speaking to me as he had to that colonel in Korea years before.

"Yes, sir," I said.

My mother had given him these clubs—Titleist irons and Hagen woods—less than four months before, and if you know anything about golf, you know that a linkster's clubs are to him what a wand is to a magician. They had leather grips and extra-stiff shafts, and they felt, even in my clumsy grip, like a product of science and philosophy: balanced, elegant, simple as love itself. They were shiny, cost over seven hundred dollars, and I told him I would begin with his wedge.

"Good idea," he said.

Snapping those clubs was neither physically nor spiritually difficult. I was strong, and I was dumb. To those folks in the hallway, my actions probably seemed as ordinary as walking a straight line. Indeed, once I started, Mr. Hightower began handing me the clubs.

"I'll be your assistant, Junior," he said. He was smiling like the helpful banker he is, and I thanked him.

"My pleasure," he said, "happy to be of service."

There was nothing in me—doubt, aggravation, none of it. Neither fear nor joy. Neither pleasure nor satisfaction. This was work, and I was doing it.

"I have your five-iron now," I said. At my feet lay what I'd already accomplished: a gleaming pile of twisted, broken, once-expensive metal. And then I heard it: the noise I am partly here to tell about. I understand now—because I have dwelled on it and because it once happened to me—that despite what was happening, he was still angry. Angry in a way that fell beyond ordinary expression. An anger that comes not from the heart or the brain, or another organ of sense, but from the soul itself. An anger that, looking down, angels must feel.

For what he was doing, while I wrenched in half his woods and putter, was speaking, in a whisper I shall forever associate with the black half of rapture, some sort of gibberish, a mutter I can only transcribe as funny-pages gobbledygook, those dashes and stars you see in newspapers when the victim of rage empties his mind. It was X, which in the tenth-grade algebra I teach stands for the unknown—as in x - 2 = y. It is everything and nothing; and that day, accompanied by twenty wiser men, I heard Daddy speak it, just as yesterday I heard Dr. Hammond Ellis, our Episcopalian minister, preach about man's need for fellowship and eternal good. To be true, when I had at last fractured his putter, I believed that Daddy was mumbling as Adam and Eve were said to mumble, in the language of Eden that Dr. Ellis insists was ours before death. Because I am old-fashioned and still a believer, I contend that my father, enraged like any animal that sleeps and eats, was speaking a babble so private, yet so universal, that it goes from your lips to the ear of God Himself; it is more breathtaking, I hold, than the wheel, fire, travel in space—all those achievements, we hope, that makes us less monkey than man.

On Daddy yammered, a phenomenon those in the hall with me found as remarkable as chickens which count by twos.

Mr. Hightower said it was Dutch. "I heard that in World War Two," he said. "Or maybe it's Flemish."

Frank Redman suggested it was Urdu, something he'd heard on TV the other night. "Junior, how's your daddy know Urdu?"

Elvis Peacock, the only one besides my father to have gone to university, said it was, well, Sanskrit, which was speech folks in piled-up headdress mutter before they zoom off to the afterlife. "Listen," he said, "I'm betting ten dollars on Sanskrit."

And so, once again, we listened and were not disappointed. My father, an American of 185 pounds and bristly, graying hair, and a reputation for mule-headedness, was in there—in that shambles of a locker room—yapping, if you believe the witnesses, in Basque, in Mennonite, in Zulu, or in the wet yackety-yak that Hungary's millions blather when they spy the vast Whatnot opening to greet them.

"Let's go in," Dr. Weems suggested at last.

From their expressions, these men seemed ready to vote on it.

"Daddy," I said, "can I come in now?"

It was midafternoon and it seemed we had waited forever.

"It's open," he said.

I sensed he was sitting, perhaps in the remains of Dr. Weems's easy chair; strangely, I expected him to be no more disturbed or disheveled than our most famous judges.

"Don't make any loud noises," Frank Redman said. "I know that man, he's liable to shoot somebody."

Slowly, I pushed open the door, stepped over the rubble of his clubs, and made room for those following me. You could see that a hurricane, a storm by the name of Hobey Don Baker, Sr., had been through there. A bank of lockers had been tipped over, many sprung open to reveal what we in the upper class dry off with or look at when doing so. There were shampoo bottles scattered, as well as Bermuda shorts, tennis shoes, golf spikes, bottles of Johnnie Walker Red and Jack Daniel's, Bicycle playing cards, chips that belonged to Mr. Mickey Clute's poker game, and a nasty paperback Frank Redman wouldn't later own up to. In one corner was a soiled bundle of lady's frilly underclothes that looked worthy of ample Mrs. Hightower herself. And then Yogi Jones noticed Memo Gonzalez, the janitor, who was leaning against the wall to our right, almost facing Daddy.

"You've been in here the whole time?" Yogi Jones said.

As a group, we watched Memo nod: Sure, he'd been in here. He was from Mexico—an especially bleak and depressed village, we thought—and the rumor was that he had been a thousand things in his youth: dope smuggler, highway bandito, police sergeant in Las Palomas, a failed bullfighter before Yogi brought him up here, on a green card, to sweep up and keep our clubs clean.

"We been having conversation," he said. "Where you been?"

Right then, you knew that all the rumors were true, even those still to be invented, for you could see by the way he smoked his Lucky Strike and picked his teeth with a golf tee that he'd seen it, and heard it, and that it—war, pestilence, famine, plague—had meant less to him than books mean to fish.

"Memo," my father said, "come over here, please."

I took note of one million things—the yellow light, the smell of the group I stood in, and the rusty taste coming from my stomach. I felt as apart from my father as I do now that he is dead. I wondered where my mother was and what was happening in the outer world. I thought of Pammy Jo and hoped she still loved me. I saw that Mr. Ikard had-n't shaved and that Rice Hershey was the sourpuss bookkeeper Daddy said he was. A thought came, went, came back, and again I heard, in my memory, the X language Daddy had used.

It was prayer, I thought. Or it was lunacy.

"Let's go," I said. "Mother says we're eating out tonight."

Standing, one arm around Memo's shoulders, Daddy looked, except for the hair slapped across his forehead like a pelt, as alert and eager as he did at the breakfast table. I wanted to grab hold, say I loved him.

"Gentlemen," he was saying, "to cover expenses, I hold here a check for ten thousand dollars."

There were ooohhhs and aaahhhs and the expressions they come from.

"If you need more, there is more."

And then he was marching past us, me running to catch up.

Now this is the modern, sad part of the story, and it is a bit about my oldest boy, Buddy—who, like me in the former story, is seventeen— and how I came again to hear that double-talk I thought remarkable so long ago. There is no Memo in this part, nor folks like Messrs. Red-man, Hightower, and Ikard, for they, like Daddy and Mother them-selves, are either dead or old and mostly indoors. Mainly, though, this section is without the so-called innocent bystander because our world is utterly without bystanders, innocent or otherwise; we are all central, I believe, to events which are leading us, good and bad, to the dry par-adise that is the end of things.

Buddy is like most youth these days—by turns lazy and helpful, stupid and smart-alecky, fussy and apathetic. Tall, too skinny through the chest, he speaks when spoken to and has a girlfriend named Alice Mary Tidwell who will one day be a fat but always cheerful woman. He reads periodicals like *Sports Illustrated* and what is required in school as advanced literature (which is *Silas Marner*, verse by Shake-speare, and made-up mishmash by New York writers who haven't lived anywhere). I love him not simply because he is my flesh but because I see that in all things—his own adulthood, for example—he will be decent-hearted and serious-minded, a man who will want, as you do, to be merely and always good. More than once we have talked about this—mostly when he was an adolescent. I used to sit at the end of his bed, as had my father with me, to offer my views on issues like relations among neighbors, what heft our obligations have, and how too often the heart never fits its wanting. One time, but without the dramatics my daddy enjoyed, I took him around the house, showing him what ought to be, not what was; later, when he was ten and mow-ing our yard, I went out, watched for a time, then stood in his path to stop him.

"What's the matter now?" he asked.

It was summer, dry but hot as fire gets, and it was partly joyful to see him sweat doing something he'd been told.

"First," I said, "you have to wear shoes. You hit a rock and no telling what'll happen."

He looked at the sandals we'd bought him in Juarez.

"And no more shorts," I added. "Long pants for the same reason."

He has his mother's blue eyes, which were fixed on me as hers often are when I rise up to put things straight in this universe.

"I'm wearing goggles," he said.

I was pleased, I told him, but then described, as Daddy did for me, how grass is cut in the ideal world.

"Starting from the outside," I began, "you go around in a square, okay? Throws the cuttings to the center and makes raking up easier."

Here it was, then, that we had a moment together, a moment which had nothing to do with yard work; rather, it was a passage of time that, to the sentimentalist I am, seemed filled with wonder and knowledge—the first things we must pass on.

"Can I have five dollars?" he asked.

He was going to the movies, he said, with Jimmy Bullard and Clo-vis Barclay. I was watching his face—what it said about his inner life—and when he took the money from me, I accepted the urge, felt in the gut, to throw my arms around him and lay on the breath-defeating hug I am notorious for.

"Come on, Dad," he said, "don't squeeze so hard."

Mostly, however, and embarrassingly, we are not close. Like my father, I tend to lecture; like me, when I was his age, he is obliged to listen. I have talked about responsibility, the acceptance of which is a measure of our maturity and not nearly the weighty moral overcoat another might say it is, and Buddy has said, "Yes, sir." I have talked about honor, which is often seen as too ambiguous to be useful, and he has answered, "Yes, sir." I have talked about politics, which— except for voting—he is to avoid; and debt, which he may accept in moderation; and cleanliness, which remains a practical concern; and trust, which he must reward in others. Other times, I have warned him against tobacco, drinking with strangers, carelessness with firearms, public displays of temper, eating undercooked or fatty foods, wasting time, rudeness, sleeping in drafts, and lying when such is not called for. I have said, in a way Pammy Jo finds most amusing, that there is hardness and cruelty, confusion and turmoil; and there is knowing what's best. To all he has answered, "Yes, sir."

I have, of course, told him about his grandfather's outburst at the country club; to be true, I told him during that father-son talk which becomes necessary when the son acquires body hair and the shoulders broaden toward manhood. I forget the point I intended, but some- where during a too-clinical discussion of arousal and penis length and courtship, I said, "Did you ever hear the locker-room story?"

We were in our living room, he holding the well-illustrated pam- phlet, *Growing Up: A Young Man's Mystery*, that Dr. Weems had given me. Outside, the August light was gladsome, and in here, among palaver that made romance sound like sport among Martians, I unloaded, taking nearly two hours telling about one. Giving him names, places, and states of mind, I watched his brain, as betrayed by his eyeballs, figure out what coitus had to do with madness. I watched him imagine my father as more than the grumpy old man he knew; and sexual congress—which, I confess, was the phrase I used—as something more than flesh attached to funny Latin words. I told him about Memo's tattoos, which were as detailed and epic as Spiderman comics, and about Yogi Jones's hole in one afterward, and about my mother pitching turkey bones at the clock that night; and then, twilight near and our neighbors home from their trades, I watched Buddy's forehead wrinkle and his hand fidget while he thrashed about in the events I had recalled, helpless as a drowning mule in his effort to establish a connection between the past and this present business of creation.

Which, in the roundabout way I think appropriate, brings us to recent hours, whose events feature a father, a son, a prophylactic, and mumbo-jumbo from the start of time.

It is early April now, rainy enough to be annoying, and Pammy Jo and our youngest, Taylor, are in the eighth day of their two-week visit to her sister in El Paso. It is an absence which means that Buddy and I eat hot dogs and Kraft macaroni too often, or we visit the Triangle Drive-in for Del Cruz's chicken-fried steak in white gravy. It is an absence I feel physically, as if what I am missing from my bed and my conversation is more body part than companion. There is a larger effect, too, specifically with reference to time—which seems to stretch forward endlessly to a future ever out of reach. Time becomes inconceivable: It is reincarnation or other hocus-pocus our wishing invents. What I am saying here is that when my wife is around, I know where I am in America; and I can say to anybody that I am forty-two years old, a Scorpio (if you care), a cum-laude graduate of the University of New Mexico (B.S. in mathematics), a shareholder in several companies (IBM, for one), a father, a sportsman who does not care for hunting or fishing, a practicing Episcopalian, and heir to nearly one million dollars' worth of baked desert rangeland (and the cattle that graze there). But when she is gone—when she visits her father in Roswell or when she attends her social workers' convention in Santa Fe—my horizon shrinks and loneliness has such weight that I am pitched forward and ever in danger of wobbling to a stop.

The other day I felt this as a restlessness to see my neighbors, a desire to be moving, so I told Buddy I was going out.

"When you going to be back?" he asked.

It was noon and there was no reason to be anywhere—here, this continent, this world.

"I don't know, maybe I'll go to the club."

He was watching Larry Bird and the Celtics make mincemeat out of the Bullets from Washington. Plus, he had a package of chocolate chip cookies and most of the milk in the house.

"Have a good time," he said, and I was gone.

Yet for the next few hours it was less I than someone else who drove around Deming. At one time, this man who was not me found himself stopped outside a shabby duplex on Olive Street where he had been violently drunk for the first time. He had been with Donnie Bobo and Dickie Greene and, in the company of Oso Negro and Buckhorn beer, he'd seen the night itself fly apart and burn. An hour later, he found himself on one of the line roads that head east through the scrub and brush toward Las Cruces. He had been here twice before with Bernice Ruth Ellis, and the sex they had had been fitful, not at all the hurly-burly described in *Penthouse* magazine—in part because he was married and because she was the confused daughter of our most celebrated Christian, Dr. Hammond Ellis. This infidelity occurred long ago, in the second year of my marriage, and is an episode I do not forgive myself for. It is one secret I've kept, and there are times, especially when I see Bernice and her husband Charlie Potts at the Fourth of July dance or at the Piggly Wiggly, when I think it did not happen at all; or that, if it did, it happened in a place—a crossroads of time and circumstance—in which there was no evil or eye looking down.

Around four, I found myself at the club, one of many husbands and fathers who seemed too bored or too free. My friend Leroy Sellers— yes, Jimmy's son—was sitting on a camp stool in the pro shop, making sense out of our war with Nicaragua. Bobby Hover was there, looking like the rich real-estate broker he is; so were Slim Sims, Spudd Webb, Archie Meents, and Ed Fletcher, all fellows I'd grown up with or met through my exploits on the football field. In time, aided by the scotch whiskey Spud brought from his locker, we fixed civilization up fine.

After eliminating poverty, we took the starch out of the diets of fat men, dealt with such dreams as are suffered by tyrants, turned winners into losers, fired two county commissioners, and agreed that in humans we liked muscle, the eagle's eyesight, voices you can hear across the room, plus what they teach in Sweden about freedom. Slim told us about his brother who was building jet fighters for LTV in Dallas, Ed Fletcher suggested a cure for flatulence, and Spud himself took the high ground in defense of intergalactic communication with, say, Venutians—a point he made by drawing our attention to the ten billion stars and planets which were said to be out there. He was standing, I remember, and his workingman's face had taken on a blissful shine, red and wet the way yours would be were you to win ten million dollars in a lottery.

"They're up there, I tell you," he said, daring each of us to contradict him. "You got to be less narrow-minded, boys."

For a moment, it was possible to believe him—to understand that out there, where light is said to bend toward time, lived creatures, like ourselves, who had our happy habits of wonder and hope.

At six-thirty, while Ed Fletcher addressed the topic of loyalty in Washington, D.C., I called Buddy to say I'd be a while yet.

"No problem," he said, "I'm going over to Doug Sherwin's."

I know now that he had already done it: that he had gone into our bedroom and had opened my bureau drawer, finding the plain drugstore condoms Pammy Jo and I used for birth control. I know, too, that his mind was filled with a dozen contrary notions—guilt and anxiousness and excitement; and I suspect that at the moment we in the pro shop were putting Mr. Nixon on his feet again, Buddy was bringing himself to that point his *Young Man's Mystery* book calls "orgasm," which is defined as a matter of friction and fluids.

I got home late, finding eight lights burning and the TV tuned to a Sunday-night movie about, near as I can tell, greed and those the victim of it.

Buddy wasn't home, which was just as well because I was drunk. I have mostly forgone heavy drinking, a crutch (Pammy Jo's word) I leaned too heavily on after my father died. Nowadays, I have wine to be polite or take my alcohol mixed, for there was a time—nearly eighteen months, in fact—when I was addled enough to be drunk virtually every night; those in my family have said that they were truly afraid of me during this period, seeing me as a desperate sort who wouldn't watch his tongue and who heaped on others the misery he'd heaped on himself.

So, unsteadily and ashamed, I made coffee and ate peanut butter, a remedy I'd heard on *Donahue* once. I tried reading the Raymond Chandler I like, but the words, not to mention the events and the people shaped by them, kept sliding off the page. I looked at *Life* magazine but could not figure out what beasts like giraffes and African elephants were doing next to the colorful vacation homes of the rich. I thought, at last, of calling Pammy Jo, but didn't. She would hear the thing I was covering up and she would be sad. So, believing I would go to bed, I scribbled this note: "Buddy, I'm going to school tomorrow to do lesson plans; you, as promised, begin painting the garage."

My father claimed, especially in his rage-filled years in later life, that he'd developed the extra sense of suspicion, a faculty he likened to an awareness old-time oilmen have: Roughnecks, it is said, know when a well is about to come in by a "harmonic tremor," a subtle shaking of our earth heralded by a noise that causes dogs to prick up their ears. I have inherited this sense, along with bony elbows and a mouth that can be set hard as a cue ball. In our bedroom, which is as big as a two-hundred-dollar-a-night hotel room, I knew immediately that something was wrong. My bedsheets looked too tight, and the clutter on my nightstand—a *National Geographic,* the Kleenex box, the clock radio, plus a water glass—seemed unfamiliar, somehow different. That organ of suspicion, which is composed, I know now, of habit and how you are taught, was well at work in me. I compare it to my dog, a pound-bred beast named Ticker, and how sometimes he becomes three parts attention, one part muddle.

I made my way around my room on tiptoe, feeling myself the intruder here. I have fist-fought twice in my lifetime—the last in the ninth grade with Billy Joe De Marco, which was when I broke my wrist—but, counting the change on my dresser and opening my jewelry box, I was ready. I heard what nighttime has to offer in these parts: Poot Tipton in his backyard next door hollering at his brother; a car going too fast on Iron Street; our air conditioner taking its own pulse. Who was here? I was thinking, and pictures came to mind of robberies and the serious prowling we suffer around here. And then, arms held as I had been taught, tight to the body, the fists on either side of the head, I went into the bathroom.

For several moments I didn't see the used condom on the water tank for the toilet. Rather, I was studying the man in the mirror who is me. It would be a cliché to say that in my face—particularly the way the cheekbones lie and how the nose goes flat at the bridge—was my father's; but there he was, at forty or fifty, gazing at me from a mirror my wife had paid too much for at the White House department store. It is also possible to believe that in his face lay the images, as well, of his father, who had gone broke at least twice. In a way quite natural under the circumstances, I let my heart and breath go free, flipped on the lights, and looked at that room as Chuck Gribble, our sheriff, looks at places that are the scenes of small crimes. I report to you now that I found the condom immediately and took note of it as in past years I have taken note of bad news that happens in big towns far, far away.

"Yes," I said.

It was a word which then meant no more to me than what is muttered in Paraguay. Yet I muttered it again and again—as if an official with important-looking documents had knocked on my door to say, "Are you Hobey Don Baker, Jr.?"

That night I behaved like an ignorant father. I phoned the Sherwin house, but Betty, Doug's mother, said Buddy wasn't there.

"You okay, Junior?" she said. "You sound funny."

For the most part, my voice was coming from my chest and, yes, it wasn't her friend talking; it was Buddy's father.

"You see him," I told her, "it's time to come home, all right?"

Sure, she said, and reminded me of the barbecue on Wednesday. "You haven't been drinking, have you, Junior?"

I watched my hand shake and attended to the rasp my breathing made.

"I'm fine, Betty, thanks."

I called Clovis Barclay and put up with Earl, his father, scolding me about how late it was. Afterward, I stood on the street, watching our neighbors' lights go off after the late news. It would be a cool night, the clouds racing up from Chihuahua, and I hoped Buddy hadn't gone out without a jacket. I was not angry, just dislocated—as unhinged as I was when I tried to quit smoking. I heard the same noise over and over: a fierce ear whine. I regarded heaven, which was up and far away, and hell, which was underfoot and near; and then I went indoors to make myself a camp in Buddy's room.

It is a truism that teenagers have the collector's spirit. In my time, I'd hoarded baseball cards and kept statistics on the Aggie basketball I listened to on the radio. I had trophies (swimming), drawings and photographs of jet planes that Grumman had sent me. I had saved coins for a while—nothing special—plus books on oceans. Buddy was no different. He possessed a Zenith record player and at least one hundred albums from Fed-Mart: Mötley Crüe, Devo, and foreign-looking groups whose lyrics were about love, or what passed for it. On the walls—ceiling, too—were charts ("Generalized," of time and rock units) of Canada and the USA. The rocks we stood on, I discovered, came from the Silurian Age. From his desk I learned that apparently he'd never thrown away a single school assignment; you could see him, represented in thousands of pages, go from one unable to spell *garage* to one familiar with what Euclid had achieved. I am not proud of this snooping, but I had to know, and isn't knowing—even if it is painful and frightful and small—better than not knowing? And then, after I'd counted his shirts and pants, he was standing at his door.

"Hey," he said, "I read the note."

I took a second, trying to strip the age out of my voice. "Who was she?" I asked. "Was it Alice Mary?"

He stepped backward, shaking his head as if he'd run into a cobweb. He was wearing a shirt like the checkered flag at the Indy 500 and pants that are too expensive and too tight.

"You had a girl in here tonight," I said. "I want to know who."

It was a shameful question, but I had to ask it again before I realized—my organ of suspicion, I guess—that there had been no girl, or woman; that, instead, he had indulged in what my 1949 edition of

Webster's New Collegiate Dictionary calls, stupidly, "self-pollution," which is masturbation and is as normal to us as flying is to birds.

"In my bathroom," I said. "On top of the commode."

He went to look and while he was gone I, in my mind, began putting his books in order. Large to small. Good to bad.

"It was Frances Greathouse," he said when he returned. "You don't know her. Her old man works for the state police, a sergeant."

Buddy looked defeated, as nerve-wracked as the time his Little League team was beaten and the world to him had gone topsy-turvy into chaos.

"Stop," I said. "I don't believe you."

It was true, he insisted. She sat behind him last year, in fifth-period chemistry. She had brown hair and was tall. "They live on Fir Street. It's a white place, I don't know the number."

The rocks we have in the world are these: Cambrian, Ordovician, Devonian. And they go back six hundred million years or more, to times that were dark, silent, and wet.

"Go to bed," I said, "we'll talk about this in the morning."

His face was flushed and open, and I could see that it, too, was mine and how I looked a generation ago.

"You're right," he said.

A fiber had snapped in my stomach—a muscle or link between nerve and bone.

"It wasn't Frances Greathouse," he was saying, "it wasn't anybody."

And then, as it had been in that men's locker, I heard it again, our X-language, a tumbling rush of speech that if put down here would be all z's and y's and c's, the crash of tongue-thick syllables and disordered parts that everywhere is laughed at as madness. It wasn't anger I was experiencing—that word can't apply here—but sadness. Sadness that had to do with time and love.

I was in the hall, several paces from Buddy's door, next to the watercolors of trees and distance we have bought as art, and the world—as it had for my father—fell away from me. Piece by piece. Element by element. A wind had come up, freezing and from twelve directions, and there was nothing hereabouts but your narrator and his fear. I wore the cotton shirt of a civilized man and the long pants of a grown-up, but I could not think, as I am doing now, of how I came to be in this century.

"What's wrong?" Buddy said. "Dad?"

My arm, as if on strings, went up. Down. Up again.

Dad," he said, "you're scaring me."

I think now I was speaking, as my father had spoken, of deceit and miserable hope and craftiness and forfeiture and my own ignorance—and of, especially, a future too weird and horrible to ponder. I was speaking, using but controlled by X, of the mud and ooze we will one day be. If I had to translate, I would assert that, victim of a grammar composed of violence and waywardness, I said this: We are flesh and it is fallen. And this: The way is the way, and there is an end. And this: We are matter, it must be saved. And this: There are dark waters all around. And this: Please stop, please stop.

In those minutes in my hallway, in a home I still owe eighty thousand dollars for, while my oldest son trembled as if I had struck him, X wasn't unknown any longer. It had hair and teeth and ancient, common desires. I knew X.

It was him.

It was me.

It was all of us.

Twenty-five years ago, Memo Gonzalez, to whom my daddy had given his ten-thousand-dollar check, stood unmoving next to Dr. Weems's splintered chair. Jimmy Sellers, who told this to me, says there was nothing at all in Memo's face. It was stone, with the impression that the nose, mouth, and eyes had been added later. He was strong, built like a toolbox, and nobody—not even Mickey Clute, who'd wrestled heavyweight in school—thought to go over there and ask for the money.

Several minutes passed—the way they do in the dentist's office—before Memo walked ("lumbered," Jimmy says) toward Yogi Jones. He set himself in front of Mr. Jones, and twenty pairs of eyes stared at the tattoos on his arms—inky, clotted designs which were of ideas he held sacred and the women he'd known. Death. Conception. Maria.

"I got to be moving along, Yogi Jones," he said at last. "I quit."

Whereupon he went out and, as in some fairy tales, was never seen again.

I like that moment. I like, too, the moment I had with my father in his Biscayne in the members' parking lot later that afternoon. I did not feel like a teenager then; rather, I felt myself to be the trustee of a dozen secrets, none of which had a name yet but all of which would be with me until there was no more me to know them.

"You drive," he said.

But before he gave me the keys, he touched me, squeezed me at the shoulder, and in that touch, man to boy, was the knowledge that we were the same: two creatures made blind by the same light and deafened by the same noise; that his dismay was the thing I'd grow into as I had already grown into his hand-me-down trousers; that we were harmless in water, or air; that we were put here, two-legged and flawed, to keep order. It is a moment, so help me, that I intend to re-create for Buddy when he gets home from the picture show. It will be brief, like the original, but I hope it will remain for him forever as it has remained for me.

ABOUT THE AUTHOR

Lee K. Abbott is the author of six previous collections of short stories, many of which have been featured in *The Best American Short Stories* and have won O. Henry Awards. His work has appeared in such publications as *The Atlantic Monthly*, *Harper's*, *The Georgia Review*, the *New York Times Book Review*, *The Southern Review*, *Epoch*, *Boulevard*, and the *North American Review*. A multiple winner of National Endowment for the Arts fellowships, Abbott splits his time between rural New Mexico and Columbus, Ohio, where he is professor of creative writing at Ohio State University.